"Sarah Adler wil̲̲̲̲̲̲̲̲̲̲

—Abby Jiminez,

author of *Just for the Summer*

"A second-chance romance and a treasure hunt? My *Goonies*-loving heart rejoiced—and this delightful novel absolutely delivered. This was my first Sarah Adler book, but it definitely will not be my last."

—Colleen Oakley, *USA Today* bestselling author of
Jane and Dan at the End of the World

"Sarah Adler once again provides the laugh-out-loud goodness that makes her books the perfect go-to for comfort reading. Resplendent with clever wit, delicious romance, and quirky charm, *Finders Keepers* truly entertains. It has real heart, too—of course it does, this is a Sarah Adler book! I recommend it to anyone who loves fun."   —*USA Today* bestselling author India Holton

"Sarah Adler never misses. With compelling characters, a pitch-perfect voice, and electric chemistry, *Finders Keepers* delivers another helping of the Sarah Adler Special: a delightfully quirky romantic comedy that had me swooning, laughing, and on the edge of my seat all the way until the end."

—Heather McBreen, author of *Wedding Dashers*

"Fun and adventurous and filled with Sarah Adler's classic whimsy, wit, and humor, *Finders Keepers* is an absolute treasure! . . . Pure joy from start to finish!"

—Naina Kumar, *USA Today* bestselling
author of *Flirting with Disaster*

"A wildly sexy and gorgeously romantic delight. Sarah Adler brings her trademark wit and addictive prose to Nina and Quentin's story, and I have no doubt readers will fall for them just as much as I did." —Catherine Walsh, author of *Snowed In*

"A gorgeously tender love story brimming with zingy humor. Sarah Adler deftly guides us through Nina and Quentin's past and present as they realize their chemistry and emotional connection are too powerful to keep buried. I love everything she writes!" —Jamie Harrow, author of *One on One*

"*Finders Keepers* proves that Sarah Adler can make me yearn. Her pairing of estranged-childhood-friends-to-lovers with a journey of self-worth and discovery was exquisite." —Rachel Runya Katz, author of *Whenever You're Ready*

"*Finders Keepers* is hilarious, poignant, and deeply romantic. . . . Beautifully written. Très magnifique." —Sarah Hogle, author of *The Folklore of Forever*

"Sarah Adler is my go-to author for charming romances that are chock-full of quirky humor and heart. Adler's voice is singular, and *Finders Keepers* is no exception! This friends-to-lovers gem sparkles with wit and warmth. I'm already waiting impatiently for whatever Sarah Adler writes next." —Ellie Palmer, author of *Four Weekends and a Funeral*

"*Finders Keepers* is one of the best romance novels I've read in ages. . . . By turns heartwarming, quirky, and scorching hot. . . . Sarah Adler's clever writing kept me riveted as I flew through the pages. Every line of dialogue is a gem. Highly recommended!" —*USA Today* bestselling author Mimi Matthews

Praise for *Happy Medium*

"Ridiculously charming and irresistible. This delightful slow-burn romance has it all: sizzling chemistry, phenomenal banter, and a voice that's both hilarious and vulnerable."

—Lana Harper, *New York Times* bestselling
author of *In Charm's Way*

"With voice-y narration and whip-smart humor, Sarah Adler has concocted a delightfully original screwball rom-com. This book had me at 'fake medium helps a goat farmer with a ghost problem'—yes, please, and thank you."

—Megan Bannen, author of *The Undertaking of
Hart and Mercy*

"*Happy Medium* is a sincere and sincerely funny romance populated by a higher-than-average number of goats and ghosts. I stayed up late to finish it and fell asleep smiling."

—Alix E. Harrow, *New York Times* bestselling
author of *Starling House*

"Adler dazzles yet again with a voice that leaps and twirls off the very first page. Equal parts hilarious, whimsical, and utterly unique in the best way, Gretchen, Charlie, Everett, and the goats stole my heart and ran away with it."

—Amy Lea, international bestselling author of *Exes and O's*

"Hilarious! This is exactly the kind of rom-com I love to read—the perfect alchemy of romance, humor, and quirky originality. Gretchen is now one of my favorite heroines. This book is going to be huge."

—Sophie Cousens, *New York Times* bestselling author
of *This Time Next Year* and *The Good Part*

"What an absolute delight. *Happy Medium* is quick, clever, and fantastically fresh. Sarah Adler just earned herself a spot on top of my auto-buy list."   —B.K. Borison, author of *Lovelight Farms*

"A funny and flirty tale of redemption, both in this life and the next. . . . A warmly addictive story of finding yourself and what you want in the most unexpected of places. Wrap yourself in your favorite sweater and enjoy this gem!"

—Sarah Goodman Confino, bestselling author of
Don't Forget to Write and *She's Up to No Good*

"A total delight from the first sentence to the last, *Happy Medium* delivers an utterly winning romance, not to mention a chatty ghost and baby goats in sweaters. Like her good-hearted con woman heroine, Sarah Adler knows how to spin a story that's exactly what her audience wants—and needs—to hear."

—Laura Hankin, author of *The Daydreams*

Praise for *Mrs. Nash's Ashes*

"A perfect romance novel . . . funny, hot, smart, and so full of love. I can't wait to devour everything Sarah Adler writes."

—Jasmine Guillory, *New York Times* bestselling
author of *Flirting Lessons*

"Sarah Adler nails the ultimate rom-com alchemy with her sparkling debut, *Mrs. Nash's Ashes*. Full of zippy banter, gorgeous prose, and tender-hearted characters who give the novel a deep, emotional core, it's a complete delight."

—Carley Fortune, #1 *New York Times* bestselling author
of *Every Summer After* and *Meet Me at the Lake*

"I laughed. I sobbed. I loved it! Soft, sweet, and utterly enchanting, *Mrs. Nash's Ashes* by Sarah Adler is a delightfully funny and poignant romance that sticks with you like a warm and gooey cinnamon roll."

—Ashley Poston, *New York Times* bestselling author
of *The Dead Romantics* and *The Seven Year Slip*

"Brilliantly constructed and full of unforgettable characters, *Mrs. Nash's Ashes* is an unequivocal delight. Fans of Emily Henry and Sarah Hogle, you've found your newest obsession."

—Ava Wilder, author of *How to Fake It in Hollywood*

"This unforgettable road trip runs on laugh-out-loud humor, deeply felt romance, a profound sense of the unexpected, and classic rock radio—we loved every mile."

—Emily Wibberley & Austin Siegemund-Broka,
authors of *The Roughest Draft*

"*Mrs. Nash's Ashes* is a delightfully fun and utterly romantic debut. Adler has it all—fresh characters, fabulous writing, and enormous heart."

—Sarah Grunder Ruiz, author of *Luck and Last Resorts*

"With an unforgettable voice, Adler crafts a tale full of humor and heart, proving that love sometimes finds us when we least expect it."

—Ashley Herring Blake, *USA Today* bestselling
author of *Astrid Parker Doesn't Fail*

"A delightful debut from Sarah Adler! This is a road-trip romance at its best, with all the forced proximity, unexpected intimacies, and questionable music playlists that come with it. . . . A journey I didn't want to end."

—Jen DeLuca, *USA Today* bestselling
author of *Well Matched*

"Adler perfectly mixes humor, heart, and steam to create a flawless romantic comedy. If you're in the mood for a true rom-com, you cannot go wrong with this book!"

—Falon Ballard, author of *Lease on Love* and *Just My Type*

"Playful, sexy, and unexpected in the very best way, Sarah Adler is a dazzling new voice in romantic comedy."

—Jen Devon, author of *Bend Toward the Sun*

"At turns both zany and heart-wrenching. . . . This is a treasure of a story that lived and breathed inside my heart."

—Anita Kelly, author of *Something Wild & Wonderful*

OTHER TITLES BY SARAH ADLER

Happy Medium

Mrs. Nash's Ashes

FINDERS KEEPERS

SARAH ADLER

BERKLEY ROMANCE
New York

BERKLEY ROMANCE
Published by Berkley
An imprint of Penguin Random House LLC
1745 Broadway, New York, NY 10019
penguinrandomhouse.com

Library of Congress Cataloging-in-Publication Data

Names: Adler, Sarah, 1991- author.
Title: Finders keepers / Sarah Adler.
Description: First edition. | New York: Berkley Romance, 2025.
Identifiers: LCCN 2024051042 (print) | LCCN 2024051043 (ebook) |
ISBN 9780593817421 (trade paperback) | ISBN 9780593817438 (ebook)
Subjects: LCGFT: Romance fiction. | Novels.
Classification: LCC PS3601.D5748 F56 2025 (print) |
LCC PS3601.D5748 (ebook) | DDC 813/.6—dc23/eng/20241205
LC record available at https://lccn.loc.gov/2024051042
LC ebook record available at https://lccn.loc.gov/2024051043

First Edition: June 2025

Printed in the United States of America
1st Printing

The authorized representative in the EU for product safety and compliance is
Penguin Random House Ireland, Morrison Chambers, 32 Nassau Street,
Dublin D02 YH68, Ireland, https://eu-contact.penguin.ie.

For Hazel—
Please don't read this until you're quite a bit older.

AUTHOR'S NOTE

—

This book is hopefully both fun and funny, with a happily ever after at the end. But it also has a main character who lives with generalized anxiety and depression, references to a parent's workplace accident and subsequent injury and medical debt (in the past, off-page), and separation/divorce (of parents, in the past). If any of these are potentially sensitive topics for you, please read with care.

FINDERS KEEPERS

LATE SELTZER MAGNATE HINTS AT BURIED TREASURE
Fountain's Will Includes Riddle

CATOCTIN, Md., May 20—Family, friends, and employees gathered at the law offices of C. A. Howe yesterday for the reading of Julius James Fountain's last will and testament learned that the notoriously mischievous industrialist had left them one final jape. The relevant passage is reprinted here:

To the City of Catoctin, I leave Sprangbur's house, lands, and outbuildings to be used for the public good, in perpetuity [. . .], entailed to the Sprangbur Conservancy, which will be established as a charity organization upon my death and funded by trust.

To Isolde Fountain Bouchard, my beloved niece, I leave $500,000, and all of the material possessions housed at Sprangbur that are visible.

One (1) item, of immense value and currently hidden (i.e., buried, disguised, covered, or otherwise shielded from the naked eye) somewhere on my estate, shall be the rightful property of whoever is first to discover its whereabouts. CLUE: "Stiff of spine, body pale, you shall find what you seek beneath the whale."

Former secretary to the late Mr. Fountain, Miss Louisa Worman, says that the unconventional bequest is in character for the man she worked for until last July, though she is less certain whether it is intended to be a true hunt or a practical joke. "Julius would have found both options to be quite amusing," Miss Worman stated. She went on to say that she did not intend to take it seriously herself.

Mr. Fountain was the founder and president of Fountain Seltzer, one of the largest beverage companies in the nation. Mr. Howe remembered his client in a short eulogy before the reading as "an esteemed member of our community, renowned as much for his idiosyncratic sense of humor and imagination as for his sharp business acumen." Mr. Fountain died at his home, Sprangbur Castle, last Monday, age 83.

1

GIVEN ALL THE change I've had foisted upon me recently, it's nice to find that Mr. Farina's naked torso is pretty much the same as I remember. Sure, the bulldog tattoo on his left pec is more faded, its jowls a tad droopier, but the egg-like shape of him and the tuft of gray hair exploding from his sternum are heartachingly familiar. And, oh god, am I really crying about a septuagenarian mowing his lawn in booty shorts?

At least I'm still in the privacy of my car. Not that I can stay here much longer. My mother keeps peeking through the living room blinds, her giddiness over my arrival broadcasting itself through that single green eye that appears, disappears, and appears again a moment later to see if I've made any progress toward the door yet. I give it five minutes before she can no longer contain herself and comes out here. Then there will be no avoiding unloading my belongings from the trunk and carrying them inside—a ceremony announcing to the entirety of West Dill Street that Patti and Dave Hunnicutt's Sad Adult Daughter is moving back home.

I slide my glasses up my forehead to avoid smudging the lenses while I dab at my ridiculous tears with a leftover napkin from my stop at the Auntie Anne's in the Jon Bon Jovi Service Area in New Jersey. Four hours ago, I was shoveling pretzel nuggets into my mouth between agitatedly whispering to a nearby pillar plastered with a photo of the travel plaza's namesake and the quote "It's ok to map out your future—but do it in pencil" that it could go fuck itself. Which might have been a little harsh. It's not like it's Jon Bon Jovi's fault that I lost my job, boyfriend, and apartment all in the span of approximately seventy-two hours. But did he really need to rub it in?

Across West Dill, Mr. Farina and his push mower come to a stop at the edge of his front lawn. He spots me as I'm adjusting my glasses back into place and gives a friendly wave. I wave back so as not to be impolite, but quickly redirect my attention to the symmetrical two-story brick duplex where I grew up in hopes it will discourage him from coming over to say hello. Small talk is not exactly something I'm up for at the moment. Mom's eye has returned, now joined by her nose and a corner of her mouth as she pushes the blinds further askew in her eagerness.

The voice of my therapist back in Massachusetts pops into my head, asking: *What is the best outcome here? The worst? The most likely?* Best would be that I make it inside without anyone (other than Mr. Farina and my mother) noticing me, and also maybe I find a winning lottery ticket on the sidewalk. Worst would be that, while walking from my car, a plane engine falls on my head and the headline reads something like "Woman Donnie Darko'd While Moving Back into Her Childhood Home," thereby broadcasting my shame to the entire world. And the most likely is that a passerby sees me hauling my belongings inside, thinks *Oh, she must be staying awhile,* and then immediately stops caring because, really, why should they?

Time to bite the bullet, I suppose. Or face the plane engine.

I open the door and get out, my body unsteady after spending so many hours in the driver's seat. A few quick stretches work out the worst of the kinks, but I still feel tight everywhere. I grab my purse, then close the door and head for the trunk and the many bags and boxes I stuffed inside of it before leaving Boston in my rearview mirror early this morning.

That's when I see movement on the porch of the mirror-image house conjoined with my parents'. There's a man there, slowly pacing back and forth. I'm not sure how I didn't notice him before, unless he only just came from inside? He's fairly tall, pale, with brown side-parted hair and rounded cheeks that prevent his strong jaw and aquiline nose from giving him too severe a look. He appears to be close to my age, somewhere in his early to mid-thirties. Mom mentioned that the Singhs moved out last month, so it's possible this guy is the new tenant. Or maybe he's from the property management company that's been taking care of the house since Mr. Bell left in '09. Could even be a real estate agent, I guess, if the place is finally going to be put on the market. That would explain why he looks like a Brooks Brothers mannequin come to life in his well-tailored navy suit, white dress shirt, and light blue tie.

Whoever he is, I have even less desire to chat with him than I do Mr. Farina. At least Mr. Farina has already seen me in all sorts of embarrassing states since I was a small child (including my baffling and ill-advised eighth-grade glam rock phase). He probably wouldn't even register my stained sweatshirt, unwashed hair, and puffy eyes as particularly notable. But this guy pacing the porch of 304 West Dill and I have not established that sort of rapport. The only thing worse than hitting rock bottom would be having to advertise the fact to a handsome, professionally dressed stranger. No thank you!

So I do the only thing I can think to do under the circumstances: squat down and hide behind my car. With my eyes positioned just above the back seat's window, I can monitor the situation like a human periscope. The man continues strolling the short span of the porch, talking into his cell phone. After a few seconds, he stops pacing and leans on the railing, focusing more intently on whoever is on the other side of the call. As he listens, he sucks on the corner of his bottom lip in a gesture that immediately triggers a memory: my childhood next-door neighbor perched atop that same railing, lip disappearing into his mouth as he practiced peeling an orange in one long, spiraling piece. One of our ridiculous, incessant competitions of who could do it the fastest (me—I won—it was me).

But Quentin Bell moved away a long time ago, and this dapper stranger bears little resemblance to the petite redheaded boy I once dared to eat an ant.

The guy shakes his head before saying something into the phone, then mimes strangling himself with his tie as he listens to the response. It's unexpected and silly, and the gesture brings a smile to my face. It's an expression I haven't worn much lately; reassuring to know I'm still capable of it.

Shit—he's looking over here! I duck farther down.

I have no idea how long I've been hiding, but my calves burn and my thighs are shaking thanks to this extended squat. Is it safe to get up yet?

Just as I'm about to declare the coast clear, a whistled tune drifts into my ears. Unfamiliar, it doesn't seem to have a defined melody so much as a refrain that chases its next note with the exuberance of a dog let loose in a room full of tennis balls. It's increasing in volume and getting closer. Fuck, fuck, fuck. The whistler must be heading straight for me. Could it be Mr. Farina? A quick glance behind me confirms he's still on his steps across the street, sipping his can of Natty Boh and listening to the Orioles game on the old transistor radio my father has repaired for him a dozen times. He's either not noticed or has already lost interest in my bizarre behavior.

The tune grows even louder. What do I do? I'm running pretty low on dignity here; it would be nice to save whatever pathetic scraps I can.

The whistling ceases at the same time the car parked behind me unlocks with a flash of its headlights and a mechanical click. Of course—because my luck is apparently on an indefinite hiatus—it's the man from the porch who steps out from between the back of my old, beat-up car and the front of his much nicer one. And now, with the late day sun shining on him, it strikes me that his hair isn't the dark brown it appeared to be from afar, but a rich, red-heavy russet. The kind of color that a youthful carroty orange might transition into over time.

He tilts his chin in my direction, the barest acknowledgment of my tragic existence. "Nina," he says prosaically, then flashes a brief, devastatingly smooth smile before climbing into his car and speeding away. All this before I can even manage to get myself out of my awkward crouch.

Frankly, I think I would have preferred the plane engine.

2

QUENTIN BELL.

    Quentin *Fucking* Bell. (That isn't his real middle name, obviously, but I think it fits better at the moment than Foster.)

I can't believe it. The last time I saw him was August 16, 2008, when we were sitting beside each other in the back seat of his father's car, absolutely silent the entire twenty-minute ride home from the police station on the outskirts of town. The last time we spoke would have been about an hour before that, when I tearfully apologized for betraying him and getting us in trouble and he responded by coolly dismissing our entire friendship as a mistake.

Now he's just *here*? Back in Catoctin and "Nina"ing me as if the last seventeen years of silence between us never happened?

This development balloons the embarrassment and hurt that have already been taking up the majority of my emotional real estate lately. But it also introduces a modicum of panic and something that feels almost reminiscent of joy. It's extremely tight quarters inside my frontal lobe. Might explain the dull headache starting up between my eyes. Well, that, the incessant crying, and the grass pollen drifting over from Mr. Farina's yard.

"Nina, sweetheart?" My mother's voice comes from the sidewalk.

Right. I'm still squatting behind my car like an action hero in the middle of a shoot-out. I surface slowly, hippo-esque, cringing at the audible pop my knee makes. "Hey, Mom. I'm here."

"Oh, I thought I saw you pull up." Have to admire the way she makes it sound like she just happened to catch a glimpse of the street at the exact moment I arrived and not that she's been glued to the window for the last hour. "But then it was taking a while for you to come in . . ."

"Yeah, I, uh, dropped some trash," I improvise. "It went under the car. Didn't want to be a litterbug." My hand dives into the pocket of my hoodie and pulls out the balled-up, damp Auntie Anne's napkin that I fortunately happened to stash in there. "Anyway, hello."

My mom practically bounces on the balls of her feet in excitement as I lean in for a hug. She squeezes me tightly for a solid thirty seconds, then takes me by the shoulders. "Oh, sweetie, I'm just so glad you're here!"

"Thanks," I say, probably a little too sarcastically. Would it kill her to sound a tiny bit less thrilled that I've seemingly dropped a marble into a sort of Rube Goldberg machine of misfortune, the end result being my arrival back in Maryland?

I guess the thought shows on my face, because her smile turns contrite as she says, "I do wish it were under better circumstances, but it's good to have you home. It feels like years since I saw my baby." She releases me and pinches my cheek.

I frown and tilt my head, attempting to escape her crab fingers. "It's only been six months, Mom."

"And look how much has happened in those six months," she says.

She has a point. When I was here for a brief visit over winter break, everything was going *so* well. My boyfriend, Cole, had accepted an assistant professorship at UMass Boston starting this fall, marking the end of three excruciating years of long distance. We'd be getting an apartment together at the beginning of the summer. And the chair of the history department at the small liberal arts college where I'd been teaching had promised me a multi-year lecturer position. I remember telling my mother how much of a relief it was to know I'd no longer need to plan my life in nine-month contractual increments.

Fast-forward to the first week of June and now there's no Cole, no shared apartment, and, it turns out, not only no multi-year lecturer position but no position of any kind for me at Malbyrne College anymore. How much has happened in six months, indeed. (Although all of that actually happened within the last three days, because I'm nothing if not an overachiever.)

"Thanks for letting me stay here," I say. "I promise it won't be for long. I've already started looking for a new—"

"Nonsense. This will always be your home too, Ninabean. You stay as long as you need."

"Thanks," I say, tears nearly spilling out again. Ugh. The only time I've ever cried this much as an adult was when I babysat a colleague's kids and they made me watch every episode of *Bluey*. "I'll grab my stuff."

She flicks her hands dismissively. "Leave it. We'll have your father come grab it all. You know how he loves feeling useful." I'm not sure this is actually true. My father loves *having a task*. Any task. Whether it's a useful one or not doesn't make much difference to him. The way I am with long-term goals, he is with extremely short-term ones. But I'm not going to complain about not having to haul everything inside on my own, in front of the neighborhood, in some sort of walk of shame designed specifically for adults upon whom life has recently shat. Mom links her arm with mine as if we're off to see the Wizard and says, "Now, let's get you settled inside. I made banana bread this morning."

I sniffle. "With cookie butter swirl?"

"Of course, with cookie butter swirl. What is this, amateur hour?"

I follow her up the walkway to the house where I grew up—the one that apparently once again shares a wall with Quentin Bell, the first boy to ever break my heart.

As soon as I enter my old bedroom after my mother has completed her maternal duty of stuffing me full of pot roast and baked goods while telling me all of the latest hot goss about locals I've either never met or don't remember, I catch a glimpse of myself in the mirror above the dresser opposite the door. My splotchy, swollen face is framed by my high school friends' senior pictures that I for some reason glitter glued to the wooden edges. All of those seventeen- and eighteen-year-olds posed in fields, leaning on fences, or draped in velvet in a photography studio, holding roses or band instruments or footballs. Those kids look ready to go out into the world, to reach their potential. And then present-day me, there in the center like Alice from *The Brady Bunch* if she'd showed up for filming the show's opening the morning after a bender. Welp. I'm officially back at the starting line a decade and a half after the pistol sounded, looking as haggard and defeated on the outside as I feel on the inside.

It's kind of hysterical. And not in a haha-this-is-so-funny way, but like a suffering-from-literal-hysteria way.

I don't have time for a full emotional breakdown right now, though, because my father has caught up with me in the doorway. Considering there was a substantial period of time when he couldn't even walk, it's always reassuring to see him up and about. In fact, it seems he's taken Mom's request to unload my car as a personal challenge to do it in as few trips as possible. He was able to grab most of it in one go; he's got my weekender and duffle slung over one shoulder, a large tote and another duffle over the other, and my suitcase trailing behind. All that's left, I think, are a few boxes with my kitchen items and sentimental tchotchkes in the trunk. The books I shipped should get here in however long media mail takes to arrive. Everything else I already sold or donated over the last few months in preparation for my imminent move.

Cole and I were supposed to move into a gorgeous Somerville two-bedroom today. I thought we were equally excited about it, but apparently he was just a little more hyped than I realized. That's the only reason I can fathom that explains why he decided to move in *two weeks early* by himself. It had to have been that and not the reason he gave me: that he came up to Boston without telling me he was in town because he "wanted to enjoy the space a bit before he had to share it with someone."

Because that's totally fine and normal when it'd been four months since we'd last seen each other in person! Not at all a problem that, when I was texting him how disappointed and upset I was about losing my job and that I wished he were around to comfort me, he responded with stuff like *Me too, babe*, when he was actually only two miles away, drinking with mutual friends at Backbar. Nothing wrong with it at all, according to him. In fact, when I told him that I couldn't be in a relationship with someone I couldn't count on or trust, his expression alternated between annoyed and confused for so long I thought I might have short-circuited him before it finally settled back into its usual flat dismissiveness. *I don't understand what the problem is, Nina. You weren't expecting me until tomorrow anyway.*

"Where'd'ya want me to put all this stuff, Ninabean?" Dad's gruff voice brings me out of my thoughts like someone turning down the knob on a stove, and I no longer feel on the verge of boiling over. Instead, I'm back to the previous slow, steady simmer of ire and pain that seems like it might never fully evaporate.

"Over there on the floor is fine," I say. "I'll put it away later."

He unloads everything at the foot of the twin bed, which still sports the bright orange and hot-pink floral comforter from JCPenney I begged my parents for when I was fourteen. It's bold, I'll give it that. Staring at the garish, narrow bed reminds me how much I already miss my queen-size mattress—the one I sold for twenty-five dollars on Facebook Marketplace last night to avoid having to strap it to the roof of my car and haul it all the way to Maryland. I have many fond memories of waking up in my small-but-sunny apartment in my soft cream linen sheets, burrowing farther beneath the soothingly neutral blush-brown duvet cover I paid too much for even on sale at CB2. I stare at my suitcase, where my beloved bedding is currently compressed within an inch of its life inside a vacuum bag. Symbols of a failed attempt at adulthood, packed away, while that orange-and-pink comforter waits for me, a print so loud it's practically screaming. And not even some fun, irreverent message, like *Welcome back, bitch!* but a steady *Ahhhhhhhhh!* that buries itself deep into my brain.

The last time I lived in this room, I knew it was temporary. I had plans—so many plans—to get out of Catoctin, to do big things, to succeed. Now I basically have to start over again, and I do not currently have the wherewithal to figure out how to go about doing that. It's possible I will still be here when I'm fifty, sleeping alone in this loud, too-small bed. That thought, however melodramatic, makes my pulse race and my stomach drop. No way can I let that happen. I quickly add, "You can leave the boxes in the trunk. No point in hauling them in just to have to haul them back out in a few days."

Dad gives a short hum of acknowledgment and a murmured goodbye as he leaves my room, almost certainly heading back to his basement workshop to fiddle with some rotary telephone or Swiss cuckoo clock he's repairing for someone or bought at a yard sale to fix up and resell. I'm left alone, in my childhood bedroom, trying to determine whether it would be more depressing to settle in and unpack or to live out of my suitcase in a state of denial for however long I'll be here.

Deciding that is a tomorrow-morning problem, I turn on a lamp and throw myself onto the bed. This place is basically a Teenage Nina Museum. I've been back to my parents' house since moving away for college, have spent nights here with the debate tournament medals hanging from the doorknob and my collection of burnt CDs stacked precariously beside the massive old purple boom box. But during those brief visits they felt like someone else's belongings—artifacts of the person I was before I grew up and left it all behind. What used to act as a reminder of how far I'd come now feels like a taunt. *Not so far after all.*

This blows.

I pull out my phone and check my email, my chest aching with the desperate hope that something good might be there. A surprise job offer, or maybe even an uncharacteristically self-aware and sincere apology from Cole (if I'm going to dream, might as well dream big). Of course my inbox is actually filled with increasingly desperate-sounding political fundraising emails and promotional messages from the fancy multi-tool store I purchased my dad's Christmas present from last year. I'm about to close the app when I hear a quiet thump from the other side of the wall. My thumb freezes, hovering over my phone screen. My pulse pounds in my fingertips as I wait in absolute stillness to see if I can pick up any other sounds. A few seconds later, there's a louder thump and the whine of a door.

Quentin.

I sit up, tossing my phone onto the bed as an intense urge hits. I don't actually *want* to do it. In fact, a distinct sense of nausea that comes with a particularly severe wave of anxiety takes hold of my stomach as soon as it occurs to me. Yet I still find myself sliding down onto the floor, sitting beneath the room's only window. It's a reflex, like when the doctor taps at your knee with the little hammer. It's as impossible to resist this as it is that involuntary kick. Embarrassingly, it was such an ingrained habit I even resorted to it a handful of times after Quentin moved away. Not that anyone answered then. No one will probably answer now.

I breathe deeply—in for four, out for six—and my therapist's voice returns. *Best, worst, most likely outcomes,* she prompts. Okay, best: Quentin isn't there at all. In fact, he never existed. He was just a particularly vivid imaginary friend that I grew out of. Worst: He's there, and he wants to talk, but only about how much I suck and/or cryptocurrency. Most likely: He's there, and cordial, but we quickly find we don't have much in common these days and this conversation winds up acting as a sort of unsatisfying closure.

Oof. Honestly, I think you could shuffle all of those outcomes around and they'd still fit whatever heading they wound up under.

Living my life never knowing what would've happened if I'd tried, though . . . that doesn't feel like a legitimate option. Not when I already have so little left to lose. And even unsatisfying closure would be *something*. More than it feels like I got from Cole and Malbyrne College.

So. I guess I'm going to talk to the Moon.

The sash is a good twenty-five years old, and it sticks at first, then opens with a banshee-like scream that will probably cause someone to post to the neighborhood Facebook group with speculations that a murder has occurred somewhere on West Dill. I poke my head out of the screenless opening (it's absolutely amazing I never fell out of here as a child). A string of globe lights my parents zigzagged across the concrete patio illuminates our long, narrow backyard. The other side of the tall dividing fence is darker, but I make out an Adirondack chair and an uncoiled hose—signs of life. The humidity that lingered when I got here two hours ago is dissipating, and the cooler, early evening breeze reminds me that summer is only just arriving. A distant car alarm and the sound of kids playing basketball in the alley behind our detached garages are the only evidence that there's still a world beyond my view. It's . . . soothing, but irritatingly so. Familiar in a way that I want to both embrace and shove away. Kind of like my mom's exuberant fawning.

I tilt my head back and look up to the sky where my supposed quarry is swaddled in a wispy cloud, glowing almost eerily. "This is stupid," I grumble to myself. Even if Quentin happens to be in his old bedroom right now, surely he's simply going about whatever business he has in there. He isn't kneeling in front of his own window, waiting to chat like the old days. But I still take a deep breath and send my words out into the blue-black dark.

"Um . . . Hey, Moon. Been a while, huh?"

The silence that follows feels pitiful. I don't actually expect a response. I'm not sure I even *want* one. So why does my heart feel like its beats have been put on hold as I wait?

Then it practically trips in its attempt to catch up again as soon as a familiar-yet-not voice breaks the silence. "Aw haw haw, indeed it has, mon amie."

I reach up and slam the window shut, barely moving my head out of the way in time. "Oh my god," I whisper. It's him. After all this time. There's absolutely no denying it now; even my expert-level ability to delude myself is no match for that offensively bad French accent. Quentin Bell is once again next door, talking to me from his old bedroom window, only a foot away from my own, thanks to the duplex's Rorschach inkblot layout.

My breathing is too shallow, the earlier nausea intensifying. I try to make my exhales a few seconds longer than my inhales even though I don't have the presence of mind to actually count, willing my nervous system to chill the hell out.

Full-blown panic attack averted, I stare at the closed window. Why did I do that? I hoist it open again, wincing at both the ear-piercing screech and the humiliating likelihood that Quentin realizes exactly how flustered I was to hear his voice.

His words are predictably teasing. "You close your window, but you cannot hide from zee Moon. Zee Moon remains in zee sky, whether you are open to receiving its wisdom or not."

This is painful. Actually, physically painful, because the floor is hard and my stomach hurts, but also emotionally. Nearly two decades of silence, and now we're jumping right back in, resuming our childhood games like nothing ever happened. Like the hurt he left me carrying only exists in my imagination.

At the same time, there's something comforting in it. Like maybe, as long as we're both willing to pretend, time doesn't really exist. We won't need to face what transpired or what's to come. We can simply drift along in this liminal, goofy space, somewhere between childhood and adulthood. Somewhere I don't need to have everything figured out yet.

"I suppose you're right," I say. "And since you're here regardless, I might as well tell you about the weird thing that happened to me earlier."

"Aw haw, I do love a good story. Oui, go on."

"I arrived at my parents' house this evening, and I noticed this guy standing outside on the porch next door. He looked vaguely like someone I used to know, but I told myself that it couldn't be. No way Quentin Bell grew up to be such a . . . what's the right word?"

"Dreamboat? Hunk?"

"Hobbit."

Laughter floats from his open window into mine, as if the idea of anyone finding him unattractive is the best joke he's heard in a while.

Collecting all of Quentin's various laughs was a pastime I thought I gave up many years ago, and yet I find myself turning the pages of a dusty, long-forgotten mental catalog until I land on the entry for this particular, achingly familiar one, listed under *When he found out I spread a rumor that he was the grandson of the founder of Taco Bell.*

"Aw haw, mon amie, perhaps you saw this man in a bad light.

The sun can be harsh and unflattering. I, on the other hand, with my soft, forgiving glow . . ."

We used to go back and forth like this forever, teasing each other, sprinkled with the occasional more serious conversations about life that we were too timid to have face-to-face. Our banter is like a second language, and even if I'm a bit rusty I'm confident I still remember enough to continue. But there's a larger part of me that doesn't have the patience to bury my curiosity about why he's back. (When I tried to ask my mother about Quentin's reappearance next door, she did a horrible job pretending that his return was news to her as well before putting another slice of banana bread in front of me even though I wasn't finished with the first.)

"What are you doing here anyway?" I ask bluntly.

"I thought we already covered zees when you closed zee window. Zee Moon is always there, even when you can't see it."

"Quentin."

"Nina." He drops the horrible accent and says my name with an emphasis on the *ee* sound in the middle like he used to when taunting me. "I just got back to the States. Needed somewhere to crash for a while, and this place was sitting here empty, so . . ."

"Back to the States? Where were you?"

"Paris. I was in my firm's office there for a couple years, advising European companies looking to expand into the US."

"You mean you've actually lived in France and your accent still sounds like Pierre Escargot from *All That*?"

"Just because I speak perfect French doesn't mean the Moon is equally fluent in English. Duh." I can hear the smile in his voice, but when I picture it on his face, my mental image is of a scrawny fifteen-year-old with freckles scattered over his cheeks. Strange to think that cute-but-dweeby kid has transformed into a man who wears ties and drives an Audi. "I'd ask what you're doing here, but your mom mentioned you were coming to visit, so I assume you're, uh, visiting."

Dammit. I *knew* she knew.

"How long you gonna be around?" he asks.

It isn't an unreasonable question, but it's also not one I want to dwell on at the moment. I've never done well with uncertainty, or things that are out of my control. I stumble over my words as I say, "Oh, just until I . . . Till my . . . I'm already looking for . . ."

This one time, when we were in first grade, Quentin proposed we race up the big metal climbing dome on our elementary school's playground. I generally never went higher than two or three feet off the ground, too worried I'd fall through one of the triangular openings to go all the way to the top. But as soon as he issued the challenge it was like my fear disappeared, replaced by such a strong urge to win that I attacked that dome with bold determination—and wound up missing a rung and smashing my nose into one of the diagonal steel bars. And that's kind of how I feel now, grasping for a next move that should be within easy reach but isn't. As if I'm slipping, falling forward, about to meet with a fate I could have avoided if I'd simply paid more attention. "It's rather up in the air at the moment," I conclude, swallowing back the tears threatening to rise for the millionth time today.

There's a pause, and then, "Neen."

Quentin's use of the shortened version of my name, especially in that soft, warm tone, makes my edges feel wiggly. "Hm?"

"I, uh, really . . ." There's a brief hesitation, as if he's carefully weighing what he's about to say. But then finally: "Urgent memo just came through the fax. The boss wants to see us both right away."

A choked, surprised laugh spills out of me. This is a more obscure throwback. When we were around eleven or twelve we thought it was hilarious to pretend we worked for a huge corporation. Doing our homework became "putting in overtime on the big Thompson file." Walking to get ice cream from the corner store was "attending the quarterly revenue meeting." Neither of us knew anything about huge corporations, of course, so it was a bunch of jargon we cobbled together from TV shows and movies. We dropped the bit at some point, and I haven't thought about it in years. But Quentin picking it back up again now feels kind of like deciding to rewatch a movie I loved as a teenager but haven't seen since—delightful nostalgia mixed with the worry that the passing of time might have made the things I enjoyed most about it fall flat.

"The big boss?" I respond anyway. Because I figure it's at least worth seeing if it holds up.

"The biggest. The head honcho himself," Quentin confirms. "Front porch. Two minutes, sharp, or Debbie says it'll be our asses."

"Debbie in accounting?"

"No, that's *Daphne* in accounting. Debbie is the big boss's assistant. She took over for Matthew in January, remember?"

"Oh. Right," I say. "I miss Matthew. He always used to bring in donuts on Fridays."

"One minute, thirty seconds, Hunnicutt. Time is money. Ticktock."

"Fine, fine, I'm coming!"

Quentin's window closes with a suction-y thud that tells me

that, unlike mine, it's been replaced sometime over the years. I imagine him sprinting down the staircase in the mirror-image house beside mine, maybe even sliding down the wooden banister like he used to. (And Dr. Bell isn't even here to yell at him about it.)

I take a moment to blow my nose, wipe my eyes, clean my glasses, and redo my messy bun. My reflection reminds me that it's been a rougher few days than a quick hair adjustment can possibly remedy, but there's not much I can do about that right now. Hopefully the porch lights aren't on and I can rely on that soft, forgiving moonglow. Maybe if I look presentable enough now I can trick Quentin into thinking that when he saw me earlier, crouched behind my car with my unruly curls half out of their elastic and pretzel salt still clinging to my hoodie, it was an optical illusion. I was actually very put-together and not acting weird at all.

Mom clangs around in the kitchen, loading the dishwasher as an audiobook blasts at full volume, and I manage to tiptoe through the dining and living rooms without her noticing me. It's all muscle memory, slipping outside onto the porch, holding the knob of the storm door until it shuts completely so it doesn't slam. Not that the sneaking is strictly necessary, but it feels proper to do this how I would have back when Quentin and I were teenagers, meeting on the porch past our bedtime to continue plotting and chatting late into the night.

He stands on the other side of the cream-painted wooden divider railing, where I first spotted him earlier. As my eyes adjust to the darkness (thank god the lights are off), I make out the outline of him bowing his head as he studies his wrist.

"Three minutes, forty-five seconds," he says, clucking his

tongue. "Punctuality is very important in this business, Hunnicutt. I'm sorry, but we're going to have to let you go."

And even though my termination from Malbyrne had nothing to do with my being on time, that's apparently all it takes to release the floodgates and get me bawling again.

3

S HIT, NINA." CONTRITE laughter. Now that one is new. I
find myself adding it to the catalog as I watch him start to
hoist himself over the divider before realizing he can simply
step over it now. "Hey, come here."

I move into his open arms, which wrap around my waist,
bringing me against his warm, strong chest. It strikes me that
this may be the first time we've ever embraced like this. Cooties
were a concern during the earlier years of our friendship, and
later there was the possibility that a hug would give Quentin a
prime opportunity to slap a CALL ME BUTTHEAD sign on my back, or
that it would provide me with the perfect angle to slip ice cubes
down the back of his shorts.

Of course, there was that last summer, when we had a tentative ceasefire and everything felt strangely charged between us.
I would remember if he'd held me like this then, though, because I would've immediately exploded into a million tiny ribbons of hormonal confetti.

"I'm really sorry. I didn't mean to upset you," he whispers into the hair piled atop my head.

I inhale deeply and find that he smells like soap and laundry detergent—an enticing and clean smell that, coupled with the heat of his body against mine, reminds me of snuggling into a freshly made bed, sheets still warm from the dryer. I pull away, thoroughly abashed by both his pity and my wandering thoughts.

Once there's distance between us, I clear my throat. "It's fine. Seriously. Nothing to be sorry about." I dab at my face with my sleeve, wondering if I might be able to somehow at least pass off the crying as bad allergies. Considering how Quentin's looking at me as if he's afraid I might break like a cold glass dunked into boiling water, I doubt it. Besides, who knows how much my mother already told him about my situation. "I'm just . . . I'm kind of going through a rough patch right now," I confess.

"No worries, I understand. Same here, actually." Quentin, arms now unencumbered, puts both of his hands behind him on the railing and leans back casually. There's the tiniest pause. It really is dark out here, under the overhang of the porch's roof, but we're standing close enough that I can make out the tilt of his lips. "In fact," he says, "I'm pretty sure I'm going through an even rougher patch than you are."

I know what he's doing. I *know*. But, even after all this time, I can't resist. It's that urge, like during that ill-fated playground climbing race and the Grape Juice Incident of '01 and so many other challenges over the ten years that we were best friends. It takes full control of me, triggering my long-dormant impulsiveness and competitive spirit, better judgment be damned.

"Oh, I doubt that very much," I say, picking up the gauntlet. And boy, does holding that gauntlet feel good. Because I might have lost everything I worked for, the life I built out of meticulous planning and hard work, but here is something I can fucking *win*.

He tilts his head and holds a hand out at his side, as if offering me the first serve in the game of shitty-luck tennis we've agreed to play.

"I was promised a promotion at the college where I'd been teaching for years, only to be informed at the last possible minute that, not only was I not getting the multi-year lecturer position they'd dangled in front of me, but due to 'unforeseen budget concerns'"—I form air quotes with my fingers as I repeat Dean Bradbury's explanation—"my usual nine-month contract wouldn't be renewed either." There's something perversely funny about someone who makes six figures telling you your $47,000 salary is the thing that's going to bankrupt the whole school.

"Hmm," Quentin hums in brief acknowledgment. "That sucks."

"Yep."

"I myself was 'encouraged to part from'"—he provides air quotes of his own—"my law firm because I broke off my engagement with the daughter of a major client, and they didn't want to risk losing his business by letting me stick around. Even though I was the one who brought the client to them in the first place."

I guess this is as good a transition as any into the personal stuff. And boy, do I have this one in the bag. "My boyfriend finally moved to the same city as me after three years of being long-distance and didn't bother telling me that he arrived in Boston *two weeks* early. Not even after I lost my job and needed his support. I only found out because I saw him in the background of a mutual friend's Instagram story at a bar down the street. He, of course, believed he didn't do anything wrong and that I was a brat for getting so upset about it."

Quentin's eyes go wider and his eyebrows shoot up in surprise at that, which makes me feel oddly warm inside. It doesn't take long for him to recover and add coolly, as if I hadn't even spoken, "The reason I ended my engagement, by the way, was that my fiancée cheated on me."

"That's unfortunate. I'm sorry to hear it," I say. And I am sorry that Quentin went through that. But, in the context of this game we're playing, I'm also thoroughly unimpressed by the cliché of it.

I know he hears the tepidness in my voice, yet my eyes have adjusted to the low light enough now to see every detail as the corners of his mouth curve farther upward, as if he's confident that he's about to win. And damn, he might, because he says next, "My best friend was the one who broke the news. He knew, of course, because he was the one she'd been cheating with. Apparently, the first time it happened was in my office. On my desk. While I was busy eating cake in the conference room. Because it was my birthday."

Geez. Can something be so cliché that it comes back around to being novel?

"My apartment was already sublet to someone else by the time I found out I wasn't going to be moving in with Cole, and I can't get another place without proof of income, so now I'm back to living with my parents in my thirties," I say.

He responds so rapidly, it's clear he's been waiting for his turn. "Without my job, I lost my work visa, and since I wasn't marrying a French citizen anymore, I needed to leave or risk deportation. So now I'm also back to living in my childhood home. All alone." He smiles wider, already amused by what he's about to say. "Because *I* am a child of divorce."

I almost muster a chuckle. That last summer living beside

each other was haunted by the specter of his parents' separation, and Quentin quickly began using it to win arguments between us. I don't think it was because he actually felt like he deserved special treatment; it was more because insisting he should get the last Oreo or that we should go to the record store before the bookstore since he was "soon to be a child of divorce" added a level of absurdity to it all that helped make it a little easier to bear.

Maybe that's what this silly back-and-forth was too. Because laying it all out like that, each of our respective bad luck streaks shared as matter-of-factly as playing a card in a game of crazy eights, certainly has helped me appreciate just how ridiculous my life has been lately. And Quentin's, apparently. We're quite the pair.

He grins at my near-laugh, then forces his mouth back into a serious straight line. His eyes still crinkle a little in the corners, like he can't fully hide his enjoyment. Pushing himself off the railing, he takes a step toward me. "You think it's funny that my life fell apart, Hunnicutt?"

My laughter bubbles over in response to his nearness, almost like a fear response. Not that I'm afraid of Quentin exactly. It's more that, from this close, it's easier to comprehend the transformations that took place during our time apart. Where the gangliness of youth has turned to solid, defined angles, or how his almost orange wavy hair darkened to a shade of deep rust. His freckles are still there, in the same arrangement I remember, petering out just under his light blue eyes, but they're more faded now. He's taller, of course, with broader shoulders, and while he isn't muscular in a hangs-out-at-the-gym way, he seems strong. A useful person to have around if you ever need a piano moved.

The similarities to and departures from the Quentin I remember conspire to make it feel like this is someone I've known all my life, and yet don't truly know the first thing about. It's . . . strange. Comfortable and intimidatingly new at the same time. An eerie echo of how it feels being back here in general.

"I mean, *I* think it's hilarious," he says. "But it's rude for *you* to laugh about it. Especially when you're not doing too hot yourself."

I shake my head now, laughing to the point of needing to gasp for air, barely able to get words out. "I'm really not! I'm doing . . . *so* . . . badly!" I have to admit, this is a nice change of pace from all the crying I've been doing, even if it is only exchanging one exaggerated emotional response for another. My eyes close as I take a few deeper breaths, trying to calm myself. When they open again, they land on Quentin's throat. He's still wearing the dress shirt I spotted him in earlier, but the top few buttons are undone and his tie—which is the exact color of his eyes, I realize—is loosened. His closeness is sobering. "So why are you dressed all business-y?" I ask, gesturing toward the half Windsor knot. "You weren't at the office, I take it."

"I had a virtual interview with a firm in Chicago this afternoon. Figured the T-shirt with the big mustard stain I'd been wearing for the past week wasn't going to cut it."

"Yeah, mustard stains are totally passé." I pull at the hem of my hoodie to expose the large brown spot where the lid on my Dunkin' cup popped off while I was drinking in the car this morning. "Coffee's what's hot now."

"Oof. Bad pun," he says.

"I wasn't trying to pun at all, but now I'm going to have to stand behind it." I don't know what to do with my hands. They keep wanting to fiddle with his tie, or straighten his collar, or muss his hair. I shove them into my hoodie pocket instead. "How'd it go? The interview."

He shrugs.

I follow the movement of his shoulders upward. He's staring down at me, as if he's been watching my mouth this whole time. It's like the residual familiarity between us disappeared as the distance shrank, and now it's just me standing a few inches away from a man with pretty eyes and an aura of magnetism. The effect only heightens the longer we stand there, until he says quietly, as if sharing a secret: "It's good to see you, Nina."

And that's all it takes for everything to come whooshing back. Our history. The silly competitions and pranks, yes. But mostly that last sweltering summer spent roaming Catoctin together, hunting for a treasure that may or may not have even existed. The night we lay in his backyard, looking up at the stars, and I thought maybe, just maybe, I could find a way to keep him. The very next night, when everything fell apart. Then all of the silence—seventeen whole years of it. Our best and worst moments, everything that I've kept carefully folded and tucked away for so long, spring out all at once in an assault that nearly knocks me off my feet.

"Is it, though?" I ask, intending for it to sound playful. But it doesn't. In fact, I think I surprise both of us with not only the question, but the naked desperation behind it. Quentin's eyebrows furrow and his head tilts. My stomach roils in the second of silence that follows, and I cross my arms, as if they might keep my insides from spilling out all over the place. My brain—which generally takes great pains to *avoid* conflict—screams, *What are you doing??*

Quentin stares at me, his lips slightly parted. He looks . . . stunned. Did he truly have no idea I'd still have some lingering emotions around what happened between us? Or maybe he assumed I would never let them show. It reminds me of the conversation I had with Cole when I confronted him. How he seemed so taken aback that I was upset about his gigantic lie by omission. Bewildered that I cared enough about our relationship to go through the trouble of ending things.

Maybe everything that happened between us didn't matter that much to Quentin, but surely he can't be *that* surprised to find out it mattered to me.

"I'm sorry," he says quietly.

"For what exactly?"

"For . . ." His sentence stalls out, as if he isn't sure how to describe exactly what happened. *For saying it was all a mistake. For ghosting you after I moved away. For reappearing in your life at one of the very worst possible moments.* So many ways he could complete the thought, and yet he chooses a noncommittal gesture, a half-hearted wave that seems to imply the brushing aside of the past as if it were nothing but a tiny, annoying gnat.

"Very convincing apology," I say with an eye roll.

His eyes drop to his feet—which I'm now noticing are bare—before coming back up to meet mine. He doesn't say anything more.

I don't have the emotional, mental, or physical energy left to continue on this journey to a destination I don't really need to revisit anyway. "Good to see you too," I lie briskly. "But I better get going. Had a long day. Good night."

And, as I go back into my parents' house, I let the old storm door slam behind me—the sound acting as an audial punctuation mark, ending the conversation.

4

AWAKEN IN THE morning, immediately aware of two things: My eyelids—along with most of the rest of my face—are puffy and painful, and I am buzzing with a renewed sense of determination to put Pathetic Nina away and start figuring out how to get my shit back together. For pride reasons. *Not* so I can get out of town ASAP to decrease the likelihood of having to talk to Quentin again.

I figure a splash of cool water will help with the former until I can get to Target and purchase several heavy-duty face masks to restore a bit of the moisture I've been shedding willy-nilly.

As far as the latter, well, I guess the first step is to figure out where Ambitious Nina has run off to. She's the version of me who is determined, driven, and mature. She makes lists and plans, and her goals are always Specific, Measurable, Achievable, Relevant, and Time-Bound. She's successful and intelligent and absolutely *not* someone who cries multiple times a day. That's the person I'm used to being, the one I've been for most of my life. Even if she's currently difficult to locate, I'm sure there's still enough of her somewhere inside me to get the ball rolling on the whole getting-out-of-Catoctin thing.

After getting dressed, I open my bedroom door to head to the bathroom and am greeted by my mom's distinctive laugh— a twinkly, melodic *haHA!* punctuated with an incredible goose-like honk—drifting up the stairs. Yesterday, that familiar sound might have felt like a kick in the teeth—a reminder of the very long chute I've slid down in the Chutes and Ladders game called life (which is also the name of a game, so actually that's kind of confusing). But this lovely early June morning, fully convinced that I may only be a single lucky spin away from another ladder that will take me straight back up to the top of the board, Mom's laughter brings a smile to my face. Because now, with every intention and hope of getting back on track, I can think of this as simply a nice and admittedly overdue visit with the lovely people who raised me. A vacation of sorts.

Just as I wouldn't allow a storm to ruin a weekend at the beach, or a lost suitcase to keep me from enjoying a trip to Madrid, I'm not going to let my circumstances—and especially not Quentin Bell's sudden reappearance next door and torpid non-apology—cast a shadow on this quality time with my family, however unexpected.

So, while brushing my teeth, I imagine all of the places I might encounter Quentin and how to coolly handle each hypothetical situation. Washing my face and applying copious moisturizer, I settle on a potential greeting: "Hi," but delivered with scathing disinterest. The need to find the exact perfect combination of hostile yet detached words to show him how little I care gives me an excuse to take an extra few minutes to add defining cream to my blonde curls instead of throwing my hair up into yet another frizzy bun. My full speech is finalized by the time I put on my glasses and apply a swipe of tinted lip balm.

The version of myself in the mirror this morning looks a lot more like the one I remember being before everything started going wrong. Quentin's presence (or lack thereof) had no effect on the life I worked so hard to build, and it doesn't need to have anything to do with my ability to rebuild it now. What does it even matter if we've found ourselves temporarily living beside each other again? It doesn't mean we have to be friends. If I can't avoid him, I'll treat him with the same icy politeness I would a door-to-door salesman.

And while I put away Pathetic Nina and await the eventual return of Ambitious Nina, maybe I can be an interim version of myself, one made for this particular moment. I can be Badass Nina, who wears real clothes and washes her face and isn't at all hung up on the distressing things that happened to her this past week, much less the ones that happened a lifetime ago.

I hold my head high as I descend the stairs. Because Badass Nina is cool, calm, and collected. She is a duchess making her entrance at the season's grandest ball. Grace personified. A goddamn *swan* of a woman.

Mom sits at the dining room table, a floral stoneware mug cupped in her hands. It looks a little off-kilter, like something she must have made herself at one of the many art classes she's been taking since she retired last December. She smiles beatifically as I appear. "There she is," she says.

"Here I am," I respond in a matching singsong voice.

"There you are," Quentin says.

Wait, what?

I blink a few times. I must be hallucinating. Or dreaming.

But no, Quentin's still here, in real waking life, sitting opposite my mother at the table and cupping a slightly wonky mug of his own. Quentin in the dining room is even more surreal than him on the porch last night, a sort of fun house mirror reflecting a distorted version of the past. He used to sit in that exact chair whenever he would come over for dinner or to work on school projects. Back then he was slender and not much taller than me, wearing two-sizes-too-large band tees with hair so shaggy he was constantly having to swipe it away from his eyes. He wasn't this . . . this . . . *man*, with his meticulous grooming and button-down shirts with the sleeves rolled up and pale, freckle-dusted forearms taking up an unnecessary amount of space in my house.

I mean, my *parents'* house. That I am visiting. Briefly.

Luckily, Badass Nina prepared for this moment. Not for Quentin being in the dining room when she walked down the stairs, of course, but the general strategy still applies. I open my mouth, ready to deploy my uninterested "Hi." Instead it comes out as "Ho . . . there? Howdy. Good morning."

Fuck.

Well. Rest in peace, Badass Nina. June 8, 8:50 a.m., to June 8, 9:15 a.m. The lights that burn brightest truly burn fastest.

Quentin manages to keep a straight face despite the absolute nonsense I've just blurted out. "Ho there, howdy, and good morning to you as well," he says with the solemnity of a faith leader greeting his congregation.

Okay, okay. New plan! It isn't perfect but it will have to do: yawn wide, state my immediate need for coffee and food, and hide in the kitchen. Forever.

Mom stands and gives me a good morning hug while continuing to look at Quentin affectionately, and it's like we've somehow time-traveled back to the mid-aughts. "You two and your inside jokes. Such silly gooses. I'll just leave you to catch up while I go make some breakfast."

Before I can protest, she's left the room.

"Hope you don't mind me hanging out with Patti while I waited for you to come down," he says. His eyes drift to where Mom is still visible through the doorway from where he's sitting, and a fond smile spreads across his face. "What a ray of sunshine that woman is. She had me seated with banana bread and coffee in ten seconds flat."

Seriously? There was only one slice left, and she gave it to *him*? The person who ghosted me for nearly two decades and then refused to even explain himself or apologize beyond a half-hearted "sorry"? I know my mom doesn't know the full story of what happened between us, or anything about our conversation last night, but come on! I fold my arms over my chest. "What do you want, Quentin?"

My attempt at boredom comes out instead as hostility. Fine with me. He blinks a few times like I've surprised him again. "To talk. I just . . . wanted to talk to you."

Oh, *now* he has something to say. "Well, mission accomplished. A number of words have left your mouth and reached my ears. You can go now. Goodbye!"

"Nina . . ." He stands and makes his way over to me. Seeing him in a well-lit room, this close up, is a real mindfuck. They may not have liked each other much, but Mr. and Dr. Bell made a very handsome couple. So it shouldn't be a shock that Quentin's become rather appealing himself. But it's still annoying. His gaze travels over my face, as if he's also observing my features, before settling back on my eyes. Am I going to get my apology now? A real one? I guess I did sort of ambush him last night. Maybe now that he's had time to find the right words . . .

He reaches up and takes one of my curls between his thumb and forefinger, pulling it down and releasing it into a bounce—an old playful gesture that feels more intimate now than antagonistic. The slight tug at my scalp sends a tingle down my spine. "I can't go yet," he says softly, seriously, before he succumbs to the amusement lurking in the wrinkles at the corners of his eyes. "Your mom promised me pancakes."

I attempt to shove him away, but it's too weak, reluctant. He barely moves an inch. "Oh, fuck off."

"Language!" Mom scolds from the kitchen.

"Sorry!" I call back before refocusing on Quentin. "I don't want to play with you," I tell him in an angry whisper that immediately shrinks me into an elementary school version of myself. It's surprising that, when I do a surreptitious glance down, I'm still wearing my floral sundress and not ill-fitting black corduroy overalls with a Tweety Bird T-shirt underneath.

He presses his lips together and nods as he reaches into the back pocket of his jeans. He pulls out a worn, folded piece of paper—the familiar looping cursive on the outside making my heartbeat accelerate before he even opens it and holds it up in front of my face.

The map we made that last summer as we set out to find Julius James Fountain's legendary hidden treasure. The thing that ultimately destroyed our friendship.

"Well, that's disappointing, Neen. Because I would really like to play with you."

Forms to be Filled out for Each Interview

FORM A

MID-ATLANTIC INDUSTRY
Circumstances of Interview

STATE .... Maryland
NAME OF WORKER .. Albert Aaron
ADDRESS .... Sprangbur Estate, Catoctin, Maryland
DATE .... June 9, 1937
SUBJECT .... Life and business of Julius J. Fountain

1. Date and time of interview

    June 9, 1937, morning

2. Place of interview

    Sprangbur Estate
    1 Riverview Drive
    Catoctin, Maryland

3. Name and address of informant

    Julius James Fountain (see above)

4. Name and address of person, if any, who put you
   in touch with informant

   Isolde Fountain Bouchard (informant's niece)
   Washington, District of Columbia

5. Name and address of person, if any,
   accompanying you

6. Description of room, house, surroundings, etc.

   A large estate atop a hill on the outskirts of
   the small city of Catoctin, Maryland, overlooking
   the Monocacy River. In the center of the property is
   a three-story Richardsonian Romanesque residence
   known as the Castle, constructed of rough-faced
   brown stone and accented with patinated copper
   turrets and towers of varying shapes and heights.
   The footprint is notably asymmetrical, consisting
   of many swells and recesses. An arched portico
   shelters the front entrance, with an elaborate star
   motif carved into the wooden door.

   Inside, the residence is richly appointed in the
   fashions of the last century, with silk-papered
   walls and elaborate woodwork trim. The library, in
   which this interview was conducted, is lined with
   overflowing bookshelves. I recognize that it is not
   standard practice to comment upon the appearance of
   the informant at this stage of the record, but I
   feel it crucial to note that Mr. Fountain attends

~~this interview wearing his pajamas, which are in the exact pattern of the fabric of his chair, resulting in the illusion upon first glance that he is but a floating head. This startled me upon my entrance into the room, causing me to drop the glass of soda water the butler inexplicably handed me upon my entrance to the house, and in response, Mr. Fountain shouted, "Six! Add another tally to the board, Marshall!" as this is apparently a game he enjoys playing with his visitors.~~ There is abundant natural light.

5

THE SLIGHTLY YELLOWED sheet of legal paper swiped from Mr. Bell's office, covered in amateur blueprints and the adolescent version of my own handwriting, takes me back to the summer of 2008 so quickly my neck twinges from the emotional whiplash. All of those mornings we spent trying to find some secret meaning behind the Fountain estate's idiosyncrasies until the heat and humidity wore us out and we fled to the library's special collections room, where the cool air-conditioning dried our sweat and made us shiver. I can almost feel the familiar resulting drowsiness from the temperature change, Quentin's elbow nudging me awake when I fell asleep combing over Fountain Seltzer Company meeting minutes.

"You still have it," I breathe.

Quentin narrows his eyes. "Of course I still have it. Who would throw away a treasure map?"

"It isn't . . ." I shake my head, more to clear it than convey anything. "It's not a *real* treasure map. We made it ourselves. Besides, it was just . . . kid stuff."

"Oh, come on. You know it was more than that."

For a moment I'm not sure if we're still talking about the map. Even so, I point to the square in the corner. "You labeled the old cemetery 'the Bone Zone,' Quentin."

He examines the words written in his scratchy small caps. "Okay, fine, I will concede that the map *itself* wasn't that serious. But the treasure was not 'just kid stuff.' And it's most likely still out there." One side of his mouth kicks up quite charmingly—a little *too* charmingly, if you ask me. Like it's something he's spent a good amount of time practicing. "I bet we could still find it."

It feels like my blood freezes in place as I process the words. I stare at him, then shakily take the proffered paper from his hands and smooth it out on the table. Our interpretation of Julius James Fountain's estate, Sprangbur, lies before me: a large amebic shape representing the eccentric mansion at its center, the various odd little outbuildings, monuments, and themed gardens scattered around it. We drew this because we were convinced the higgledy-piggledy layout of the property might provide some clue we were missing. Why else would Fountain have built so many bizarre structures with seemingly no rhyme or reason unless they actually formed a symbol or something from above? What we didn't understand at the time—but I certainly do now that I've gone to school with and taught some of their children—is that sometimes rich people do strange, outlandish, expensive shit simply because they can. Looking over our makeshift map again, that certainly seems to be the case here.

"What are you thinking?" Quentin asks softly.

I glance up at him. "I don't even know . . ."

"Don't even know what?"

If I believe it's actually there. If I could do this again, knowing how much pain it wound up causing me. Why you *want to when you said yourself it was all a mistake.* But before I can choose how to respond, Mom comes in with a precariously tall tower of pancakes, a flour sack towel draped over the plate so it looks like she's carrying a small, slightly inebriated ghost. "Breakfast is served!" she announces with a flourish.

Quentin takes the map from the table before Mom can set the plate atop it and refolds the paper along its deep-set creases. He doesn't look at me as he tucks it back into his pocket.

"Oh, Nina, you don't have anything to drink." My mother is already turned back toward the kitchen, pancakes still in hand. "Remind me how you take your coffee?"

"No, no, Mom. Sit. Eat. I've got it," I say, putting my hands on her shoulders to physically guide her toward the table as I scoot past and out of the dining room, finally escaping but much too late to do me any good.

I WOULDN'T HAVE believed it possible to be this tense while eating pancakes, but I'm certainly managing. Each bite has to practically fight its way through my clenched teeth to make it into my mouth, and I can feel my jaw working against my shoulders, which have been up by my ears since I returned to the table.

The unfairness is what's getting to me. It's not like I was naive enough to expect everything in my life to go swimmingly forever, but I also didn't expect to almost drown so close to what I've always considered my destination. And then I *really* didn't expect to climb into a lifeboat only to have to share it with Quentin Fucking Bell and a goddamn makeshift treasure map.

Quentin Fucking Bell and a goddamn makeshift treasure map and that stupid *smile* that he's flashing at me from across the table even as he chews. He doesn't look tense at all. He looks . . . loose. Relaxed. Annoyingly okay, considering his own recent string of misfortunes. What is his secret? Maybe it's time. Maybe his wounds aren't as fresh.

"So how long have you been back in town, Quentin?" I ask conversationally.

He's in the middle of a sip of his coffee, but at the tail end he says, "Not too long. About a week and a half."

Further confirmation that my mother is a traitor. Didn't know he was here, my ass. The wall between our houses isn't thin enough to hear conversations word for word (unless someone's screaming at the top of their lungs, the way the Bells often did before they separated). But they're certainly thin enough to know if someone's in residence next door. The one fact about my mother that no one on earth would dispute—not even Patricia Hunnicutt herself—is that she is nosey as heck. No way she wouldn't have figured out that 304 West Dill was once again occupied, and by exactly whom, within three hours of the first stair tread squeak.

"That's *very* interesting," I say more to her than to him. Mom looks away guiltily, her eyes drifting from her plate to her mug, then finally settling on the painting of what I think is supposed to be a still life of fruit hanging on the wall across from her. I don't remember it being there before, and quality-wise I'm going to assume it's yet another product of her recent arts and crafts spree.

Quentin takes a big bite of pancakes and watches me watching my mom, his eyebrows—slightly lighter than his hair—elevated in interest.

The door beneath the staircase swings open, and my dad surfaces from his basement workshop. Even when I was a kid, he spent a good bit of time down there. But since repairing stuff and tinkering around became his sole focus after the settlement from his accident at the quarry finally came through and allowed both my parents to retire, it feels like kind of a big deal whenever he graces us with his presence. Like actually spotting a whale on one of those whale watching tours—you hope it might happen, and there's a greater-than-zero chance, but everyone makes it clear ahead of time that nothing's guaranteed.

"Morning," he says gruffly to the room at large, then: "Quentin, come on down when you're done. I'll show you that record player we were talking about yesterday."

Oh my god. Et tu, Father?

So *both* of my parents have been *cavorting* with Quentin for the past week and a half and for some reason kept it a secret from me? Great. Wonderful. Why not add a little extra annoying cherry to top off this nightmare sundae.

My fork clatters onto my plate, and everyone's attention turns in my direction. "Excuse me," I say, politely dabbing at the corner of my mouth with my napkin. "I think I need some air."

My mother's failed attempt at a whispered explanation for my behavior follows me through the living room as I head for the front door. "She's had some setbacks lately. Poor baby."

Outside, I grab the porch railing and bend forward, forcing myself to take a deep, steadying breath. The midmorning air is heavily scented with sweet honeysuckle courtesy of the gigantic bush that grows against the side of the house. It clears the now-cloying smells of maple syrup and coffee from my nose, and a tiny bit of the tension I've accumulated slips from my muscles. When I glance up, I notice Mr. Farina once again sitting on his steps across the street, dressed in the same too-short shorts from yesterday and an Ocean City tank top with oversize armholes.

He spots me over his newspaper and holds up his smoothie in my direction, a sort of frozen fruit–based salute.

"Think those legs of his go all the way up?"

Startled, I turn too quickly and my elbow makes hard, pointy contact with Quentin's stomach. He lets out an *oof* as the wind is knocked from him, then places a hand over the spot. "Jesus, Nina. I admit it was a pretty bad joke, but I'm not sure *that* was necessary."

"Sorry," I mumble. "It was an accident. You snuck up on me." I turn back around so he won't see the small smile on my face, which would probably not do much to bolster my apology.

"I'll make sure to approach loudly next time." After he's recovered, he moves to stand beside me at the railing. "Wanna tell me what's wrong?"

My resulting scoff is weirdly screechy. "What's wrong? What's *wrong*?"

"Other than the obvious, I mean."

"Isn't the obvious enough?" I ask, incredulous.

"Oh. I see." He turns around and tucks his hands into his pockets. "You're still mad at me." His tone is casual, like someone noticing that they've run out of milk.

"I'm not mad at you!" Good job, Nina. Shouting about not being mad is a surefire way to convince someone you aren't mad. "But if I were, wouldn't I deserve to be? I mean, you were my best friend and then you—" *Almost kissed me but didn't, even though I really wanted you to, and* . . . Nope. Let's just skip ahead, why don't we . . . "—disappeared from my life! And now you're hanging out with my parents and asking me to go treasure hunting like we're fifteen again."

I take a step back. Having to look up to meet his eyes makes me feel like such a child. *All* of this makes me feel like such a child. Why can't I control my emotions anymore? It's like I left all of my coping skills back at that rest stop in Jersey.

Stupid Bon Jovi.

"Nothing is going right for me," I say. "*Nothing*. Not even this. I was supposed to at least be able to come back home to lick my wounds, but instead you're here tearing open old ones."

My voice is too loud, too raw. But hey, at least I'm not crying again. Yet.

"I'm not trying to tear open old wounds, Nina. I'm trying to heal them." That look of surprise and contrition from last night is nowhere to be found on Quentin's face. His lips are a flat line, and his cheeks are flushed. "Do you think you were the only one who was hurt that summer? That you're the only one hurting now?"

The emotion in his voice manages to pull me out of my pity spiral. I blink, and suddenly standing before me is my old friend, a little boy trying to make everything into a challenge, into a game, so he doesn't have to confront it head-on. He's going through it just as much as I am. And this—the treasure hunt—must be something of a coping mechanism. It's like in 2008, when we spent those long days researching at the library, making the map at my dining room table, exchanging theories late at night over AIM, exploring Sprangbur's grounds over and over again as if the X that would mark the spot might magically appear if we were persistent enough.

We wanted to find Fountain's riches, of course. But I always suspected that it was about more than that for Quentin. That he was using the hunt as a distraction. One that got him out of his house, away from his parents' ice-cold silence and the moving boxes that reminded him that everything was about to change. In that light, it's easier to understand that his proposal to resume the search may not be the provocation it felt like a moment ago.

It may be him grasping for a way to navigate another challenging period in his life.

Or a way to make amends.

"You know I've always had my doubts," I say, finding myself willing to be gentler. "We did enough research on Julius James Fountain to know that he was . . . whimsical."

Quentin snorts. "Sure, let's go with that."

True, it's a gross understatement. Fountain existed somewhere beyond whimsy. He was like a turn-of-the-century Willy Wonka, minus the child endangerment. A man known for his shrewd business sense but also for doing things purely because he found them amusing. Quirky, original, a little bit annoying. Sort of a manic pixie dream industrialist.

"So what makes you believe he actually hid a treasure at Sprangbur?" I ask. "Wouldn't he have equally enjoyed the idea of everyone searching for something that never existed? We know he loved pranks. Remember the thing in the oral history interview about him always trying to scare the shit out of visitors by blending in with his furniture?"

He frowns, considering. "I hear you. I just don't think he was the sort of person who would lie about something like this."

"But he *was* the sort of person to hide something of immense value somewhere on his property and construct an elaborate treasure hunt for strangers to find it?" As soon as the words are out of my mouth, I shake my head. We're talking about someone who claimed to be the monarch of a pretend kingdom and was notorious for breaking into pig latin at board meetings just to keep his employees on their toes. Not hiding a treasure and hiding one do seem equally in character. "Okay, yes, he probably was that sort of person," I admit. "But then why hasn't anyone cracked this yet? Doesn't it seem more likely that it isn't actually there than that no one has managed to find it over the last eighty-whatever years? We know we aren't the only ones to ever search for it. Not even the only ones this century. There were plenty of people who looked after the reward was announced."

Quentin shrugs. "Not that many, though, and who knows how seriously they took it. We know that even back when Fountain died, most people thought it was nothing but a silly legend. And they still do. Mr. Long definitely did."

Our tenth-grade social studies teacher assigned us a short research project about local folklore and used an overhead projection of the original newspaper article reporting the unusual contents of Fountain's will as an example of a primary source we could use. Somehow, in a class of twenty-two bored teenagers, Quentin and I were the only ones who latched onto the idea that a hidden treasure might actually exist in our hometown.

Or, rather, Quentin latched onto it. Then persuaded me. Not completely dissimilar to what is happening right now.

He takes a step closer, and the honeysuckle in the air mixes with that clean, soapy smell I picked up while hugging him last night. I have to admit it's certainly an upgrade from the Axe Body Spray he (and most of the other boys at school) used to wear like a heavy jacket. There's something about the scent of him that makes my bones feel like they're made of pudding.

"Isn't it tempting?" he asks, and it takes me a moment again to realize we haven't switched topics. "An item of *immense value*, according to someone who was one of the wealthiest men in the United States. We could be talking thousands, hundreds of thousands, *millions* of dollars! Split fifty-fifty, I assume that kind of cash could be very helpful at this particular moment in your life."

"Would we even have the legal right to keep something

discovered on someone else's property?" I ask. "Or would we have to turn over whatever we find to the Sprangbur Conservancy anyway?"

"I actually have no idea," he confesses happily.

"Aren't you supposed to be a lawyer?"

"Good lawyers admit when they need to do some more research. And, believe it or not, this isn't exactly a straightforward situation." He pauses. "But I can see a world in which someone would be able to make a case that 'finders keepers' applies here."

"'Finders keepers,'" I repeat. "And that's an official legal term?"

He grins. "Surprisingly, sort of yes?"

I place my hands flat, palms up, as if about to shrug. "So, I could spend my time looking for a new job and a place to live that isn't my childhood bedroom, *or* I could go on a fool's errand with you that has a half of a percent chance of helping me out if the treasure actually exists, if we can find it, if it's actually worth something, and if the law happens to be on our side." Perhaps it's a bit much, but I make a show of it before settling the look-for-a-new-job hand up toward my ear and the go-treasure-hunting one somewhere near my waist. "Yeah, sorry, no, I will not be doing that."

My smile is tight-lipped as I turn to go back inside.

Quentin's hand comes to my upper arm, gently stopping me in my tracks. A delicious tingle dances along my skin where his fingers rest. "Neen. Wait."

I spin around, facing him, crossing my arms to protect myself from the contact. "What?"

"Five thousand dollars."

I wait for him to explain why he has said an amount of money at me, eventually gesturing for him to go on when the natural time for him to do so elapses.

"What if there was still a guaranteed ten thousand dollars if we found it? Would it be worth it then?"

My eyebrows dive in confusion. "What are you talking about? The reward expired." It's true that there was once one offered for information leading to the treasure's discovery. But that was just a publicity stunt concocted by the Sprangbur Conservancy and the gigantic beverage conglomerate that now owns Fountain Seltzer in an effort to drum up interest in the old property when they started their renovation fundraising in the early aughts. It wasn't even in effect when we were hunting in '08 (not that it kept us from dreaming that we would still be lauded as heroes and showered with money regardless).

He shakes his head. "Not technically. There's an obscure legal loophole I learned about in Contracts. It's called Charlie's Law. You know, because of the whole golden ticket, chocolate factory situation. And it says that if a corporation announces a contest where the prize is dependent on finding something, it cannot officially end until said thing is found."

I let out a bizarre, unamused laugh. "And you think we could actually hold Aera-Bev to that? They wouldn't just laugh in our faces?"

"Charlie's Law is very straightforward in this situation, and ten grand is basically nothing to a billion-dollar company," he says. "Definitely not worth the expense and bad PR of a court case they know they'd lose. I don't anticipate any issues."

"What do you even need me for, then? Go look by yourself."

"I need you to tell me what you were doing that night and why," Quentin says. "I also know you probably remember a lot more than I do about what sources we've already consulted, and where we've already checked."

I frown.

Quentin steps closer, looking down at me, his eyelids lowered and his mouth serious. "We agreed to hunt for Fountain's treasure together, Nina. As far as I'm concerned, that agreement still stands." He lays a hand on my forearm as if to keep it from making any sudden movements. I try to resent the warmth that returns to my skin like a sensual boomerang. "What do you have to lose?" he asks softly.

It's a good question. For the life of me I can't think of a single thing except my heart. Again.

"Well, last time we did this, we lost our friendship," I quip.

"Yeah. And maybe this is how we find it again." Quentin lets his fingers fall from where they were resting above my wrist. He walks past me and smoothly steps over the porch's divider railing. As he opens the front door on his side of the duplex, his eyebrows shoot up and his lips settle into an even more contemplative expression than before. "Five thousand dollars, Neen. Just think about it."

6

Mom sits on the couch in the living room, her attention fully on her e-reader so she doesn't notice me until I'm in front of her. Which is good, because it keeps her from making a quick getaway like earlier when I tried to talk to her and she slipped out the back door, mumbling something about meeting a friend for lunch before I could point out that it was after three o'clock.

She clutches her chest as I appear in her field of vision. "Nina, sweetheart. Goodness."

"We need to chat, Mother."

"Okay, all right," she capitulates, placing her e-reader on the coffee table. "Go ahead." Her chin goes up, probably to get a better view of me standing in front of her, but it also makes her look like a little kid trying to put on a brave face.

"Why did you pretend you didn't know he was back?" I ask.

"Who?"

"Slim Shady," I say, folding my arms in annoyed disbelief. She returns my stare, one eye narrowed as she tries to make sense of the reference. To be fair, my mother isn't particularly known for her knowledge of early 2000s rap. "Quentin, Mom. Quentin Bell. You know, about six feet tall, reddish hair, big fan of pancakes and getting on my nerves?"

Mom presses her lips together primly.

"When I asked you yesterday, you acted like you'd never heard of him in your life, much less noticed him living next door for the last week and a half. Then this morning he's sitting in our dining room, chatting away like it's part of his daily routine. Why didn't you just tell me he was here instead of being so weird about it?"

She sighs. "I didn't mean to be *weird* about it. It's only . . ."

I have to admit, it feels wrong to interrogate my mother like this. But she's left me no choice. "It's only what?"

"Well, you were so sad after he left, Nina."

"What? I was *not* sad."

Mom gives me a long look that says she vividly remembers me playing No Doubt's "Don't Speak" on repeat for weeks after Quentin moved to Michigan to live with his mom. Which, considering he wasn't speaking to me at all, is actually quite ironic now that I think about it.

"Okay, fine, I was a tiny bit sad, but it wasn't . . . It wasn't all about Quentin. I was fifteen. A lot was happening, like, hormonally and life-wise." I've always believed that it wasn't losing Quentin himself that made that fall and winter so awful so much as losing the steadiness of having him around. Especially with my father's accident at the quarry; his long, painful recovery; our resulting financial struggles; and the court case that took a decade to settle. There was a lot going on, and I found myself in a dark place. Without Quentin to talk to and to compete against, I had all of this nervous energy and nowhere to focus it except into catastrophizing. It was the perfect breeding ground for my burgeoning anxiety disorder. Until I realized I could make myself so busy and future oriented that I wouldn't have to think about the present outside of what I needed to do to achieve my goals. If my academic success also made my parents proud, gave them something to talk about other than my dad's chronic pain and overdue bills, and took some of the weight off their shoulders when it came to paying for college, all the better. "Regardless," I add, "it doesn't justify you not telling me he was back."

"I was only trying to look out for you, baby. I didn't want to upset you when you have so much going on," she says.

"So much going on?" My laugh is small and filled with a probably unfair amount of bitterness. "I don't have *anything* going on anymore. That's kind of the whole reason I'm here, remember?"

"I am sorry for not telling you." She folds her hands together in her lap, then unfolds them again. "But I . . . Never mind." The intensity with which she's keeping her mouth closed is visible at the corners of her thin lips.

I groan. "Mom. Whatever you're thinking, just say it."

"The biggest reason I didn't want to bring him up was that I was afraid it would embarrass you."

"Why would Quentin being back in town embarrass me?"

"I know kids like to believe their parents are stupid, but you think I didn't notice how you were inseparable for months only for him to leave you and never mention him again? It's obvious something went wrong between you two, and I've always figured it had to do with your crush on him."

My eyes go wide at Mom's words, and all I can do is let out an unconvincing *ha*. Sure, I may have developed *some* no-longer-strictly-platonic feelings for Quentin over those three months we spent treasure hunting. And the night before everything went wrong, when we were lying side by side on a blanket in his backyard, looking up at the stars as we finalized our plans to search Sprangbur one last time, I can't say I didn't want him to lean over and gently press his lips against mine. For a split second, I even thought he was going to.

But it's not like I filled pages of a notebook with hearts or practiced signing my name as Nina Bell or anything like that. I wasn't, like, *pining* after the kid.

She tilts her head, as if saying, *Really, Nina?* "It was clear you were gone for him."

I scoff, not very convincingly. "I was absolutely not *gone* for Quentin." In fact, I'd be willing to bet that those feelings were nothing but the product of my aforementioned teenage hormones and forced proximity. A crush I will admit to. But there's no world in which I was *in love* with Quentin. Any thoughts I had about us becoming more than close friends were simply the inevitable outcome of being young and having spent so much time together—nothing more, nothing less.

Like, if I had hung out with Francesca O'Brien from down the street as much as I hung out with Quentin, I'm sure I would have had recurring dreams about making out with her too.

"You and he were together nearly every single day that last summer, from dawn to dusk . . ." Mom continues.

"Yeah, because we were hunting for treasure."

She flaps a hand, waving away what I've said. "Whatever you want to call it, it was none of my business. I made sure you knew about safe sex well before that, and I trust that you took precautions—"

"Ahh! Stop!" I cover my ears and close my eyes. "That is not a euphemism for anything! Quentin and I spent that summer *literally* hunting for the Fountain treasure at Sprangbur." My mother has become much more sex-positive in recent years after joining a local romance book club, but I am still not mature enough to find the ease with which she now attempts to talk to me about it anything but mortifying. Maybe when I'm thirty-five.

Three deep breaths later, I explain, "We agreed to look for it after reading about Fountain's will in social studies that spring."

"Oh, I remember hearing about that," she says. "When they were renovating that mansion, people were joking about what they might find in the walls."

In my mind, Sprangbur Castle is still shuttered and dotted with DO NOT ENTER UNDER PENALTY OF LAW warnings. But I suppose the renovations they started right before I left for college must be done by now. Is it open to the public? I wonder what it's like inside.

"Anyway," I say, returning my focus to explaining to my mother what happened in 2008, "even though we were supposed to be looking together, I went rogue and started doing some solo research to find the treasure on my own. Quentin found out the night we went—uh, the night before he left for Ann Arbor, and I never heard from him again. He wouldn't respond to my emails or texts. Not even a peep from him until the other night when I got here and he's just—surprise!—next door." *Also, we got caught trespassing and taken to the police station, which I have never told you and will not be telling you now. And also I sort of thought maybe he was interested in me the same way I was interested in him, which he wasn't, so my ego was pretty bruised on top of everything else.*

Mom's mouth falls open with a shocked gasp, and she brings

a hand up to cover it politely. But is she taken aback that I hurt Quentin, or that he hurt me? "I can't believe he *goblined* you," she says from behind her palm.

"Goblined? What does—Oh, geez, Mom. Do you mean ghosted?"

"It's 'ghosted'? Really? Hm, I suppose that does make more sense. What is a goblin, again?" Her gaze drifts off to the side as she mines her mental bank of imaginary creatures, trying to recall. Then she remembers the point of our conversation and her eyes meet mine. "Well, that was very rude of him."

"Yes, it was. I agree."

"But . . ."

I sigh. "But what?"

"You were both very young, Nina. And fifteen-year-old boys aren't known for their emotional intelligence."

"We haven't been 'very young' for a while now, though. He could have tried to reconnect with me at any time. The internet would have made it pretty easy if he cared to bother." Part of me always expected it to happen. But at some point it became less of a "when" and more of an "if." Then each passing year of silence nudged it closer and closer to the "if" side until it seemed on par with pigs flying. So that's why I was so flabbergasted to find Quentin here, ready to pick up where we left off. It was like looking into the sky and finding Babe and Wilbur waving to me from the cockpit of a 747.

"Well, maybe it's time to think of it as water under the bridge. He seems to want to, considering how eager he was to see you this morning. Kept asking when you'd be down." She smiles slyly, like his impatience to talk to me is the equivalent of asking for my hand in marriage. "Besides, holding a grudge never helps you get where you're going. It only holds you back."

This is actually quite poignant advice. It's also unexpected and notably hypocritical, considering my mother hasn't talked to one of her cousins for thirty-five years over a minor dispute concerning the flavor of her wedding cake. Then again, who better to know, I suppose.

"I'm not holding a grudge," I protest. "I don't even *care* about it." Maybe I did a long time ago, back when losing Quentin's friendship and any possibility of more felt like the worst thing in the world that could happen. When it was the rug pulled out from under me, making me stumble and fall into a big puddle of anxiety and depression. But over time it slipped places in its importance, falling farther and farther behind in the Grand Scheme of Things. I figured out how to harness my angst, my heartbreak, and my worries, and transform them all into something more productive. That's when Ambitious Nina made her debut, with her big dreams and determination to work her ass off to get where she wanted to go. Moping over a stupid boy certainly wasn't part of the plan. Quite frankly, it still isn't.

No. Thinking about the past, Quentin-related or otherwise, isn't a good use of my emotional energy. Because all of that stuff happened to a different person, one who doesn't exist anymore. Badass Nina may not have lasted long, and Ambitious Nina may or may not return, but it doesn't mean I need to unearth that old, sad version of myself. I don't know who to be right now, but I know I don't want to go back to who I once was.

"I'm sorry for not telling you he was here, especially when you asked directly," Mom says.

"Thank you." I bend to wrap my arms around her and squeeze lightly.

"My sweet baby." Her soft, familiar voice and the warm cucumber melon–scented squishiness of her hug loosens some of my tension. It doesn't last long, though, because as soon as I pull away she says, "In the interest of full disclosure, I feel like I should tell you that Quentin and your father are currently at the hardware store together."

Right. Because of course they are.

7

WITH EACH PASSING day, it becomes increasingly clear that I need to get back to Boston as soon as possible. Or, if not Boston, somewhere else that has the infrastructure to help me locate Ambitious Nina. I can't linger in Catoctin, with its limited opportunities and reminders of the past. I love my parents to pieces, and I know that I am extremely lucky to have them both still alive and well—something I try not to take for granted, especially since Dad's accident, which could've been so much worse. But I can already tell that spending the next month or two doing nothing but applying to jobs I'll never hear back from and hanging out with my mom and dad (mostly Mom, though, given Dad's basement troll tendencies) is not going to be good for my mental health.

Priority number one is figuring out how to get enough money to cover a security deposit and first month's rent.

Quentin's proposal that we continue looking for the treasure clangs around in my brain. Five thousand dollars of reward money. That would be enough, or at least close to it. I wonder if there's a way to make it more . . .

We agreed to hunt for Fountain's treasure together, Nina. As far as I'm concerned, that agreement still stands.

And maybe I do owe Quentin this. Maybe I owe it to myself too. Because, other than how it ended, that summer was an absolute blast. The best I ever had. I always thought it was because we spent it exploring and doing research—ideal for a little nerd like me. But now I think maybe what made it great was that, for those few months, we were a team. Quentin and I stopped being two people competing to be the best at everything and started working together. As much as I enjoyed him being my perpetual rival, I enjoyed having him as my closest confidant more. Our nightly window conversations became deeper, more serious, the candid thoughts of two kids grappling with the world around them and their place in it. Then there were the long walks through downtown and along the river. The afternoons in the library's special collections room trying not to piss off Mrs. MacDonald, the grumpy old archivist. The nights before his mom moved out, when Quentin's parents fought too loudly and we'd sneak out to simply sit in silence side by side on my front steps. Sunday mornings eating Mom's homemade cinnamon rolls while we updated our map of Sprangbur.

It was the intimacy of knowing him, enjoying each other's company. That's what I mourned when he left and didn't keep in touch. That's what I missed and then eventually convinced myself to stop missing.

Is that something I could have again? Something I would even want to have again?

I'm really not sure. But it doesn't matter because tonight, when my mother mentions over dinner that she saw the local steak house is hiring a hostess and also that she heard from a friend that her very nice, very handsome accountant is newly single, it acts as a double underline under the as-soon-as-possible part of my plans.

That's why, the minute I'm finished doing the dishes, I hurry up the stairs to my room and throw the window open. It once again does an impression of a distressed seagull. Gotta see if Dad can fix that. At least it's an easy way to alert Quentin to my presence. His own window slides open a foot away, much more mellowly, and I'm annoyed by the jolt of relief I feel knowing he's there. I'm probably just glad I don't have to sit with this stupid decision for too much longer. Either he agrees to my terms and we do this, or he doesn't and I can finally stop thinking about it.

"Hey, Moon," I say, feigning more nonchalance than I feel as I fold my arms atop the windowsill and rest my chin on them.

"Bonjour, mon amie."

"You know, I used to worry sometimes about the pane slipping and guillotining me, but now I think that, if that's what fate has in store for me, at least it means never having to upload my résumé before manually reentering all of the details ever again."

"Aw haw, Nina, zat is very dark." He pauses. "But très relatable."

The moon is large and perfectly round tonight, glowing bright and hanging heavy in the sky like it weighs more than usual. "This fullness is a good look on you."

"Merci, mon amie," he says. "I've been doing zee squats."

The way he says "squats" forces me to cover my mouth for a moment so I don't bark out a laugh. It feels like giving him that will take away some of my bargaining power, and I'm going to need everything I can get; international business lawyers are probably better trained in negotiation tactics than eighteenth-century US history PhDs. "Your hard work is certainly paying off."

There's a brief silence. I'm surprised that, when Quentin talks again, he's already switched over to his normal voice. "Have you considered my proposal?"

"I have."

"And?"

"I have an . . . amendment."

Another pause. "Okay, shoot."

"We only search for four weeks. If we don't find anything by then, the agreement ends. And if we *do* find it, I want sixty percent of the reward."

He scoffs. "What? How would that be fair?"

"Because . . ." This made a lot more sense when I was thinking about it while scrubbing pans downstairs. "You'd be paying for my expertise."

"Expertise, huh?"

"Yes. Not only do I have a better sense of where we've already searched and what sources we've consulted, as you said, but I have an actual degree in this stuff."

"Oh, did you study treasure hunting in grad school?"

If I thought about it for a while, I could probably make a decent case for how archival research and treasure hunting have quite a few similarities—including the inhalation of a surprising amount of dirt and dust. "Ha ha," I say sardonically. "I spent years learning how to find information as efficiently as possible. And I'm damn good at it."

I can hear the smile in his voice as he says, "I don't doubt it." There's a hint of pride, of something like admiration, that feels like a quiet echo of the past. It sends an unwanted warmth to my cheeks.

"I'm just going to be blunt," I say. "I could use the money, Quentin. And I need the potential payout to be worth enough to make fucking around with you a good use of my time."

He hasn't moved from his spot at his own bedroom window, but there's a distance imbued in his tone when he finally responds. "Seventy percent and eight weeks."

"What?"

"You can have seven thousand. But only if you commit to 'fucking around with me' for at least eight weeks."

"Eight weeks! You want me to stay here until August?"

"Only if we don't find the treasure before that." He continues, "I also want to note that you only asked me for six thousand. I'm upping it to seven. You're welcome."

"But it's double the time commitment!" I protest.

"That's the offer, Nina," he says. "Take it or leave it." There's a strength and a confidence in his words that make it easy to imagine him at a conference table, wearing that perfectly tailored navy suit, negotiating mergers or whatever the hell it is that international business lawyers do.

Best outcome if I accept? We find the treasure and we get to keep it, it's worth a bajillion dollars, I never have to work again, and also maybe Quentin and I reconcile. Worst? We don't find anything, I've wasted eight weeks of my life, we wind up hurting each other again, and I walk away with nothing. Most likely? The treasure doesn't exist but we spend a week or two occupied, at least, while getting on slightly better terms and I find a real job in the meantime.

If I don't agree to Quentin's proposal, then the best outcome is that I immediately find employment and this is all moot. The worst is that I spend the entire summer in bed, alternating between refreshing Indeed and sobbing into the too-bright comforter while my mother tries to set me up with every semi-attractive person she hears about while incessantly inviting me to read high-heat romance books with her and her friends. Most likely? Well, that looks a lot like the worst, but maybe only through, like, the end of July.

Never in a million years would I have guessed that willingly taking part in an eccentric dead guy's practical joke with someone who completely stomped on my heart when we were teenagers would seem like a smart way to spend my thirty-third summer on the planet. But until I can find Ambitious Nina again, I'm in a sort of holding pattern. And this at least will get me out of the house and away from my mom's well-meaning smothering.

"Fine. I accept."

"What was that now?" I know he heard me. He's just being a shit.

"I said *fine*," I repeat, not bothering to hide my annoyance. He better get used to it because I plan on being very annoyed for the next few weeks. "I accept your terms. We'll hunt for the stupid treasure."

"Ah haw, ma chérie," he says, taking up the Moon's outrageous accent again. "C'est magnifique!"

MID-ATLANTIC INDUSTRY
Personal History of Informant

STATE .... Maryland
NAME OF WORKER ..... Albert Aaron
ADDRESS .... Sprangbur Estate
DATE .... June 9, 1937
SUBJECT .... Life and business of Julius J. Fountain
NAME OF INFORMANT .. Julius James Fountain

1. Ancestry

   Of English extraction

2. Place and date of birth

   Baltimore, Maryland, January 31, 1855

3. Family

   Lifelong bachelor. Niece, Isolde Fountain Bouchard,
   is closest living relative.

4. Places lived in, with dates

   Primary residence in Mt. Vernon, Baltimore, until
   completion of Sprangbur Castle in 1890. Spent ten
   months in Europe in 1875.

5. Education

Eight years of formal schooling as a child. Six months
of unofficial enrollment at the École des Beaux-Arts
in Paris to learn basic principles of architecture.

6. Occupation and accomplishments

Founder of Fountain Seltzer Co., currently the
largest beverage company in the mid-Atlantic. Holds
four US patents relating to siphon technology.
Honorary doctorate degree, Johns Hopkins University.
Knight, Order of the Oak Crown (Luxembourg).
Co-monarch of the Kingdom of Edlo. [AA: Informant
wishes this recorded, but will not elaborate.]

7. Special skills and interests

Languages--German, French, Luxembourgish,
"Edlosian" [AA: Hearing it briefly spoken, I believe
this may be pig latin?]. Interests--Architecture,
camouflage, astronomy, viola da gamba.

8. Community and religious activities

Supports several charitable causes, including
hospitals and orphanages throughout the region.
Does not regularly attend any house of worship.

9. Description of informant

Approx. five feet ten inches, slender, with a
shorter torso and long limbs. Eyes are gray. Hair

is white with natural curl. Wears distinctive,
old-fashioned large mustache. Dressed in silk
pajamas with a fuchsia paisley print and slippers.
Sitting in matching chair with one leg tucked
beneath him and the other splayed over the
chair's arm.

10. Other points gained in interview

Informant would like it formally noted that he
thinks interviewer's tie is "atrocious."
[AA: Tie is a unique shade of green and was a
birthday gift from my wife. It admittedly may not
be what I would have chosen myself.]

8

WHYYYYY?" I WHINE, sitting up in bed. It's only . . .
Okay, it's actually almost eleven in the morning, so the
loud power tool sounds happening outside aren't as egre-
giously inconsiderate as I thought. But still, it's not my preferred
alarm clock.

I clear the crusties from the corners of my eyes and roll over to
grab my phone from the nightstand. There are three emails from
job search sites, helpfully informing me that there are no new
posts matching my criteria, and a missed video call from my best
friend, Sabrina. Shit. We were supposed to chat this morning.
But since I'm now living on Unemployed Sad Person (USP) time,
I completely slept through our usual Monday eight a.m. catch-up.

If it's eleven here, it's . . . twelve, one . . . four p.m. in Belfast?
She used to teach a class around this time, but I'm pretty sure
her semester also ended last week, so hopefully she's free. I call
her back, and my phone very rudely turns on my front-facing
camera as I wait, prompting me to sit up so that I'm at least
looking less like a blobfish when Sabrina answers.

"She lives! Hooray!" she shouts, throwing an arm into the air and almost dropping her phone. For a second all I can see is the top quarter of a row of beautiful old brick townhomes and a rectangle of light gray sky.

"Sorry," I say. "I forgot what day it was and slept in. Is it too late to talk? Are you busy?"

"No, no, not busy at all. Just off to Malcolm's for the night," Sabrina says, then seems to recall that Malcolm is her boyfriend (a thing I no longer have), and winces. "Anyway, he can wait." Her eyes dart around as she examines the framed poster hanging over the bed behind me—David Bowie jumping in the air while reading Dostoyevsky. "Ooh. That's a strangely sensual picture," she says, tilting her head.

"Bowie was a strangely sensual man."

"Too true. You know, I think *Labyrinth* was my sexual awakening." She holds in a laugh as an elderly woman in the midst of entering her house, a fluffy dog cradled in her arms, gives her a stern look for saying the word "sexual" on the street like a hooligan. "How's it being back home?"

"Mostly strange," I say. "My parents seem glad to have me here. Almost *too* glad. Well, Mom at least. Dad spends most of his time in his workshop, appearing only for food and to do whatever chores my mom asks him to do." I pause, unsure if I want to mention Quentin. He feels like a can of worms, and even if I don't provide a can opener I know that Sabrina will happily pry it open with her bare hands. Then again, not telling her feels like I'm hiding something. No reason to hide something that really is no big deal. So I add, "Also, an old childhood friend who lived next door has coincidentally just moved back too."

"Ooh. What are they like?"

"He's . . ." It's hard to answer this question, I realize, because I'm not sure whether to base it on what I know of young Quentin or this new, grown-up version. I eventually land on, "Mostly very frustrating."

"Hmm. Now that's interesting." Sabrina brings her topaz-colored eye closer to the phone, like a detective leaning over a clue with a magnifying glass.

"What's interesting?"

"Oh, nothing. It's only you paused before 'mostly very frustrating.'"

"There was no pause," I insist.

"There most certainly was. And, well, I don't know if you remember, but that was also how you used to talk about . . . That's what you said before . . ."

I know she means *before you and Cole got together* but isn't sure how I would feel about her bringing up my ex less than a week after our split.

"Quentin is a very *different* kind of frustrating," I say, freeing her from having to finish her sentence. I found Cole frustrating back then because he always seemed to swoop in and check out whatever books I needed from the university's library before I could get to them. Eventually that led to a realization that, if he wanted the same obscure monographs I did, we probably had a lot of things in common—including the areas we were focusing on for our comprehensive exams. Which led to me suggesting we study together. Which, perhaps inevitably, led to us doing a lot more than studying.

It's sort of mortifying, now that I think about it, that I somehow managed to stretch what Cole must've intended as nothing but a three a.m. coffee-fueled convenient hookup into a six-year-long relationship.

"Yeah, yeah." Sabrina verbally waves away my words before grinning. "So. Is this very frustrating old neighbor friend of yours single?" she asks. While I'm not a huge fan of this line of questioning, I'm glad to at least shift my focus away from Cole and the uncomfortable mixture of sadness, anger, and shame that intensifies whenever I start remembering the way things were between us. All the red flags to which I was apparently oblivious.

"Sabrina," I chide anyway.

"Well, *is* he?"

"Yes. Newly," I admit.

"Hmm," Sabrina hums, and I know it's a placeholder for *just like you.* I both love and hate the way I always know exactly what she's thinking even without her saying a word. "Wait. Is this the same guy who moved away after some sort of treasure hunt–related drama when you were in high school?"

I tuck my hair behind my ears as I try to recall which margarita-fueled night in grad school resulted in me spilling my heart about Quentin. Probably the one where I wound up puking in the bushes behind a church and insisting I could speak Portuguese. (I cannot.) "Ugh. Don't you ever forget anything?"

"Never." She pauses. Then amends, "Almost never. I did have a student this past semester, could not remember her name for the life of me. Kept calling her Emma, but she was actually . . . Amy? I think. I still really don't know!" Sabrina's beautiful round face lights up as she smiles, and I realize that the scenery behind her hasn't moved for some time.

"You're outside Malcolm's now?"

She looks over her shoulder quickly, as if checking to confirm. "Oh. Yes. That's his flat. But I don't need to—" The sudden return of the buzz saw's screaming drowns out the end of Sabrina's sentence.

"No, no, go on and have a nice evening with Mal. Some asshole is using power tools outside and making it hard to hear you anyway."

"If you're sure?" she says. "I don't mind . . ."

I know she's offering to talk more about what happened with Cole, since it happened so recently that we haven't been able to discuss it outside of a few quick messages.

But no part of me feels the need to rehash that mess right now. Maybe it's like when you injure yourself and it takes a second for your body to register the extent of the pain. I'm still in that infinitesimal lull between cause and effect. Sabrina is offering up her kit of best friend emotional bandages, but I'm not sure what size I even need yet, so I respond, "I'm sure. Besides, it's nearly afternoon here already. I should really get up and get moving. Find something to occupy myself with so my parents don't start worrying about me." Also so I don't start worrying about me. My memories flash back to the fall of 2008, sobbing into my pillow at night as I felt my sadness like a physical thing spreading throughout my body. The heavy, dull ache that would flood in after the numbness I felt during the day. Hopelessness that things would ever get better mixing with the anxiety that they would keep getting worse. Clinging to my ambition was the way I dug myself out of that hole then, and if I lose the ability to do it now I don't know for sure that I won't stumble right back in.

"All right, then," she says. "Till next week, unless you need me before. Love to my Neen." She blows a kiss toward the camera.

I blow one back. "Love to my Breen."

"Chat soon," she says, before hanging up.

For a moment, I allow myself to imagine the scene unfolding 3,300 miles away: Sabrina unlocking Malcolm's door with the key he gave her an almost worryingly short amount of time after they started dating. Her kissing him hello. Filling him in on the conference paper she worked on between meetings with students. Listening to a funny story about one of his patients. Them settling on the couch, limbs tangled as they discuss their dinner plans. Giggling as they fall into bed a few hours later.

Jealousy blooms deep inside my stomach, like a digestive juices–immune lotus flower. I hate feeling this way about someone I love so much. It's just that, since we met at orientation for our PhD program, Sabrina has been not only my closest friend but also a helpful yardstick by which I can measure my progress toward the life I want. We've both been working toward the same things for so long: A university faculty position. A supportive partner. A beautiful home and a bright future. All things Ambitious Nina worked her butt off to secure—was so close to finally having. Sabrina and I used to be inches apart at most, but now it seems like she's miles ahead, and it stings to see her disappearing into the distance while I collapse from a sudden muscle cramp.

That Bon Jovi pillar from the rest stop pops into my mind. *It's ok to map out your future—but do it in pencil.*

At least remembering the overly smug expression on the rock star's face plastered above that quote gives me enough of a spite-powered burst of motivation to actually get out of bed.

I glance out the window to check the day's weather as another high-pitched buzz cuts through the air and draws my attention downward and to the left, into Quentin's backyard. Which is where I find him meticulously running a circular saw over a piece of what appears to be laminate flooring. He's wearing a raggedy Modest Mouse T-shirt with athletic shorts, and even from up here I can see the sweat rolling down his forehead.

I kneel and lean against the sill, watching him work. Just so I know when it's safe to open the window and holler down without the risk of startling him and making him slip and cut off a finger or something. Not at all because I'm enjoying the view of a hot, sweaty Quentin Bell using power tools.

Okay, I can admit, it's extremely attractive, but it feels wrong to be thinking about Quentin that way.

Just because we've made a deal to continue our search for Fountain's treasure doesn't mean I've forgotten what happened. It just means I'm willing to bury it back down in the deep, dark underbrush of my heart where it dwelled quite contently before Quentin's sudden reappearance so rudely flushed it out from its hiding place.

I watch as he tosses the cut piece of flooring atop a small pile beside the sawhorse. He takes a step back and wipes his forehead with his arm. Now that he's standing at a safe distance from things that could maim him, I hoist the window to declare my presence so I'm no longer covertly staring like a creep. The screeching draws his attention upward, and he squints against the powerful near-midday sun.

"Well, ho there, howdy, and good morning to you," he says, bringing his hand up to provide some shade and, presumably, get a look at me. Perhaps I should have changed out of my cats-with-yarn-balls nightshirt and fixed my hair before getting his attention. Not that it really matters. He can't see much of me while I'm crouched. And it's not like I'm trying to *impress* him.

I ignore his teasing and respond with a simple, sharp "Hi" like I intended to the other day before I got all flustered. Maybe I can somehow resummon Badass Nina, now that I haven't been taken by surprise. I prop my chin on my hand, trying to look as uninterested in him as possible.

Yet something must give me away, because he says, "Been watching me long?"

"No," I retort, realizing too late that I've fallen into a trap. "I mean, I wasn't *watching* you at all, really, so much as thinking about how every time I see you, you're dressed more and more casually. What's next? Swim trunks? A strategically placed fig leaf?"

Why on earth did those words just come out of my mouth?! If Badass Nina were coming back to life, that's definitely killed her again.

Quentin flashes that too-charming smile in my direction. It really gets under my skin, for some reason. And not in the way that Sabrina would tease me about. It legitimately irks me, and I can't figure out why. Maybe because it doesn't look fake, but it does look practiced. Like a trick he picked up somewhere. A third-party add-on to the genuine, original Quentin Bell experience. It reminds me of all the time I missed. All the things I no longer know about him. How he *chose* not to let me keep knowing him.

"Would you like that?" he asks. "The fig leaf?"

"Absolutely not."

It doesn't come out very convincingly, though, and that vexing smile of his grows as he steps closer to the house, into the thin band of shadow on the patio so he can continue looking up at me without needing to use his hand as a visor.

I scramble for something else to say to change the topic to something safer and land on, "So, what's all this, then?"

"You sound like the police in a Monty Python sketch. 'Wot's all this, then?'" he quotes. His next smile is smaller, but easier, more natural—more *him*. This one I like a lot. I always have. "I'm replacing the floors on the main level."

I didn't spend nearly as much time at Quentin's house when we were kids as he did at mine. My mom—who worked as a secretary in the high school's front office—was home in the afternoon, while Quentin's parents, a lawyer and a scientist, often worked long hours. So it made sense for him to come over after school most days, sometimes staying through dinner. And, to be quite honest, the vibes at Quentin's were just *bad*. I didn't understand it at the time but felt the tension nonetheless. Mr. and Dr. Bell's marriage was like a Jenga tower of resentment and bitterness sitting right out on the coffee table. Even while it was still standing, everyone seemed aware that it would only take one small move to topple. It was all very uncomfortable. Not the kind of place kids wanted to hang out. (Also, my house always had baked goods. So it was really no contest.)

Still, I think back to the few hours I did spend inside 304 West Dill. I recall the pale green linoleum squeaking beneath my cheap Old Navy flip-flops as we crossed through the kitchen on the way to the backyard, and I imagine it replaced with the dark gray faux wood on the sawhorse. It feels a bit like a renovation of old memories, and I wonder if that's what Quentin is out to do—both with his childhood home and with me. "I didn't know you were handy," I say.

He throws his arms out in an enormous, sloppy shrug as he flashes another one of those stupid smiles. "Probably lots you don't know about me."

"And whose fault is that?" I intend it as a joke but realize too late that it isn't.

"Ah. Touché," he says, bowing his head for a moment. A more neutral expression is in place when he raises it again. "I'll be finished here in another hour or so. Want to grab lunch?"

"Lunch?"

"Yeah, you heard of it? Been all the rage for a couple centuries now."

"Are you always this annoying?" I ask.

He wipes his forehead with the bottom of his shirt this time, obscuring his face but revealing a pale, strong stomach bisected by an auburn line of hair. My eyes instinctively follow it down to where it disappears behind the waistband of his shorts. "Depends who you ask," he counters, reappearing as his shirt falls back into place. "I'll get cleaned up and meet you at that new café by the toy store at twelve thirty. Unless you're in the mood for something else?"

He almost definitely means in the mood for something else food-wise, but my brain takes the prompt and runs with it in the uncomfortable direction of the fig leaf again.

Okay. I really need to stop thinking about Quentin naked, because it's only making things weird.

Or, rather, it's making *me* weird. That's really the only explanation I have for why it seems perfectly normal and reasonable to shout, "Sure. I desire a large salad!" before slamming the window shut.

9

THE CAFÉ WHERE Quentin and I are supposed to meet is located in one of the historic buildings on Main Street, about four blocks away from our houses. If I remember correctly, it used to be a RadioShack. While there are a few long-time businesses on this strip, including the toy store next door and the menswear shop across the street, most of the storefronts around here were either empty or occupied by some sort of un-sexy retail chain back when I was growing up. But there's been a downtown renaissance in Catoctin over the last decade or so, and now there are bubble tea places and hip vintage stores and microbreweries and bougie restaurants called, like, Fate/Happenstance. (How do you even pronounce that? Fate Slash Happenstance? Fate Divided by Happenstance?) Apparently they have vintage bicycles on the walls and give you an origami crane with your check.

This place is cute, cozy. There's lots of exposed brick, and the sun streaming in through the large windows reflects the café's name—Best That You Can Brew—backward in shadow on the hardwood floor. Yacht rock plays just loud enough to get my brain humming along with it. It's the kind of place where I might come to grade research papers, if that was something I still did.

"Can you imagine Catoctin having a place like this when we were kids?" The combination of Quentin's sudden appearance and the relevance of his question to my inner thoughts makes me turn around so fast that I nearly knock my drink off the table.

Once I've ensured the cup isn't going to topple, I take in his hair, still a bit damp from showering, and his new outfit of mauve chino shorts, black T-shirt, and Converse high-tops. Those were the shoes he always wore when we were kids too. Has he been wearing them steadily over the last seventeen years, or are they another thing he left and came back to later?

"You're late," I point out. He's only about five minutes past our agreed-upon time, but I'm feeling petulant.

"Blame your dad," he says. "Ran into him on my way out the door and he wouldn't stop chatting."

"*My* dad? *Chatting*?" If ever there was a man of few words, it would be Dave Hunnicutt. His best man speech at my uncle's wedding famously clocked in at a cool ten seconds.

"Surprised me too. But I asked him a question and it turns out he has a *lot* to say about electrical wiring fill capacity." He nods toward my sweating glass of iced tea and the overflowing plate of greens in front of me. "I see you already got your desired large salad."

Really, *why* did I say that? I must've sounded like some sort of strange, prim, lettuce-loving monarch, issuing a formal declaration from my window. Of course Quentin wasn't going to let that go unacknowledged. What I would give to be able to control my bodily response to his teasing so that he didn't get the satisfaction of seeing this hot blush overtake my face.

"Want me to grab you anything else while I'm up there?" he asks, drumming his fingers on the table.

"I'm good, thanks."

"Mkay. Be right back." Quentin makes his way to the counter, where he stands with his hands on his hips, head craned to read the chalkboard menu positioned high on the wall.

I find my gaze once again drawn to the new shape of him, because frankly I still haven't fully processed it. As a kid, he had this awkwardness he seemed to carry around like a physical burden. Now Quentin Bell exudes nothing but confidence. Paired with that stupid charming smile that he keeps wielding like a weapon, I have to admit he's a real presence in a room. And there's definite strength there, his forearms and biceps hinting at it, even at rest. Plus his butt—

"Nina? Nina Hunnicutt?"

My shoulders jump and my mouth produces a swift, panicked, "No!" as I whip my head around.

The woman who said my name narrows her dark eyes at my bizarre response. "Oh. I thought—"

"I mean, yes. I'm Nina Hunnicutt. That is me and I am . . . sorry?"

She smiles, and my brain calms down enough to actually take in the person standing in front of me. Her previously long black hair is now short and streaked with light pink, and she has a septum piercing that wasn't there before, but she's unmistakably the same girl I sat beside in countless homerooms, at graduation, and whenever else our grade was arranged alphabetically by last name. "Oh my goodness, Hanako Hughes! How are you?"

"I'm well! And also sorry too, since I seem to have interrupted you . . ." Hanako trails off as she glances in Quentin's direction with a knowing smile.

"You weren't interrupting anything," I insist. "I was just . . . checking out the menu." My peripheral vision catches on the salad in front of me, and I quickly add, "For next time I'm here."

"Ah, can't go wrong, to be honest. I'm a big fan of the potato leek soup. And the apple fritters, but those are Sundays only and they sell out within, like, the first hour of opening."

I sneak a heavy exhale of relief, grateful that she's either believed my lie or is polite enough to go along with it. "I'll have to set my alarm early this weekend and try to make it in time."

"It's worth it, I promise." She grins at me like I'm a long-lost favorite purse she's found in the recesses of her closet. "It's really so nice to run into you. And unexpected! I didn't even know you were in town."

"Oh, I'm not. Not really." I shake my head a little too vehemently, and my glasses slide down my nose. After pushing them back up, I force a chuckle. "I mean, I am. Obviously. But not for too long. Just like, apple fritter long, I guess." Does that even mean anything? I don't know. Might as well keep going. "I came down to help my mom with some, uh, reorganization projects. As soon as we finish those, I'm headed home." This second lie spills from my mouth before I have any hope of catching it. I generally don't make a habit of telling untruths, but I'm finding it a lot easier than honesty these days.

Hanako adjusts the neon-green yoga mat tucked under her arm. "Things are good, though? My aunt took some pottery class with your mom this past winter, and she said she heard you were doing really well."

At the time my mother and Hanako's aunt chatted, I probably

was. That was back when everything was coming up Nina. But I'm not about to confide in a random high school acquaintance that my life sucks now. "Yeah," I say. "Everything's good. Great, really."

"You've been living in . . . New England somewhere?"

"Boston."

"Oh, nice. How do you like it there?" she asks, probably just as a courtesy.

"Bit cold," I say. I have genuinely been a resident of that city for ten years, yet suddenly I remember absolutely nothing else about it. "But it's really nice. Good, um, parks. And . . . beans."

Hanako laughs as if I've made a joke, which I appreciate. "You're a . . ." She searches her memory. "A history professor, right?"

"Sure am!" I respond too enthusiastically, then quickly switch over to "And what are you up to these days?" to avoid having to talk about my currently stalled-out career.

"A surprising amount, actually. My partner and I opened up a cocktail bar just up the street from here last fall, right on the river. It's called Flow State."

"Wow, that's awesome," I say. "And business is good?"

"Good enough." Her smile seems more forced this time. "One of our bartenders was in a car accident last week—" The concern must plainly show on my face, because she hurriedly explains, "No fatalities, thank god. But he has a broken pelvis and will be out for a while, so we've been scrambling to cover his upcoming shifts, and he can't really afford to be out for five months, so we're organizing a fundraiser night to benefit his family." She shifts her yoga mat as she exclaims, "Oh, you should totally come if you're still around! It's on Saturday the twenty-first, and it's going to be a ton of fun. Drink specials, DJ, the works."

"Absolutely, yeah. I'd love to." I'm not sure how much I mean this. This is my first real venture outside of the house since I arrived in town and I managed to run into someone I know within half an hour. A local bar owned by a former classmate is probably a prime stomping ground for all of the people who stuck around here after graduation. The ones who will douse me in either pity or smugness if they find out the circumstances under which I've returned to Catoctin. *Poor Nina*, I can hear them whispering. *I always assumed she'd amount to more.* Or, *Serves her right, leaving, thinking she was better than us.*

Then again, as my therapist used to say, people aren't thinking about me nearly as much as I imagine they are. A hurtful yet reassuring truth whenever I remember it.

Hanako looks up, her eyes settling somewhere right behind and above me. "Maybe you can bring your friend?" Her voice makes it sound like she's winking, even though she isn't.

"I'm in. Where are we going?" The unanticipated nearness of Quentin's voice sends a shiver up my spine.

"To my bar," Hanako says, and holds out a hand. "Hi, I'm—"

"I know who you are, Hanako Hughes." I look over my shoulder to find Quentin smiling that practiced smile again, a hand laid over his heart. "And I'm absolutely crushed that you don't remember me."

She makes a show of squinting, examining him from a few more angles. I'm tempted to address Quentin by name and put an end to this unnecessary playfulness, but he speaks before I get a chance to ruin their fun.

"Tyler McMaster's pool party, summer after sophomore year?" He says it like a question, and I spot a twinkle in his light blue eyes.

"Quentin Bell? Holy shit!" Hanako throws herself at him,

wrapping her arms around his torso. He sets down a numbered table tent and his mug so that he can return the embrace. She's even shorter than I am, with a much more petite build. I can't help but compare the way she fits against Quentin with how I did that first night on the porch, when he held me close, and wonder if he has a preference.

She steps away and they spend a moment catching up. I don't hear much of what they're saying because I'm busy trying to reconfigure my memories to accommodate this new connection. Quentin and Hanako . . . knew each other? I mean, of course they did. We all went to school together, and it wasn't exactly a huge graduating class. But that they knew each other in a way that would generate this sense of nostalgia and camaraderie after all this time is news to me. Hanako was so *cool*, and we, distinctly, were not. I mean, if we hadn't had to sit beside each other so often over the course of thirteen years, I'm not sure she'd even know my name. So how did she and Quentin get to be besties? What exactly went down at this pool party?

My stomach lurches unpleasantly at the thought of them having hooked up. Not because Quentin isn't allowed to have been involved with another person—truly none of my business then or now, really—but because if that's what happened, it means he deliberately kept it a secret. The knowledge that he could've been holding back an important part of himself from me, even when we were the closest we'd ever been . . . It's impossible not to start wondering if I was imagining that closeness in the first place. If the whole thing with Cole has shown me anything, it's that my perception of reality cannot always be trusted. Sure would explain a lot, including how easily Quentin cut me out of his life. And how surprised he was to find I still carry around some hurt over his ghosting me.

"Sooo . . ." There's a suggestiveness in Hanako's tone as she leans in closer to Quentin again and stands on her tiptoes to whisper something in his ear that makes his pale, freckle-dusted cheeks turn an impressive shade of scarlet. When she mentioned a partner earlier, I assumed she meant life partner along with business partner, but I guess that isn't necessarily the case. Or maybe they do the whole ethical non-monogamy thing. Or maybe she's just flirting with Quentin because the universe relishes watching me squirm.

He shakes his head, a weak smile on his face as it fades from deep red to light pink.

Hanako's attention bounces back to me. "Tell you what," she says. "Let me give you my number, then you two can let me know if you're going to swing by and I'll make sure to give the staff a heads-up in case I'm busy. First round's on the house."

"Oh, cool. Thanks," Quentin says, handing her his phone so she can text herself from it. "Looking forward to checking it out."

"Oh, shit. Speaking of the bar, I was supposed to be there five minutes ago. Gotta run—literally—but it was so good to see you both." She waves over her shoulder as she heads out the door.

"You too," we return in unison.

Quentin takes the seat across from me at the small wooden table. He doesn't speak for a long time, simply stares at me with a hint of humor at the corners of his mouth, as if he can read my thoughts and finds them amusing. "Well, that was interesting," he says at last, sounding a lot like Sabrina. He takes a long sip of his coffee while his eyes remain focused on my face, watching for my reaction.

I stare blankly in response, not wanting to give him the satisfaction of asking to what he's referring.

"I didn't know you had a problem with Hanako Hughes."

He leans back in the wooden bistro chair and props his ankle on his opposite knee.

I chew a bite of salad a bit longer than strictly necessary for digestion, then respond nonchalantly. "I don't have a problem with her. She's fine. I mean, I don't know her as well as you do, apparently. But what I do know is fine. Lovely, even. She's a *lovely* person."

"Just seems like running into her bothered you."

"What? It didn't bother me. I am completely *un*bothered."

He tilts his head and gives me a dubious expression as he takes another rather pointed sip.

I might have been able to conceal my duplicity in our treasure-hunting research that summer, but that was an exception to the rule. I've never had much luck hiding things from Quentin. So I concede, "I was just . . . flustered."

It's tempting to tell him that the idea of his having kept whatever happened between him and Hanako a secret feels like a final, long-delayed nail in the coffin of our old friendship. That I'm wondering now what else he never told me, and if I'm misremembering how close we were. What if what I thought of as the implosion of our relationship was actually more of an anticlimactic fizzling out, like the time we tried to do the Mentos and Diet Coke experiment without realizing the bottle of soda we found in the back of his pantry was three years old and mostly flat? Considering how badly I'm realizing I must've misread things with Cole, it isn't impossible. But that's not a path I want to go down, not after having agreed to spend time with him again. I decide to settle for another explanation that is also true, if not as pressing. "I don't like having to lie to people about my situation."

He rotates his mug slightly, glancing up as he speaks. "Feels like an easy solution to that problem is, you know, not lying."

"Don't you understand how embarrassing it is to be back here with almost nothing to show for the years since I left?"

"Uh. Yeah. I do, actually."

"Right," I say. "But it's different."

"Is it, though?" he asks.

"Well, yeah. Did you know I was one of only a handful of kids in our entire grade to leave the state for college?"

He shakes his head.

"Out of those ten, two went to super Evangelical schools—"

"Christa Goodman and Mary . . . Fortune, was it?" he guesses, naming two of our more ardently religious classmates.

"Christa, yes. Mary, no. But she is one of the ten, incidentally. She wound up going to circus school in Philadelphia."

Quentin is about to take a drink but freezes with the mug an inch away from his lips. "Are you . . . joking?"

"I am not. Last I heard, she's a member of a traveling troupe called Clowns for Christ."

"Didn't have that on my bingo card, I'm going to be honest." His brow crinkles. "I can kind of see it, though."

"Anyway, four others went to state schools on sports scholarships. Which leaves four that left for academics—including me."

"You know that there are really good universities in Maryland too, right?" he asks before finally taking his postponed sip.

"Yes. That isn't the point. The point is that leaving here is the exception to the rule. Leaving makes a statement—that you are going off to do things you can't accomplish here. Except now everything I accomplished has suddenly disappeared. I'm not much better off than I would have been had I never left. It's like having to come crawling back to someone you publicly announced you didn't need."

Quentin frowns. "Without discounting your feelings, is it possible you're overthinking this?"

"Of course I am. I have an anxiety disorder."

"What?"

I suppose this would've come up sooner or later. I just didn't think it would come up right *now*. Whatever. If he can't understand, then he can go join Jon Bon Jovi in fucking himself.

"I started dealing with some mental health stuff after you left. Depression, anxiety. It was pretty bad the last half of high school."

I pause, waiting for him to joke about how it must have had to do with his no longer being around. But he surprises me by asking, "Because of Dave's accident?" Considering it happened a few weeks after he moved away, I wasn't aware that Quentin even knew about that. As if reading the thoughts on my face, he adds, "Your mom told me about it when I first got back to town."

I nod slowly.

"I don't think there was any one cause, but I'm sure that didn't do anything to help," I explain. "Things were hard. I felt . . . crushed. Trapped beneath an avalanche of sadness and worry. And no one . . . no one really noticed. Because my parents were so busy dealing with my dad's stuff, and I put up a good front." *And because you weren't here to see through it.* "Eventually I figured out that, with a lot of things feeling so out of my control, I could focus on stuff I did have some control over. Like my schoolwork, my extracurriculars. By the time I left here, I had a feeling I was going to be a success. I didn't know what that would look like, but I just *knew* there would be something good at the end of it all for me. And now I am . . . *this*." I spread my hands.

"A salad?"

"A loser," I correct.

He frowns more deeply. I can tell he's about to argue or dismiss what I'm saying as a bunch of self-absorbed rambling. And it probably is. "Even if no one truly cares about what became of me," I say, "even if *they* didn't have any expectations, I had a ton of them. And the funny thing is, I was actually a bit proud of my life until a few days ago."

"Nina . . ."

He reaches for my hand and I subtly move it away by using my finger to wipe away a tear caught at the corner of my eye. "I know. This is something to discuss with my therapist, not you." (Not that I can even see my therapist anymore, now that I'm out of state and no longer have health insurance.) "Forget it. Let's move on. Should we talk about the treasure hunt?"

"Thanks," he says to the woman who places his food in front of him and swipes the number from the table. Then to me he says, "Nope."

"Nope?"

"Not here."

"Not here?"

He picks up his sandwich. "Is this a new game where you repeat everything I say but add a question mark at the end?" Quentin takes a bite, and I resent how my eyes are drawn toward his mouth even when it's doing something as basic as eating. His teenage braces did their job; his teeth are straight and even. Those light pink lips that were a bit too wide on his youthful face are now perfectly sized (for what, other than consuming a BLTA, I refuse to acknowledge). After he swallows, he says, "You know we don't talk about the"—he mouths the word "treasure" before continuing at his previous volume—"in public. In fact, if I remember correctly, that was *your* rule."

"Then why did you suggest lunch?" I ask.

"Because I was hungry and I figured you might be too." He takes a bite out of his sandwich's accompanying pickle spear. "Is it really that awful to spend time with me?"

"No comment."

He shifts his jaw back and forth subtly. "Look, after this we'll go to Sprangbur, start getting our bearings again."

The idea of returning to Fountain's estate with Quentin makes my stomach drop. I can't tell if it's guilt, anxiety, or excitement. But it forces me to put my fork down, my intended next bite still speared onto its prongs. "You can't expect me to spend all day, every day roaming around with you for the next eight weeks. I have other things to do, you know."

"Do you?"

Well. He's got me there.

"Come on, Neen," he says as he reaches to take a cherry tomato from my plate. "We had fun that summer, didn't we?"

I wonder if his mind also goes straight to that night in his backyard, staring up at the inky, star-scattered sky, my right arm and his left pressed together under the guise of the blanket being too small to allow for space between us. Then again, I'm not sure I would call that fun so much as . . . paradigm shifting. *This could be something*, I remember thinking. *Maybe we can find a way to keep it.* I just never expected the paradigm to shift in the direction it did. As if following my exact train of thought, he adds, "Up until the end, at least."

I let out a small, humorless laugh.

Quentin lets out one of his own. "Don't be too grumpy. It's a treasure hunt! Fountain would want us to have fun with it. And we could both use a bit of fun right now, I think."

He's right. Having fun won't counteract everything else

that's gone wrong lately, but moping around isn't going to help me get out of here any faster. It's time to stop feeling sorry for myself and take action. To be someone who is worth paying seven thousand dollars for her expertise. Preferably also someone who can handle eight weeks of close contact with an attractive but frustrating man without doing anything stupid like kissing him or pushing him into the river. "Okay. Fine," I say, smacking away his hand as he attempts to reach for something else off my plate. "I'll hunt for the treasure. I'll even try to have fun. But it doesn't mean I have to like it."

TEXT OF INTERVIEW (UNEDITED)

STATE .... Maryland
NAME OF WORKER ..... Albert Aaron
ADDRESS .... Sprangbur Estate
DATE .... June 9, 1937
SUBJECT .... Life and business of Julius J. Fountain
NAME OF INFORMANT .. Julius James Fountain

I

Guess how old I am. Guess! Never mind. Don't. You'll
either guess low on purpose in hopes of flattering
me, or high to insult me. Not that you would take
that opportunity, would you, Mr. Aaron? Don't seem
the type to seek out petty revenge, no matter how
much a man insults your necktie. Ha ha!

Well, I'm eighty-two, not that it's any of your
business. Eighty-two and a half to be precise. And
I like to be precise whenever given the
opportunity. So much of life doesn't allow for
precision, you know.

I've spent sixty-one of those eighty-two years
running the Fountain Seltzer Company. The idea of
it, like so many great ones, came to me in a dream:
I was napping upon the spout of a massive whale,

and a prodigious stream of water shot out and
lifted me into the sky! I ran my hands through the
clouds, caressed the stars, tickled the moon. Then,
slowly, I was lowered again to the whale's back.
"My, what heights you can reach!" I exclaimed.

"Seltzer, my dear boy!" the whale responded.
"The bubbles lift you higher!" And that's the
origin of our famous whale logo and slogan--
"Fountain's bubbles lift you higher!"

Fordham Jones was my business partner and
friend for many years. He sketched the first
version of our logo. Brilliant man. Fordham fled
North Carolina and settled in a freedmen's camp
outside DC during the war, made his way up to
Baltimore sometime in the seventies, which is
where we met. Had a real head for numbers, Ol'
Fordham did. Greatest fellow I ever met, and like a
second father to me. When he died, I thought
surely the company would follow.

Thank goodness for Lou [AA: Louisa Worman,
informant's longtime secretary]. Yes, thank
goodness for Lou. Now, that's my own personal
slogan.

10

THERE ARE TWO ways to get up to Sprangbur on foot. Sometimes Quentin and I would take the same route we would
have in a car, following Main Street all the way up to where
it forks, turning right onto Carmichael Chapel Road, and then
eventually right onto Riverview. It's kind of the long way round,
though, and the sidewalk stops for a long stretch on Carmichael
Chapel, so we were forced to walk single file on the narrow
shoulder with cars zooming past (there is, notoriously, no posted
speed limit, which, according to local legend, means that the
limit does not exist; the police occasionally beg to differ). Then
there's the more direct route through Riverside Park. It's a mile-
long stretch of trail that starts downtown and ends at the base
of Sprangbur, copying the curve of the Monocacy River. Despite the prime real estate, it's never been particularly scenic; the
county often neglected maintenance on the bordering land, so
the view was mostly overgrown grass and invasive trees growing
between the path and the water.

Or, at least, that's how it was the last time I was here.

When Quentin and I approach the unassuming trailhead, a few minutes' walk from Best That You Can Brew, I look at him like *Is this right? Did we take a wrong turn somewhere?* Because Riverside Park is nothing like I remember it. Instead of hard-packed dirt, the pathway is now paved with dark, fresh asphalt. More surprisingly, the area to the left is freshly mowed grass dotted with benches and a picnic pavilion, while to the right is a lovely unobstructed view of the water and the forested land on the opposite bank.

"Whoa, they made this nice," I say.

"Yeah," Quentin agrees. "The lady behind me in line at the post office was telling me about it the other day. She said they're putting a bunch of big new houses where the old middle school was, and the builder wanted to advertise proximity to the park as an amenity. So the company gave the city a big donation to be used toward ongoing upkeep."

"Oh. That's good, I guess."

"Not according to the post office lady. She wasn't particularly happy about it, or any of the other changes happening around here. She was there to mail a letter to the county disputing her property tax increase."

"I wonder if my parents' has gone up," I say, swallowing hard. Mom hasn't mentioned anything about that, but I suppose property tax increases will likely affect them too, if they haven't already. There's a small lurch of fear, supported by the memory of overhearing my mother on the phone with the mortgage company after Dad's accident left him unable to work, begging them to give her a few months to catch up on payments. The piles of bills marked with big red overdue stamps that sat on the dining room table for most of my junior and senior years. But, no, things are different now. They have the settlement money. This won't make or break them. Which is good, since I'm in no position to help them out.

"Probably. Ours is ten percent over the next three years." Quentin pauses before continuing, "That's one of the reasons Dad agreed to let me get the house ready to sell."

I almost trip as I take my next step but am thankfully able to play it off as avoiding a small puddle leftover from last night's thunderstorm. "Oh, I didn't realize you were," I say. But that doesn't sound right, so I add, "Doing that." Which doesn't sound right either. I try again. "That . . . that's why you . . . with the flooring and stuff." Geez. A bunch of high school debate championship ribbons, thirteen conference presentations, three job talks, and a dissertation defense under my belt, and yet, in Quentin's presence, I can't even string together a coherent sentence.

It was never like this before. I blame his forearms.

"Yeah, that's why I with the flooring and stuff," he says with an infuriating slight smile. "Figured it would be a productive way to spend my time between jobs. Help get more money for the place, give me a roof over my head and something to focus on that isn't directly related to the horrible crushing despair of existence. You know."

"I do know, yes."

Something heavy shifts around in my stomach as we continue forward. At first I assume it's my body rejecting my lunchtime salad, but then it becomes clearer that it's not related to anything I ate. No, it's a response to the thought that whatever Quentin and I manage to rebuild between us won't matter, because he'll be leaving again. And I'll be leaving too. At least we are mutually leaving this time, and I know what to expect. Or rather, what not to expect. In a way this is great news; less pressure to get things right.

It's also an important reminder: I can't let myself get too comfortable with him. Definitely can't get *invested*. We might be living in the same houses we used to, hunting for the same treasure, but so many things have changed. The town has changed. *We've* changed. Everyone and everything has moved on, and this is hopefully just a summertime pit stop on the way back to regularly scheduled programming for both of us.

We're mostly quiet then as we stroll along the river. There must've been a good amount of rain here this spring, because the water flows a few inches below the bank, and everything is lush and verdant. A hawk takes flight from a CAUTION BLIND CURVE AHEAD sign, and by the time it disappears into the woods across the way, I notice that Quentin has stopped walking.

Because now that the county has cut down the massive half-dead oak tree that used to be near this part of the trail, you can actually glimpse Sprangbur from here. It's just the top of one of the Castle's octagonal turrets, but even that hits me in the heart the same way Boston's skyline used to when I'd be driving back from somewhere outside of the city and see it up ahead in the distance. This loosens something in me I didn't realize had been tightened, almost as much as stepping inside my parents' house and sitting down to banana bread the other day.

Quentin lets out a little chuckle that sounds almost like a "huh." I find that one in the mental catalog—the same wonder-filled sound he made the first time I ever beat him at chess—before I can think better of it. And the incredible ease with which I can still recall that annoys me enough that my hands find their way to my hips.

Mom's advice pops into my head. She was right that holding grudges isn't going to help us find the treasure. It will only make this not-entirely-comfortable joint venture feel more interminable. Now is as good a time as any to clear the air. Or rather, cover up the worn linoleum of our old friendship—and all of its highs and lows—with almost aggressively neutral faux wood that will give us a blank canvas. A fresh start.

"I think we should declare a truce," I say.

My words interrupt the step he's about to take, and he comes to a stop again. "Are we . . . at war?"

I throw my hands up in frustration that he doesn't know exactly what I mean. "A truce, a clean slate, whatever you want to call it. I think we need to agree to keep the past in the past if this is going to work."

"Our past, or like, the entire past? Because I don't think we can find a dead guy's treasure if we pretend he never existed."

"You know what I mean. Everything that went down between us was ages ago. It basically happened to other people. We're different now," I say. "Grown adults. So let's just forget it all and move on, okay?"

"'Different now,'" he repeats, as if he might be skeptical. After five seconds of intense eye contact that feels much longer, he says, "Okay," and holds out his hand. "Clean slate, then."

"Clean slate." I take his hand and shake it. The warmth of his palm against mine is subtle, a few degrees' difference from the surrounding early summer air; I can't help but notice it nonetheless. How would it feel to have that hand cupping the back of my neck, or sliding up my thigh . . .

No, no, no. No thoughts like that.

Although letting myself lust a tiny amount, while clearly

some sort of irrational mental rebound from the recent end of my relationship with Cole, certainly would help keep me in the present. Remind me of all the ways we are different now. Very, very different . . .

"Nina?"

"Hm?"

Quentin looks from my face to our still-joined hands and back again, amusement dancing in his eyes.

I release him and turn abruptly in the opposite direction. "Oh. Sorry. I got distracted by . . . a bird," I say. "I think it flew that way . . ."

"Ah," Quentin replies, clearly humoring me.

We continue along the trail, and I keep my eyes locked on the turret's spire poking up from the trees along the edge of the crag to avoid noticing Quentin's every movement.

"Oh, hey," he says, and points to an old brick warehouse up ahead, on the other side of the grassy area. "Is that where Hanako's bar is?"

It's basically as close to being waterside as local zoning will allow. I bet the large patio with its assorted seating and globe lights is absolutely packed in the evenings and on weekends now that it's warm. A sign for the complex indicates there's also a burger place, an upscale Italian restaurant, and an interior design studio in the same building. The offshoot path toward the big, expensive new houses Quentin told me about is right nearby. "Dang. Really great location," I say.

"Should we see if it's open on our way back?"

"I'm not a big day drinker," I say. Which I'm not; it mostly makes me sleepy now that I'm in my thirties. I am also still reluctant to commit to spending even more non-treasure-hunting time together. Despite our recently declared clean slate, who knows how this will actually play out once we return to the scene of the crime. Literally.

Because we were definitely trespassing when we went to Sprangbur that night in 2008. (I more so than Quentin, if we're being technical.) That we got sent home with nothing but a few stern words from the deputy sheriff is thanks purely to luck, privilege, and Quentin's father being a state prosecutor who was owed a favor by someone high up in the Catoctin City Police Department. My parents were out of town for their anniversary that weekend, trusting me to stay home alone overnight for the first time, and as far as I know they still have no clue I was ever—however briefly—on the wrong side of the law. I plan to keep it that way.

We finally reach the downside of traveling through Riverside Park to reach Fountain's estate: The last leg of the trip is up a steep stone staircase built into the side of the hill. Think the *Exorcist* steps in DC, but like, narrower, and with a single railing that leaves your hands smelling like iron if you use it. Quentin and I attempted to race up it exactly once—the first time we explored Sprangbur that summer. It ended with me having an asthma attack and him throwing up in Technicolor thanks to the two bowls of Trix he'd had for breakfast. Which is why when he turns to me at the base of the stairs and suggests we see who can get to the top first, all I have to do is glare at him to send him into a fit of laughter. It's boisterous and unrestrained, and I find it in the catalog filed under *When we were six and he bet I couldn't jump over a huge ditch full of mud and it turned out he was right.*

He concludes with a fond sigh. "You know, I have not eaten

fruit-flavored cereal since that day," he reminisces. "I don't know about you, but I'm feeling pretty old and tired lately. *Last* one to the top wins."

And with that he moves ahead of me and leisurely ascends toward Sprangbur.

II

My niece Isolde was quite young when my brother
and his wife died. They were aboard the Titanic,
you see, on their way back from visiting my sister-
in-law's family in England--Rebecca was the
daughter of an earl or some such. I was never able
to discover exactly what happened, how Issy became
separated from her parents. Whatever chaos
unfolded, I am glad of it because it meant that she
at least survived.

Rebecca's family quite reasonably didn't want to
put the babe through another trans-Atlantic
crossing after what happened, so she came to live
with me as I was the only stateside relative with
the means to care for her. I would be lying if I
said it was an easy or particularly pleasant time
for any of us. I was a bachelor and business
owner; I didn't know the first thing about raising
a child. I hired nannies, of course, but Issy
always managed to escape the nursery and find her
way into whatever room I was in. She was like a
little homing pigeon who'd decided I was to be her
roost. She'd appear beside me at all hours of the

day and night and simply cry and cry, flashing her
big doe eyes my way and reaching up as if trying
to grasp the ceiling.

Then one day Lou saw this, and she said to me,
"I think she wants you to pick her up and sit her
on your lap."

"But why?" I asked. "Issy, dearest, there's a
perfectly good empty chair over there."

I see that look on your face, Mr. Aaron. You're
thinking I was impossibly dim. Well, yes, and
imagine how I felt! I thought myself to be a fellow
of above-average intelligence. The New York Times
called me one of the greatest business minds of
the new century! Then tiny Isolde Fountain arrived
at Sprangbur and I discovered that I knew very
little at all. About anything that mattered, at
least.

But I did learn. We learned together.

11

QUENTIN AND I both pause on the top step. He looks at me and raises one eyebrow. "What do you think, Hunnicutt? Should we go at the same time and call it a draw?"

It's kind of him to offer. A very "clean slate" sort of thing to do, I guess. Then again, not having these stupid competitions in the first place is an even *cleaner* slate. I ignore him and take the final step, onto the grounds of Sprangbur.

We've arrived at what is technically the rear of the property, near the small eighteenth-century graveyard that Quentin labeled "the Bone Zone" on our map. Fountain left it mostly as it was when he purchased the land. Whether that was out of respect or some superstition, I don't know. I used to find it spooky, but the historian in me lingers for a moment outside the little iron-fenced corner, attempting to read names on the eroded tombstones. I make a mental note to look up two of the ones I can glean to see if there's any interesting research to be done there, then head for the gardens.

It's an interesting contrast. Now, in the early summer, everything on this part of the property is so vibrant and alive. The extensive formal plantings are like a great undulating ocean of green, Sprangbur Castle rising up behind it like a curious sea monster made of stone and wooden shingles with mismatched turrets for arms. I turn to Quentin but find him yards behind me, his attention focused on the small, boxy stone structure off to the right.

Julius Fountain considered architectural design one of his hobbies. Unlike most amateurs, though, he actually had the resources to build the bizarre things he dreamed up. I do have to hand it to him—most of his creations are still standing, as far as I'm aware, so at least they're structurally sound if not always aesthetically pleasing. There's the mushroom folly in the gardens that lost the red and white paint on its cap long ago, so it's now more like a phallic gazebo, and a gigantic brick arch flanked by bronze statues of haunted-looking soldiers he constructed in honor of the (relatively few, as far as I'm aware) Luxembourgian Americans who fought for the Union in the Civil War. Three freestanding Greek Doric columns, identical in height and spaced five feet apart. A tiny stucco pagoda. And the thing that's captured Quentin's attention: the tomb Fountain designed to be his final resting place.

It's where I was supposed to meet Quentin that final night but didn't.

I slowly make my way to where he stands lost in thought. "Quentin . . ."

"Did you ever come back here?" he asks, his voice distant. "After everything?"

It's tempting to lie and say that I did. That I used to come here to fool around with my crushes, like the goth kids were rumored to do. But the truth is that the wound of Quentin's abandonment was easily reopened if I wasn't careful; I spent most of the two years before college staying away from anything that might be even a little sharp. Instead I organized my life in such a way that I was always too busy with SAT prep and debate team practices and extra credit essays to even tempt myself. "No," I say. "Never."

He nods once, twice. It's almost like he appreciates that I never reclaimed this place as my own, as somewhere that meant anything to me beyond what it meant to both of us. I consider saying something that might hurt him, something about how I was too busy living my life and didn't have time for childish games after he stopped goading me into them. That isn't very clean slate of me, though. Nor do I think it would fool him. So I resecure the hurt that's threatening to come loose from its chains and instead go with "Why do you ask?"

He seems to come to, refocused on me now. "I figured we shouldn't waste time rechecking the places we already checked. I wanted to see if there was anywhere else you'd already covered."

"No," I say. "I only checked . . ."

"Where you went instead," he finishes for me. But there's no heat in his words, not even the subtle, repressed kind, so I order the defensiveness rising up in me to take a hike.

"And I assume you checked the cenotaph that night?" I ask.

"The what?"

I gesture in the direction of the little cave-like building.

He squints at it. "You mean the mausoleum?"

"A mausoleum that doesn't actually hold any remains is called a cenotaph," I say, enjoying the way Quentin's eyebrows still get that deep dividing line between them when I've said something that annoys him. "And Fountain wound up being buried in Baltimore, in the same plot as his brother and parents, remember? So technically . . ."

"Then yes, I checked the *cenotaph*," he says, and pauses before continuing, "inside and out."

The only clue Fountain left was that the treasure was hidden somewhere at Sprangbur, and the riddle: "Stiff of spine, body pale, you shall find what you seek beneath the whale." Much of our time on the estate that summer was spent looking for carvings or markings that even remotely resembled a whale. The problem wasn't that we couldn't find one so much as we found about two hundred. Whales were second only to stars as Fountain's favored decorative motif.

But in early July, we found a newspaper article talking about Fountain's burial in Baltimore and learned that what we assumed was just another weird stone outbuilding was actually what Fountain had once intended as his final resting place. "Stiff of spine, body pale" certainly seemed to apply to a dead person. So we started focusing on the cenotaph, which, frustratingly, was the one place on the property we couldn't seem to find anything whale-related. We figured we were on the wrong track and went back to researching and wandering aimlessly around Sprangbur together in hopes of having an epiphany.

Then, on Quentin's penultimate night in Catoctin, as we were talking through our windows, he switched over to his normal voice and asked me to meet him out back. I snuck out of the house and went around to the gate at the end of his yard, where he directed me to a fleece blanket flung over the grass near the garage, where it was darkest. We lay there, arms pressed together, the air still warm and humid despite it being near eleven. The memory of how my heart kicked up when he asked if I'd stargaze with him, beating so hard it felt like it was trying to knock its way out of my chest, is still surprisingly fresh in my mind. I tried to bury every other memory of that summer after it became clear Quentin wasn't going to be in my life anymore. But that one I've kept a bit closer than the rest.

Quentin reached over and handed me something. It was a planisphere—one of those star charts where you adjust it to the right month and time and you can see what constellations are in the sky above you. He said, "I found this while packing up my bedroom."

I spun the planisphere to August, eleven p.m., and adjusted it so the cardinal directions around the outside lined up with our position.

"I bet," Quentin started, "that I can accurately identify more constellations than you can."

It turned out he could, and I didn't really mind, because it meant I got to lie there beside him while he pointed up at the sky and taught me about the stars.

When he finished with what we could see, I thought he would stop. Instead, he continued, taking the planisphere and rotating it to different dates, telling me stories about the constellations currently in hiding.

"That one, there, is Cetus," he said quietly. "The sea monster, or whale."

"The whale, huh," I said. "Wait. Quentin. *The whale!*" I sprang up then and grabbed the planisphere. "What if this is what Fountain meant?"

Which is how we realized there may be a whale on the cenotaph after all.

I feel the sudden and urgent need to explain myself. To confess what I discovered on my own and why I never made it to the cenotaph that night as we'd agreed. But before I can decide how to start, how to phrase it, Quentin walks to the outer edge of the gardens, where his fingers graze against the top of a well-manicured hedge. It sends a shiver through me, as if my skin can't help but imagine being one of those waxy leaves.

"I thought about this place a lot when I was overseas," he says matter-of-factly. "I visited a bunch of the grand European estates while I lived over there. Versailles. Boboli. Schönbrunn. Keukenhof. And even after seeing all of those much bigger, much older mansions and gardens, I couldn't help but compare them to Sprangbur and find them . . . well, lacking."

I let out a surprised laugh. The gardens here are beautiful, and the county and volunteers have always done a great job with their upkeep, even when the Castle itself was a condemned eyesore. But the property is also much less ornate and, like, one-twentieth the size of the famous ones Quentin mentioned.

"I didn't say I thought Sprangbur was *nicer*," he clarifies. "There's just . . . something really special about it." He smiles fondly as his gaze sweeps over the large house and the land surrounding it.

Maybe that's what I've been missing about that summer whenever the memories of it have managed to slip through my defenses. In my head, it was the time Quentin and I were closest, inching toward some precipice that was terrifying and exciting all at once. I thought that maybe I was developing romantic feelings for him, that *we* might have been developing those sorts of feelings for each other, and that's one of the reasons it hurt him so much that I went behind his back. But now I'm wondering if it wasn't that Quentin and I were falling in love, but simply that we were overcome by the surprising magic of this otherworldly domain that Fountain built.

It *is* magical. Not literally, obviously. But I can't deny that there's this sense here that anything might be possible. Even when the Castle had broken windows, flaking paint, and a partially caved-in roof, it still exuded this quiet yet enticing playfulness. I suppose that's why Fountain loved living here so much. And why it's always felt like such a touchstone for Quentin (and, I guess, for me) as we went about the rest of our lives.

Maybe all of my overwhelming feelings back then weren't even about Quentin at all. They were just grief over the end of my love affair with this fascinating place.

Even more reason to put the past behind us and finish what we started so we can move on without the risk of becoming enchanted again.

"So," I say, still feeling the need to explain myself. It's part of our agreement, after all. The word comes out croaky, so I clear my throat, then point down the path. "That night. When you were at the cenotaph. I, um, went inside the house."

Quentin's eyes go wide in disbelief. "You . . . Jesus, Nina. That was stupid."

"Excuse me?"

"What if you'd gotten hurt? The place was falling apart and—"

"I was careful," I argue. He shakes his head in exasperation.

My left knee twinges, thanks to the long walk and many stairs it took to get here. I sit down on a small bench tucked among the rosebushes that make up the southwestern edge of the formal gardens, hugging one of the mansion's rough-hewn stone walls. The fragrance drifts through the air and a pink petal falls at my feet as if saying hello. "I didn't find anything. Obviously."

"Okay. And . . . ?" he responds, as if still waiting for more.

"And what?"

"I always wondered, why did you decide to search there instead of meeting me?"

"You didn't have to wonder. Nothing was stopping you from asking." I immediately kick myself for the waspish tone of my voice.

He responds steadily, "I'm asking now."

My eyes wander back toward the cenotaph, over the gentle crest of a hill. If I'd met Quentin there as we'd agreed, would we still have gotten caught? Would he have still declared it all—our friendship, the time we spent together—a mistake? Everything that happened that night may very well have been all my fault. Guilt feels like a pile of worms wriggling inside the pit of my stomach.

Quentin leans casually against a portion of the Castle's wall not guarded by the rosebushes, examining his thumb as he bends and straightens it a few times, as if my answer to his question isn't that important, really. As if he hasn't actually been waiting for me to give him this information for nearly two decades. Then again, maybe his "I always wondered" was less like "I frequently lie awake at night pondering why you did what you did" and more the kind of idle curiosity that accompanies that thing you want to look up on Wikipedia but can never seem to remember at a convenient time.

Clean slate, I remind myself. *Clean slate*. These thoughts are the opposite of that. In fact, my slate has all of the ghostlike chalk impressions of the past, smeared all around to make the black surface more of a smoke color. I take a deep breath and close my eyes to recalibrate—what I hope will be the mental equivalent of taking a wet paper towel to the whole thing and trying again.

As I breathe in through my nose, the faint rose smell becomes thicker. My eyes open again to find Quentin crouched in front of me, his face inches from mine. He slides a large, fluffy pink rose into my hair, above my left ear. His fingertips brush against my cheek as he lowers his hand again, and it takes all of my strength not to lean into the touch.

"I hope that doesn't have any bugs hiding in it," I say, my words coming out a little breathless.

"I shook it out first."

Even so, I slip it from my own hair and tuck it into his, which has just enough length and body to hold it. "It looks better on you," I say. He smiles slowly and lets out a little hum of satisfaction that I don't remember ever hearing before but decide deserves a place in the catalog of his laughs, forever filed under this moment: him looking unfairly delicious, smelling of soap and flowers and the light musk of exertion, staring back at me with a confidence that's entirely proprietary to this grown-up version of him.

"So are you going to tell me why you thought it could be there?" he asks.

Oh. Right. Focus, Nina. No, no, not on his lips. On words.

I swallow before continuing. "We thought we might find Cetus among the constellations on the cenotaph. But I'd also seen another collection of stars in one of the rooms inside the Castle." Glancing back at the external wall of the mansion, I fold my hands in my lap and speed through the rest of my words when I land on the right ones. "I came here one day without you . . . sometime at the end of July, I think. You were at your grandparents' for the week, and I figured it wouldn't hurt to poke around a bit. See what I could find. It had stormed pretty bad overnight, and the wind forced a side door ajar just enough for me to slip through. I knew it was illegal, and probably not even safe, but . . . I couldn't pass up that kind of opportunity, could I? To see what it was like inside Fountain's Castle?"

I can't say what gave me the courage to be so uncharacteristically bold, so brave. But it felt like something I had to do. For Quentin. For *us*.

That deep line in his forehead reappears. "You never told me that you came out here by yourself."

I flap my hands and say, "Clean slate." I'm grateful that seems to work as a get-out-of-jail-free card, Quentin simply rolling his eyes. "I only did a quick walk-through, since I was pretty anxious about getting caught or running into a ghost. But one of the rooms upstairs had this . . . I don't know if it was wallpaper or painted directly on the plaster, but the walls were covered in stars. Really faded and dirty, but they were definitely stars. I didn't think much of it at the time, but then you told me about Cetus when we were in your backyard and my very first thought was that room. How the stars hadn't been positioned willynilly, but like, arranged in specific patterns. Constellations. I was going to go along with your plan to check the cenotaph again, because there *are* a lot of stars on the back of it, and you could've been right."

"But you didn't," he says flatly. "Go along with it."

"No. I didn't."

He simply waves this away, as if this recounting of my betrayal is a minor flub that can be edited out later. Quentin is way better at the clean slate thing than I am, it seems. Unsurprising, considering how good he is at forgetting things. And people.

"So. You thought you'd find it in that room. That you'd cracked it," Quentin says, staring off into the distance, looking deep in thought.

"Yeah," I admit. "I thought I had."

He blinks a few times before looking at me again. His lips curve into a small smile. "That's really brilliant, Neen. Amazing work." There isn't any sarcasm in the statement. Just the same admiring tone I heard him use when we were kids and I managed to best him at something. That's what made competing with Quentin so addicting, come to think of it. Don't get me wrong—the boy loved to win. But he also never seemed to mind too much when he didn't. In fact, he often looked . . . proud of me. The way he's looking at me right now.

And I know deep down that's why I tried to find the treasure on my own. Because I thought he would be so impressed that that pride would transform into something else. Something that might survive the upcoming distance between us. Not love, maybe, because when he didn't kiss me that night in his backyard I figured he must not return my feelings. But I still thought that his admiration, his respect for my mind (and the hustle) might leave a lasting impression. That it would only strengthen what we had.

Then again, I'm realizing that maybe what we had wasn't as strong as I believed it was. Maybe the outcome wouldn't have changed, regardless of what I did or didn't do that night.

"I was wrong, though," I say. "The treasure wasn't there."

"Are we sure about that?" he asks after a short pause.

"All I found was the skeleton of some small, unfortunate animal beneath a newspaper, and an empty Bubble Tape container."

"No chance you missed something?"

"I mean . . . I was as thorough as I could be, but it was dark and the walls were too damaged for me to figure out if Cetus was actually there. I didn't get to check every single floorboard or anything. Honestly, after finding the skeleton I was a bit less enthusiastic in my search. And then . . . you know . . ." I wiggle my finger in the air and say, "Wee-woo, wee-woo."

He lets out a responding laugh that I recognize as the earliest entry in the catalog. It's the same one from the very first conversation we ever had, in front of our houses while the movers were lugging the last few boxes into 304 and one full of his sister's underwear dropped and split open on the sidewalk. I still find it tucked inside a subfolder labeled *Reluctant favorites*.

"I don't think the treasure was inside that room," I reiterate. "I'm like ninety percent certain it wasn't. Don't patronize me by telling me it was smart for me to look there."

"Okay, fine. You were wrong to look there and it was a stupid thing to do. And also you suck."

"Thank you," I say, feeling somewhat relieved to have that over with, even if he is being facetious.

"But also maybe you were onto something. That summer, almost all of our search focused on the property."

"Yeah, because we didn't have access to the house." I'm aware of the irony that I am the one saying this, so I add, "Technically."

"Right. But that's a pretty massive oversight, don't you think? He *could* have hidden it inside the house."

It's true that, aside from my solo search in July and that last night, we almost solely focused on the gardens and outbuildings. Probably because it was a lot more fun as teens to wander around, tapping on various stones and covertly digging small holes, than to try to reconstruct the Castle's original interior based on old photos. That, and we hadn't exactly planned to trespass at the beginning, especially not into a spooky-ass mansion.

"Hmm." I stand and start following the brick pathway through the gardens. Quentin follows close behind me; I can tell because he's started whistling idly, the way he did my first day back in town when he made his way from the porch to his car.

I turn abruptly as we reach the ornate asymmetrical front of Fountain's mansion. "Is that even a real song?" I ask.

He doesn't respond, only quirks the corner of his mouth.

"If you're just going to try to get on my nerves all summer, we don't have to do this at all," I threaten.

Quentin tucks his hands into his pockets and takes a step closer, tilting his head down. His mouth is only inches from my ear, and when he speaks, the heat of his breath sweeps against the sensitive skin there. "I'm not trying to get on your nerves, Nina." His voice is quiet, intimate. The way it might be if we were in a crowded room and he wanted to ensure his words were for my ears only. "I'm succeeding."

"Okay, that's it," I declare, turning on my heel again. Sure, I'm only confirming his assertion, but I can't stand here and convincingly insist he isn't getting under my skin. Because I've rarely been more annoyed. Not just with him, but with the hot pressure curled in my stomach like a cobra, unsure whether to take a nap or strike. There's no way I can handle an entire eight weeks of spending time with this man. He is . . . frustrating. *Very* frustrating.

"Neen, wait," he says, lunging forward. His hand grabs mine and gently pulls until I'm back at the base of the stairs leading up to the Castle's entryway. "I'll be good. I promise."

I narrow my eyes. I find that doubtful, especially because his own eyes are once again crinkled in the corners in the stupidly handsome way that means he's finding this very funny. I'm about to tell him so—that I doubt he'll be good, not the stupidly handsome part—when one side of the front doors creaks open, revealing a small, plump, middle-aged white woman.

"Oh, hello!" she calls to us. "You're just in time! We're about to start our two o'clock tour."

Shall we? Quentin asks with his eyebrows and a quirk of his lips.

As tempted as I am to be contrary for the sake of it, I am much more intensely curious about the interior of Sprangbur Castle now that it's been restored. And if we might be able to get a good look at that parlor with the stars. "Fine," I grumble, and follow him inside.

TEXT OF INTERVIEW (UNEDITED)

III

Have you been to Edlo, Mr. Aaron? No, I don't
suppose you have. Don't look like the sort of
person who could make it there. Now, that's not a
slight--the journey simply isn't for the faint of
heart.

I will be honest with you and confess that it
took me several attempts to get there for the first
time myself. Isolde and Lou, they took to it right
away. No braver hearts than those two ladies. The
land opened up before them and welcomed them with
open arms. For me, it took more coaxing. More time.
Some growth.

You see, Edlo only appears to those who can
believe in its magic. I wanted to believe, very
desperately. I wanted to join Issy and Lou in that
wonderful place. It wasn't until I rediscovered the
lightness in my heart that I had packed away after
Fordham's and my brother and sister-in-law's deaths
that I suddenly saw the same fantastic world they
were seeing.

Would you like to go there, Mr. Aaron? Of course you would. No place better.

Well, we'll have to work on your lightness, then. Your heart's altogether too heavy at the moment. I can see it in your shoes.

12

THE WOMAN WHO beckoned us inside introduces herself to the small group of assembled people in the foyer as Sharon, the deputy director of the Sprangbur Conservancy and our tour guide. She's very pleasant, if a bit scattered. Clearly someone who knows a lot about Julius Fountain and his estate, but isn't necessarily well-versed in delivering that knowledge in a way that is organized and concise. The historian portion of my brain appreciates the information and stories, but the rest of it wishes she would hurry up already. We've been here for fifteen minutes so far and are only now getting to our first room of the tour, the library. At this rate, it's going to be at least an hour before we reach the second-floor parlor I tried to search as a kid.

I'm not sure I can handle standing beside Quentin for that long. His proximity has a strange effect on me. It's like he's a freak weather system sweeping through, leaving me somehow simultaneously cold, hot, and wet all at once. My brain is aware that this is the same person who left me feeling abandoned seventeen years ago, but my body refuses to believe it.

Perhaps it's because I've been through so much lately, with losing my job and breaking up with Cole and returning to this town, and my subconscious is trying to protect me from falling into a deep depression by distracting me with an attraction to someone convenient. Yes. I'm sure that's all it is! A way to keep myself occupied so I don't start anxiety spiraling. Nothing more.

It's just a coping mechanism, I tell myself when he positions himself directly behind me as Sharon tells us about a dinner party during which Fountain apparently faked his own death twice (and his butler's once). I remind myself as the radiant heat of his body caresses the back of my neck. *Coping mechanism.* When he leans forward to whisper a joke into my ear, his fingertips brushing over my arm. *Coping . . . coping . . .* what's the word again?

Thank god. We finally reach the Star Parlor. I shake my head, clearing it of the lust-induced fog that seeped in through my brain's cracks so that there's space to process my surroundings again. We've been ceding the position directly in front of each doorway to the three elderly women with whom we've been sharing the tour, but this time I slip in front of them so that I'm the one against the velvet rope cordoning off the room.

It's both gorgeous and discombobulating. I recognize the room's distinctive shape—a sort of half circle with a rectangle tacked on—from when I broke in, but otherwise I'd never guess it was the same space. It's a lot like when I saw Quentin on the porch from my car—newness with the vaguest, nagging hint of familiarity. There are still stars on the walls, but instead of the faded and torn panels my cheap flashlight revealed as I searched, it's smooth and vivid, pinks and oranges and the darkest navy like the most beautiful sky at dusk. The constellations themselves are painted in subtly shimmering gold. It's breathtaking.

"Wow," Quentin says from beside me. We're practically alone, the rest of the group gathering at the base of the wide staircase in the hallway as Sharon shifts to sharing fun facts about late nineteenth-century advancements in household technology.

My eyes work their way from left to right over each grouping of stars. It's been a long time since I had reason to think about Cetus, so I can't say I know exactly what I'm looking for here. "Do you see it?" I ask.

He takes a moment to answer. "No. And I doubt we will." Quentin points in the direction of a portion of wall with stars positioned in a backward question mark. "I'm almost certain that's Leo. Which is only visible in spring and summer. Cetus is wintertime. I don't think it would be here. Not if it's accurate, at least."

And it most likely is. Fountain was big on accuracy and preciseness. It was one of the first things he told his interviewer in the oral history transcripts we read, and everything else we learned about the way he ran his business corroborated his claim. Apparently he insisted on monitoring the carbonation levels of his seltzer daily by having employees count the number of bubbles that appeared in the first three seconds of pouring a glass.

"What if, when they renovated, they chose a different pattern of constellations than Fountain originally had in here?" I suddenly want very much to have been correct about this, to have simply not searched thoroughly enough that night. For my betrayal and everything that followed to have not been for nothing.

Quentin shrugs. "I suppose it's possible."

"We'll talk to Sharon after," I decide. "See if she knows anything about it."

A tiny ball of nausea bounces around my stomach. It's guilt—something that's always been there, hidden behind the anger and hurt—resurfacing as I remember that night in more vivid detail than I've let myself in a long, long time.

Quentin and I were supposed to meet at 11:30 at the cenotaph to check if there was a loose stone or anything else among the constellations etched there. Instead, I borrowed one of my dad's hammers and pried the nails out of three of the new planks covering the same side door I'd snuck through earlier that summer. It was 11:50 when I heard Quentin whisper-yelling my name outside. By then I was getting pretty freaked out being alone in an abandoned, crumbling mansion with only a (squirrel?) skeleton for company, so I decided to get out of there and go meet up with him after all. I'd managed to squeeze my upper body back through the hole I made when a throat cleared loudly to my right. "Quentin?" I asked quietly. But it wasn't Quentin. It was Deputy Kramer of the Catoctin Police. Who definitely didn't buy that I was there alone after hearing me say someone's name. She made quick work of finding Quentin, who was basically a sitting duck. (Or a roaming duck, I guess, since he was still wandering around the property quietly calling for me.)

Sharon is now telling the group about Louisa Worman, Fountain's secretary, and I try to push aside the memories of what came next that night: my tearful apology in the back of the police cruiser, and Quentin's cold, angry words: *This was a mistake. It was all a mistake.* Followed by silence. The loudest, longest silence of my life. One that might have never ended had fate not simultaneously knocked us down several pegs.

And all because I made the stupid decision to look inside the Star Parlor. Which probably didn't even feature Cetus among its constellations.

I look back now, and all I can think is *Stupid. Stupid. Stupid.* "Nina," Quentin says, his voice farther away than expected. I blink, refocusing on the present, and find that I'm still lingering in front of the parlor while Sharon leads the rest of the group back downstairs. Quentin is halfway between me and them, as if he started in that direction before noticing my continued stillness. "You okay?"

"Who's to say!" I answer, not willing to commit to a solid yes at the moment.

In the basement, Sharon tells us about Fountain's domestic staff, who were paid double the going rate in the area at the time. Which seems like the very least Fountain should do for his employees, considering one of his favorite pastimes in his final years apparently included filling his claw-foot tub with various non-water substances to see what it would feel like to soak in them. Thankfully, this anecdote is so unexpectedly weird that it reboots my struggling brain and allows me to get through the last ten minutes of the tour without becoming lost in the past or turned on in the present.

Once everyone has returned to the main level, Quentin and I linger in the foyer, waiting for Sharon to bid the elderly women goodbye. He leans in toward me again, and this time the clean scent of him is such an intense contrast to the musty basement we recently vacated that I take a startled step away.

"What's going on with you?" he asks, giving me a puzzled look. "Have you been possessed by a maid who tragically drowned when she fell into Fountain's molasses bath?"

Thankfully, Sharon's attention turns to us now, freeing me from having to enumerate the *many* things going on with me at the moment.

"Great tour!" I say with too much enthusiasm.

"Oh, thank you for saying so. I haven't given one in a while, believe it or not."

Oh, I can definitely believe it, considering it took over an hour to get through ten rooms.

"We had a few questions about the house, if you don't mind?"

Sharon practically glows, happy to keep talking about Sprangbur Castle. "Absolutely! What can I answer for you?"

Quentin takes over with, "We were wondering if you knew more about the Star Parlor. It's beautiful."

"Isn't it?" Sharon's glow intensifies, as if she designed the room herself. "It was one of the most complicated—and expensive!—parts of the Sprangbur Castle restoration. You see, we had a few photos of the room to go off of, but they were all black-and-white, of course. Thankfully a specialist was able to pull samples from the walls before we replastered them to identify the approximate colors used. Imagine our delight when we saw how wonderfully it came together."

"Incredible," Quentin says. "I noticed the constellations seem to be spring or summer ones. Do you know anything about that? If Julius Fountain chose that time of year deliberately?"

"Oh, I can't believe I forgot to mention! It's one of my favorite facts. The Star Parlor was redecorated in 1917 as a birthday present for Mr. Fountain's niece. The constellations reflect those in the sky on the evening she was born."

"Wow, what a sweet gift," I say lightly despite the increasing heaviness in my stomach at this confirmation that I hadn't been onto anything at all when I broke into this place, thereby fucking up my closest friendship.

"Yes, Mr. Fountain could be very thoughtful when he wanted to be." Sharon smiles affectionately at a portrait visible through the open library doorway, hanging over the mantel. The glint in his eyes and the seltzer bottle tucked into the crook of one arm mark him undeniably as Julius James Fountain, but it was painted when he was much younger than I'm used to seeing him. His hair is slicked back and dark, his face clean-shaven. He bears only a passing resemblance to the wild white-haired and mustached man I know mostly from twentieth-century photos.

"Interesting portrait," Quentin says, reading my mind.

"Wasn't he a handsome one?" Sharon asks. "I've always been surprised he never married."

It isn't particularly surprising to me; Fountain was shockingly open about his reasons. Sure, he didn't use the terms or labels we might use today, but he was clear that sex and romance were not high on his list of priorities in life. I'm not about to "well, actually . . ." the deputy director of the foundation keeping the man's estate running, though. Nor do I want to publicly declare that Fountain was a babe, even if he sort of was (in this portrait at least). So instead I say, "It's a very striking painting. Lovely . . ." I search the recesses of my mind for the art history intro course I took in undergrad and settle on "composition," even though I don't fully remember what it means.

"Yes, I've always thought so," Sharon agrees. "An interesting story behind it too. It was a gift from a friend of Mr. Fountain's, a Canadian painter named John Claude Whale. His father was—"

Quentin cuts in before I can. "I'm sorry, what was that name again?"

"John Claude Whale," she repeats, over-enunciating each part as if trying to give important information over the phone. My eyes find Quentin's quicker than two magnets in sudden proximity. *Whale!* I mouth as Sharon's attention is focused in his direction. "As I was saying, his father was much more well-known. He painted a very famous version of Niagara Falls. It actually helped lead to conservation efforts. I read a great book—"

"Sorry to interrupt," I say. Under other circumstances, I might be interested in the book recommendation, but not right now, with excitement whirring through my veins like it's being powered by tiny turbines. "We have to get going, but before we do, I'm really fascinated by the way the Conservancy worked to restore this place so authentically. How you decided what to keep, knew where to put things. Like the portrait. Has it always hung there above the fireplace in the library?"

Sharon's face transforms from confused and slightly irked by my obtrusion to overjoyed to share more of her knowledge. "Oh, no, I don't believe this is where it was during Mr. Fountain's time."

"Do you know where it would have been originally?" Quentin asks when it becomes obvious she isn't going to share the information unprompted.

"I haven't a clue," she says slowly, almost as if she can't believe we've asked about something she doesn't know. "A contractor found it wrapped in a sheet inside an armoire up in the attic." A cell phone rings, the tune echoing strangely down the hallway as if the walls themselves find the technology unfamiliar. "Oh, that's mine! Excuse me, I have to get this. Sorry I can't show you out, but thanks for visiting!" Sharon calls behind her as she hurries toward a door by the dining room marked OFFICE.

With wordless looks, Quentin and I agree that we can't linger here. Nor would it do us much good without having any idea where the Whale portrait hung at the time of Fountain's death. So he drops a ten-dollar bill into the donation box sitting on a table in the foyer, and we head back outside into the slightly sticky late afternoon air.

At the bottom of the steps, where Quentin whispered in my ear and took my hand only an hour and a half ago—really, that was quite the thorough tour Sharon gave us—he puts his hands on his hips and tilts his head back, his eyes closed, letting the sun shine down on his face. He lets out a long, pensive sigh.

I let out one of my own, though it comes out as more of a groan. "I can't tell if that was productive or not."

"I would say so. We now know the Star Parlor has never had the Cetus constellation on its walls, so signs point to the treasure not being in there. But there *is* a portrait painted by a man named Whale, which is a huge lead."

"Yes, but we have no idea where the portrait was at the time of Fountain's death. Unless it was in the attic even then?"

"Maybe it's like some sort of reverse Dorian Gray situation where Fountain aged normally and his portrait remained youthful," he remarks.

"That's . . . just how normal portraiture works," I say.

"Oh. Right." Quentin stretches his hands high toward the sky. I do my best not to stare at the sliver of stomach that's appeared between his T-shirt and shorts. But it's like my eyes can't resist. There's that trail of hair again, barely visible in the small gap, but I know it's there now. I know it's there, and where it would lead and—

"Nina? Did you hear me?"

My eyes jump to Quentin's, as if I can mislead him into thinking that's where they were directed all along. "Huh?"

"I said I have a plumber coming tomorrow morning to give me a quote on a few things, but we could probably go to the library in the afternoon if the special collections room is open."

"Yeah. Um, sure." Why are we going to the library? Exactly how much did I miss while ogling him?

"Wow, you really weren't listening, were you?" he asks with an affectionate smile—the kind you might give a small child with ice cream all over her face.

"Sorry, I was just . . . thinking. About how hot it is. Outside. In the environment."

"Only June too. Probably going to get a lot worse," he says, sounding endearingly like an old man making small talk with a grocery store cashier. "What I was saying was that we should go to the library to look through those photos they have of the Castle, see if we can spot the portrait in one of them."

"Oh. That's a good idea."

"I do have one on occasion," he says. The lift at the corner of his mouth turns into a full-blown smile, but the not-quite-right one that makes me feel like I'm looking at a version of Quentin that someone tried to "fix" with AI.

I suppose it's also possible I just don't know Quentin anymore. Like, it would be absurd if he was still the same boy who incessantly quoted *Talladega Nights: The Ballad of Ricky Bobby*. He has a law degree. He's lived overseas. He was going to marry someone. Is it really so impossible that he's actually grown to be as charming as he now seems? No, not impossible. But dangerous. My subconscious is probably trying to protect me by making me suspicious that it's all an act because it knows a genuinely magnetic Quentin would be way too much for me to handle in my fragile state.

"Library tomorrow afternoon," I agree.

I'm still not convinced this treasure exists. But for my sake, I hope it does and that we find it as soon as possible. That way I can stop dwelling on Quentin at all.

13

THE LIBRARY'S ALSO changed since I was last here, which I think was a few months before I left for college. There's still a wide spiral staircase leading up to the second floor at the center of the main level, but the area surrounding it has been fully reimagined. It's now open and sunlit, the floors smooth and shiny instead of covered in threadbare carpet tiles.

It's also a lot noisier than I remember it being.

"'O, what a noble mind is here o'erthrown!'"

In the center of the space is a gathering of teenagers standing in front of an audience of senior citizens, probably bussed in from a local retirement community considering how many there are, plus one or two kids their own age who are likely here out of friendly obligation. The actors are each wearing one or two accessories to denote their characters, but otherwise it's as low-budget a production as it gets.

A flyer taped to a nearby pillar helpfully explains that I have stumbled upon the library's Summer Teen Drama Club rendition of "Selections from *Hamlet*."

Quentin left to procure a new library card and is still chatting genially with the desk staff, so I lean against the wall and watch from afar for a moment longer. The kids overacting their hearts out are a bit younger, but they remind me of the students I had in my freshman classes at Malbyrne. That patented mixture of over-assuredness and insecurity that spikes around that age, making teenagers somehow both the cringiest and coolest people you'll ever meet.

The thought that I almost certainly won't be going back to a college classroom in August hits me anew. It was relatively easy until now to push it to the back of my mind, summer being my usual time off anyway. But seeing these teens here now makes me recall reality, and my heart aches.

I may not have won awards for my teaching, but I did manage to keep the attention of a bunch of hungover eighteen-year-olds at 8:30 in the morning—no mean feat.

"Do you remember," Quentin whispers, suddenly beside me, "when we read *A Midsummer Night's Dream* aloud in sophomore English?"

A smile tugs at the corner of my mouth. "How could I forget? You had a fantastic Bottom. Were! *Were* a fantastic Bottom." Oh god. I stumble for more and land on, "The ass. The guy with the ass head."

Man. This not-being-able-to-talk-without-making-a-fool-of-myself thing sucks. If I could die from embarrassment, I'm pretty sure I would've done it like six times over by now.

Quentin grins, clearly wanting to comment on what I've said but deciding it's too easy of a joke. "You ready to head up?"

It's tempting to stick around for another few minutes, to support these kids who are admirably spending their summer being cute little drama club dorks instead of getting into mischief.

But I also don't want to keep being reminded of how much I'll miss my students, even if they did sometimes whine about their grades and leave inappropriate comments on my teaching evaluations.

Also, if we're busy looking through the Fountain files, I am less likely to accidentally compliment Quentin's ass again. Or be thinking about his ass at all.

"Let's go."

We travel up the winding staircase and head to where the special collections room is still tucked in the library's back corner as if it's in its own secret world. The door is closed, adding to the feeling that there's something particularly valuable or sacred within. A sign taped onto it assures us that it's open, though, so Quentin reaches for the handle and turns it. The familiar scent of a place filled with old paper hits my nose, and I breathe it in with relish. I scan the room, which is almost exactly the same as I remember it, right down to the scowling face staring back at us from the desk in the corner.

Mrs. MacDonald sits completely still, like a creepy animatronic waiting her turn to speak in a theme park show. If her eyes weren't open, I would assume she was asleep.

Unless . . .

"Oh my god, is she dead?" Quentin whispers, voicing my exact thought.

"I'm never dying!"

We both jump in response to the sudden exclamation. I hold a hand to my chest, trying to keep my heart from making a run for it. "Mrs. MacDonald," I say. "Hello. Good to see you, um, well."

"Who says I'm well?" she snaps.

"Sorry to hear that you aren't?" I try.

"Who says I'm not?"

My eyebrows dive as I attempt to figure out what exactly I'm supposed to say here. I land on, "Either way, it's good to see you."

"I don't know if you remember us," Quentin chimes in. "We came here a lot back in 2008, when we were researching Julius Fountain."

Mrs. MacDonald stares for a long time. Long enough that I'm worried she has actually passed away in this very moment. Then she slowly extends a knobby finger in Quentin's direction.

"The gum boy," she says accusingly. "I thought I banned you."

Oh. Right. Quentin is technically not allowed in here. Not since the Trident Tropical Twist Incident. I suppose that's another reason we didn't concern ourselves much with the house itself—lack of access to research materials after about mid-July.

"Wow, what a memory you have!" Quentin says, flashing her his most charming smile. If I had any lingering doubt about it being an intentional trick, it's laid to rest as I watch him summon it. "That was almost twenty years ago. I mean, I can barely remember—"

"I remember it like yesterday." She narrows her eyes as she says it, and it somehow sounds like a threat. "And you, young man, are not allowed in my special collections room."

Quentin's responding laugh is a nervous one—filed under *The time he stapled our second-grade teacher's calendar together and she threatened him with lunch detention*. "Mrs. MacDonald . . ." he starts, but I cut him off. The old archivist has always had a soft spot for me. Or as soft of a spot as the woman possibly can. "I think what my friend is trying to say is that he is incredibly sorry for his reprehensible actions as a youth and hopes you can find it in your heart to give him another chance now that he has grown up and learned from his past transgressions."

"Yes," Quentin says with a nod. "Thank you, Nina. That's exactly what I'm trying to say."

Mrs. MacDonald deliberates for a few seconds that feel eternal, then grumbles, "Fine."

"I promise I won't disappoint you," Quentin says earnestly.

"I even catch you looking like you might start chewing and you're out of here," she warns. "Both of you."

"Understood," we reply in unison.

"Now, what do you want?"

"The Julius Fountain papers," I say. "If you have a way to search the catalog, I'm happy to give you the exact record group—"

"We don't do that here," she says, and is off into the stacks of bankers boxes before I can finish.

Quentin says, "Sorry. I forgot about the gum thing."

"So did I. Although I don't know how. That was super gross. Why did you even do that?"

"The trash can was too far away and I thought I'd just stick it under the table until I got up again. But then I forgot to grab it. It wasn't like . . . I didn't make a habit of it or anything."

"Still extremely gross."

"It was far from the grossest thing I did as a kid, believe me."

"Ew." I give him a light shove. "That in no way helps your case. What did I ever see in you?"

I say it without thinking, and Quentin's smile shrinks and his brows come together as the words register.

"Did you see something in me, Nina?" he asks. And there's no teasing in his tone, no flirtation. Just a sort of confusion and . . . curiosity?

"I . . . Well, no, I just meant . . ." I am not about to confess to having had a crush on Quentin Bell when we were fifteen. Why would I? So he can laugh at how stupid I was to think we meant something to each other?

Thankfully Mrs. MacDonald saves me with her reemergence from the stacks, hunched over and pulling a yellowed box inch by inch toward her by its handle. It drags along the old, rough carpet, making a sound like someone loudly and prolongedly shushing us.

"Let me help you with that," Quentin says, moving forward.

Mrs. MacDonald stops for a moment, out of breath. "No. You sit. I'll be there when I'm there."

"Really—" His outstretched hand is actually slapped away as he tries to take the box.

"I said *sit*," she commands as if we're overexcited beagles instead of two adults attempting to do historical research.

And, I don't know, maybe there's some part of us that is beagle-esque, because damned if we don't both immediately go to the table in the center of the room and take a seat on perpendicular sides of it.

"I feel really bad that she's doing this," Quentin mumbles. "Like, every single instinct I have tells me to intervene, but to be honest I'm kind of really scared of her."

"She's terrifying," I confirm.

Mrs. MacDonald hoists the box onto the table in slow motion before dropping it between us with a thud. "I'll go get the second one," she says, turning away and shuffling back toward the stacks.

"Are you sure we can't help?" I ask.

"Did you go to library school?" she barks. As if an MLS degree is required to move boxes from shelf to table.

"Not exactly," I say. "But I do have a PhD in history, with a minor field in archival studies. If that counts."

"You do, do you? Huh." The slightest hint of a smile curves her thin, dry lips. Or maybe that's a sneer. But she does sound somewhat impressed. "All right. Come with me."

Quentin and I exchange raised eyebrows as I stand, then follow Mrs. MacDonald into the aisles of shelves holding the library's special collections. I glance back at Quentin before turning the corner and find him leaning back in his chair, balancing on its rear legs in the exact way that earned him six stitches in the back of his head when we were eleven.

Something that definitely hasn't changed about Quentin Bell is that he has never once in his life learned a lesson.

In the stacks, I immediately notice something I didn't when I was younger, simply because I had nothing to compare this collection to: there is absolutely no system of organization here. Some boxes have a word or two scribbled in faded pen on the side of the lid, but others are completely blank. The accordion files interspersed don't seem to be labeled at all. How on earth does Mrs. MacDonald know what to pull? What's inside each? The only thing I can think of, which I'm pretty sure is accurate despite how horrifying it is to the part of me that appreciates order and best practices, is that all of the information about the Catoctin Library's special collections is stored solely in Mrs. MacDonald's brain.

I'm about to ask her about her organizational system to confirm my suspicions, but she speaks first. "Went to some fancy school to learn how to do this job, did ya? Where are you working now?"

"Um . . ." I consider lying and telling Mrs. MacDonald I'm still at Malbyrne College, the way I did when I ran into Hanako. Something—fear and awe, probably—keeps me honest, though. "I'm actually between jobs at the moment."

"Oh, that's good," she says, which is a strange response. Was she maybe not listening? Is she hard of hearing? I don't think so, considering how easily she made out Quentin's whispering from across the room.

"Um. Is it?"

"Could be," she responds cryptically, then points to a box on a high shelf. "That one."

"Okay." A step stool is already nearby, and I pull it over and climb up. I pull the bankers box from its place while trying not to fall over. I can't believe Mrs. MacDonald—who must be in her eighties, at least—is still doing this. Sure, I expected her to be here since that's what I was used to, but I didn't actually *expect her to be here*. She's an institution, I guess. And this place runs on pure institutional memory. Which is impressive but also a big problem.

But not *my* problem. It can't be. I don't even live here. I'll be gone as soon as I can catch a break and get things in order again.

Even if I did have more time, considering how challenging it was to convince Mrs. MacDonald to let me carry a box for her, I don't think an offer to help her organize the special collections room would be well received.

She trails me to the table, as if, without an escort, I might inadvertently light the box on fire or something. I set it down and she gives me a nod of approval. Then she creakily ducks down and checks beneath the table where Quentin is sitting. It's clear, of course, but she still shoots him a warning look. Then she shouts, "No pens!," making us both jump an inch in our chairs, before heading back to her desk in the corner.

I slowly, carefully lift the lid on the first box, and the smell of old documents and dust increases tenfold.

"Hello, old friends," I whisper to the contents before I

remember I'm not alone. Quentin's mouth quirks at the corner, but he thankfully doesn't comment.

It's what it feels like, though, being back in a library's special collections room, digging around in a bankers box. Like a reunion with someone I've missed maybe more than I ever realized. The same way I felt with Quentin when we met on the porch that first night I was back in Catoctin, if I'm honest with myself (which I prefer not to be).

When I decided to continue in my PhD program instead of accepting the position I was offered at the historical society archives where I interned, I consoled myself with the fact that I would still be spending a ton of time working with primary sources. But once I finished the archival research for my dissertation and it was just a matter of writing the dang thing, my funding dried up and I took the temporary teaching position at Malbyrne to support myself. I finished my dissertation, but just barely. Definitely no time or institutional support for jaunts to the National Archives. My last few years have been so focused on new course proposals and serving on committees and advising while balancing a 4-4 course load that combing through a bankers box feels like a sort of homecoming. One less imbued with the sense of failure than arriving at my parents' house with all of my belongings, and more with the what-if-things-had-been-different wistful feeling of seeing an old lover after a long time.

I pull out the finding aid—the one that Mrs. MacDonald had me and Quentin put together "if we insisted on digging around in her things." It was the first work of this sort I'd ever done, and looking at it now . . . well, it's far from perfect. It's also handwritten, on notebook paper. And why is it being kept inside the box? At first I thought Mrs. MacDonald organized everything in a way that makes it unintelligible to pretty much anyone who isn't her because she didn't know better, but now I wonder if it's because she wants to make life extremely difficult for anyone who might try to replace her. I highly suspect the latter.

"I assume this kind of thing is old hat for you nowadays?" Quentin asks, gesturing to the finding aid in my hand.

"I haven't actually done any archival work in a while," I say. "But I did do a whole lot of it in grad school." I pause, trying to decipher a spot where my description of the box's contents smeared under my fist as I wrote. "You know, I almost didn't finish the PhD. I fell in love with archival management while completing my coursework, and I had a great summer internship that turned into a job offer."

"What made you decide to turn it down?" he asks.

"Ah . . ." This is another one of those decisions that, at the time I made it, seemed extremely logical. But now I'm not sure. It may be yet another instance of me making the wrong assumptions, focusing on the wrong things. "My ex. Cole. He said I had too much promise as a scholar, that I wouldn't have the resources to reach my full potential without the PhD. My faculty adviser agreed that my work was strong enough to be competitive on the academic job market, and I, uh . . . You may not realize this about me, but I enjoy a challenge."

"You don't say?" Quentin grins back at me.

"I knew it would be difficult. There are way, way fewer tenure-track jobs than there are candidates for them. But I thought I could be the exception to the rule if I just worked hard enough. That I would be letting Cole down, letting *myself* down, if I didn't try."

And I did try. So, so hard, for so, so long. But what I loved about academia was also the worst part of it: There's no real end point. You're never finished. You published a paper? Great, now get started on the next one. You won an award? Nice, but there are still more out there to work toward. Got a faculty position? Now you get to bust your ass until you have tenure. Got tenure? Bust your ass a bit more and you get a promotion. Or maybe a more prestigious university will come and scoop you up, make you an endowed chair or give you your own institute. There is always more work you can be doing, new benchmarks to set, things to achieve.

It's easy, I'm realizing, to fall into a trap where it feels like the work can counteract the aspects of it all that actually come down to luck or connections or institutional politics. To believe that, if you don't succeed, it's only because you didn't do enough. Didn't want it enough.

And maybe I didn't.

"Anyway. Guess it didn't work out exactly as I planned."

Quentin nudges my arm very gently with his. "I'm sorry about your job."

"It's fine. I'll find something new eventually, I'm sure. It'll all work out for the best." If I say it often enough, maybe I'll really start to believe it. Right now, my best idea is to reach out to a bunch of different history department chairs across New England and hope they're all in desperate need of an adjunct. Even if they all came through, though, I'm pretty sure it would cost me more to commute to each university than I would be making.

At least I'm not the only one here with career problems. "What about you? Hear anything back from that firm in Chicago?" I ask.

"Yeah. They want me to do an in-person interview next week."

"Oh. Congrats. That's great."

"Eh," he says, tilting his head to the side.

"Eh?"

"I think I'm going to withdraw my application. I'm not sure I'm interested."

"Why not?"

"I don't think I want to do international business law anymore. I didn't really mean to land there in the first place. It was just easiest to get into when I graduated, the area where I'd inadvertently made the most connections. And I'm not going to lie and say the money wasn't a factor. I know my dad made peanuts working for the government." He stretches his arms behind him as he rocks his chair back again. "Maybe it's because I'm in my thirties now, and my priorities have shifted, but helping shitty rich people be shittier and get richer doesn't feel like a good use of my time on earth anymore, you know?" He brings his chair back down with a thud, and it makes him bite his tongue. "Ow."

"Actions have consequences," I sing softly, mimicking what Quentin's mom used to say whenever he hurt himself doing something stupid. I'm surprised how quickly and easily it finds its way out of my mouth after all this time.

Quentin shoots me a look before deciding to ignore this taunt. "Besides, the partner I was talking to on the video call looked like a foot and it creeped me out."

"He . . . looked like a foot? How?"

"I don't know. His hair was all—" He gestures with his fingers upward, presumably to represent something toe-like. "It was something about the shape of his head."

"I don't think you should turn down a job opportunity just because a guy looks like a foot. I doubt he can help it."

"Well, he also made a joke about a paralegal's legs that made me feel pretty uncomfortable."

"What the hell, Quentin. Why didn't you lead with that? That's a way more legit reason than 'he looks like a foot.'" I nudge the toe of his sneaker with mine beneath the table. We're being inappropriately loud, but when I glance over at Mrs. MacDonald she's once again staring into the distance. Is she sleeping with her eyes open? Unnerving.

I thumb through the box and retrieve several envelopes filled with black-and-white photographs. "Well, if not Chicago with the creepy foot guy, where *would* you like to land next?" I ask.

"Good question," he says, looking down at the pile of photos I place in front of him. "One I don't have an answer for yet. I'm hoping that while I'm working on getting the house together it will magically come to me."

Considering how lost I feel without Ambitious Nina at the helm, not knowing the exact steps ahead, it's difficult for me to understand how he can choose to be so casual about his future, but I say, "As good a strategy as any, I guess."

We fall into a mostly comfortable silence as we review the old pictures of Sprangbur. These shots were taken for a feature in *Life* in the mid-1930s, and Fountain requested copies for his own personal collection. They date to a few years before his death, so if we can find the portrait in one of these, that may be where it was located when his will was read. If we don't find Whale's painting in any of the photos, then . . . Well, I don't know what we do.

"What's next if this doesn't turn up anything?" I ask.

I fight off a smile as I notice Quentin sucking at the corner of his bottom lip, deep in concentration. He seems to notice he's doing it at the same time he comprehends my question and stretches his neck instead. "I can't believe you're losing hope already."

"What makes you think I had any to begin with? You know I doubt this thing even exists."

"Don't lie to me, Hunnicutt," he says, finding his smile. "I saw the way your eyes lit up when Sharon said the artist's name was Whale." He leans in, close enough that his breath ruffles a few loose strands of hair by my ear, making me shiver. "I know you want this just as much as I do."

"What I want is to be done with this," I manage, only stumbling on two of the nine words in the sentence. Which isn't bad considering the distracting heat pooled between my legs. *Coping mechanism*, I remind myself.

I wish someone would inform my body that this is all in my head, though, because right now it sure feels pretty much indistinguishable from being genuinely attracted to him. I squeeze my thighs together, trying to alleviate the incessant ache.

"Right." The word—or rather, the way he says it—sounds off, but I can't quite figure out how. It's strangely clipped, tight. I turn my head to catch his expression, but find him staring back down at the dwindling stack of photos in front of him, once again sucking his lip.

"Quentin . . ."

But instead of responding he starts laughing, slowly, almost maniacally. I've heard it before, and there it is, right under *When he managed to extract DNA from a strawberry for the ninth-grade science fair after several failed attempts*. "Look," he says, sliding a photo over to me. "Nina, look. There. In the corner." He points to the edge of the picture, where part of an ornate frame is visible. It's hard to tell for sure, but it looks very much like the one we saw yesterday around the portrait.

I take off my glasses and hold it closer to my face to inspect. "But where is—" I don't need to finish the question. Because I've noticed the decoration on the walls.

Of course. The portrait used to hang in the freaking Star Parlor.

IV

You said that your wife recently delivered your
first child? Is that why you look like you haven't
slept in ages? Or perhaps that's simply the way you
always look, in which case, my apologies, Mr.
Aaron.

I never married or had children myself. Isolde,
of course, is the light of my life and I love her
as I would have my own progeny. But she came into
my life quite unexpectedly, as I mentioned.

I simply never felt any strong urge to have a
family of my own. I was content by myself. And
really, when one is wealthy, one doesn't need to be
alone if they wish not to be. But I usually wished
to be. Therefore, I was.

Sometimes I think about how my life would have
been different had I not become Isolde's guardian,
not discovered Edlo. It's the fastest way to give
myself the morbs.

Yes. I do believe that this life I've lived has
been quite a happy one, but one I lived quite by
accident.

14

PULL UP THE Sprangbur Conservancy website on my phone. I have to say, the modern iteration is much easier to use than the old version that was hosted on Geocities and involved a lot of too-large text and rotating word art. Now there are a few photos of the Castle's current decor to entice people considering it as an event venue—how I assume they pay the bills, since I'm sure the suggested donations from tours don't go very far. It really is such a gorgeous place and an exemplary house museum. The Conservancy has done an incredible job keeping Fountain's distinctive aesthetic while including enough modernization for practical use.

I click on a photo of a woman wearing a crown of peonies and a sleek ivory satin gown, leaning ethereally against the curve of a Syrian arch. The next shot in the slideshow was taken in the library, with a man in a white tuxedo sitting in a hot-pink paisley chair with his elbows on his widespread knees, smoldering at the camera. Then there's one of the couple together in the Conservancy, smiles lighting up their faces.

To think, that could have been me and Cole had things been different. Or Quentin and his ex, more realistically, since they were actually engaged before things fell apart.

"So when are the tours?" I jerk at the sound of Quentin's voice, like I've been caught looking at something naughty.

"Oh, um. Must've hit the wrong thing," I say, embarrassed that I somehow wound up deep in the wedding gallery page. I select *Visit* from the menu and scan the information. "Looks like they do them on Mondays and Thursdays at ten and two."

"You up for Monday at ten, then?" Quentin asks.

"I'll have to check my calendar," I say, already knowing that it's completely clear for the foreseeable future. "But that should work for me."

He pauses for a moment as if mulling something over. Then he says, "I was thinking about painting the living room this weekend, if you want to come over and help." The invitation is issued as he hovers his cell phone over the photo of the Star Parlor that shows the sliver of portrait and takes a picture. A good idea, and one I don't know why I didn't have.

There's a part of me—Smitten Nina, I guess—who wants to accept. Anything to spend more time with Quentin and watch those forearms of his flex while they move the paint roller over the wall. But Smitten Nina is clearly an idiot when it comes to this man, so instead I say, "I don't think me doing manual labor at your dad's house was part of our deal."

"Just figured I'd offer."

"How very kind of you."

Quentin takes it upon himself to combine the piles of photographs and return them to the envelopes in which we found them.

"Do you want me to—"

"I've got it," he says.

I stand there, watching the way he takes care to keep everything in the bankers box in the proper order despite the contents having very little rhyme or reason. It unlocks something in my nerdy little heart that I don't want to inspect too closely. Smitten Nina is already too powerful; she doesn't need Quentin meeting the very low bar of being basically responsible to add fuel to her fire.

"Anyway, I should probably get home," I announce when we're outside the library. "Mom wants to spend some time together." I mean, I assume she does even if she hasn't said it. Not technically a lie.

He gives me a tight-lipped smile that feels as false as the charming one. It isn't nearly as practiced, so it's much more obvious that it doesn't belong there. "Have fun."

I'll admit that I've never completely stopped caring about Quentin, unable to fully give him up no matter how many years passed without a word. There's part of me that wants to lay a hand on his arm and ask him what's going on. If I've done something wrong. But I need to keep my distance. I can't let him start to mean something to me again.

"See you next week," I say. I'm deciding right now that I will not intentionally see Quentin until I absolutely need to for treasure-hunting purposes. This boundary feels necessary, not only to keep Quentin from thinking I want to spend time with him, but to protect myself. Because if I'm not careful . . . Well, that's how I got hurt seventeen years ago, isn't it?

Which is why, even though I linger downstairs until after my parents go to bed, and even though I press my ear against the wall their house shares with Quentin's, and even though music drifts ever so slightly through the layers of plaster and

wood separating our living rooms and I can hear Quentin sing-
ing along enthusiastically, and even though he's probably standing on a ladder, back muscles tight as he reaches up to run his
paintbrush over the edge of the blue tape cordoning off the wall
from the ceiling, I do not give in to the urge to go over there and
offer him my assistance. Because unlike *some* people, Nina
Hunnicutt *can* learn a lesson.

15

My Monday morning starts off inauspiciously, with a rejection email from a long-term boarding school sub job I had high hopes for arriving minutes after I wake up. *Unfortunately, you do not meet our minimum qualifications*, it says, which is not only disheartening but baffling because I'm pretty sure I exceeded all of the ones listed in their posting. Then there's a text from a former Malbyrne history department colleague around nine, expressing her distress that my contract wasn't renewed and that they gave me such late notice of the fact. Which is kind of her, I guess, but it also reignites my anger over the whole situation, which had taken a back seat during the whole Cole debacle and, until now, had mostly presented itself as disappointment and worry. So I thank her when she says she's going to put in a good word for me with a friend at Williams—a nice but futile gesture. Then I throw my pillow across the room. It knocks a porcelain ballerina figurine my grandmother gave me when I was six from its spot on the edge of a shelf, and

I watch the girl's head come clean off as it hits the floor at an awkward angle.

On my way to the basement to deliver the broken figurine to my dad in hopes he can glue it back together, I overhear my mom on the phone with one of my aunts, talking about how I'm home now and probably will be through the summer "at the very least." I'm annoyed by both her lack of faith in my prospects and how correct she probably is, which prompts me to close the fridge a little too forcefully in annoyance after getting the almond milk out for my cereal, resulting in being reprimanded like I'm thirteen again. And, to be fair, I am acting like a teenager, so I don't really blame her. It doesn't stop me from rolling my eyes and stomping back upstairs anyway.

I need to go to Sprangbur with Quentin for our second tour today, even if my brain is telling me it would be better to stay in bed and alternate between napping and catastrophizing. Because there's a chance that we've already cracked this, that the treasure will be beneath the area where the Whale portrait used to hang in the Star Parlor. Depending on what we find, it's possible we can be done with this. Then I will have a bit more money to get out of this town and rebuild my life. The thought isn't quite as rejuvenating as I'd hoped, but it's enough to get me downstairs and outside to meet Quentin.

"Nice car," I say as I climb into the passenger seat of the shiny black Audi A7. I don't know anything about luxury vehicles, but I'm assuming this is one based solely on the fact it has multiple touchscreens. I only mention it to make conversation about something innocuous. Well, and also because I'm only slightly less nosey than my mom. How did Quentin wind up with such an expensive ride? This can't be the car he had while living in France, can it? How much would it even cost to ship over here? And if it's a newer purchase, or a lease, why? Does Quentin have the kind of savings that allows him to afford something like this while unemployed? Just how much money is in international business law anyway? Inquiring (former) low-paid college professor with ten-year-old Hyundai Elantra minds want to know.

"Yeah," he says after a brief silence in which he monitors three young children chasing a cat across the street ahead, making sure to slow down to allow them safe passage. "It's actually my sister's. She's letting me borrow it in exchange for babysitting whenever she needs me for the next ten years."

"How is Lexi these days?" I don't add *besides financially comfortable enough to have a high-end car that's apparently so nonessential to her daily life that she can lend it to her younger brother for a few months*, though it's definitely what I'm thinking.

"She's good. She's a software engineer and her partner is a VP at a tech startup that's in the process of selling for a decent chunk of change. Two-year-old twins and a baby on the way. Lives in Pittsburgh right now, but they're talking about moving back to Maryland soon."

"Wow. So she's doing like the exact opposite of how we're doing," I joke.

He sighs. "As my mother enjoys reminding me whenever we talk lately."

Ouch. Poor Quentin. It isn't difficult to imagine Dr. Bell being critical of his current circumstances. I remember her being almost coldly logical. Probably a helpful attribute for a research scientist, but it didn't make for a particularly affectionate or understanding partner or parent. I wouldn't be surprised to learn she doesn't believe in things like bad luck, only cause and effect. Surely, in her mind, Quentin must have done something to bring this all upon himself. She probably thinks he didn't work hard enough to keep his job. Didn't love hard enough to keep his fiancée.

"Hey," I say softly, and my hand starts to rise of its own accord, wanting to land somewhere comforting. But I know that's a dangerous instinct, so I let it fall back to my lap, then brush away an imaginary speck of lint from my shorts.

"No, it's fine. That's just how she is. I came to terms with it a long time and about a hundred therapy sessions ago." There's a notable period of silence as we navigate through downtown. He doesn't want to talk about his family anymore. Which is fine, because we're here to find some treasure, not have the types of intimate conversations friends have.

Yet by the time we turn onto Carmichael Chapel Road, I'm desperate to clear the tightness from his jaw. Before I even think it through, I turn my head and say, "So, is this baby fast?"

I can't believe I just said that. I have never once referred to a car as a baby in my life. It feels wrong coming out of my mouth. Which is probably the real reason why a slow smile spreads across Quentin's face.

"Fast enough, I'd imagine," he says.

"Bet you won't go above a hundred." I can't believe I've said that either. In what world do I dare Quentin to drive dangerously?

The challenge must take Quentin by surprise too, because he turns to look at me for a split second, eyebrows raised, before looking back at the road. And then he floors it.

We're both jerked back as the car accelerates quicker than either of us is ready for. The digital speedometer climbs to one hundred and one as we hit the longest straight stretch of the road, then falls as Quentin coasts us the rest of the way to Sprangbur.

He clears his throat and pulls into a parking spot along the edge of the grounds. And that's when I realize that, at some point during that silly little dare, I grabbed onto Quentin's leg, right where the hem of his shorts ends and the wiry hair of his thigh begins.

Oh my god. I even left pink crescents in his skin with my fingernails. "Oh. I'm . . . sorry about that."

"It's okay," he says. "I, uh . . . You made a really fun sound I've never heard before. Kind of . . . *Eeeeeeeep.* Like a Muppet."

"I did not."

"I would say I'll floor it again on the way back to see if you'll repeat it, but honestly that was way more harrowing than I expected."

"Yes, let's not," I agree as I get out of the car, my legs wobbly as if they aren't sure what speed to expect when I start moving. "I don't know what I was thinking. We could have died." *Hey, at least we would have died with my hand on Quentin's thigh and a smile on his face,* an incredibly fucked-up voice in my head says. That must be Unhinged Nina. I am in no way interested in spending time with her right now. I direct my focus to the Castle, trying to will my hand to stop doing a Darcy-esque flex in memory of having touched him. "It's still surreal that we actually get to go inside this place now. Legally."

"It's really something," Quentin says, staring at the towering asymmetrical building. "Somehow exactly and nothing like I expected."

After Fountain's death, his mansion—under the care of the newly established Sprangbur Conservancy—was used as the local library for about a decade before the much larger current building was constructed downtown. It then did a short stint as the town's historical society before the Conservancy, hoping to increase their income, decided to rent portions of the Castle out as offices to various other nonprofits. Except the upkeep was way too expensive to be paid for with what they could reasonably charge as the aging building became less and less desirable (especially after the blizzard of '96 caused the Conservatory's roof to cave in). The tenants all left at the end of their lease terms, and the place fell into utter disrepair. There was a brief legal battle in the late nineties, when a developer tried to buy the land. That drew attention to the property for the first time in a while, and a new generation of leadership at the Sprangbur Conservancy began making plans to renovate the Castle to its original splendor. That's when they teamed up with Aera-Bev to offer the reward. But they'd hit a lull in their fundraising when Quentin and I were hunting for the treasure the first time around, having raised enough to keep the gardens and outbuildings in order but not enough to tackle the house yet.

Quentin nudges me lightly, his elbow barely grazing my upper arm. The paltry contact leaves an unreasonable amount of heat in its wake. "Come on," he says. "Let's go see what we can find."

What we find is, of course, Fountain's house pretty much exactly how it was when we toured it last week. This time, though, we know that the landscape hanging above the navy-blue velvet divan in the Star Parlor was once the location of a portrait painted by a man named Whale. The treasure, if it's here, could very well still be behind it. Or under it? It's kind of hard to tell what exactly "beneath" means in the context of something hanging on a wall. We'll have to be thorough.

There's just one problem that we did not anticipate. And her name is Gladys.

"We call this the Star Parlor, due to the star motif on the

walls. We carefully reconstructed the design based on photos and remnants of the original. The house's blueprints have this room labeled as a bedroom for the lady of the house, but as Fountain never married, it was instead kept as an upstairs sitting room. Fountain's secretary, Louisa Worman, often used the space as her personal office when working from the Castle, which she did frequently as Fountain aged and became less inclined to travel to his factories to take care of daily business." Gladys smiles warmly as she takes a well-rehearsed breath. She told us when she introduced herself that she's been a volunteer docent at Sprangbur Castle since the house reopened to the public ten years ago. That's a whole lot of Monday tours. She's basically the opposite of Sharon, in that she has the spiel down to an art. This is the tight five version of a historic house tour. Also, Gladys seems extremely aware of where all seven of her visitors are and what they are doing at all times. "Nowadays we use it as one of the dressing rooms for wedding parties. Events are a big part of what we do here at Sprangbur, so if you know anyone looking for a venue . . ." She trails off cheekily and everyone chuckles on cue. "Take a peek inside, then we'll travel down the hall to Mr. Fountain's bedroom."

Quentin and I allow the other five people on the tour with us—a family of three and an elderly couple—to stick their head through the doorframe to look at the parlor and wait until they've all proceeded down the hall before Quentin leans in himself and whispers, "Go. I'll keep a lookout."

I swallow against the nerves telling me this is a bad idea and slide around the velvet rope to enter the room. One step. Two steps. That's as far as I get before Gladys's voice dashes down the hallway, almost as if it's grabbing me by the upper arm. "We okay back there? Ready to move on?" she asks. Which, I will give her, is a very nice way to say "What do you think you're doing? Get your asses over here with the rest of the group this very instant."

So I turn around and head back out of the Star Parlor, Quentin's heavy exhale audible as I pass by his outstretched arm.

The idea that we could simply detach ourselves from the tour and enter one of the Castle's rooms without anyone noticing suddenly feels like an extremely poorly thought-out plan. At least it is with Gladys in charge. As we rejoin the group, the older Black woman begins telling us about Fountain's bed, which is no longer here but was particularly extravagant and so heavy they needed to construct it in pieces and assemble it in place. Quentin leans down to whisper into my ear again. "What if I ask her a bunch of questions after the tour and you can sneak back upstairs while I keep her busy?"

I put my hand on his shoulder to tug him down to me so I can whisper back. One of his hands lands at my waist in response, and I try to ignore the familiarity with which he touches me. Like it's the most natural thing in the world. "Why am I the one sneaking back up?"

"Because you're cute."

Oh.

Hey, wait. What does that have to do with anything? Before I can ask, Gladys says, "Now we'll head down into the lower level. If the gentleman by the stairs will lead the way . . ."

It turns out that Quentin is the gentleman by the stairs, which gives us no chance to linger behind. Not that Gladys would let us anyway. It's probably just paranoia brought on by the fact that the last time I did anything even remotely against the rules was over a decade ago, when I stole a fork from my university's dining hall. But I feel like this sweet little lady is aware of every breath I'm taking, every move I'm making, and maybe also every other lyric from that Police song.

Down in the basement, she tells us more about the staff who worked at the Castle. Sharon might win for breadth of knowledge about this place, but Gladys definitely has the presentation down much better. And thankfully I'm able to focus, despite the residual jitteriness in my limbs from getting caught going into the Star Parlor earlier.

I cannot believe I'm about to try to sneak back up there. Best-case scenario: I make it inside and am able to do a thorough search, during which I find the treasure and I'm suddenly seven thousand dollars richer. Worst-case: I get caught and sent to jail for a million years for, I don't know, cultural site defacement? Is that a thing? At the very least, I'll get banned from Sprangbur forever. Most likely: I guess I go in, look around briefly, find nothing, and slip back out without anyone the wiser. That wouldn't be so bad.

"And that concludes today's tour of Julius James Fountain's home, Sprangbur Castle," Gladys announces. "We'll return now to the foyer, where I'm happy to answer any questions or provide you with a map of the grounds, which you are welcome to continue exploring at your leisure."

Quentin gives me a speaking look before we start up the narrow servants' stairs. Back on the main level, he sidles up beside me. "So, am I distracting her or not?"

"If it's in that room, don't you think they would've found it during the renovations? I mean, maybe they did and it was so boring they didn't even bother—"

"Nina," he says more sharply. "Are we doing this?"

Ugh. If I don't go now, when will we get another chance to check it out? We can't just keep coming here for tours until we eventually happen to get Sharon again. That would be seriously suspicious behavior. "Okay. Fine," I say. "Let's do it." My stomach dips as I remember the worst outcome is not a completely far-fetched one. If I get banned from Sprangbur, I'll have deserved it. I feel a bit like a traitor to Sharon, Gladys, and public historians everywhere. But I'm going to do it.

Quentin plasters on that hardworking charm of his, then takes a step toward the docent. "Ms. Gladys. Such a wonderful tour. Thank you so much. I do have a few questions, if you don't mind . . ."

I turn around and quietly but quickly make my way back up the stairs. There's a moment halfway there where I nearly trip over my own feet, my nerves making me feel like I've suddenly grown six more of them. It's a relief when I reach the second floor without any major incidents.

I'm about a yard away from the Star Parlor when a door marked STAFF ONLY at the far-left end of the hallway creaks open and a woman with a small cleaning cart pushes through. She smiles at me, and I smile back. But in my head, all I can think is *Shit, shit, shit.* Because I've been caught up here when I'm not supposed to be, and even if she isn't about to sound any sort of alarm, I am now officially conspicuous. Which is generally the opposite of what you want to be when doing something against the rules. Or maybe the law. I'm somewhat unclear on what constitutes trespassing. Quentin presumably knows more. Probably why he made me do this instead of going himself.

Maybe this is all an elaborate attempt at payback for getting him in trouble that night. As if the loss of him in my life wasn't punishment enough.

My smile wobbles as the weight of what I'm doing sinks in further.

"Hello," I say.

"Hello."

"Hello," I repeat.

"Hello?" she answers, understandably confused.

There's an awkward little pause while we continue smiling at each other. "Um. Bathroom?" I ask at last.

She points downward. "Beneath the stairs."

"Thank you."

My heart pounds even harder than it already was as I hurry back down. I pause on the landing, peeking around the banister to make sure Gladys is still occupied. Quentin has very smartly arranged them so that her back is to me. His eyes briefly meet mine over Gladys's short gray hair, just long enough for me to give him a subtle headshake. He returns his attention to the woman in front of him, who is gesturing widely and with enthusiasm.

"Oh, hey, there you are," Quentin says, making more direct eye contact with me now that I'm down the stairs and in the foyer.

"I had to run to the bathroom," I volunteer—perhaps unnecessarily.

His eyebrows rise as if they're speaking a language of their own, attempting to communicate something to me. "I was just talking to Ms. Gladys about the wedding."

"The wedding?"

His eyebrows jump farther up, emphasizing his original intended message. "Yes. Our wedding."

It takes me a full two seconds to register what he has said and why he has said it. "Right, yes! *Our* wedding." I draw the words out strangely, emphasizing the wrong syllables.

Quentin holds a business card between two of his fingers.

"She very kindly gave me the event coordinator's information so we can set up a time to come back and check out the place more thoroughly." It must be my imagination that he stresses the last word, because Gladys doesn't seem to notice.

"Oh, great. That's . . . great. Thanks . . . lovemuffin." Lovemuffin? What the actual fuck? I'm pretty sure I've never even thought that combination of words in my life, so why did I just say them?

Quentin smiles to conceal his urge to laugh, then schools his features expertly as he responds, "My pleasure, cookiepuss."

"Oh, aren't you cute together!" Gladys exclaims.

"Some might say too cute," I mutter under my breath. Quentin must hear, though, because the side of his shoe makes not-exactly-soft contact with mine.

"Ms. Gladys told me that they usually hold ceremonies outside. Do you want to go check out the gardens while we're here, since the weather's nice?"

"Definitely," I say, grateful for the excuse to get the hell out of here.

We thank Gladys again for the tour, make a show of putting another ten-dollar bill into the suggested donation box on the front table, and reemerge into the rising mid-June heat.

I assumed we'd actually head to the parking lot, but Quentin was apparently serious about lingering in the gardens. His hand comes to my lower back and he steers me toward the brick path leading around the side of the Castle. I want to be annoyed about it, but it's a difficult feeling to muster when liquid warmth is seeping through the entire lower half of my body in response to his touch.

"In case she's watching," he explains. I sort of doubt Gladys is peeking out of a second-story window to make sure we're going where we said we would and acting properly in love on the way there. But whatever.

I don't feel like meandering around, the humidity making the temperature feel about ten degrees hotter. So I settle on the bench inside the shade of the mushroom folly, the concrete cool against the backs of my thighs. "So we're engaged now?"

"Yep," Quentin says. He doesn't sit beside me, choosing instead to lean against one of the bulbous support pillars that hold up the mushroom's cap. "Hope you don't mind too much."

"Perhaps you can explain to me how that came to be, then I can decide how much I mind."

"I figured it wouldn't hurt to have a backup plan in case you were unsuccessful with your sneaking. Which I assume you were, considering how quickly you came back down. What happened?"

"Ran into a cleaning lady, so I had to pretend I was looking for the bathroom. Got out of there as fast as I could."

"Ah. Well, then it's lucky I realized us being a couple interested in Sprangbur as a potential wedding venue gives us a chance to contact their event coordinator for a tour. A *private* tour."

"You don't think the event coordinator might be even more eagle-eyed than Gladys, considering we'll be the only people they'll need to keep track of?"

"Probably. But don't worry. I have a plan."

I groan. "Oh god." Now I'm extra worried. "Quentin, your plans have historically not been particularly successful."

There was the time he tried to catch a local cryptid called the snallygaster when we were eight and he wound up stuck inside a net suspended from the tree in his backyard for three hours. Or the time when he constructed an elaborate plan to sneak candy after bedtime only to fall down the stairs and knock out one of his teeth. Once, in eighth grade, he was convinced that if he kept talking nonstop about a fake huge snowstorm coming at the end of the week, he could trick the district into closing school preemptively. (It obviously did not work.)

"That isn't even—" He stops himself, thinking for a moment. "Okay, that may have been true. But my plans are much better these days, I promise."

"You literally just had one that failed!" I protest. "You're the one who had me go back upstairs, remember?"

"Hey, you can't blame me for that. Isn't my fault you didn't execute it correctly."

I narrow my eyes, ready to tell him to shove it. But he stops leaning on the bit of mushroom stem and starts walking away. "I'll email them tonight and try to set up something—maybe for Friday," he says over his shoulder. And before he turns his head back around, I notice a grin spreading slowly across his face. "If that works for you . . . cookiepuss."

16

QUENTIN DROPS ME back off at my parents' house before continuing on to run some errands. The discombobulated feeling plaguing me can't be blamed completely on the grocery store sushi I had as a late breakfast. Sure, that might account for the bubbling in my stomach, but it doesn't explain the bizarre urge I have to run upstairs the moment I walk into the house, close the door to my bedroom, and look at the Sprangbur wedding gallery until the images are permanently burned into my retinas. It's easy to tell myself it's because I need to study for our upcoming venue tour, but the fact that I want to do it in secret and slight shame, like I'm a teen who's just discovered porn, alerts me that it's also probably not the healthiest impulse I've ever had. And speaking of porn . . .

"Is that a penis?" I find myself asking the question before I realize I may not actually want to know the answer.

"It is indeed," Mom says cheerfully from where she has her tablet, zoomed in quite tightly on a man's genitalia, propped in front of her on the coffee table as she uses light strokes to shade her approximation in a sketchbook.

"But. Mother. Why?"

She removes her reading glasses and sets them to the side. "I've signed up for a life drawing class at the new community center in Derring Heights. We'll be working with nude models, and I wanted to practice the awkward parts on my own so I'm less flustered in person."

"I . . . I think . . . Okay."

"Oh, Nina! There are still a few open seats in the class. Why don't you join me? Wouldn't that be fun?"

"Ah, I'm . . . I don't . . ." *I don't want to draw naked people with my mother* is going to hurt her feelings, which I think are already a little tender after I turned down her neighborhood walking group invite this morning. "I have plans then," I say instead. "But maybe some other time." A lie, of course, but I'll just have to cross the excuse bridge for that when we get to it.

"But I didn't even tell you when it was."

"When is it?"

"The first class is next Saturday evening. On the twenty-first. It starts at eight."

"Yep, I definitely have plans then." The date does sound familiar, in truth. *Do* I have something going on then? Other than the upcoming venue tour with Quentin, I'm not sure there's anything on my schedule. Oh, right. That fundraiser at Hanako's. I hadn't particularly wanted to go, but it's a perfect excuse. "I ran into an old classmate last week. Hanako Hughes. Remember her? The one who came right before me alphabetically, who was really good at cross-country?" I pause, waiting to see if my mom knows who I'm talking about. Since she worked at the high school when I went there, she usually remembers my classmates better than I do.

"Hmm . . . Oh! Yes. I think I took a pottery class with her aunt a few months ago."

I nod. "Yeah, exactly, her. She owns a cocktail bar in a converted old warehouse near Riverside Park. Quentin and I promised to stop by for this fundraiser thing." I admit that it feels a little scummy, all this fibbing to my mother. But the spirit—if not the details—of what I'm saying is true. We did tell Hanako we'd try to come. Even if I didn't really mean it then, it doesn't mean I can't now.

Mom's smile is so bright and unexpected that I find myself repeating my words in my head in an attempt to figure out what I said that could have been so intensely pleasing to her. As far as I know, my mom is ambivalent toward cocktail bars, converted warehouses, and Riverside Park. *Quentin and I promised to stop by.* Dammit. Yep, that would've done it. I invoked her current favorite person on earth and implied that he and I have repaired our relationship enough to make plans together.

"That's wonderful. I'm so glad he and you have mended things," she says, turning back to her enlarged penis image and picking up her pencil before exclaiming and sliding it behind her ear. She looks so genuinely pleased that I can't bear to tell her that Quentin and I haven't "mended things" so much as I've decided to completely suppress all of my long-carried animosity and pain (and a surprising amount of fresh physical attraction) in pursuit of hopefully getting some extra cash and the heck out of Dodge ASAP.

I respond with a brisk, "Yep, me too. Anyway, I have to—"

"That reminds me. The class instructor sent out an email

asking us to let people know they need models for the next few weeks . . ."

How did anything I just said remind her of that? My mother's thought processes are a mystery. "I'm going to stop you right there, Mom," I say, holding my hand up as if physically keeping the idea away from me. I did a lot of work with various therapists around body neutrality over the years, and most of the time I feel pretty content with myself. But posing nude in front of a bunch of people—one of them being my mother—is not a thing I'm up for at the moment. Or probably ever. "If you're about to suggest that I—"

"No, no, of course not. I know you get nervous in front of an audience. Like when you had to sing that solo at the fourth-grade chorus concert and you fainted right off the stage."

God, Quentin made fun of me for that one for literal years. His reenactment was an artful physical comedy piece that I would have appreciated a lot more had I not been the butt of the joke. I think that's also what prompted me to pay his older sister twenty bucks to freeze his favorite Game Boy game inside a block of ice (inside multiple Ziplocs; I'm not a complete monster).

"I remember," I grumble.

"Anyway, when you see Quentin again, maybe you could ask him if he's interested?"

"Excuse me?"

"What? He's a handsome man, Nina. And he seems confident. Just ask him for me, okay?"

"Why don't you ask him yourself at one of your daily breakfasts, since you two have apparently become such close friends?" I immediately regret the bitterness in my voice as soon as the words hit the air. My mother frowns at me in quiet admonishment, and I bow my head. "Sorry. I'm still a bit . . . Yeah. Sure. I'll ask him." It feels easier to break that promise—and I am *not* going to ask Quentin to be a nude model for my mother's drawing class, it just isn't going to happen—than to argue.

"Thank you. Tell him I can forward him the potential dates." She grabs her pencil again, replaces her reading glasses, and zooms in even closer on the penis's base. Mom sketches out a thick, veiny line as she says, "I'm going to make those little frozen IKEA meatballs for dinner."

"Great," I say. "And I'm going to pretend we never had this conversation."

At least my interest in being extremely weird about the wedding photos on the Sprangbur site has now been obliterated by distressing thoughts of my mother and a naked Quentin in the same room. I head upstairs and throw myself on the bed. My phone buzzes, alerting me to a new text.

My heart jumps up a few centimeters at the thought it might be Quentin (*coping mechanism*) before plummeting to new depths as the name COLE DIXON appears on my phone screen. Then it bungees back up an inch. What if he's trying to mend our relationship? Or at least put us on civil terms moving forward? Maybe even good enough ones that we could manage to be roommates until I find a new living situation! That would be immensely helpful—to have a Boston address on my résumés, to be easily and promptly available if I ever do get called in for an interview . . .

Of course, my luck being what it is these days, the message winds up being the exact opposite of that.

Emailed you a form to fill out in order to take you off the lease. Complete and return asap. Thanks.

Really? Not even a "How are you?" I would have even accepted a cursory "Hope you're well." Like, that's a bit trite, but
it's the bare minimum you should send before asking someone
to do something. Not that this is even an ask—it's more like an
order. The kind of message he'd send to his department's administrative assistant. Although I bet she would at least get a
"please" thrown in somewhere.

I have had a weird day full of treasure hunting and sneaking
around a historic house and fake engagements and Quentin
being . . . enticingly, frustratingly Quentin-y. There was already
enough going on without Cole adding his asshole-ish tendencies
to the mix. So I am deciding here and now that this text is the
last straw. I need to press pause on keeping it together for a moment, or I'm liable to burst at a much more inopportune time.

I'll let Pathetic Nina back out. But only for a few minutes.
Like letting a little kid go to the playground to wear themselves
out before naptime.

Stomping heavily around my room only results in my mom
calling up the stairs to ask if I'm okay and also if I could please
stop because it's distracting her from her drawing. If that's too
distracting for her, then I assume releasing a primal scream is
out. I very responsibly take off my glasses before I throw myself
back on the bed, folding my arms across my chest and kicking
my legs as hard as I can against the mattress. But after the initial
burst of angry energy, I'm left pretty beat. Which I guess was
sort of the goal all along.

I must have actually fallen asleep, because my room is darker
when I open my eyes again. There's also that gross post-nap whole-
body grogginess that makes me feel coated internally with a
wispy layer of cobwebs. As I attempt to move around enough to
clear some of it away, the scent of Swedish meatballs and mashed

potatoes finds my nose and sends my stomach growling. A little after eight o'clock, my phone says. I missed dinner. Knowing my mom, she came up to find out why I wasn't responding to her shouts that it was ready, saw me asleep, and decided not to wake me (though I wish she would have, since I'm going to be up all night now). She'll have a plate saved for me in the fridge, covered with a shower cap she swiped from a hotel five years ago, the way she does for my dad whenever he can't be pulled away from whatever he's working on. I'll head downstairs in a second and—

The quiet yet unmistakable slide of Quentin's window opening makes me freeze mid-stretch and mid-thought.

I could ignore it. Could simply get up and leave this room, refusing to engage any further today. Yet the same part of me that was pissed off at Cole a few hours ago now feels . . . hollow. Noticeably numb. It's a sensation too reminiscent of a bout of depression for my liking. The thing about Quentin Bell, though, is that, for better or worse, he's never once failed to make me feel *something*.

So I move to the floor and lift my own window's sash, wincing in anticipation of the screeching before it even happens.

"Bonjour, Nina," he says, almost as if he was waiting for me.

"Hello, Moon." I sigh heavily.

"What iz zee matter?"

"Nothing. Just . . . Men are the worst."

There's a slight pause before the answer comes. "Aw haw, oui, indeed zey are."

"Oh. A little surprised to hear you agree. Figured you'd side with them, because, you know, the man in the moon."

"Aw, haw, gender is a, how do you say, social construct. And I am zee Moon, which belongs to no one society."

"That's a good point."

"Regardless, zee men . . . zey often disappoint. Tell me, what have zey done zis time to . . ." Quentin seems to struggle here to keep up the horrible accent as he settles on, "irk you?"

How do I even explain it in a way that doesn't make me sound whiny? Poor me, my ex wasn't friendly when he requested I do a necessary administrative task. But that's not really the issue, is it? It's that once I send Cole that form, everything becomes officially over between us. Even if I can see now that we weren't good together, even if I have no desire to reconcile and try again, there's something painful in the finality of it all. Something that Cole's message doesn't give its proper due. "My ex-boyfriend and I were together for six years," I say at last. "But now that things are over, I wonder if we really were ever together at all, or if I just assumed things and he didn't care enough to correct my assumptions."

Quentin's voice is soft, accent fully dropped as he responds, "I know the feeling." There's a brief pause, then: "I'm here if you want to talk about it."

He is here, and god, I still can't quite get over that. The way I still want to confide in him, despite everything. The way I do want to talk about it, because talking to him about my worries was once as natural as breathing and some residue of that old easiness has managed to linger over the years, even though it would be simpler if it hadn't. It's sort of like a stubborn price sticker on the glass part of a picture frame.

"I thought . . . I mean, I don't know, I guess I thought that he cared about me? That we were in love."

"Reasonable assumption after six years," Quentin says.

"Except now that it's over, it's like I'm finally waking up and seeing things for how they truly were. Which was . . . very one-sided. Which makes me wonder about all of the other times I've misjudged or misunderstood situations and relationships in my life." I let out a small huff of sad laughter, thinking about mine and Quentin's. "How do I trust my memories when six whole years might not have been what I thought they were? How do I trust myself?"

I wait for him to answer. He doesn't, but I know he's still there, listening. So I continue, not wanting to linger on the question any longer. "You know, when Cole and I started dating, he said what he liked about me most was my ambition. He said it equaled his, and that together, pushing each other to be our best selves, we could be unstoppable."

"So you guys were supervillains set on taking over the world, then?"

I roll my eyes, somehow certain Quentin knows I'm doing it despite being unable to see me. "Shut up," I say.

His softest, kindest laugh drifts through my open window. It brings with it a corresponding memory: *when my popsicle slid off its stick and onto the sidewalk, so he went back into the corner store and bought me another.*

"You told me it was his idea that you finish the PhD?" Quentin's voice pulls me out of the too-sweet recollection.

"I mean, I wanted to do it too. I'd left Catoctin eager to do something big, something impressive with my life. But I only had the vaguest idea of what that could look like before he came along. He talked about becoming an academic like it was his birthright. And then he started talking about it like it was ours. He seemed so *certain* we both could do it, and it made it easy to buy into what he was saying. To let him push me to do better. To think bigger. Whenever I'd start to settle in, get too comfortable, he would go and do something impressive and remind me what we were working toward. He'd apply for the same jobs and fellowships and grants, even if he didn't really want them, to motivate me to work harder. To keep me on my toes." I pause, making a connection I was never brave enough to make before. "It was kind of like the way you and I used to be."

"No."

"What?"

"We weren't like that at all," he says, and there's an obvious impatience to it, almost verging on anger.

"How do you figure? You were constantly goading me into stupid little competitions. We were always competing against each other."

"I competed *with* you, Nina. Never against you. It's an important distinction." His voice sounds sharp, and there's something balancing on the knife-edge of it. "This jerk stood in your way and called it making you stronger. That's not what support looks like. That's not what love looks like. He wasn't there for you the way he should have been."

"And you were?" I ask, not bothering to hide my bitterness. How dare he judge my (admittedly shitty) dynamic with Cole when he single-handedly decided to end ours? Our clean slate is all very well and good for treasure hunting, but it seems like the stray lines leftover are more noticeable when we talk like this. When we act like friends again. "I'm trying to let it go, Quentin. I am. And I know it's partly my own fault—"

"It isn't. It's not your fault." I don't know if he's talking about what happened between us or between me and Cole, and I'm not sure what I'm talking about anymore either.

I'm tired of this conversation, and tired in general. Tired of sleeping in a twin-size bed with an ugly comforter. Tired of being surrounded by memories everywhere I look. Tired of not being able to trust the past or see a clear path toward a future. "I told my mom that you and I are going to Hanako's bar for that fundraiser next Saturday to get out of drawing naked people with her," I say wearily.

There's a moment of hesitation before he asks, "Is that something we're actually doing? Or are you just informing me of the lie in hopes I'll keep a low profile?"

I sigh. "I prefer not to lie to my mom, but it's your choice."

He takes a moment—whether genuinely thinking it over or trying to add some suspense, I'm not sure. "I'll text Hanako to let her know we're coming. I'm sure she'll be happy to see us."

I wonder if what he means is that he'll be happy to see her. The image of her throwing herself into his arms at the café reminds me that the two of them have some sort of history. My throat feels unaccountably scratchy as I speak. "Great."

"Great," he repeats.

"Well. Good night," I say, and reach for the window.

"Neen, wait," he says before it's fully closed.

I pause, listening through the remaining crack. "What?"

He's silent long enough that I'm not certain he's going to actually say anything. At last he says, "Do you remember when we were seven, we were playing outside and lost my baseball in the Jankowskis' yard?"

If it's the same time I'm thinking of (because when were we *not* losing things in the Jankowskis' yard?), we decided it would be fun to toss around a big rock instead. And it was fun. For about five minutes. That's when I threw it a little wild and Quentin came at it too low and got hit right dead center in the eye. He had to go to the emergency room to make sure he didn't scratch his cornea or break any of his facial bones. One of the few times our parents talked about punishing us formally, though they ultimately decided that Quentin's gnarly black eye and my guilt were effective enough lessons on their own.

"Sometimes," he says, voice soft, "not intending to hurt each other isn't enough to keep it from happening anyway."

Oh.

I don't know what to say, especially because there are so many ways he could mean that. So I lower my window the remaining inch without saying anything at all.

V

I can tell you're curious, so I shall spare you from asking.

Edlo is a kingdom made of magic and mayhem. There are fantastic trees of every color, and they grow any food one could wish to eat. All of the birds are granite statues until the exact moment you glance upon them, when they animate for a time until you look away again. The seltzer river that makes up the eastern border launches bubbles into the air, and they drift, drift around the kingdom, immune to bursting for quite some time. If you're quick and careful, you can slip inside one and use it to travel around--if you have no destination, of course, since they cannot be steered. And sometimes there are fearsome monsters who must be vanquished. But usually all they need is a bit of a tickle and a mild scolding.

Old as I am, Issy grown, I find myself visiting Edlo rather less frequently than before. Besides, I know the way by heart. So perhaps I should hand it over to you and your boy, so that he may grow up

knowing what it is to float above the trees in a
perfect, iridescent bubble.

Where is it located? Well, right here, of
course! On the other side of yesterday, with a
sharp right before you reach tomorrow.

17

QUENTIN'S CAR IS missing. Or rather, it hasn't been parked out front for the last several days. Not that I'm watching for him or anything. Just something I noticed, along with the complete silence emanating from the other side of the duplex since we spoke Monday night. Like maybe he's gone missing too.

My anxious mind keeps imagining him in various scenarios ranging from innocuous to disastrous. Mostly it oscillates between him being dead in a ditch somewhere and having accepted the Chicago job and left without a word. They both feel like worst-case scenarios. A best-case with him suddenly absent from my life again is hard to land on, and I don't want to examine why.

I'm sure it's just the strangeness I've been feeling since our most recent window conversation. That's the closest we've come to discussing the fallout from that summer since Quentin's half-hearted apology that first night on the porch. It didn't help; all it did was make that dull ache in a long-ignored corner of my heart turn into a sharper twinge. *Sometimes not intending to hurt each other isn't enough to keep it from happening anyway.* Was he saying that he knows I wasn't trying to hurt him when I went rogue that night, but that I still did? Or was he acknowledging that he hurt me, but claiming it was unintentional? Whichever way he meant it, it's a reminder that we managed to wound each other deeply and that the scar left behind might never fully fade away.

All this remembering makes me feel small and vulnerable and young—things that, as Ambitious Nina, I thought I would never feel again. She was a suit of armor I got used to wearing, and Quentin's reappearance in my life at a time when I've been left unprotected feels like the universe has an unfair advantage over me.

As a distraction, I've thrown myself into preparing for our tour of Sprangbur that's coming up this weekend. That's why I've spent so much time staring at the events gallery this week, thinking about the people in those photos. And I guess all of those images of weddings against the setting of the Castle are really messing with my brain, because I've decided that *something* is wrong with them. I just can't put my finger on it. They look . . . weird. Off. At first I thought they'd been Photoshopped. But now that I've spent the last hour reviewing them all again (hey, don't judge), I think I've finally figured it out: The people in them look happy. Like, genuinely, truly *happy.* Especially in the photos where the couples are together.

That's what my brain is having trouble comprehending. And, god, that's sad.

Because I'm realizing that the reason it looks so foreign is that I have zero pictures of Cole and me looking even remotely that happy. I even check to make sure I'm not—what's the opposite of sugarcoating? Salt-coating? Citric acid–coating?—

the truth. Ignoring the bubble of nausea that floats up inside my stomach, I open the digital folder filled with all the photos of the two of us. There are a couple from early on where there's a slight hint of it. Maybe. If you squint. But especially in the most recent one, from a grad school classmate's wedding we went to in October, we look like we might not even know each other. There's a noticeable amount of space between our bodies, and his hand hovers near my shoulder without touching it. If I didn't know better, I'd think we'd just met an hour before the photographer asked to take our picture.

That releases a whole bunch of stuff I kept in a corner cupboard in my brain. Because now the memories of countless instances where it was clear we weren't working but I insisted we continue soldiering on in some attempt to force it are spilling out, threatening to bury me. It's the conclusion of a long, drawn-out epiphany that started the other night as I was talking to Quentin. Cole and I weren't interested in each other as much as we were invested in creating an ideal *us*—one that he envisioned but that I wanted just as much. As soon as it became apparent that I was falling behind, that I wasn't going to have the career we both expected of me, he started losing interest. I think I saw the signs but didn't want to accept them. Breaking up with Cole would feel too much like giving up on myself. Admitting defeat. And that's what's hurting now—not that I lost someone I care about when we split, but that I lost the version of myself I'd grown so used to being.

Ambitious Nina was so wrapped up in Cole's expectations, and the expectations I had for myself because of him, that I'm not sure she can exist outside of those confines. I'm not even sure I want her to.

I send a message to Sabrina even though it's late in Belfast:

I don't think I was ever really in love with Cole, just the idea of who he thought we could be together.

I get a response about thirty minutes later: Didn't your therapist suggest that last year and you got really indignant about it?

Oh. Right. That did happen. I guess I was unhappy for a lot longer than I wanted to acknowledge. Yes, but it's rude to bring that up when I'm in the middle of a breakthrough.

Sabrina sends back a kissy face emoji, followed by a heart.

It sounds terrible but . . . I don't know if I know who I am without him, without my job. As soon as I press send, my pulse races as I recall that Sabrina was friends with Ambitious Nina, not this lost, sad version of me. What if she doesn't like whoever I become next? What if she can't relate if we're no longer on the same path?

Reading my mind as any good best friend does, she immediately responds with, It doesn't sound terrible. Those things were major parts of your life for a long time. But they were just that: parts. They weren't YOU, Neen. And I know it's scary to feel like you're starting over, but isn't it exciting too? The world is your oyster!!

My heart slows slightly as I read Sabrina's supportive words. But I don't like oysters, I type but don't send, because just then I hear a quiet thud on the other side of the shared wall. Quentin. He's back?

Unless it's only someone coming to gather his belongings. A moving company or his family, depending on if he's vacated or dead, I guess.

No. It's him. Something in me recognizes his presence, even through the wall.

My heartbeat revs familiarly as I go to the window, which I already opened earlier when my room got too stuffy.

There's a good chance he won't know I'm here without my window's distinctive siren call. Or maybe after the other night, when I didn't have anything to say in response to his cryptic pronouncement, he won't want to talk at all. "Hello there, Moon," I say, only half expecting an answer.

I guess he must already have his window open too, because I hear a few noises that sound like him coming closer, followed by a tired "Bonsoir, Nina."

"I've missed you," I say before I can think better of it, "these last few nights."

"Oh? Zee, uh, zee feeling is mutual," Quentin says, sounding distracted. There's another little thud.

"What the heck's going on over there?"

He replies, dropping the Pierre Escargot impression for a moment, "Taking off my pants and almost fell over, if you must know. I'm about to hop in the shower." I have the immediate mental image of him standing there naked, water sluicing off his skin, darkening that trail of hair on his stomach, leading lower . . . He picks the accent back up again, pulling me out of the fantasy. "Ça va, mon amie?"

"I'm fine," I say, digging deep into the one semester of high school French I took after I exhausted their German offerings and hoping I've responded correctly. "Spent the last few days being dragged to every flea market in the tri-county area by my father. What about you? Where have you been?"

"I, zee Moon, have been right here, of course, despite zee silence." His normal voice returns, sounding even more tired than before. "But I, Quentin, have been on a plane for the last ten hours."

"Oh. Where—"

"Paris."

My nerves kick up as my brain scrambles for reasons he might have gone back to France and keeps landing on *He's getting back with his ex*. Not that it should matter to me if he is. "I didn't realize you had a trip planned."

"I didn't. But Tuesday morning I woke up to an email from Charlene." My heart and stomach drop as one, plunging into the depths of my torso. I try to muster some semblance of happiness for him so that he won't know how disconcerted I am. Why *am* I so disconcerted, anyway? He continues, "Turns out she and my former best friend are moving in together. How very wonderful for them!" I've never heard this biting, sarcastic tone from him before. Is it wrong that all I feel is relief that we get to continue being miserable together? "She was writing to tell me Jean-Luc doesn't like having Faustine around. Charlene was going to give her to a neighbor unless I came to get her."

"Who's Faustine?"

"My daughter," he says.

"Excuse me?" His ex was going to give his daughter to a neighbor? Wait. Quentin has a *daughter*?

"Hold on, I'll send you a picture," he says.

My phone vibrates on the nightstand and I snatch it up. On it is a photo of the most hideous cat I have ever seen. It's one of those super wrinkly, hairless ones, mostly beige with some black splotches on its head and tail. She's wearing a striped sweater and an expression that might actually give me nightmares. Frankly, it's even more shocking than him having a human child.

"Jesus Christ," I say.

"She's sweeter than she looks," he insists.

"She'd have to be, considering she looks like she's possessed by Satan's even eviler cousin."

"Faustine is fourteen years old. Her days of torturing souls are behind her. Now she mostly sleeps and summons minor demons."

"I can't believe you flew to Europe to bring home an ugly, elderly cat," I say. Except that I can absolutely believe it. After all, this is the grown-up version of the boy who tried to send an envelope filled with loose change to the World Wildlife Fund when he was seven. It was returned to sender for insufficient postage (obviously—twenty-six dollars in coins isn't exactly light), but my mom was so touched by the gesture that she personally exchanged his nickels and quarters for a thirty-dollar check and a fresh postage stamp.

"She may be ugly and elderly, but she's my baby and I love her," he says defensively. "It broke my heart to leave her before, but I didn't want to put her through the long plane ride, and I thought she'd be happy enough with Charlene." His voice goes quieter. "I didn't think she'd give her up so easily."

If I've learned anything over the last few weeks—not to mention the last seventeen years—it's that it's a lot easier for most people to get rid of someone they supposedly value than one might imagine. But that is a thought I am not going to voice. "Tomorrow . . ." I start instead.

"Oh, right. Shit. The venue tour. I almost forgot."

"Do you want to reschedule?" I ask.

"No, no, it's fine. The trip was so short I didn't even bother trying to adjust to the time difference, so I'm not jet-lagged, just exhausted. I should be fine after a good night's sleep. Also, that reminds me," he says. "I have something I need to give you. Can you come over in about half an hour?"

"Um. Yeah, sure."

"Okay, cool." There's a moment of silence, and I'm worried he's about to say something else vague and profound to end the conversation. But then it's just, "Let me go shower so I can put my fig leaf on, then."

Heat engulfs my cheeks as his window quietly slides shut.

18

QUENTIN, OF COURSE, does not come to the door wearing nothing but a fig leaf. But he does open it wearing gray sweatpants, which might as well be the same damn thing as far as my libido is concerned. He also has on a black Franz Ferdinand T-shirt, and I mentally cling to it like the ivy climbing up the side of Sprangbur's westernmost turret.

"Did you listen to their collaboration with Sparks?" I ask, gesturing to his chest. Music is a much safer topic than anything else my brain currently wants to conjure. "Came out in 2015, I think."

"Of course," he says. He aims a rueful smile toward the floor. "You know, when I heard that album, one of my favorite bands melded with one of yours . . . I actually started drafting an email to talk to you about it. It felt like a sign to reach out."

"You never sent it." It comes out quiet, almost inaudible.

"No," he confirms. "I didn't."

"Why not?" I ask before I can remind myself that's a path littered with shards of broken glass.

Quentin raises his chin slightly and glances past me, giving it more consideration than I expected. "I was worried that it had already been too long. That the door I closed would be locked. I thought it might . . . hurt . . . if I tried to pry it open again."

This feels different from the other night. The past doesn't feel as sharp-edged and dangerous to talk about right now, looking into his exhausted eyes. It mostly feels . . . sad. "Maybe," I admit. "But I wish you'd done it anyway."

He runs his fingers through his damp hair.

I step into his space, into a cloud of his just-washed scent. "Even if it hurt a little, something would have been better than nothing."

He inclines his head to look into my eyes. "You say that now, but . . ." Quentin lets out a sigh, followed by a tired chuckle as he runs his hand over his face. I notice he hasn't shaved recently, leaving a ruddy shadow coating his jaw. My fingers tingle with the desire to touch it, to see how it feels against my skin. "God. It's been a long couple of days," he says, instead of finishing his thought.

"Yeah," I agree, even though I'm not the one who had to see my ex again and bring a naked-ass cat on an international flight. Speaking of . . .

I glance around the living room for the first time, Quentin's stupid sweatpants having distracted me when I first arrived. Faustine is nowhere in sight—probably hiding upstairs, busy plotting the destruction of all human life. There's also no furniture. Just four freshly painted light gray walls, a stepladder, and a drop cloth. It's sparse, temporary. Easy to leave, to move on from. Probably how I should think of our current relationship if I don't want to wind up bruised again.

"Anyway, you have something for me?" I ask.

"Right." Quentin holds up a finger. "One second," he says, hurrying upstairs.

"I hope you don't plan to give me Faustine!" I call out.

A faint laugh drifts down from the second floor.

He returns quickly, something clenched in his fist. "Definitely not. But it *is* something else I grabbed from Charlene while I was back in Paris, since she hadn't gotten around to mailing it yet." His fingers unfurl, revealing a beautiful diamond engagement ring.

"Oh, wow. That's . . . Quentin, it's gorgeous."

"Glad you think so."

"Why on earth are you giving it to *me*?"

He presses his lips together and raises his eyebrows sardonically. "I figured you could borrow it for the venue tour of Sprangbur tomorrow. For authenticity."

"Oh. Um, sure, but . . . That isn't going to be . . . weird for you, is it?" I ask.

"Not weird for me. Is it weird for you?"

I take the ring from his hand and turn it, letting the overhead light fixture pick out the sparkle. "Everything is already weird for me at the moment. What's one more drop in the ocean, right?" It slides onto my finger with ease; very convenient for our shenanigans that Quentin's ex-fiancée and I have the same ring size. "Nice of . . . Charlene, was it? . . . to return it," I say instead.

"She didn't seem to feel too strongly about it one way or the other. Kind of like how she felt about me, I guess." He doesn't laugh at his joke, and I realize it might not be one. Quentin walks back over to the stairs and takes a seat on the third one up. "Those long-ass, back-to-back flights gave me a lot of time to think," he says.

"Yeah?" I join him, sitting on the bottom step. I have the weirdest, thankfully fleeting, urge to wrap my arms around his outstretched leg and rest my head on his thigh.

"I thought it would be painful seeing Charlene again. But the only thing I felt was . . . stupid." He grips the edge of the stair tread as he talks, his fingers growing whiter as he squeezes harder. "I knew, Nina. I knew practically from the beginning that she didn't truly give a fuck. That she was with me mainly because her father approved of the match, and that meant enough to override the general ambivalence she felt for me personally. I knew all of that, and yet I stuck around. Made sure we checked off the milestones her parents expected of us, stayed on schedule with the life they wanted us to build." I swallow, feeling Quentin's words deep inside my heart. Both of us were stuck in relationships that were better on paper. I can't help but be glad fate crumpled them up and threw them in the trash. "But she wasn't happy," he continues, "and neither was I, and instead of doing something about it, doing *anything* about it, I started finding excuses to work longer hours, to give her more space. And now I'm not sure if I hoped it would make her realize she missed me, or if I was trying to give her an excuse to finally put me out of my goddamn misery."

"I'm so sorry, Quentin," I say, tucking my hands beneath my thighs so I won't lay one on his.

He shakes his head. "I wish it hadn't had such a domino effect on every other aspect of my life, but it's actually better this way. I'm . . . I'm grateful. To get to start fresh. To have a redo at some things." Quentin pauses for a long moment, staring at the ring on my hand. "What about you?" he asks eventually. "How are you feeling about things since we last talked?"

The question startles me. "Oh, about my things?"

"Unless you have feelings on mine?"

I do, actually. A surprising number of them. Most prominently, I'm baffled by the concept of anyone feeling ambivalent about Quentin Bell. I don't know how you know this person and not have a strong sense of *some specific* feeling toward him. I know I always do at any given time—even though it's often annoyance or frustration.

Not always, though.

"Well," I say slowly. "I also wish everything hadn't gone to shit all at once. But I actually had a similar realization today, about my relationship with Cole. I think we both felt it was a decent partnership—when we first got together at least—but that he considered the romance aspect sort of . . . optional."

"But you don't," Quentin says. His eyes sweep over my face, as if really seeing me for the first time since I walked through the door. He must be exhausted.

"I don't need candlelit dinners and rose petals on the bed, no. But I do want to be . . . *wanted*, I guess." Ambitious Nina was fine with putting romance second (or third, or sometimes eighth), prioritizing the hustle with the understanding that affection and togetherness were something to enjoy at a later date, when the work was done. In academia, the work is never really done, though, and I simply went without for so long I stopped noticing. But now, with Quentin sitting so close that I can count his faded freckles, I'm noticing again. Noticing quite intensely. "I don't mean wanted sexually, although ideally that would also be the case. I mostly just want someone who genuinely enjoys being with me. Someone who wants to spend time together. Who feels like I'm equally worthy of their attention and love, whether I'm a massive success or a huge failure or doing just fine." I think back to the first time I visited Cole after he moved to Alabama for his first tenure-track job. How I spent most of the trip alone in his house because he said he didn't want to introduce me to anyone there "until I had some good news to share." God. I completely understand what Quentin means about feeling stupid.

I look down at the glinting ring again and let out an overwhelmed chuckle. "It's such a relief Cole and I hadn't gotten this far yet. Breakup logistics are already annoying enough with the new place we were leasing together. Can't imagine how much of a pain it is to move out of a shared space and also cancel a whole wedding."

"I do not recommend," Quentin says with a tight smile. "Very expensive and not super fun."

There's a beat of silence, and then softly, I say, "You are worth a lot more than it sounds like she would have given you. And maybe it makes me a jerk, but I can't help but be glad that you've wound up here instead of there." I have apparently lost control over my words and also my hands, because one is now resting on his knee. At least I am touching a relatively innocuous part of him instead of doing something egregious, like licking his jaw.

His sleep-heavy eyes go wide for a second before his expression turns warm and his hand comes to rest over mine. Our fingers weave together, and the sudden rush of electricity through my system sets off a mental siren. The feelings coursing through me hold an echo of familiarity. They're the grown-up version of the ones that once led me to believe that I loved Quentin Bell. And I *definitely* do not have any business going back there, to that long-ago, foolish version of myself.

"So!" I say with a nervous smile as I yank away. "Thanks for the . . ." I hold up my hand—the right one at first, the one that was touching him, and have to quickly switch it for my left, where the ring sits on my finger like it belongs there. "Definitely a nice touch."

"Yeah. Sure. No problem." Quentin nods, and it might be my imagination, but he seems slightly muddled too. He follows me to the front door. "It is worth, like, *several* thousand dollars, though, so please take care of it."

"Thank god you said something, since I was planning to be extremely careless," I retort.

The corner of his mouth kicks up. He takes my left hand and rubs his thumb over the diamond on my finger, twisting it back and forth for a moment, his mouth in a straight, pensive line. I'm expecting him to be serious again, but he says, "If for some reason they ask . . . I was thinking we'd combine our names into a new one. We could be the Bellicutts."

"I think I prefer the Hunnibells. Less violent sounding."

"Mr. and Dr. Hunnibell," he says. "That's delightful."

"Did you want to come up with more of a backstory? Make sure we're on the same page about any other questions they might have?" I ask.

"Nah," he says. "Too tired. Let's just wing it."

19

WINGING IT WAS probably not the way to go.

Our vibes are all over the place. We can't seem to settle on if we're madly and disgustingly in love, or if we
actually hate each other a little and just don't realize it yet. As
we head upstairs with Avanti, Sprangbur's event coordinator, I
lean over to Quentin and ask, "So are you going to tell me exactly what your plan is here?"

"We're going to make things super awkward until she leaves
us alone for a minute."

Oh. Well in that case, we could not be doing a better job. We
are being nothing if not off-putting.

"Here on the second floor we have rooms where you and your
bridal party can get ready before the ceremony," Avanti says.

"Very nice," I say, eyeing the Star Parlor.

"Speaking of the ceremony," Quentin says, "if it's usually
outside in the gardens, what happens if it rains?"

"It's up to the couple. Some people decide to get a tent just in
case. Others choose a backup space indoors. Depending on the

final guest count, we use either the conservatory or the downstairs sitting room that opens up into the drawing room."

"Oh, the conservatory! That would be beautiful, wouldn't it?" I lay my hand on Quentin's arm and look up at him. "All the windows. Like being outside without being outside, you know? And with the rain dripping down the glass . . ."

"Eh. I think I'd rather the tent," he says without looking back at me.

"Except a tent rental would be an added expense"—I elongate the word as if teaching it to a toddler—"while the conservatory is—"

"Wait, why would we rent? We can just buy one," he says. "I'm sure it's more cost-effective."

"You want to *buy* a tent that will cover eighty people?" I take a step away and put my hands on my hips. "To use one time? And you think that will be *more* cost-effective?"

He matches my indignant posture. "Eighty? I thought we were only inviting close family and friends."

"Yeah, and that's about eighty guests. I told you, it adds up. Especially if we're including children and plus-ones."

"But that's way too many people. Didn't we agree we wanted something more intimate?"

This is all definitely uncomfortable for Avanti, but probably nothing she hasn't dealt with a million times before. We're going to need to up our game to get her to excuse herself. I meet Quentin's gaze, and there's this glint in his eye. One I know quite well. *I bet*, it says, *I'll be the one who gets her to leave us alone.* I'm more than happy to accept the challenge.

"Well, I'm sorry," I say. "But you're the one who wants to invite all of his college buddies."

"How many times do I have to explain this to you?" He

raises his voice slightly and spreads his arms. "It just isn't a party without Frankie J. and Goober!"

"I cannot believe you want to invite a grown man who goes by Goober to the *happiest day of our lives*." I imbue the statement with as much drama as I possibly can, trying to sound like I'm on the verge of tears.

"Well, I can't believe you want to invite a woman who keeps trying to seduce me."

Oh, that's good. But I can do him one better.

"For the last fucking time, Quentin, my grandmother is not trying to seduce you!"

Quentin almost busts out laughing then. He shifts so that his back is to Avanti, because he's having trouble keeping a straight face. Which in turn makes it difficult for me to retain my angry look, because it's hilarious watching him struggle.

Fortunately Avanti chooses that exact moment to hug her iPad to her chest and say, "Um, I'm going to just . . . check on something." She points downward. "Downstairs. Give you two a moment to chat. And I'll . . . be back." Avanti turns and takes the stairs more quickly than is probably prudent in her high heels.

As soon as we're sure she's made it to the first floor, we both break, laughing noiselessly, leaning against each other for support.

"That was inspired," Quentin whispers.

"Thank you. I had a great scene partner," I whisper back. "Frankie J. and Goober?" I burst into another round of quiet laughter, resting my forehead against Quentin's shoulder.

"Actual friends of mine from college," he says. "But they're just Francis and Steven now. They actually just got married. To each other, I mean. It's a funny story, really."

"You can tell me later," I say, turning him around. "We don't have much time."

"Right."

We rush into the Star Parlor and head straight for the Impressionist painting of wildflowers along a river that's taken the place of Whale's portrait of Fountain. Quentin gently lifts the frame up and toward him until its back wire slips off the heavy-duty mounting hook. Unfortunately (but unsurprisingly), there isn't an obvious safe or secret compartment directly behind it. Propping the painting on the divan beside him, Quentin and I lean in toward the constellation-covered surface, inspecting it for any clues.

But it just . . . looks like a wall. A prettily painted one, but a wall all the same.

There are no obvious seams or places where one might push or pull. I slide onto the floor and wriggle beneath the divan, where I hastily search the lower portion and then lift the rug as much as I can to check the floorboards. The riddle does say *beneath*, after all, and I want to be thorough.

"I don't think there's anything here," I say, sitting up, my glasses askew and my hair in my face.

Quentin takes a few steps back to scan the area from farther away. "Not unless there's something we're missing . . ."

But neither of us have any clue what that *something* could even be, and our time before the event coordinator returns is finite. So we both sigh, wordlessly agreeing that we've reached the point where we need to give up looking here. That's when we hear Avanti in conversation with someone, closer than expected.

"Fuck," I whisper, jumping back from the divan in a panic. My fight-or-flight instinct fully kicks in, and I find myself briefly and irrationally wondering how injured I would get busting through and leaping out one of the room's large arched windows.

Quentin, who is apparently much cooler under pressure, grabs the landscape and hastily hangs it again—a little crooked, but it'll have to do. We hurry toward the Star Parlor's doorway, hoping to make it back to the hallway where Avanti left us so she won't suspect anything. Before we get there, the creak of the stairs and the soft thud of her approaching heels alert us that we're too late.

"Fuck!" I whisper more emphatically this time. Maybe the window wasn't such a bad idea . . .

Before I can fully process what's happening, I'm pressed against the gold star–covered wall, the cherry wood wainscoting digging lightly into my back. One of Quentin's hands has found its way to my hip, where it squeezes, and the other flattens on the wall beside my head, obscuring my view of the open door. "Play along, cookiepuss," he whispers into my ear, sending a shiver through my body that's an odd contrast to the intense rush of heat between my legs. He nuzzles his face into the crook of my neck as if kissing me there, his nose brushing against the skin briefly. Having his lips hovering so close without actually making contact, his quick breaths hot and tickly . . .

Clearly this is supposed to be for Avanti's benefit, and Quentin's positioning does a great deal on its own to imply what's happening without me having to do anything. At the same time, it might look strange if I'm literally standing here, sandwiched between my supposed fiancé and the wall, with my arms awkwardly hanging at my sides. Maybe it wouldn't hurt to just . . . touch him a little. You know. For authenticity's sake. He did tell me to play along . . .

I splay my right hand across his shoulder blade and slide the fingers of my left hand up the back of his neck until they're threaded into his red-brown hair. I involuntarily give it a soft tug, and Quentin lets out a quiet sound that I'm not sure he intended to let slip. I'm surprised to feel it echo against my pulse as his lips close the small amount of distance and make contact. Even though he keeps them still, doesn't actually kiss so much as rest there, the knowledge that his mouth is against my skin prompts a primal, subconscious reaction that makes me tilt the lower half of my body forward, searching for contact, for pressure. I find it as I'm pinned harder against the wall, his hips subtly grinding into mine.

We are doing an excellent job here. Such a good job that it seems both of our bodies have forgotten it's all a ruse. Either that or Quentin has an unripe banana stashed in his pocket.

His ragged exhale against the place where my neck meets my shoulder sends heat cascading through me, making me whisper once more, "Fuck," the panic now completely stripped from it and replaced with something huskier.

A throat clears and my eyes open (though I hadn't realized I'd closed them).

Quentin takes a few steps away from me, swallowing hard before he manages to speak. "Uh, excuse us. Sorry. We got . . ." He glances back at me with such heat in his gaze that I suddenly feel like an ice-cream cake left in front of a fireplace. "A little carried away."

"You know how planning a wedding can be," I say, my voice sounding reedy and unfamiliar to my own ears.

"Emotions run high," he continues. "And . . ."

"And so do other things. Right? Haha." I squint, unsure if that made sense.

Quentin reaches over and faux-discreetly fixes the strap of my dress where it slipped off my shoulder during our, um, pretending. "Anyway, we appreciate you taking the time to show us around, but Nina and I have discussed things and we're not quite ready to put down a deposit. We're going to have to talk a bit more about what we want, make sure we're on the same page before settling on a date."

"I understand," Avanti says. "We'll be here and happy to host your special day whenever you're ready." Her smile is professional and practiced. But her dark eyes show her true thoughts: *You people are a nightmare.*

Quentin grabs my hand and brings it to his mouth to kiss it, hiding a smile.

"Whenever we're ready," I echo mindlessly.

20

ND . . . SCENE," QUENTIN says as the front doors close behind us. His voice is quiet, and his shoulders rise and fall a little more rapidly than makes sense for the amount of exertion it took to walk down the stairs and out of the Castle.

"Good work in there," I say, patting him on the back, then snatching my hand away as if that might somehow undo the gesture. Contact between us right now feels extra charged, and I'm already addled enough. "Um. I mean. We did good work. Improvising. Everything. That we improvised." At least my cringing is of the inward variety and doesn't seem to show on my face.

"Nina . . ." he starts.

"Because that would be ridiculous. If we . . . If you and I . . . I mean. We could . . . we could never. Right?"

"Right." His lips press together, making his smile look slightly pained. He bows his head and more quietly repeats himself. "Right."

"Um, I think I'm going to walk home," I say. "I need to get

some . . . air. In my lungs and, um, also the compressed kind from the hardware store, for my dad." Dad has not asked me to do this, but I can't imagine he'll mind a surprise can of it considering he goes through one every two weeks or so. Mostly I need an excuse to get away from Quentin for a minute, to experience a break in the lust coursing through me so I can think straight again. Until now, any attraction between us felt so farfetched, it was easily dismissed as me clamoring for a distraction from my woes. But after what just happened, the desperation to have him is charging at me full force. There's no dismissing what I'm feeling at the moment as a coping mechanism, because it is not helping me cope with anything at all. The opposite, really.

"Oh. Sure. I have some errands to run anyway," he says, eyes focused on the car door's handle instead of on me.

"I'll meet you at Hanako's tomorrow night?" I ask. "And we can figure out next steps while we're there. For the treasure, I mean. Not for . . . us. We're . . . we're good." The ring on my finger suddenly catches a beam of sunlight, creating sparkles in my peripheral vision. I nearly forgot it was there. "Oh, you can have this back now." I twist it off and attempt to tuck it into his palm, but it falls onto the gravel at his feet.

He bends down to pick it up. When he's upright again he has that annoyed crease between his eyebrows and it looks like he's about to say something. Whatever it is, I don't think I can handle it right now. I cut him off with a quick "See you tomorrow" before I turn and speed walk away.

"See you tomorrow," he agrees, although I can barely hear him with how much distance I have successfully managed to put between us in the last two seconds.

I consider going straight home, where I can at least dig out one of my sex toys from the bottom of my still-packed suitcase. But my mom might be around, and she's going to *know* that something happened just by the expression on my face. It is her superpower, and one I do not want to risk encountering.

Instead I head over to Best That You Can Brew, where I snag a place at the raw-edged wood bar stretching across the front window. I get a fancy latte and an almond croissant and slowly consume both while reading over the draft of a journal article Sabrina sent a few weeks ago and has been expecting comments on.

It's well written and interesting and hits me with a sudden wallop of sorrow. This was how Sabrina and I bonded over the years. By looking over each other's drafts. Sharing a hotel room at conferences. Taking turns giving pep talks before important meetings. And now she's still living that life, spending the summer putting the finishing touches on her first monograph and getting published in *The American Historical Review*, while I'm spending it traipsing about my hometown looking for something that might not even exist and being intensely sexually frustrated. Will she still want my notes on her work if I never find my way back to academia? Still tell me stories about her students when I can't counter with ones of my own? Leaving the field, even inadvertently, often makes you a sort of pariah. Sabrina might still want to be my friend, but I can't help thinking about the ways that friendship might change and fizzle out now that I'm no longer the same Nina she's used to.

It's getting more and more crowded in the café as Catoctin's surprisingly large young professional population pops in for lunch. I look around, expecting to see a bunch of familiar-but-older faces, yet . . . I don't recognize a soul. For the first time, it strikes me that this might actually be a desirable place to live.

When I was young, it seemed like a sort of vortex—a place that sucked everyone who was born here into it and made it almost impossible for them to get out. Because why else would people stay? I didn't understand it. But now, with eyes used to urban sprawl and a biological clock that ticks a bit louder when I see a couple with a baby walk past, I think I'm starting to get why someone might choose a life here.

Huh.

Once I respond to Sabrina's email with my scant suggestions for improvement (seriously, she's brilliant) and reach the dregs of my mug, I decide to head out and free up my seat for the many people now waiting for a spot.

I continue up Main Street, checking out what is here now. A plant store called Leopold Bloom's advertises a sale on fiddle-leaf fig trees on its sidewalk sign. I wish Quentin were here so I could nudge him with my elbow and flirtingly joke about getting him one.

I really wish he were here in general.

Wait. No. I don't mean that. He isn't someone I can let myself become attached to. Not only could he wind up hurting me again, but he's too much of a distraction. One with pretty eyes and strong hands and a warm mouth and that stupid charming smile that makes me so *mad*, and . . .

The point is, Quentin Bell is trouble. I knew it from the moment I saw him pacing on his porch three weeks ago. And okay, maybe I was wrong about what kind of trouble he would be, but he is trouble nonetheless.

Clearly we need to speed this up a bit, and the only way within my control is to find the treasure as soon as possible. Then I'll have enough money to take whatever opportunity comes my way. More important, I won't have to spend the whole eight weeks here. Because if I do . . . I can't trust that I'll be able to stay out of trouble. Or that trouble will stay out of me.

As I stroll back in the direction of my parents' house, my body tingles in all sorts of distracting places as it plays a highlight reel of the few moments I managed to collect today: the heat of Quentin's breath on my skin, his hardness pressed against me, his fingers gripping my hip . . .

Oh god. I'm out here giving a whole new meaning to getting horny on Main.

That's it. I take a hard left instead of continuing down the street. I'm going to the library. I need to figure out if this treasure exists and where it is. And there's nothing sexy about the special collections room, so I'll be safe there.

A whispery voice that may be my conscience asks if I should be doing this without Quentin, or without at least giving him a heads-up. But it's only research, and if I find anything promising I'll make sure to tell him. It's not like I'm going to Sprangbur and hunting for the thing alone.

Not this time at least.

Besides, the special collections room is open today but closed on the weekends. I am simply saving us time. Also, Mrs. Mac-Donald is not Quentin's biggest fan because of the whole gum thing. Which is why it makes no sense to text Quentin to let him know I'm doing this. I can't let him invite himself along, for both Mrs. MacDonald reasons and my needing space from him reasons.

So really, this is the best thing I could be doing. For both of us.

Especially because of how badly I wish we were doing it together.

21

EVEN THOUGH THE special collections room is supposed to be open from noon to four on Fridays, when I arrive at half past twelve, the door is locked and no one seems to be inside. *A sign that I am not supposed to be doing this?* a tiny guilty voice in my brain suggests. Just as I'm about to go to the circulation desk and ask if they know what's going on, Mrs. MacDonald appears from the direction of the elevator, breathing heavily and moving slowly.

"I'm here," she says.

It takes a while for her to dig through her bulging leather purse to find the key, and even longer for her to fit it into the lock and turn it. What her hands lack in steadiness, her pride more than makes up for, and she refuses my offer of help.

"Back again, huh?" she asks as I finally follow her inside. "Where's your little boyfriend?"

My cheeks go hot. "He's not my boyfriend."

"Whatever you want to call him, then. I'm not hip to the current slang," she says.

It's probably easier to answer her question than to both find and explain a label that fits the strange friends-but-not-but-yes-but-there's-definitely-chemistry situation Quentin and I have found ourselves in. "He's busy today."

"Probably sticking gum places it doesn't belong," she mumbles with a sneer.

I press my lips together, trying not to smile. "I don't want to bother you too much," I start.

Mrs. MacDonald gives me a look that says I'm already failing. It's the same one she used to give me when I would ask her research questions or about archival practices when I was here as a teen. And I suddenly understand that it's all bluster. She's never once actually been put out by my curiosity or requests. This has been her job for decades, and despite her hard demeanor, she must love it immensely to have continued doing it all this time. Lord knows it can't pay that well.

"I was hoping to look at the Fountain materials again," I say as she lowers herself into the chair behind her desk.

She pauses. "Of course you were." I wince, knowing she's now going to have to get right back up. But to my utter shock, she says, "You know where they are. Help yourself."

"What?"

"It's going to rain tonight," she says by way of explanation.

"Uh . . ."

"My arthritis. Feels like someone's kicked me all over while wearing steel-toe boots."

"That's . . . a vivid description," I say. "I'm sorry that you're dealing with that."

She waves off my sympathy. "I finally made it here, and I'm not getting up for nobody. Especially not when I know you're perfectly capable."

Mrs. MacDonald calling me perfectly capable rivals the first time my PhD adviser called me Dr. Hunnicutt after I passed my defense. An actual tear wells in my eye. "Thank you," I say, omit the *I promise to make you proud* that nearly follows, and head into the stacks.

Once I've brought the boxes to the table in the center of the room, I reexamine our amateur finding aid. I start with the photos again, searching them for anything we may have missed last time around while we were focused on the Whale portrait. An hour later, when picture after picture of Sprangbur starts blending into a bunch of black-and-white blobs, I switch over to the Fountain Seltzer administrative and governing documents. I pause for a moment when I reach a parenthetical note at the bottom of typed meeting minutes that Julius Fountain's opinions on the matter at hand had been primarily shouted from an adjoining room while he watched the proceedings via strategically placed mirrors. Louisa Worman must have been an absolute saint to put up with him for as long as she did.

By three o'clock, I decide that if I read another conversation about bottling logistics or wholesale marketing strategy I will scream. I stand and stretch toward the ceiling, my neck clicking as I finally look up after hours of looking down.

"I'll be right back. I'm just going to the bathroom," I tell Mrs. MacDonald, who, as promised, has not moved from her chair since taking her place in it.

"Do you want a medal or something?" she snaps as she slowly rubs her right hand with her left. I pause outside of the special collections room, listening to her sigh heavily and mumble to herself about "these damned fingers" and "that damned doctor" not sending in a refill for her pills.

"Can I get you anything? Do anything for you?" I make sure

to ask when I return. I know it's a long shot, but considering she let me grab the materials on my own, maybe she's in enough discomfort to say yes.

"Yeah," she surprises me by saying. "You can take this god-forsaken job so I can finally retire."

I blink at her. "I'm sorry?"

"You're an archivist."

"I'm not . . . I mean, I was, or I'm technically qualified to be, but I—"

She waves away my bumbling protest with a slightly clawed hand. "I've been doing this job for sixty years," she says.

Sixty?! I knew she'd been here a good long time, but *sixty* years?!

"I thought about retiring back in 1999. All that Y2K bullshit. Didn't want to deal with it. But then there was talk about closing down the special collections room completely if I left. Deaccessioning everything. I couldn't let that happen, could I?"

"Of course not," I say.

"So I stayed. And stayed. And stayed. And now it's 2024, and—"

"2025," I correct. She frowns. "Happens to the best of us," I assure her.

"Whatever year it is, I shouldn't still be here. I should be in Arizona with my great-grandchildren. Now that you're here, you can take over. I don't have to worry."

My first emotion at her words is elation. Like Santa Claus has hand-selected me to be his successor. Quickly, though, it dissipates as I remember I can't accept. "But Mrs. MacDonald, I'm *not* here. I don't live in Catoctin. I'm only visiting for—"

"You got a job back wherever you came from?" she asks bluntly.

"No."

"You got a husband there? Kids?"

"Um. No."

"A house?"

"Ha. Definitely not."

"And your parents are here?"

"They are."

"So what's the problem?" The way she says this, it's as if she thinks it's all very simple.

And maybe it would be, if I were the person I was when I first discovered this room and everything it held. Or even the person I was when I considered archives as a career. But so much has happened since then that taking over for Mrs. Mac-Donald would feel like a step backward. Settling for something I told myself wasn't worth wanting. If that was a lie, if I didn't really mean that, then the last few years of my life were a waste. That's a bit too much to swallow right now.

"I am extremely flattered that you think I'm a good choice. Really." Mrs. MacDonald has always held a place in my heart as the first person to introduce me to the world of archival research. Everything I decided to throw myself into later might not have ever been an option if Quentin and I hadn't spent time with her in this room in the summer of 2008. Her wanting me to be her successor is truly an honor I would never have expected. "But I'm sorry, I can't."

"Can't, can't, can't," she says dismissively. "Don't talk to me about can't. There's a difference between can't and won't. I *can't* run a marathon. I *can't* talk to my dead husband. I *can't* live on my own much longer. Lots of things you can't do when you're my age. And lots of things you can do but won't when you're young."

I try to absorb the lesson while also figuring out the best way to counter it. Before I come up with my response, Mrs. Mac-Donald lowers her voice to something gentler. "Let me know if you change your mind. But don't take too long. Don't want to get to my granddaughter's house in Tucson only to croak on her doorstep."

"I don't think you need to worry about that," I say with a small smile. "I have it under good authority that you're never dying."

"Well, you will, one day," she says bluntly. "So figure out what it is you want in life before the real 'can'ts' come to get you."

22

THE UNIVERSE IS clearly not done trying to punish me for some unknown offense. Because according to the sign outside Flow State's front door, this isn't just any fundraiser they're throwing. It's a *themed* one. NOSTALGIA NIGHT the sign reads. Capri-Sun and Hi-C cocktails. Fifteen percent off for anyone dressed as a Spice Girl or wearing JNCOs. Pog tournament at eight. And a DJ spinning the greatest hits of the '90s and early 2000s.

It's like the past heard I'm trying to avoid it and decided to come along and smack me in the face in retaliation.

I turn to Quentin. "Did you know about this?"

"About what?" His innocent look is not nearly as persuasive as that practiced smile he flashes so often. I glare in response until he confesses, "Hanako may have mentioned it when I texted her."

"Why didn't you warn me?"

"And miss out on this wonderful conversation?" He grins.

"Come on. What's the big deal? I seem to remember you really liking *NSYNC back in the day. We can ask the DJ to play 'Bye Bye Bye.'" He opens the door and gestures for me to go inside.

For a second, I consider turning around and walking home alone without another word. But that's a little more dramatic than the circumstances call for.

Plus, it's 6:40. I'm not sure Mom has left for her drawing class yet. If I get home too early she'll want to know what happened, promptly followed by an excited pronouncement that now I can come with her after all. As tempting as it is to put space between me and my youth, and me and Quentin, and me and Quentin *in* our youth, I fully recognize that this doesn't actually warrant a tantrum. Especially when he didn't have to come out with me tonight at all. He's doing me a favor, helping me not be a complete liar to my mother. The least I can do is not be a jerk in return.

"Are we sure we want to go here?" I ask instead. "We could just Venmo Hanako some money, grab something from that taco truck, and call it a night."

Quentin releases the door and lets it close. "Nina," he says. "What's up?"

I sigh. "Nothing. Nothing's up."

"You can tell me, you know," he says softly. "Anything you're feeling—it's always safe with me." *You are always safe with me* goes unspoken but seems to linger in the air between us until one side of his mouth lifts. "Like, clearly right now you're worried I'm going to demolish you in Pogs like the old days. But I promise I'll take it easy on you."

I close my eyes and take a deep breath, telling myself I don't *need* to engage. But just because I don't need to doesn't mean part of me doesn't want to.

So I reach past him, open the door, and head inside Flow State. The space is unexpected. I figured an old brick warehouse would be industrial and sleek. Instead it's sumptuous—plum and hot pink, velvet and silk and tassels and fringe everywhere. Jutting into the center of the space is a large, antique U-shaped mahogany bar. A long booth stretches along the right wall, tables and chairs lined up with it to create more intimate seating.

It's almost Fountain-esque, really, both in its richness and the way it seems to play with the concept of power clashing. Not just in the patterns of the throw pillows scattered along the banquette and the heavy drapery on the wall behind it, but in the crowd. There's a guy in a smart suit looking like he just came from an accounting firm in DC sitting at the bar beside someone dressed like the guy in the "Virtual Insanity" video. It's admittedly pretty cool.

"Sweet place," Quentin says as we head toward the bar. "Cozier than I thought it would be."

"Let's get our drinks and go out to the patio," I say, remembering the friendly-looking space outside that's likely less packed with tipsy women screeching along to Christina Aguilera's "Beautiful."

Quentin raises one eyebrow at me and the side of his mouth quirks again. "And miss out on all this nostalgic fun?"

"Exactly," I say grouchily.

"Nina! Quentin!" Hanako calls from behind the bar at the same time one of the tipsy women shrieks near my ear.

Once I've recovered from the auditory assault, I manage to paste on a smile. "Hey!"

Quentin leans over the bar and gives Hanako a kiss on the cheek like they see each other all the time. Maybe they do, for all I know. "Thanks again for inviting us," he says. "This is great."

"Of course! I'm so glad you could stop by," she replies, then slides us a menu. "Like I said, first round's on the house."

"Are you sure?" I ask. It feels sort of counterproductive to not charge us when this is supposed to be a fundraiser.

"Definitely sure. I have a soft spot for the two of you." She winks at Quentin. God, could the flirting be any more obvious?

I peruse the options and settle on a yuzu paloma, while Quentin gets one of the specials. As Hanako mixes our cocktails, Quentin leans casually against the bar with his arms folded atop it.

"So, Nostalgia Night, huh?" he asks, voice gaining in volume to be heard over the DJ's introduction of the next song.

"Yeah, it was my partner, Kell's, idea." Hanako flashes a smile as her eyes search the room and land on a tall, slender figure with bronze skin and a shaved head gesturing enthusiastically while talking to a group of three Scary Spices. "They're in charge of getting people in the door, and I'm in charge of making sure everyone has a good time once here."

"Definitely seems like mission accomplished on both counts," I say as someone accidentally brushes against my butt as they navigate the crowd. I'm not sure he's even fully conscious of it, but Quentin repositions himself behind me, protecting me from further inadvertent touching. Thoughtful.

What if I were to lean back, rest against him? Best-case outcome: He'd wrap his arms around me and kiss the top of my head. Worst-case: He'd push me away . . . No, no . . . worst would be he whispers something mortifying in my ear like, "Um, Nina, did you remember deodorant this morning?" Which I did. I'm like ninety-eight percent certain. Most likely is that he'd go stiff (not in the sexy way) and take a step backward, either assuming I'm requesting more space or to politely remove himself from my proximity.

Just going to stay right where I am, I think. (And maybe turn my head to take a subtle sniff of my armpit to make sure everything is all hunky-dory under there.)

"I like to think we make a pretty good team." Hanako beams as she sets our drinks in front of us on the bar. The love absolutely radiates from her as she flashes her left hand, which sports a tattooed infinity symbol on her ring finger. "Ten years together and counting." So maybe she hasn't been flirting with Quentin after all. Then again, I still haven't completely ruled out the whole non-monogamy thing.

Quentin tries to hand her a twenty-dollar bill, but she shakes her head and instead gestures for him to lean in. She whispers something in his ear like she did at the coffee shop, and Quentin goes pink again. Or maybe it's just the moody lighting in here, because the color is gone by the time he straightens. Then he bends back down to whisper something to her that makes her grin, then roll her eyes. He drops the cash into a cigar box being used to collect extra donations and grins back at her.

Whatever this moment is, I am clearly not a necessary part of it. So I grab our drinks and move to the door leading out onto the patio, pushing my hip against it. Quentin appears behind me, arm stretched over my head to prop the door open, and his scent and the light breeze coming off the river combine into something so summery and sensual that I feel like my kneecaps have turned to jam.

At least it's less packed out here—only an uncomfortable first date happening at one of the picnic tables and four guys playing a game of cornhole in the nearby grass. Even though the music the DJ is playing inside is still piped over an outdoor speaker, it's quiet enough to have a conversation without needing to raise our voices.

I sidle up to an empty cocktail table made out of an old barrel. "You and Hanako sure have a lot of secrets, huh?"

"Nah, not a lot. Just one, really." Quentin takes a sip of his drink and emits a hum of appreciation. "This is super good. It's the Hi-C one. Wanna taste?" he asks, offering me the glass.

I shake my head and instead try my own. It's tart and crisp and refreshing on this sultry evening. "One secret can be a lot." *It certainly was for us*, I don't say but definitely think.

Quentin leans in. "You jealous, Hunnicutt?"

"Hardly," I say, grabbing his drink and taking a swig despite having just turned down his offer.

He's sucking the corner of his bottom lip, as if he's concentrating on something. Then he says, "You know, Thursday night, after you left, it struck me that I don't know what style pizza you prefer."

"What?"

"Or the best concert you've ever been to. Or if you studied abroad."

I finally relinquish his Hi-C cocktail (which is indeed super good). "Um . . ."

"I know that a lot happened over the last seventeen years. For both of us. But it's easy to forget sometimes."

"It is," I say. Because that period of time when he was absent from my life feels like a fever dream lately. There's us before, and there's us now, but everything in between feels kind of like a series of endnotes that neither of us have skipped ahead to examine.

"So maybe . . . What do you say that tonight we try to catch each other up? We can treat it almost like a first date. Pretend we're two strangers getting to know each other over a drink or two while enjoying this scenic setting, and . . ." He pauses, listening to what's now playing over the outdoor speaker. "Harvey Danger's 'Flagpole Sitta'?"

My brain latches onto the word "date" and doesn't want to let it go. *Like* a date, I try to tell it. *Like* one, not that it *is* one. Even so . . . "I don't know if—"

"Forget everything you know about me." He holds a hand out over the barrel, and it takes me an embarrassingly long time to realize he wants me to shake it. When I finally do, he smiles warmly. "My name is Quentin Bell," he says. "I'm a lawyer, currently in town renovating my dad's old house."

When I don't respond automatically, he prompts, "How about you?"

"Nina," I say. "Nina Hunnicutt. Historian. I'm here visiting my parents for the summer."

He's gracious enough not to point out that this is a gross simplification of the reason I'm back home. Instead, his smile widens. It isn't that too-charming one that bothers me either, but something much more natural and unguarded. Something that, even if he were actually a complete stranger, I would know right away is genuinely, one hundred percent *him*.

"I hope to get to know you better . . . Nina, was it?"

I narrow my eyes at him, but then my gaze goes softer as I say, "Yeah, I hope to get to know you better too, Kevin."

Joking aside, I do mean that. Because Quentin is right that there are a lot of gaps in my knowledge of the adult version of him that's sitting across from me. I've been so preoccupied trying to reconcile that he's the same boy who hurt me with my undeniable attraction to the man he is now that I've neglected to consider the time we spent out of each other's lives was actually longer than we spent in them. So much happened during those years, things that shaped us both. And now I have a million questions. Like, what does he like to do on a lazy weekend? Does he know how to cook? Does he like IPAs or porters? Does he even drink beer at all? How many times has he had his heart broken? Or broken others'? I might know his origin story, but that isn't enough. I want to know the person he's grown into and everything that's made him that way.

I want him to know me too. Which may be difficult, considering *I* barely have any clue who I am right now. But maybe this is the first step in figuring it out. And maybe it will take away some of the mystery, some of the *allure* of him.

So Quentin and I spend the next few hours just . . . chatting. Catching up on the time we missed. Filling each other in on where we were, with whom, why. Funny stories, new hobbies, the music we listen to these days. I learn that he spent two summers in college volunteering with Habitat for Humanity— hence the comfort with power tools. I tell him about when I got stuck in my apartment building's elevator for an hour and that I learned to drink black coffee in grad school because someone kept stealing all of the sugar and creamer from the student lounge. We talk a bit more about Dad's accident, the emotional and financial uncertainty of it all. The aftermath of his parents' divorce, and the resentment he used to feel toward his sister, who was already out of the house and much less affected by it. We agree that Neapolitan pizza is the best, but disagree on the order in which we rank Detroit-, Chicago-, and St. Louis–style pies.

And it's frankly better than any real first date I've ever been on. Not that I've been on that many. Or any at all for the past six years. Also, not that this is a date at all. It's only *like* a date.

We're just two strangers who already sort of know each other, getting drinks to support an old classmate's injured employee, and so that one can avoid drawing naked people with her mom. A tale as old as time, really.

It's dark before we know it. I'm sure we missed the Pog tournament—for the best, as Quentin definitely would've trounced me. Solar lanterns and café lights keep the patio illuminated, but not brightly enough to block out the stars.

"Hey. Wanna dance?" Quentin asks.

"What?"

"Do you want to dance? With me."

"Really? Here? Now?" I don't bother adding "To S Club 7's 'Never Had a Dream Come True'?" because it feels like that part goes without saying.

My hesitation to slow dance with Quentin must be obvious, because he pulls a very dirty trick. "Unless . . . Well, if you don't think you can keep up . . ."

I scoff. "Oh, please. I remember the homecoming debacle. How many stitches did you wind up needing that time?"

He grins, running his finger over a barely visible scar by his left eyebrow. "Only three, which is practically the same as none. And that was mostly Edgar's fault anyway. Who wears spiked leather cuffs to a formal dance?" He holds out his palm, waiting for mine as if it's an inevitability I'll give in. Which I hate to admit, it is. "Besides," he adds, "I've lived a lot of life since then, as we've spent the evening discussing. My coordination and balance have improved quite a bit."

"I'll believe it when I see it," I grumble, laying my hand atop his.

He pulls me in quicker and closer than I expect, and I laugh in nervous surprise as I place my left hand on his shoulder. "Do you remember Mrs. Mann coming around with a ruler during our middle school dances to make sure everyone was at least a foot apart?"

Quentin's response sends a delicious tingle down my spine, his voice only inches from my ear as he brings me even closer to his warm body. "Thankfully, she doesn't seem to be here tonight. Unless she's the person in the Daft Punk helmet I saw in the bathroom."

We exchange smiles as we settle into a nice swaying rhythm. It isn't long before his eyes on mine become too much to bear. I clear my throat and tentatively rest my forehead against his jaw, which strikes me as even more intimate but somehow soothes my nerves. "So, uh, when and where did you learn to dance without incurring or inflicting injuries?"

"I took a class senior year of college," he says, his words fluttering the curls framing my face. "Needed a phys ed credit to graduate and it was the only thing available that worked with my schedule. I also learned how to waltz . . ." He adjusts us into a more formal posture and spins us around the patio. "And cha-cha." His hand on my lower back leads me into a few unfamiliar movements before we fall back into our previous low-key sway, matching the sedated rhythm of the music. "A lot of it's muscle memory," he tells me. "But I did get to practice a few times over the years. Lots of friends' weddings." He pauses. "Huh. Guess I would've been dancing at my own wedding in just a few months, if things had been different."

"I'm sorry things didn't work out," I say. Because that's the polite response, even if it's not strictly true. I'm glad he isn't with Charlene. Quentin might have hurt me in the past, but I've never stopped wanting only the best for him. And she certainly wasn't the best when she didn't even understand how lucky she was to have him in the first place.

"Yeah?" He looks down at me, and I'm startled to find his eyes filled with heat. My tongue darts out to sweep across my lips in unconscious response. "I'm not," he whispers as his thumb dips beneath the hem of my tank top and strokes back and forth along the exposed skin above the waistband of my shorts.

I think . . . Are we actually . . . ?

Best-case outcome: He kisses me. Worst-case outcome: He kisses me. Most likely outcome: He kisses me? Or maybe I kiss him? I am internally screaming at the near certainty of what's coming. I've never wanted something as badly as I want his mouth against mine at this moment. Even if the worst outcome were the end of the world, it would be challenging to talk myself out of it as long as our lips still made contact for a split second beforehand. My eyes flutter closed as I lean in, waiting, waiting for the contact I've been craving so intensely it feels like an intrinsic part of me.

There's the warmth of his exhale, of his nearness as inches between us turn into centimeters into millimeters and—

The song transitions abruptly, the speakers seeming suddenly louder as they blast out *SomeBODY once told me* . . .

Goddammit. We've been mouth-blocked by Smash Mouth.

Our laughter erases the remaining tension. I rest my head on his shoulder, and he wraps his arms around me for a moment before stepping away and downing the rest of his third drink. He pulls my empty glass toward his and pinches them both between his fingers. "Want anything else?" he asks.

My brain immediately responds: *You. I want you.*

I shake my head, feeling said brain rattle around a bit in my skull. "No. I'm good. Probably should have stopped earlier, really."

"Same. I blame Hanako. These things go down way too easy." He bangs his hip into a stool as he passes by and mutters an apology to it—the most endearing evidence of his tipsiness. "I'm going to run these in and we can head home."

"Sounds good," I say. As soon as he's out of sight, I press my fingers to my lips, trying to ease the anticipatory buzz. But I suspect nothing is going to do it except finally, *finally* kissing Quentin Bell.

TEXT OF INTERVIEW (UNEDITED)

VI

No, I never did marry. Friends suggested that it
might be good for me to have a wife, that it might
be good for Isolde to have a maternal figure. For
myself, I saw little point in it--I have never felt
the need to wax rhapsodic about anyone's hair or
eyes, nor do I crave physical affection the way most
men seem to do. There's a German doctor friend of
mine, Hirschfeld, who calls it "Anästhesia
sexualis." Perhaps that is more information than you
wanted, but there you are. What you get for letting
an old man speak at length about whatever his heart
desires. Or does not desire, as the case may be!

[AA: Informant was reminded at this point that
this interview was primarily to be about his
experiences in business and industry.]

Oh, it's all business and industry, Mr. Aaron.
All intertwined, don't you see? Life imitates
seltzer, sir! Clear and fizzy and good for all ages.

Anyway, I don't believe that my bachelorhood
ever caused Issy to want for anything. She had all
of the love and guidance a girl needs. Lou and I
made sure of that.

23

MAYBE IT'S THE moonlight reflecting off the river, or the sticky air settling on my flushed skin, or too many tequila-based cocktails, but tonight feels different. Magical. Full of possibility. Almost like being at Sprangbur. Even though the place is half a mile behind us, it's as if we've stepped inside one of the magical Edlosian bubbles Fountain talked about and now we're drifting somewhere new and exciting, unable to steer but open to wherever it takes us.

All I know is that, when I look at Quentin strolling beside me along the water with his pale skin glowing and his hair fluttering in the breeze, our history collapses into something folded so small I can tuck it away. I'm able to store it out of sight and fully focus on the man beside me. Up until now, it was like the teenage version of Quentin was a ghostly image projected over the adult version. But now the projection has been shut off, and I don't have to try to figure out which parts of what I'm seeing are from the past and which are present. Everything tonight is stripped down, simplified into *him* and *now* and *want*.

Instead of feeling lost, I'm starting to feel . . . free.

"Hanako," he says out of the blue.

"What about her?" I ask, stomach dropping.

"Do you want to know our secret?"

Yes. But also no. It really depends on what it is, I guess, but I can't admit that without sounding jealous. "Sure. If it's yours to tell."

"She was my first kiss," he confesses. The streetlights illuminating the trail reveal a deep blush spanning his cheeks and continuing to the tips of his ears.

I'm officially nauseated. "Oh. I assumed something like that."

"Really?" Quentin raises his eyebrows as he glances over at me. "It wasn't because we had any sort of connection or anything. I wasn't particularly, like, interested in her—not that she isn't attractive, of course."

"Of course," I repeat. I'm not sure why he's telling me this. It doesn't make my stomach hurt any less. And the magic feels like it's dissipating by the second, like the bubble might be about to pop and drop us somewhere inconvenient, like into the river.

"It only happened because we got to talking that night, at Tyler McMaster's pool party."

"Why were you even there, anyway?" I ask. "No offense, but you weren't exactly a cool kid."

A low rumble of laughter rolls through him—that *Taco Bell rumor* one. "Offense very much taken! I have always been cool, Nina." He claps a hand to his chest as if I've wounded him, then lets it fall. "I was at Edgar's playing D&D when Tyler IM'd to invite him—they were on the varsity soccer team together, remember?—and Ed asked if he could bring me along. Anyway, we went over there. I had like half a Bud Light, so I was feeling *wild*, and I wound up spilling my guts to Hanako about how I had a huge crush on someone but was terrified to make a move because I'd never kissed anyone before and didn't feel like I knew what I was doing. She suggested she give me a quick lesson, just platonically, so that I'd be confident enough to shoot my shot before I left at the end of the summer. It was all very technical and unsexy, to be honest. But helpful. And really kind of her."

My pulse is going a million miles an hour. Not only did I not know about his kissing Hanako, but there was a whole crush on someone he never mentioned? Even though I actively feel like I might vomit, I can't help but ask, "So, did it work? Did you work up the nerve to kiss your crush?"

He shakes his head, grinning down at the trail beneath our feet as we walk. "Not yet."

Not . . . yet? I try to think of who is still around that he might be in contact with, but the only person that comes to mind is . . . me? But that doesn't make sense, because then why wouldn't he have made his move that night in his backyard? Or one of the zillion other times we were alone together that summer?

The toe of my shoe hits a small divot in the asphalt as I take my next step. I wobble before stumbling slightly in the direction of the riverbank. I regain my balance quickly, but not as quickly as Quentin reaches out and grabs my arm.

"Geez. Didn't realize you were that drunk," he says.

"I'm not!"

He playfully narrows his eyes as if he doesn't believe me. "Well, I'll feel better holding on to you. Just to be safe." He lets go of my arm and instead interlaces our fingers.

Oh my god. Quentin Bell and I are holding hands again. We are holding hands as we walk home on a beautiful night, and he and I are two adults who are getting to know each other better, untethered by whatever happened to those kids we used to be. This could be the beginning of a new chapter. One in which this attraction I feel toward him is something that can be acted on. Something that doesn't have to be a fantasy I resent, or dismissed as a coping mechanism, but a real possibility.

I should be more anxious about that. Why am I not more anxious?

Probably the tequila.

Heat from his palm transfers to mine, and thinking about it makes it spread faster and wider until I feel it in my arm and my chest and my face and between my legs. We walk and chat idly, letting our joined hands swing as if this is a normal thing that we do. Or maybe it's actually the start of a game of intimacy-based chicken in which we each keep pushing ever so slightly forward until the reality of it becomes too much and one of us backs off. Another competition between us.

More likely, I'm completely overthinking it and Quentin is truly worried I might stumble into the river.

Except when we reach the end of Riverside Park and turn onto East Baltimore in the direction of our houses, no more water in sight, he doesn't let go. Neither do I.

When we're standing in front of our duplex on West Dill ten minutes later, I figure this is the moment when he'll finally release me, laugh it off. But we keep our fingers threaded together as we go up the stairs to our respective porches. The support column at the top of the steps forces us to finally part, and we make a big, goofy, tipsy show of it. I do a little lopsided pirouette on my porch, nearly falling over. Once I regain my balance, Quentin takes my hand again. This time he gently tugs me toward him until we're standing mere inches apart, the wooden railing the only thing separating our bodies.

"I had a lot of fun tonight," he says. "It was nice to just . . . be with you."

"It was," I agree, vaguely aware that the words echo what I said I was looking for in a partner. *No, shush, brain.* This is lust, pure and simple. *Not* romance.

"And you look . . ." His eyes sweep over me briefly, as if refreshing his memory, before closing hard, an almost pained smile on his face. "You look so fucking beautiful, Neen."

I know that my hair is gigantic from being outside in the humidity, the eye makeup beneath my glasses is probably smudged, and my lipstick is just a light stain clinging to the edges of my lips. The fabric of my tank top sticks to my back, and my thighs are slightly chafed where they rubbed as we walked. It's hard to believe I'm particularly pretty like this, but when he opens his eyes again, they're all honesty and reverence, almost daring me to argue.

Okay, maybe it is roman*tic*, but still, not romance. This is not a romance.

But, god, he's beautiful too. The way his hair shifts from red to brown depending on the light. The small, nearly vanished scars near his mouth, his eyebrow, his hairline—marks of childhood misadventures. Deep lines sunbursting from the corners of his eyes, evidence of how often he smiles. The faded freckles sprinkled over the very tops of his rounded cheeks. It's like his face is its own sky full of constellations and corresponding stories, and I think it would be nice to spend this warm summer evening committing each one to memory.

For the life of me, I can no longer come up with even one reason why I shouldn't.

My stomach dips and my heart pauses. My mind can't help but wonder if there's someone else out there he might wish he were with right now. Someone he's been waiting to kiss for years and years. But whoever they are, they aren't here.

I am. I'm the one he said it was nice to be with. The one he said looks beautiful.

The wanting is stronger than my doubt, than my anxiety—stronger than anything that could stop me—and I'm leaning in, in, in, once again.

Quentin meets me halfway, our fingers still entwined atop the railing, his free hand settling on the side of my neck while his thumb comes to rest sweetly on my chin. And then we're kissing. The hint of heat I felt at Sprangbur yesterday is nothing compared to the volcanic eruption happening inside me as my body registers the sensations of his mouth pressing against mine. His lips are soft, wide, perfect. He tastes of warmth and sweetness and a hint of rum.

How far will this go? How far do I want it to go? *All the way, all the way*, my body chants. My brain, however, is like, *Hold up a second*. Because I'm not supposed to want this. It's admittedly hard to remember why that matters right now, but I'm pretty sure it does. I pull back ever so slightly and let out a small hum. "I'm . . . a little bit drunk," I say.

"Same," he whispers as his lips find mine again. His stubble is deliciously abrasive against my bottom lip as I gently suck on his. It adds another dimension to the sensation that grounds me in the moment. My hips press into the railing, as if they hope maybe it will disappear and bring our lower halves flush if they're persistent enough.

"I'm sure we'll laugh about this in the morning," I add when his mouth slides to my jaw.

"It'll be hilarious," he mutters into the sensitive spot below my ear before taking the lobe between his teeth.

I spent so much of the summer of 2008 hoping Quentin would kiss me. I wanted that kiss between us more than I wanted anything up until that point in my life. But in this moment, as he unthreads our fingers so he can slide his into my hair, tongue swiping over the seam of my lips, requesting entrance, I am so immensely glad that it's happening now instead. That we saved this for when we truly understood how to do it. What it could lead to.

Like my hand beneath his shirt, making his breath catch when I brush over his nipple.

If I invited him inside right now, I know he'd come. Come in, I mean. And also, well . . .

"Nina," he says, pulling back, though his voice matches the dark, drugged appearance of his eyes.

I try to close the distance he creates, to lean in and put our mouths back together—where they belong—but he slides his hands from my hair and cups my face, gently keeping me at bay.

"Nina," he repeats. "Wait." And while his pupils are still blown out, his gaze is focused now. He's a man regaining control of himself. Putting a stop to this.

Well. Fuck.

I remove my hand from his shirt and take a few deep breaths, our eyes connected as we see each other through the comedown. As the lust clears, I decide I agree with Quentin that we need to stop before things go too far. We're still in the middle of hunting for the treasure. We don't need sex derailing our efforts. Like, best-case outcome if we followed this to its logical conclusion: We don't make any progress on finding a new lead because we've wasted our remaining weeks in bed. Worst-case: We wind up complicating this too much and obliterate the small amount of trust we've managed to rebuild. Most likely: I don't know, but probably some combination of the two. None of those outcomes include me winding up with my portion of the reward money or a way out of Catoctin.

Also, while neither of us are wasted, we aren't exactly sober either. The inside of my skull still feels a little too light and fluffy, like it's filled with cotton candy. That alone is a decent reason to hold off.

"Oh. Um, okay," I say. "Yeah."

"I don't want to stop," he says quickly. "I *really* don't want to stop. But we can't—I can't—"

I lay my hands over his and fake a smile as I take a step back, slipping out of his touch. "No, no. I get it. It's for the best."

"Nina, wait," he says again. The exasperation in his voice is corroborated by that vertical line between his eyebrows. But I don't want to wait. I don't want to linger in this feeling of awkward incompleteness. I don't want to stand here looking at him, wanting him, without any possibility of relief.

And I don't want to give him the chance to say it was a mistake.

"It's fine, Quentin. Thanks for the drinks and, um, stuff," I say, moving backward until my butt hits the storm door's handle. "Good night!"

His voice is quiet, no louder than a sigh, and I barely catch it as I go inside. "Good night."

24

AS SOON AS I'm inside the dark living room, door closed and bolted, I collapse backward onto the couch with my arms crossed like a vampire going to bed for the day. It feels like I need to gather everything close to my heart and hold it there for a minute. I've never been more grateful that my parents consistently go to bed at ten and sleep like the dead. If mom had been peeking through the blinds and caught sight of that? No way would she give me even a minute of silence to process what just happened.

And what *did* just happen, exactly? Oh god. I *kissed* Quentin. I kissed *Quentin*. And he kissed *me*. *We kissed*. And I liked it *so* much. Holy shit.

My body is alive with desire I haven't felt in years. Maybe ever! Sex is easy for me to push to the very back of my mind most of the time. It isn't usually a need so much as a want that surfaces on occasion. But Quentin's touch, his scent, his everything . . . it feels beyond need. It feels crucial. Something certain and solid when few other things are these days. Not that it matters, since he put a stop to it. But still. It's novel, to feel this vibrance inside me. I sit there with the sensations, enjoying the low hum of arousal that hasn't yet stopped vibrating just beneath my skin.

I am also exhausted, though. If I wind up falling asleep here and smear makeup on mom's hand-embroidered throw pillows, she will actually kill me. So I trudge up the stairs. I need to take care of this distracting, almost painful ache so I can get some sleep.

In my warm, stuffy room, I slip out of my clothes. I sigh in relief as my bra unhooks and my breasts fall into their rightful gravitational place. There are grooves in my skin around my rib cage where the band sat, and I soothe them with my fingertips as I make my way to the window and open it.

I do a quick, too-late inspection of the house across the alley. The blinds there are all drawn, so I'm assured no one can see me.

I didn't realize as we were walking back, our path illumi-nated by the lights along the trail and streets, how dark it is tonight. Sure enough, there's only a sliver of moon in the sky.

When we were young, I always assumed Quentin intended to be a constant in my life. That even during times when we might not be face-to-face, he would always be around—ever present regardless of if I could see him, like the moon he pre-tended to be. Maybe that's why it hurt so badly when he didn't stay in touch after moving away; I took his constancy for granted, like I do the fact that night always turns to day.

But if I don't make that mistake again, if I keep in mind that we'll both be going our separate ways soon and don't have any expectations . . .

No, that's not the reason it's a bad idea to have sex with Quentin. The reason is . . . it's that . . .

He didn't want to?

No, I don't think that's true. *I don't want to stop. I really don't want to stop.* That's what he said. There was a "but" afterward—"but we can't—I can't," sure. Whatever it was doesn't negate the fact he did want to continue. His huge, dark pupils, his heavy breathing, the way his lips caressed and pressed and sucked and soothed . . . I was not alone in what happened out there.

So, tomorrow, with our heads clearer and in control again, we will talk about it. I will find out what the "but" is. Maybe it's . . . *because I'm trying to get with this other person I used to like, so I shouldn't be hooking up with you. I'm not fully over my ex. I've decided to take a vow of celibacy. I don't actually think of you that way, this has all just been an elaborate prank. A mistake.*

Well, there's the nausea.

Unless . . . it could be something easily fixable? A temporary obstacle, like . . . *because I don't have any protection. We've had too much to drink. I want to take things slower. To know that we're both sure.*

My stomach calms as I remember how he looked when we first broke the kiss—hair tousled, his eyes darker, a shade of blue like a pool inside a grotto. Even if being with him in that way isn't in the cards, I can hold tight to that memory, pull it out when I need to remember I'm capable of this all-consuming feeling of want.

Because my body still wants, badly and thoroughly. Especially with the lightest breeze on my bare skin, and the thought that there may be a world in which I get to kiss Quentin again. Do more than kiss him.

Perhaps he's standing at his window now, much like I am . . .

"Hey, Moon?" I ask, my voice quiet. Like that first night I came back here, I'm not sure if I actually want him to answer or not.

And this time he doesn't.

But it doesn't keep my tipsy brain from imagining him there anyway. Not as the Moon, but as Quentin. Imagining him giving me instructions on how to touch myself. *Run your fingers over your nipples*, he might say. My hands move before I can process that thought, and I sweep them over the tips of my breasts. Then, deep and almost confiding: *Slide a hand into your underwear, Nina, and make yourself come for me.* As soon as I make contact with my clitoris, I shiver. I haven't done this manually in so long, resorting instead to toys that will get me off as efficiently as possible on the rare occasions I feel turned on enough to bother at all, but the self-attention feels good. Luxurious. Sensual instead of clinical. My eyes close so I can better focus on the sensations—of the nerve endings coming alive and rejoicing, of the muggy nighttime air caressing me as if it wants me to feel good too. *You look so fucking beautiful.*

And I don't even have to imagine him saying that one, because he did. Quentin Bell told me I looked beautiful, and then we *kissed* and it was like nothing else I've ever experienced.

A screen door slams shut and my eyes spring open to see Quentin walking out into his backyard, a glass in his hand.

Eeep!!

I'm not sure if the startled noise is in my head or if it actually comes out of my mouth as I drop to the ground and cover my head for some reason, like I'm in the middle of an elementary school tornado drill.

"Neen? Was that you?" Quentin's question drifts up through the still-open window.

Okay. I must've actually made the noise. I don't think he saw me, though—at least not fully enough to process what I was doing. If I ignore him, he won't know that I was standing almost completely naked in front of an open window. Doing more than *standing*, really. But . . . This is fine. I can stay like this until he goes back inside. Or I can army crawl away, maybe.

Except, some daring part of me whispers, *what would happen if I just . . . stood back up.* My arousal raises its eyebrows and cocks its head in interest at the idea of how he might react.

I'm going to start with the worst case, because it does seem important: Quentin finds the situation extremely uncomfortable and asks me to please cover myself. Or, no, an even worse outcome would definitely be that he's not alone and I expose myself to him and like, Mr. Farina, whom he's invited over for a late-night chat. Most likely: It's less sexy and more awkward than I'm imagining, and we wind up having a perfunctory conversation about the weather or something, with me in nothing but my underwear, before saying good night again. Best-case outcome, though? I guess best-case would be that he's into it and I orgasm so intensely that I discover another dimension.

My therapist once told me that sometimes big rewards involve big risks, and while I'm sure this is not the particular circumstance to which she was referring, I am still just drunk enough to decide it can apply here.

I turn back toward the window and slowly rise up in front of it, cupping my breasts in my hands so that I'm not immediately inflicting them upon the unwilling or, god forbid, our elderly across-the-street neighbor. There's barely enough light to see Quentin lowering himself into an Adirondack chair, a whiskey tumbler in his hand. He glances up at me and freezes for a moment before dropping the rest of the way into his seat like the wind's been knocked out of him.

"Hi," I say. It's the complete opposite of the uninterested version I practiced in the mirror a few weeks ago. In fact, it's probably the most interested "hi" I've delivered in my whole life.

"Hello again." His voice is deep and rough like it was when he said my name earlier, before he completely came back to his senses.

There's a long silence. Quentin brings his glass to his lips and takes a sip from it, eyes never leaving mine.

"Nice night," I say conversationally, regret blooming in my chest. Guess it's called *most likely* for a reason.

"Seems to be getting nicer by the second," he answers with a small smile. He takes another long drink. Quentin stares into his glass for a moment, looks back up at me. Then he says with a casualness I can tell he doesn't feel, "If your hands get tired . . . Don't feel the need to keep them there on my account."

Oh my god. Are we veering toward best-case outcome? There's so much heat running through my bloodstream. At first I think it's embarrassment, and I am a little embarrassed. Which feels reasonable considering I am about to basically flash Quentin from my upstairs window. But it has more in common with the hot thrill I get whenever he touches me. It's as if I can feel him near me, against me, all the way up here. My anxiety is still working under its usual impression that everything is about to go horribly wrong, but my body's excited thrum is enough to drown it out, leaving only an easily ignored murmur.

"Turn on a light first," I order. "I want to see you too."

If I'm going to do this, I don't want the dark obscuring anything. I want to see every minute change in his expression. I want to look into his eyes and know they're on me. There's a vulnerability in this, and I need to know he's there too, as exposed as I am.

Silently, he moves his glass to the chair's wide armrest and stands. He makes his way toward his house, out of my sight for a moment as the light beside his back door flicks on, illuminating the small patio.

Quentin returns and stands with his arms outstretched. He changed into those gray sweatpants and a white T-shirt after getting home, and said sweatpants are undeniably already tented. His posture is somehow both playful and daring. An unspoken *Light enough for you now?* as he sits again, downs the rest of his drink in one go, sets the glass on the ground, and brings his hands to the armrests, waiting for something.

Waiting for me.

I take a deep breath, then slide my hands from my breasts. My nipples harden immediately against the night air even though it's still in the low eighties, and every part of me resonates with even stronger need. The only reassurance is that Quentin doesn't seem to be faring much better down there. His eyes are so hungry, it feels like they're trying to swallow me whole.

"Nina," he breathes. "What exactly were you doing before I came out here?"

"What do you think I was doing?" I respond, trying to imbue that with the sensuality it deserves, but I'm unsure if I succeed. I'm so out of my element here. Maybe even out of my right mind. But my body continues cheering me on. *Keep going, you're doing just fine!* "I was touching myself. Obviously."

His laugh hits my ears, a new one that I'm going to file under *Can't believe his luck.* "Obviously," he repeats. There's a long, charged silence. "Want me to go back inside and leave you to it? Or . . . ?"

"I wouldn't mind some company," I say. Who is this woman?

She's brazen and sexy. She's no version of myself I've ever met before. I like her a lot. "If that's . . . amenable to you," I add, not wanting to leave any room for doubt.

There's probably fifteen feet of height elevation between us, but thanks to the light I can see how that hungry look in his eyes shifts into something else as my words float down to him. I recognize what it is right away. It's possible I even know what he's about to say before he says it, but that doesn't lessen the impact as he quietly calls up, "Not only am I amenable, but I bet . . . that I'll finish first."

A laugh spills out of me at the absurdity of turning this into another one of our competitions (and one where the goal is to be fastest, no less). But at the same time the part of me that loves a challenge—especially a Quentin-issued one—comes roaring to life, joining the lust coursing through me and creating something new and even more enticing.

"Bet not," I say, my voice unintentionally breathy.

"I guess," he says, "we'll just have to see." The way his voice teeters between self-assured and nervous is so human and so sensual I am pretty sure I would come right now if my fingers were still in the proper location.

"I guess so."

Quentin's resulting smile is somewhere between amused and wolfish. It suits him much better than the practiced charming one, in my opinion. Much more dangerous too, because this is a smile that would probably convince me to do anything he asked.

We make eye contact for a second before either of us moves, and the challenge momentarily eases from his stare—*Are we really doing this? Are you sure?* it seems to ask. I recognize it, because it's the same look he gave me when we agreed to trespass onto Fountain's estate seventeen years ago.

But no, I don't want to think about that. About things that happened before. Only now. Only *right* now. This very instant. Not yesterday, not earlier tonight, not even tomorrow.

I am fully committed to seeing this through as far as it will go. I feel like exactly the version of myself I'm supposed to be in this moment in time—the one who can smile down at Quentin in response, lips tilted upward in flirty confirmation. Someone who knows what and who she wants and doesn't hesitate when it's in reach. I slip my fingers back beneath the waistband of my underwear and find the same place that made me moan before. Except now it feels even better, because I don't need to imagine what it would be like to do this with Quentin listening or watching from next door. Because he is. He's watching with one hand in his sweatpants, stroking slowly, as if he has all the time in the world.

And maybe he does. Maybe he truly doesn't care about winning this little challenge. I mean, I'm not sure I do. Which is good, because when I bring my other fingers to my left nipple to pinch it, then run my thumb over it in circles, mimicking what my other hand is doing lower, it gets me closer but it also seems to bring him there with me. His pace increases in response, his eyes wide and dark, and he lets out a muffled sound that might be "Fuck."

Then Quentin takes the hem of his T-shirt in his fist and raises it up his stomach, giving me a view of that trail of hair that's been taunting me for days. My entire focus zooms in on his movements, every thought turning to anticipation. How much seeing Quentin lose himself to pleasure will increase mine. It's going to happen soon, I can tell. Even from this distance, I can see his chest rising and falling more quickly, his arm pumping faster, his eyes still glued to me.

"Quen—Quentin—" His name tumbles from my lips un-
bidden as *oh*, oh god, I'm—

Before my eyes shut involuntarily as every single nerve in my
body lights up simultaneously, I catch him jerk forward as he
lifts the T-shirt higher. I can no longer see him, but I hear him
repeat, "Fuck," and then groan, ending in a long, stunned sigh at
the same moment I'm finally able to take a deep breath myself.

Well.

I suppose that will have to count as a draw.

25

'M SURPRISED TO find my head doesn't split right in half when the alarm I accidentally set goes off at nine-thirty Sunday morning. That's what having three drinks will do to you in your thirties, I guess. I wonder if Quentin is equally miserable.

Quentin.

Oh shit. Last night.

I cannot believe Quentin and I . . . What exactly do you even call what we did? The most technical description, I guess, would be that we mutually masturbated from a distance. At a distance?

No English class ever prepared me for this particular grammatical conundrum.

After I get dressed and ready for the day and brush the furry feeling from my tongue—which goes a long way toward making me feel more human—I climb back into bed and message Sabrina: Quentin and I hooked up last night.

Then I add, Sort of. The exact circumstances are a bit unconventional.

Her response comes a few minutes later: ????

My phone buzzes in my palm before I can reply, an incoming video call on the screen. I answer and Sabrina's flushed, cherubic face appears. She's walking on the treadmill at her university's gym.

"Hey, I figured this would be—"

"First we were mouth-blocked by Smash Mouth and then I was standing naked in front of the window because I was drunk and it felt nice! And then he—"

"Wow. Hold please." She pops in her earbuds. "Now that your strange sexcapades will not be broadcast to the entire Queen's University gym, you can proceed."

I flop down on my bed. "You're the one who called me! You should've been prepared."

"How was I supposed to know you were going to launch right into 'we were mouth-blocked by Smash Mouth and then I was standing naked in front of the window'?" she counters, her voice lowering to a whisper as she quotes me. "And what does that all even *mean*, Nina? Take a very deep breath and start over."

In through my nose. One-two-three-four. Out through my mouth. One-two-three-four-five-six. The breath exercise is like a partial system reboot, the energy coursing through me much less frantic. "Okay. So."

I fill her in on everything that happened yesterday between Quentin and me. The slow dance to S Club 7—"Oh man, I freaking loved their show," Sabrina interrupts, then sings the chorus of the *S Club 7 in Miami* theme until I ask her if we can get back to my story, please—and the hand-holding on our walk home. The kissing on the porch. How, at first, I thought things wouldn't progress any further, but then . . .

"Oh. Wow. That's . . . hot? Weird? I'm not actually sure." Sabrina pushes a button and the treadmill slows until it comes to a stop. "David Bowie would approve, at least." She raises her eyebrows as she glances over my shoulder at the poster on the wall. "What did Quentin say after? What did *you* say?" she asks.

"Neither of us said anything."

"You just stared at each other? Creepy."

"No, we didn't stare. Not for more than a second or two anyway. I didn't really know what to say or do, though, so I waved, and then I closed the window and went to shower."

"You *waved*?"

I groan as I cover as much of my face as I can with one hand. "I panicked, okay?"

"And he hasn't texted you or anything?"

I check my phone again to be certain I didn't miss it in a half-asleep state at some point overnight, but my last message from him is the picture of Faustine. "Nope."

She grimaces.

"That look is not helpful," I admonish.

"It's all I've got," she says with a regretful shrug. "This is an unusual situation. One I am grateful I am not in myself."

"Thanks. Very reassuring as always."

She sighs. "I guess the way to proceed," she says slowly, "is to ask yourself: What do I want to happen next?"

"I don't know."

"You *do* know," she counters. "You just don't want to admit it."

"Okay, fine. I want to have sex with him. Badly. But it's a horrible idea."

"Why?"

"Because there's a lot of history between us, and this whole treasure hunt, and someone from high school he might still like, and . . . it's just complicated."

"There's no way to have a chat, try to uncomplicate some of it?"

"I mean, probably." That was basically my plan last night, wasn't it? Before the whole window situation escalated.

"So do that," she urges. "Remember, the world is your oyster. You're unconstrained. You can be anyone you want."

"Sexy Nina," I whisper.

Sabrina nods. "Exactly! Sexy Nina. And if Sexy Nina wants her hot neighbor to pound her into the mattress—"

"All right, I'm done. Goodbye." I hover my finger over the button to end the call.

Sabrina laughs. "Wait. Don't hang up! I'm sorry."

"No, you're not," I say, unable to keep the fondness from my voice.

"I'm not," she agrees as she sits on the edge of a weight bench, a towel flung around her shoulders. "I just want you to be happy, Neen. Would hot animal sex with Quentin make you happy?"

"I don't think you should be allowed to use words anymore." Nomenclature aside, I'm sure sleeping with Quentin would indeed make me happy, in the immediate moment. But I'm not convinced being together that way wouldn't unlatch my emotional storage cupboard, sending all sorts of other feelings tumbling out too. Mushy feelings, and angry, wounded feelings. Lots of things to trip and fall on when I eventually go to make my escape. "I'm worried I'll get hurt again," I say quietly.

Sabrina gives me a look that's tinged with both affection and pity. "I know, love. But when was the last time you wanted something, *anything*, this badly?"

I'm about to cite the long-term contract at Malbyrne, or some fellowship or award or whatever. Except it hits me that this isn't the same feeling at all. Those were things I wanted because I was supposed to want them. Because they were the next rung on the ladder I was climbing, driven by some mixture of my own and Cole's expectations for me (it's hard to tell where one stopped and the other began, looking back).

I want Quentin infinitely more than I ever wanted those things, and for literally no good reason except that I do. He won't help me get ahead in anything. In fact, having sex with him is bound to be a hugely unnecessary distraction from my efforts to get back on my feet. It feels a lot like seeing a bottle labeled HOTTEST HOT SAUCE THAT EVER EXISTED and having a soul-deep desire to chug the whole thing just to find out if I can.

The doorbell rings, and I realize that I haven't heard my mom clanging and clomping about downstairs since I woke up. She must be out and about this morning, and Dad is undoubtedly already combing yard sales for cool stuff to repair and re-sell, as is his usual weekend routine.

"Gotta run! But thanks for the pep talk. Love to my Breen," I say hastily, already charging down the stairs.

"Love to my Neen. Follow your heart and keep me updated!" She blows me a quick kiss before ending the call.

When I open the door, I'm out of breath and a bit worse for wear (the brisk movement was a bad idea; my head feels stabby again). Which is why my voice sounds breathier than I intend when I say, "Quentin."

"Ho there, howdy, and good morning," he says with a small smile.

I stand there stupidly, staring for way too long and saying nothing. It's just that, framed by the doorway, wearing a light pink button-down, his hair haloed with amber as the sun manages to catch a few strands despite the overhang of the porch, he reminds me of a Mucha painting. An also slightly hungover Mucha painting, judging by the sunglasses and hint of tension in his jaw. But it's still a sight to see.

He clears his throat and tries again, sounding less certain now. "Good . . . morning?"

"Sorry," I say. "I don't think my parents are home."

"That's . . . fine? I'm not here for them. I'm here for you."

"Oh. What's that?" I ask, gesturing to the cardboard drink carrier he's holding, with its two iced coffees and the white paper bag stamped with Best That You Can Brew's logo of a large moon with a coffee cup resting on its crescent, the New York City skyline smaller beneath it.

"Breakfast."

I'm still unsure how to act, what to say, how to *stand*. I shift on my feet.

"You know," Quentin continues, "the thing after you wake up, before lunch. I figured we could have it together this morning. Unless you already ate?"

I shake my head as I keep staring down at what he's holding, baffled by his presence. Everything that happened last night and now . . . he's here. With breakfast. I peek into the bag and spot two apple fritters.

"So, can I come in or . . . ?"

The question flips a switch, turning me into a fully functioning social being again. "Oh. Right. Yeah, sure."

He takes off his sunglasses and hooks them onto the pocket of his shirt as he follows me inside. I put the bag down on the coffee table and take a seat at the other end of the couch, not wanting to be too close.

"I thought these were impossible to get unless you got there right when they open," I say.

"Usually, yes. But Hanako gave me the heads-up last night that if you use the online ordering and choose a later pickup, they'll put them aside for you."

"Smart."

"She said you wanted to try them. So." He smiles again. It's a smile that makes him look a little unsure of himself. The exact opposite of that practiced one. My heart feels covered in condensation—either that or it's actively melting. Quentin takes his own apple fritter from the bag and sets it on a napkin atop the coffee table. Then he grabs two macramé coasters—that Mom made in a class, of course—and places our drinks on them.

Bon Jovi's stupid handsome face staring off into the distance pops into my mind. *Do it in pencil*, he taunts. So much of my life is currently up in the air. The things I have control over have dwindled to almost nothing. This could be my chance to have a say in something again. To prove to Bon Jovi that there's this one aspect of my journey—a physical relationship with Quentin that operates in a neat, mature fashion—that I *can* map out in pen, goddammit.

Sabrina is right. The world *is* my oyster, and now I just need to figure out how to go about eating it.

The silence between us as we enjoy our apple fritters isn't awkward so much as anticipatory. Like we both know that after we're finished, we're going to need to figure out how to handle what happened. I know what I want, and I think I'm ready to go after it. But what does *Quentin* want? Does he want anything at all? It might be my imagination, but it seems like we're both taking smaller bites, chewing slightly more slowly than usual, trying to put off the conversation.

Which is why I watch, rapt, as he balls up his napkin, sprinkled with flakes of sticky glaze, and tucks it into the empty bag. He does it slowly, meticulously, with reverence—as if he's performing some sort of sacred ceremony.

He stares straight ahead for a long moment.

"Thanks for bringing breakfast," I say, sucking sugar off my fingertip.

"I have never come as hard as I did watching you touch yourself." He drops this absolute bombshell of a non sequitur, then turns his head to look at me. It seems like he's waiting for a response, except by the time my lips part (not that I have any idea what to say), he's already continued, "But it's okay if that's all that ever happens between us."

"These signals seem . . . mixed," I say slowly.

Quentin hangs his head. "What I am trying to say is, I enjoyed last night. Very much. It was the most erotic moment of my life, to be honest, and I will treasure the memory. I don't know if you intended—"

"I did. I did intend. I would like . . . again," I interrupt. "More." Okay, so those were not even real sentences, but I do still seem to get my point across because Quentin inhales deeply and rubs the back of his neck, as if hoping to cover the flush sweeping up it. "But you . . . You did say last night on the porch that you couldn't. And it sounds like you're still unsure now . . ." This feels suddenly too vulnerable. It leaves too wide a space for something that could devastate me. So I tease, "It's because you're afraid you'll lose the next round, isn't it?"

He lets out a low chuckle that gets added to yet another new subfolder—*Hot as Hell*. "Oh, believe me, Nina. If we aimed for first again, I would be victorious in like, three seconds. It took every ounce of willpower I had to last as long as I did."

And the memory of exactly how long it took both of us

reminds me that there is a part of me that was bold enough to stand in front of that window mostly naked. A sensual, less anxiety-driven part. Someone I enjoyed being. Someone I'm not sure exists when not powered by the electricity between us. "Then if we were to give it another go, maybe instead it should be who can come last?"

He visibly swallows. "Maybe." Quentin's face has gone a delightful shade of pink to match his neck. He turns his head to look at me, smiles, and sighs before bowing it again. And I can tell there's still hesitation there. Something beyond being slightly flustered or caught without protection.

I rush to reassure him. "Listen. All joking aside, I know what I intended, but maybe you . . . I don't want to pressure you. If you don't want to—"

"I do. I want . . . so much. I'm just . . . I need to . . ." He lets out a frustrated-sounding exhale, as if the rest of his words are being held up somewhere along the route from brain to mouth and he isn't sure how to get them unstuck. His eyes focus downward and I follow them to my hand, where the engagement ring was the other day.

"Oh." I lean back, no longer intruding into his personal space. "Right. Charlene. I'm sorry. I sometimes forget that you guys were like, living together and everything. Cole was so far away, and we didn't even . . . Anyway, I understand. It's too soon. I'm sure you're still dealing with that, with your feelings for her."

"No," he says firmly. "It's not about Charlene. At all. There aren't any feelings left to deal with there, I promise."

I hesitate. "About me, then? About what I did when we were kids?"

"About what *I* did," he says.

I'm surprised that he's taking any of the blame. Up until now I assumed he thought of his harsh words and silence as justified punishment for my betrayal, not their own separate harm done. "Well," I say, but don't know where else to take that thought.

"Nina, I want you. I do. But I'm really trying not to make any more mistakes."

"Mistakes. Right." And there it is, the devastating thing I was expecting earlier. I force a smile and a lighthearted laugh, even though the pronouncement feels like a dagger to the chest. "Which is what it would be if we had sex. A mistake."

"That isn't what I meant." He catches my hand, as if sensing my instinct to move away from him.

"What did you mean, then?" I ask.

"It's only . . . I promised myself I wasn't going to fuck this all up again. That this time we would end the summer with the treasure in hand and our friendship intact. And if we continue down the path we started down last night, I'm not sure I'll be able to deliver on either of those." He absently strokes his fingers over mine. "I am trying to do better by you than I did before. But kissing you, watching you last night . . . It's very hard to remember what doing better looks like when all I can think of is, well, doing *you*."

"We could just fuck without it meaning anything," I suggest, making it sound bright enough that I can play it off as a joke if needed.

He pauses for a moment, then says, "No, I don't think I could. I think it would have to mean something to me." The hand not holding mine tucks a curl behind my ear. "*You* have always meant something to me, Nina."

I swallow hard against the sentiment. It's tempting to lean into it, to explore what he means by that. But apparently there are still tiny pieces of the person I was back when we were young, resting like shrapnel somewhere inside of me, better left alone than pulled out. And those all twinge in harmony, alerting me to their presence. I want to scream, to cry, *If I've always meant something to you, how could you disappear from my life so completely?*

"I see," I say instead.

"I hope you do," he says quietly, as his fingers drift from my ear to my chin, nudging it upward to make me look him in the eyes. "I don't want to lose you again." Then he leans in and plants a soft, sweet kiss on my cheek.

Which is the moment my mom bursts through the front door. "Sweetie, are you—Oh!" she exclaims as she takes in the scene before her: Quentin and me on our living room couch, springing apart as if we've been caught in flagrante delicto. She literally takes a step backward, back out onto the porch, and closes the door in her own face. It looks almost like someone pressed rewind on the scene, in real life.

Quentin and I remain frozen for a second or two, staring at each other. We're wearing matching blushes, his a shade deeper due to his paler skin. The fact that we *weren't* doing anything almost makes it more mortifying than if she'd actually caught us with our clothes off.

My phone vibrates on the coffee table. I reach for it and find a text from Mom: I wasn't there. I didn't see anything. Please proceed.

I respond, Nothing was even happening. Come back in.

"Oh geez," Quentin says in a voice that's so comically alarmed yet understated it sends me into a fit of laughter. He quickly joins in. "Do you think she'll believe that it wasn't what it looked like?"

I cover my face with my hands. "Even if she does, I doubt it will stop her from relaying an exaggerated version to every person she meets for the rest of time. Or until something juicier comes along." Quentin frowns, and I lean over and rest my head on his shoulder. "Thank you for breakfast. And for last night. It was . . . very good for me too. But I don't want to lose you either."

He lets out a long sigh that sounds like relief.

"Maybe after we find the treasure . . ." I start. And I say it with the certainty that it does exist somewhere out there. Because I can't believe otherwise anymore. The idea that we're holding off on exploring our connection for something that might not even be real is not one I'm willing to entertain. I simply refuse.

"Maybe after we find the treasure," he repeats in agreement. "If you still want."

I lift my head and turn toward him, laughing. "Why if *I* still want? Why is it only up to me?"

He looks me dead in the eye, pupils as dark as they were last night on the porch. "It will be up to you because I can tell you now, I already know I am going to want to, Nina. Do not mistake my circumspection for lack of interest. If you knew how many times I've imagined bending you over this couch in just the last five minutes—"

"Oh. Goodness." Our heads turn toward the voice by the door. Dammit, Mom. Of course she chose that exact moment to come back into the house. I bury my face in my hands again and groan.

Quentin grabs the bag from our apple fritters and holds it strategically in front of him as he stands. I have never seen him turn quite this red before; a strawberry held up to his face would blend right in. "Good morning, Miss Patti. I was, uh, just heading out. Have a great day!"

My mom and I both watch as Quentin escapes out the front door. Then she turns her attention toward me, eyebrows raised in question.

I glance at my phone without registering what's on the screen and say, "Oh wow, that time already? I have an important phone call with my . . . insurance agent. Gotta go!" Before she can question it, I hurry upstairs to my bedroom, where I guess I will now have to hide for the rest of my life.

26

OWARD, I TEXT Quentin once I'm safely ensconced in my bedroom with the door locked.

Yep, he replies. Then: Library again tomorrow?

Sure, I send, and attempt to swallow down the guilt and anxiety that come rising up in my throat. Should I tell him I was there alone the other day? My finger hovers over my phone, ready to type a message. It's just . . . I didn't find anything (well, except an informal job offer and a sudden hyper-awareness of my own mortality). So why bother telling him? I'll keep on keeping it to myself. Maybe that makes me a coward too.

And if that doesn't, I'm sure the fact that I continue avoiding my mother for approximately six and a half hours does. I would go on for longer, except that's when the spicy, tomato-y scent of crab soup and the sweet, buttery one of blackberry cobbler reach beneath my door. My stomach growls in excitement. I haven't eaten since the apple fritter this morning, and my lingering embarrassment turns out to be little defense against the siren call of dinner.

Thankfully—and surprisingly—Mom says absolutely nothing about Quentin when I make my way down the stairs. She simply looks up from where she's sitting on the couch and says, "Soup's ready if you're hungry."

"Thanks. It smells great." It's weird to have her acting like she doesn't want to ask me a million questions. I thought this would be the most interesting thing that happened to her all week, and she's treating it like it's as ho-hum an occurrence as Mr. Farina sitting on his porch. "Do you want me to make you a bowl too?" I ask. Maybe she's just waiting until I'm comfortable and full of crab and vegetables to spring it on me.

She shakes her head as she bends to tie her sneaker. "I'll eat when I get home. I'm off to pickleball with Theresa. She cheats horribly, but it's good exercise."

"Ah. Okay. Well, have fun."

Mom stands up, grabs her bag, gives me a noisy kiss on the forehead, and heads out.

The next few days are filled with dead ends on the research front. We go back to the library to comb through everything yet again. I don't tell Quentin I've already done that on my own, and Mrs. MacDonald thankfully doesn't make any comments that give me away.

When that bears no fruit, we take another two trips to Sprangbur, just to walk through the gardens with our eyes out for anything interesting. There isn't much point to it when we have no new information to go off, but it does feel a lot like the old days, in the very best way. Just Quentin and me, hanging out, joking and teasing, challenging each other to inconsequential competitions, chatting among the plants and strange structures. I can't pretend I'm not overjoyed to have this friendship returned to me when I once believed it was lost for good.

Every once in a while, we accidentally brush hands as we walk and my entire body lights up like an arcade game. But hitting a jackpot doesn't mean much when the machine isn't loaded with tickets, so I've gotten pretty good at ignoring the bells and whistles going off inside me. And I guess Quentin has too, because other than a few wistful smiles when I'm pretty sure we're both thinking the same thing, he shows no sign of changing his mind about holding off.

Friday morning as I'm getting ready to meet him outside to go back to the library yet again, he texts me: Sorry for the late notice but can't meet up today. Found a great deal on some specialty tile for the kitchen backsplash and have to go pick it up in Baltimore.

Oh, okay, I respond.

My phone vibrates again with the message: You can come along if you want?

It's tempting. In fact, even though when I first got here I fussed about hanging out with Quentin to hunt for the treasure, I can't deny the simple fact that being around him has always been better than not. That was true when we were kids, and it's true now. Even when we were apart, I wanted more than anything for him to reach out and make things right. Because I miss him when we aren't together. Even when it's only for a day.

That's . . . less than ideal, though, isn't it? To be this attached to someone who has let me down before.

So I text back, Thanks, but I should probably apply to more jobs. Have fun!

I've spent too much time with him lately, being the undefined, simplified version of myself he's always drawn out. This is a good reminder that I need to keep trying to figure out who I'm going to become now, which Nina will emerge like a phoenix from the ashes of my old life.

But first I need lunch.

I try Best That You Can Brew but find it absolutely packed. There isn't a free seat in the whole place. I pull up the map on my phone to review my other options for food in walking distance, because even after a few weeks of being back here, I'm not fully aware of what is and isn't around anymore. Instead of looking at the places that pop up when I select *Restaurants*, though, my eyes drift toward the green space labeled HISTORIC SPRANGBUR CASTLE & GARDENS.

Maybe after we find the treasure . . . The memory of Quentin's voice in that moment makes warmth spread low in my belly.

After echoes tauntingly in my brain. Ugh. Too much of my life is on hold until we find this damn treasure. The one that better actually exist or I might explode in frustration—the sexual kind and also the regular kind that comes with having wasted time engaging in a futile task.

I zoom in on Sprangbur until the strange, abstract outline of Fountain's mansion appears. Would it really be so bad if . . .

Yes.

Yes, Nina. That would be bad. That would literally be what screwed up everything last time. This is a lesson that was already learned.

My feet have already carried me in the direction of Riverside Park, though, and I still need to eat. I guess I could try the burger place next to Flow State . . . if it didn't turn out to be closed for emergency repairs to the kitchen. The fancy Italian restaurant isn't open till five, and there's no sign of the taco truck that was parked outside Flow State last time we were here either.

I am now hot and hungry, and my laptop bag keeps twisting and banging against my thigh with every step. I'm seconds away from admitting defeat when I remember that Hanako's bar did have a small food menu.

Okay. I didn't plan to go to Flow State today, but there's no reason not to. It isn't weird that Quentin and Hanako kissed when they were fifteen and Quentin and I kissed last weekend. No reason to make it weird either, especially when she's my last hope for immediate nourishment.

The bar is nearly empty, which makes sense, I guess, considering it's 11:30 in the morning on a Friday—not exactly when most people are going out for cocktails. It makes it extremely easy for Kell to spot me as soon as I walk in. "Hey! Nina, right?" they say in greeting. "Good to see you again."

We were never actually introduced, so I'm not sure how Hanako's partner recognizes me on sight.

"Um, hello," I say, propping myself on a barstool.

"Hanako's in the office. I'll go get her."

"Oh, no, it's—" But before I can say it's not necessary to disturb her, Kell has disappeared through a doorway beside the bar.

"Nina!" Hanako greets me with the same enthusiasm she showed when we came in last Saturday. "I didn't know you were coming by today."

"Me neither, actually. But I was in the area and starving, and the burger place next door is closed, but I remembered you had some small plates . . ."

"Of course! Let me get you today's menu." She slides me a paper with their specials.

"The hummus plate sounds great," I say.

"Anything to drink?" she asks.

It's tempting to see if she still has the stuff to make one of those Hi-C concoctions, but that feels like a poor choice, especially before noon. "Just water," I say.

A few minutes later, she slides a highball glass in front of me. It has a paper umbrella sticking out of it. "Just because it's water doesn't mean it can't be fun," she explains with a smile.

Kell comes out of the kitchen with a plate full of vegetables and pita chips surrounding a ramekin of hummus.

"Do you want me to open a tab, or just pay when I'm done?" I ask Hanako.

She waves her hand dismissively. "Oh please. It's on the house."

"You don't have to do that," I say. "You really should let me pay for stuff."

"Hey," she says in faux offense. "It's my business. I'll run it how I want." Then she leans over the bar, folding her arms, a grin spreading across her face. "But something that is absolutely *not* my business that I'm going to ask about anyway is what's up with you and Quentin, hm?"

I pretend to be absolutely fascinated by the carrot stick in my hand. "Oh. Um. Nothing much."

"Really?"

"Really," I say.

Hanako gives me a look that says she isn't going to pry, but doesn't believe me for a second.

"Okay, okay. Fine. We kissed. The night of the fundraiser here. And there was some . . . other stuff that happened. But we talked about it and decided that we should hold off on anything more than friendship for now." It's always been an unspoken rule that we don't tell anyone we're treasure hunting, and I can't mention that our lives are currently in flux because I didn't tell Hanako that I lost my job. So I settle on, "We both recently got out of long-term relationships and are still getting to know each other again." Which is absolutely the truth, even though that's far, far down on the list of reasons we're not hooking up.

"Very practical," she says, reaching for another glass and filling it with Sprite for herself. "I'm glad he finally did it, though."

"Did what?"

"Kissed you," she says with a small laugh that seems like a kind substitute for *duh*. "He's been wanting to for-freaking-ever, you know."

Wait. It *was* me? *I* was his crush? Then why didn't he . . . and then how come he . . . "But . . ." I'm cut off by a loud clang, something shattering, and raised voices coming from somewhere in the back room.

"Yikes," Hanako says. "That sounded bad. I better go check it out."

She leaves me alone with the startling realization that I was right about being wrong about my relationship with Quentin when we were younger—just not in the way I thought.

27

'D PLANNED TO apply to more jobs while I was out (hence bringing my laptop), but my brain has felt like the mint I watched Kell muddle for another customer's cantaloupe mojito since Hanako inadvertently revealed that I was the person Quentin had a crush on in high school. All I can think about is him, and me, and every moment we've ever shared—then and now—trying to reanalyze each one to see if there were signs I missed. And there are, I'm sure, but it's hard to keep it all straight because I keep getting stuck, circling images and sound bites of Quentin from the past few weeks like a little kid going through a toy catalog before Christmas. I want that version, and that version, and that version. The one dressed for an interview, his hair perfect. The one in gray sweatpants, jaw unshaven, with dark crescents under his eyes. The one from Saturday night, staring up at me with a look of awe and focus as he took his cock in hand . . .

Living in my body right now is torture. I hate being on edge like this, needing something that only someone else—only

Quentin—can give me. Can, but won't. Not until we find the treasure.

Once again part of me whispers that I could go to Sprangbur right now, on my own. It's just down the street, probably even visible from the patio if I go outside and squint. I can't tell if the nausea that accompanies the thought is the exciting sort of anxiety or the ominous kind.

Okay, best-case outcome: I go and I somehow find the treasure. Quentin's excitement is enough to overpower any negative feelings he might have about me going rogue again. We have amazing sex to celebrate, and then the Conservancy tells us there was actually a misprint in the article about the reward all those years ago, and instead of ten thousand dollars it was for one million dollars, which they will happily honor because of that law Quentin mentioned. I buy a great condo with cash and become a freelance historian like that girl who starred in *Penelope to the Past* I met at the American Historical Association conference last year. Worst-case: I go, find nothing, someone calls the police again, Quentin comes to bail me out and represent me in court but is so angry with me that he does a bad job and then I wind up in jail forever because the judge, who takes a liking to Quentin, decides the usual trespassing punishment is too lenient for a repeat offender like me. Most likely: I go to Sprangbur alone, find nothing, and simply keep it to myself, with Quentin none the wiser, just like when I went to the library. And, I mean, that does seem the most realistic of the outcomes . . .

No. No, no, no. There's no denying it's the wrong thing to do. If I find it solo, I see now that it's taking something away from him. Something he's wanted for a long time. Something he's wanted us to do *together*.

But finding a clue that might help us know where to search next . . . That would be all right. A small way I can help write our future in pen. Suck it, Bon Jovi.

While the special collections room has a great deal of Fountain's original files, it's not the only place that has primary sources related to his life. Nowadays, there are a few digitized materials through the National Archives, including the oral history interview he did with Albert Aaron in 1937. I pull it up on the website, looking around as it loads, making sure none of the patrons who have come into the bar are watching, as if they would even know or care. There are twenty pages of transcripts, and hopefully by the time I'm finished rereading them something will either have clicked or the worst of my overwhelming urge to make bad decisions (like going to Sprangbur on my own right now and digging a massive hole or something) will have at least passed.

Fountain sure does mention his secretary, Louisa Worman, often. Quentin and I never did do much research on her as a person, which now strikes me as a massive oversight. And I'm not just saying that as someone who's spent the last four years incessantly thinking and teaching about all the ways women are often forgotten in the archive. I open a new window to search her name and find it mostly paired with Fountain's or his company's—in the newspaper article about his surprising will, as the originator of the meeting minutes cited as a primary source in an article about the beverage industry. Never married, no direct descendants. It's depressing, seeing how little of a mark she left on the world. Too busy helping Fountain play around in his, I suppose.

There are so many casual mentions of how Louisa—Lou, as he called her—took care of him and his young niece, as if it were simply another part of her job as Fountain's secretary and not something very far outside her scope of work. So much on her shoulders, and no doubt assumed of her because she was a woman. A tiny, featherlight fleck of anger floats up inside me, burning out as it hits my heart. This poor lady.

Then again, she did choose to continue working for Fountain for several decades. Perhaps it wasn't all bad. I think back to the informational tours we took of Sprangbur Castle, the stories Sharon and Gladys shared. Perhaps the salary made it worth it. However much it was, though, I bet it wasn't enough recompense for everything she did for and gave to this man until she left around the time of this interview.

I continue in the transcripts, reading more about Edlo—the magical land Fountain liked to pretend he ruled over as monarch. From what I can tell, it was a game that he played with Isolde that kept growing and growing until it became something he continued enjoying on his own. He must have, since Isolde was in her twenties and married by the time Albert Aaron arrived at Sprangbur.

Isolde. We looked her up when we first started researching Fountain and learned she died in 2002. We never bothered to investigate further. I do so now and quickly discover that, though she married twice, she outlived both husbands and had no surviving children. One of the search results brings me to a page for a hospital to which she apparently left her entire fortune—a charitable streak she must've inherited from her uncle.

I turn my attention back to the transcripts and find a line that I suppose we must have read back in 2008 but didn't strike me as particularly interesting then: *Old as I am, Issy grown, I find myself visiting Edlo rather less frequently than before. Besides, I know the way by heart. So perhaps I should hand it over to you and your boy, so that he may grow up knowing what it is to float above the trees in a perfect, iridescent bubble.* Hand Edlo over to Albert Aaron? How does one hand over a place? Especially a make-believe one?

And Albert Aaron—there's someone else we never bothered looking into very deeply. Which I don't kick myself nearly as much over, since his only known interactions with Fountain happened over the course of these pages. They didn't even particularly seem to get along (another reason why Fountain's insistence on transferring Edlo to Aaron and his son sticks out to me upon this reread). Fifteen-year-old Nina, whose research skills came primarily from tightly structured, secondary source–heavy school assignments, didn't think much about the man hired by the Works Progress Administration to travel from Baltimore to Catoctin to record what Fountain had to say. But thirty-two-year-old Nina, with two graduate degrees in this stuff, has a gigantic, intensely glowing lightbulb over her head.

Because depending on what became of Albert Aaron after he worked for the WPA, he might have papers of his own. Either in a collection somewhere official, or even passed down to his relatives. It's a long shot, but it's *a* shot. And it's definitely more than we had a few hours ago.

Another search doesn't turn up any official archives that hold anything of Aaron's beyond interview transcripts and a novella he wrote that's now in the public domain. But the library's database page allows me access to a genealogy site that helps me determine that, though Albert died in 1988, his son Eugene is apparently still alive and, according to the 2020 census, lives in Richmond, Virginia. I continue down the family line and find several adult grandchildren, including a granddaughter named

Emily who is a children's book author and illustrator. And she has a website with a contact form.

My heart thuds with a combination of eagerness that this will result in something big and worry that it will be yet another dead end. Either way, I need to tell Quentin.

There's a tiny part of me, the same one that desperately wanted to go to Sprangbur an hour ago, that whispers, *What if you don't? Not yet, at least. What if you just . . . contact the grand-daughter and scope out how worthwhile it is ahead of time?*

But I recognize the voice as the same one that convinced me to keep secrets from him before. The one that masquerades as something more innocuous than it is. Behind the competitiveness that always drew me to accept Quentin's challenges, there was a desperate need for approval. His approval. For him to tell me I did a good job.

At what cost? It was high enough last time. I suspect it's even higher now that the knowledge of how he kisses is one of the few good things I have going for me. As close as we were as children, it wasn't anything like this. It wasn't this feeling that we're connected by something more than the history between us. There was only a vague notion of what *more* would even mean then, and now I know it's what I feel in every fiber of my being whenever his fingertips brush against my skin.

I can't keep this from him. Can't risk ruining whatever comes next for us before it even has a chance to start.

"Can I grab you anything else?" Kell asks as they pass me on their way back from delivering drinks to a table nearby.

"No, thanks. I actually . . . I have to go. Right now." I hastily grab my things, throw a ten-dollar bill on the bar, and call out, "Bye! Thanks! Uh, bye!" as I rush out the door.

28

THANK GOD, QUENTIN'S car is parked out front when I arrive back on West Dill Street. I ring his doorbell, then ring it two more times.

"I'm coming, I'm coming," I hear him call through the door. It swings open and his eyebrows come together. "Nina?" he says. "What . . . Are you okay? Did you . . . Have you been running?"

I gasp for air and hold up a finger. I didn't run so much as speed walk all the way here, but running sounds more impressive, so I nod. "I found something," I say. "Something that might lead us to the treasure. I don't know yet for sure, because I wanted to wait to talk it through with you before I did anything, but I really think this could be it, Quentin."

"When?" he asks.

"When what?"

"When did you figure this out?"

"Just now. Or, like, fifteen minutes ago." My words slow as I realize I have made an error. That, in my excitement, I forgot the part where he might actually be super mad at me for researching without him.

But his face isn't angry. It's just very . . . serious. "You figured it out, and you immediately came to tell me?"

I nod. "I mean, I was at Hanako's bar, and I had to get back here. But yes, as immediately as possible."

We look at each other, our gazes acknowledging the significance of the decision I made to include him this time. The fact that I didn't have to, yet I did.

"Don't look so surprised," I joke. My smile is somewhat sheepish. "We're in this together, aren't we?"

"Yes," he says. "We are." He opens the door wider and motions for me to come in. "Come on. Don't hold me in suspense. Tell me what you found, Dr. Hunnicutt."

I step inside. My legs ache and my lungs still burn. I want to sit down, but . . . Right. Quentin doesn't have any furniture here. I start making my way toward the stairs. "Okay, but give me like, two minutes to recover. It's like ninety degrees out and I—"

"You can go up to my room if you want," he says. "There's a bed there to sit on at least."

"Oh, so *now* you want me in your bed?" I tease, though I'm sure I'm not that attractive with sweat running down my forehead, conspiring with my heavy breathing to fog up my glasses.

He smiles anyway, then says, "Go up and settle in. I'll grab you a glass of water and be right there."

When he said there was a bed in here at least, he meant it literally. There is a queen-size bed in here, and very little else. I take my laptop back out of its bag, then set my things on the floor. The mattress is thick foam, probably of the purchased-online variety. I sit on the edge and toe off my sneakers. There are two pillows, one more indented, and before I can think it through, I grab it and hold it up to my nose, breathing in deeply.

I drop it back where it belongs just as he enters the room. "Were you being weird with my pillow?" he asks as he hands me a glass of ice water.

"Nope," I say, and take a long drink as he watches me with suspicion. I drain the glass before long, and he takes it from me to place on the floor. "Nice bed, by the way."

"Thanks. I had an air mattress at first, but it kept deflating on me. Also, as an unemployed single man in my thirties, I got tired of feeling like a sad cliché." He moves to the other side of the bed, where he stretches out with his arms behind his head. "Okay," he says. "Tell me what you found."

I open my laptop and show him the passage that caught my eye at Flow State. Then I take him to the contact page of Emily Aaron's website. "Maybe Fountain did give Edlo to Albert Aaron, whatever that actually means. And maybe Emily or her grandfather or someone else in the family can tell us more about it."

He's quiet for a long time, simply staring at the web page until the screen goes dark and I have to swipe the trackpad to wake it up again. "What are you thinking, Quentin?" I ask. "You don't seem . . . You're mad at me, aren't you? That I reexamined the transcripts on my own. I'm sorry, I—"

"No," he says. "I'm not mad. Just . . . trying not to get my hopes up too much, you know?" He turns over and props himself up on his elbow. "You're a genius, Neen. This is a solid idea. Good job, cookiepuss."

My heart fills with joy at his words, even though his expression doesn't fully line up with them. "Why do you keep calling me that?"

He grins, and I'm glad to see the shift as his expression relaxes. "Because I know it bothers you."

"Maybe it doesn't. Maybe I love it. Maybe I'm thinking about adopting it as my legal name." I try to joke around with him, but the fact that he's *not* upset that I did research on my own somehow makes the guilt of having gone to the library alone more intense. If he finds out later . . . "Quentin," I say. "I need to tell you something else."

His grin deflates as he registers the sudden seriousness in my tone. "Okay."

"After the Sprangbur venue tour, I went to the library. To the special collections room. Without you." I turn to face him more completely, folding my legs under me. "I was . . . I was feeling desperate to get this over with, because I wanted you so badly and I . . . I didn't find anything then, I promise. It was completely uneventful." I remember Mrs. MacDonald trying to coerce me into taking her job. "Except for Mrs. MacDonald thinking I should replace her."

Quentin frowns. "She's leaving?" he asks.

"She wants to. But she's been waiting for the right successor. And, uh, she thinks I'm it."

"Do you think you are?"

"I think you're focusing on the wrong thing here. I am telling you that this was not the first time I researched without you, and—"

He holds up a hand, stopping me. "It's fine. When you found something you came to me. I'm much more interested in this whole you-replacing-Mrs.-MacDonald thing."

"I mean, it's not a thing. It's not happening."

"Why?" he asks.

"Why?" I echo. "Because . . . because . . . it's ridiculous."

"What's ridiculous about it exactly?"

"You think I should just stay in Catoctin and spend the rest of my life sorting through Mrs. MacDonald's hoard of unlabeled bankers boxes?"

"Well, I don't know," he says. "Would that make you happy?"

And, fuck, put that simply, I think it might. Especially if Quentin were the one waiting for me at home each evening, kissing me hard when I walk through the door, even if I were covered in dust and cobwebs.

Where did *that* thought come from?

"Why is everyone always asking what will make me happy all of a sudden?" I say too loudly, my voice breaking.

"Nina." Quentin's hand comes to rest on my knee. Soothing. Supportive.

I move to lie down beside him with a heavy sigh. "I don't really know what will make me happy because I don't even know who I *am* anymore," I whisper. "I've been a certain version of myself for so long. Ambitious Nina. But she was all wrapped up in my old life, in Cole and in academia. I don't think I'm going to get to be her again, or that I want to be, but I'm not sure who to be instead."

"Why can't you just be you?" he asks, running his fingers lightly up and down my arm. "Why do you need a modifier? What's wrong with just Nina?"

"Because . . . just Nina isn't enough. She's never been enough." His fingers pause where they are, and that line forms between his eyebrows. "She wasn't enough for you to want to stay friends, and she wasn't enough to keep my dad safe, or to know how to help when we almost lost our house and—"

The tears come all at once, a deluge. They feel alien against my cheeks. Probably because they aren't current tears, but very, very old ones that I've held back for seventeen years. Quentin takes me in his arms and holds me tight as I sob and sob.

"Ambitious Nina is who I had to be after you left," I murmur into his chest when I can catch my breath. "She let me feel like I had some semblance of control again. And people liked her. My parents were proud of her. She was the best daughter, their high achiever who could take care of herself and, one day, hopefully, them. It felt good to lessen their burden, even if it was only that they didn't have to spend their limited energy and resources worrying about me."

I sniffle and Quentin rubs his hand in slow circles over my back. I've never felt this combination of safe and emotionally raw and slightly turned on before. I continue talking, trying to explain everything I'm only now understanding myself. "She served me so well, for so long, that I started thinking that's who I actually was. That her goals were my goals, and I don't know, maybe they were, because I did enjoy a lot of what I accomplished. But happiness wasn't . . . that was never part of the equation. It seemed like something to keep striving toward, something I'd get eventually. A one-day sort of thing I had to earn. Something I dangled in front of myself so that I would keep going instead of . . . instead of stopping. Instead of risking having to feel all those horrible things again that I felt that fall."

"Nina," he whispers. "Neen, look at me." I lean back and look into his eyes, blinking away the moisture still clinging to my eyelashes. The hand that was on my back comes up to cradle my face. "I'm so sorry. I am so sorry that I made you feel like you weren't enough."

"It wasn't just you—" I start.

"Hush," he says, pressing his thumb against my lips. "The

silence between us, that was not your fault. It was mine. Do you hear me? It was because of *my* failings. The Nina I grew up with was enough. And the Nina you are now—the one who still can't say no to a competition and who loves her family and who stands topless in front of windows—she's enough too. More than enough. She's everything."

With that he leans in and presses his mouth to mine, so sweetly and gently it feels like a dream. He slowly ends the kiss, and we simply stare at each other for a moment.

"You're a lot better at this than my therapist back in Boston," I say, trying to lighten the mood.

"At kissing? I don't think you're supposed to be doing that with your therapist."

I give him a small shove until he's flat on his back. This is dangerous, us in his bed, me still feeling vulnerable, and him looking like . . . well, like he always does, which is really hot. "We need to figure out what to write to Emily Aaron," I say, sitting up.

Quentin shakes his head subtly, as if resetting himself, then reaches for my laptop. "You talk, I'll type," he says as he enters our names into the contact form along with his email address. I dictate the message, and he dutifully transcribes it:

Hello Emily,

    We hope this message finds you well, and that it isn't a problem we're contacting you through your business site. We're doing research on Julius Fountain, the turn-of-the-century industrialist, and have been relying heavily upon your great-grandfather Albert's oral history interviews with him. There's a part of the interview we don't fully understand and were hoping you (or any other relatives you might have on that side of the family) would be open to chatting with us. We're happy to do so virtually, by phone, or in person—whichever is most convenient.

Thank you for your consideration,

Nina Hunnicutt, PhD, & Quentin Bell, Esq.

"Hey, wait," Quentin says as he finishes typing. "Why does your name get to be first?"

"Because I'm the one who figured this out. And my doctorate makes us sound more legitimate. Which is probably helpful since we're just two randos contacting this woman out of the blue about her family history. That's also why I think we should include our honorifics, even though it looks a little douchey."

"Good points all around," he says. "All right. Send." He presses the button, then stretches his arms as a confirmation page appears.

I suppose our treasure-hunting business is over, and it's best if I leave. Before I can announce my intention to head out, he says casually, "You could stay for a while. If you want. We could get takeout and watch a movie."

I'm about to turn him down for the same reason I've turned him down most of the other times he's tried to get me to hang out outside the scope of our agreement—it's too dangerous for my heart. But I think that ship has sailed. Whether it was that tender kiss a moment ago that hoisted the anchor or something long before now, all I know is that I'm waving to it from the shore. All I can do is hope the journey is smooth from here. "Sure," I say. "That would be nice."

29

WAKE UP AT seven in the morning, fully dressed in the clothes I wore yesterday and . . . Where am I? Oh. Right. This is . . . I'm still at Quentin's. In his bed. Okay. The last thing I remember is the "Galaxy Song" in *Monty Python's Meaning of Life*, then I must've fallen asleep. We spent a large chunk of the evening daring each other to eat progressively spicier Thai food and then moaning in pain on the living room floor, so it was pretty late when we finally started watching. And Quentin ate more of the khua kling, so the movie was his pick, and he took forever to choose. I turn over and let out a small squeak of terror, because instead of Quentin's head on the pillow beside mine, I find the tightly wrinkled forehead and threatening-even-while-sleeping expression of Faustine, curled up in a tight, somehow angry donut. "Uh, good morning," I say, and give her a tentative pat on the haunch. Between the thin skin and the wrinkles, it feels a bit like touching a disconcertingly warm raw turkey. One eye cracks open, just barely, and stares at me without any other sign of her waking.

"Glad you two have finally met," Quentin says from the doorway.

"Where's she been, anyway? There aren't that many places for her to hide."

"Under the bed, most likely."

"Or in the shadow realm," I mutter.

"Don't be too rude to her," he chides. "She likes you."

"How can you tell?"

"Because she won't sleep beside just anyone. Back when Charlene and I were together, Faustine would only come up on the bed if it was just me."

"Oh," I say. "Well. I'm honored, I guess."

"You should be," he says, and moves into the room. He's showered since he woke up, and changed into a different pair of sweatpants and that Franz Ferdinand shirt he wore the night he came back from France. He's also holding a mug. "Coffee, if you want it," he says, and holds it out to me as I sit up.

"Thanks," I say, taking it from him. "Did you . . . were you in here with me and Faustine too at some point?"

"I was, until about six. Is that okay?"

"Yeah, it's fine. Of course. I just . . . don't remember it."

"Well, you were *out*," he says. "I didn't know you still slept so heavily." Until now, the last time Quentin and I had a sleepover was when we were six and camped out with my father in a tent in my backyard, during which I notoriously slept through a surprise severe thunderstorm. Dad picked me up and hauled me inside, and I never once stirred.

"Sorry if I snored."

"Oh, you certainly did," he says with a smile. "But it was cute. Like Shemp in the Three Stooges. *Honk-mee, mee, mee, mee, mee.*"

"Cut it out," I laugh, reaching for the pillow to throw at him, but Faustine has stretched out to take up both pillows now, and I don't have the heart to displace her.

"You fell asleep on my chest," he adds quietly.

"Oh. Sorry about that."

"Don't be. It was . . . it was nice." He smiles beautifully, genuinely, and I realize I haven't seen that too-charming version of him in a long time. He's only showing me this side now—the real Quentin. "Well, it was," he adds, "until you shifted and kneed me in the balls."

"Geez. I really *am* sorry about that."

"That you can be sorry for," he agrees.

He watches as I drain my coffee, then takes my mug back and hands me my glasses from where he thoughtfully placed them on the windowsill after I drifted off.

"I, uh, I should get home. I'm sure my mom . . ." I grab my phone from where it's shoved beneath the pillow. There are indeed three missed calls from her.

"She texted me when she couldn't get ahold of you," he says. "I told her you were spending the night here and not to worry."

Oh, great. Now she's probably even more convinced that Quentin and I are sexually involved. Somehow her thinking that when it isn't the truth, though I wish it was, is worse than if she thought it and we actually were. I get out of the bed and Faustine spreads farther into the space I've vacated as if she is liquid and the boundaries of her container have changed. "Still, I should . . . Thanks for dinner and um, the nice things you said to me and uh, letting me crash in your bed and uh, into you. Into your testicles with my knee, I mean. Not like in the Dave Matthews Band allegorical way . . . Anyway! Thanks for a fun time."

I look up from my rambling to see such fondness in Quentin's smile that my heart stutters. "Thanks for sharing what you found with me," he says. "And for hanging out. It really means a lot to me that you wanted to."

"Of course I wanted to," I say, sliding my laptop into its bag and putting my shoes back on.

We exchange a quick kiss on the cheek, and I head over to my own house, ready to face the music. And I guess the name of this song is "Patti Hunnicutt."

My mother has always been an early riser. Which means she's wide awake and already knitting on the couch, watching one of the morning shows, as I attempt to creep into the house. She turns her head, registers that it's me and not an intruder, and . . . goes back to clacking her needles together while Savannah and Carson talk about their Fourth of July plans.

I guess that's coming up in a few days. Weird that I've been back in Catoctin for almost a month now. Time flies when you're treasure hunting and platonically sleeping with a sexy man and his hairless cat.

Mom's lack of interest in where I've been feels almost insulting. More so than when she had no questions after thinking she caught Quentin and me fooling around on the couch. Not that I *want* to talk to her about any of it. I just thought she'd be more curious at the very least.

"Lovely morning," I say.

"Too hot," she disagrees. "And the sun's barely up. Won't be good for my tomato plants."

"I was at Quentin's."

"I know. He told me. I wish you would've answered your phone." But that's all I'm going to get, it seems, because she continues her knitting. "They just did a segment about how to grill corn. Looked pretty good."

"Mom."

"Hm?"

"Are you feeling okay?" I ask.

Her mouth pinches, the question catching her off guard. "Little sore from all the weeding I did yesterday. But otherwise fine. Why?"

"I'm concerned about you."

"About me? Why would you be concerned about me, Nina?"

"Because you're . . . you're . . . not being nosey. You're being distinctly *un*-nosey, actually. It isn't like you."

She sets down her needles and yarn, mutes the television, and turns to face me more. "I am choosing not to take offense to that." Her face goes softer. "Ninabean, I know things have been hard for you the last couple of months. But I'm glad that it's at least brought you and Quentin back together. You know I've always adored that boy. It doesn't take a mathematician to put two and two together here as to what has . . . developed . . . between you. And since I hardly need or want the sordid details, and you haven't asked for my opinion—"

"You're my mother," I say. "I didn't think I needed to ask for your opinion. It's always been freely given."

"Not with your love life," she says.

I scoff. "In college you literally once called to tell me not to get involved with a guy you saw in the background of one of my Facebook photos because you thought he looked 'rude.'"

"Well, that was a long time ago. And also, he did."

"You offered to set me up with Mrs. Bernstein's grandson. While I was dating Cole."

"And maybe you should've taken me up on that offer. He's a very good ophthalmologist. He did Karen Harmon's cataract surgeries last winter. Had it in both eyes, poor woman." She picks up her needles again. "It's about time I stayed out of your business," she says.

I go over and sink down onto the couch beside her. "But Mom, I don't *want* you to stay out of it." As much as I was dreading having to answer her questions this morning, I realize now that part of me was looking forward to it. Because my mom isn't just my mom; she's also one of my closest friends. And getting to talk out this strange situation might give me some much-needed clarity. I let out a heavy sigh and lean against her. "I think I'm in over my head," I confess. "I don't know what to do. I need help."

"I know, baby," she says, and kisses the top of my head. "But I don't think I'm the right person to give it this time. I know both of you too well. And while of course I love you more, I don't think I can be impartial if push ever comes to shove." Her arm goes around me and squeezes me into a hug. "Now go shower. You smell awful."

"Thaaanks."

Upstairs, the water falling onto my head and running into my eyes, I wonder what my mother meant by her not being the right person to help me with Quentin. Wouldn't her knowing us both so well be helpful in this case? Who would even be the right person if not my mother? Sabrina's no help; when I text her and tell her I spent the night at Quentin's but we didn't do anything beyond kiss very chastely, she sends a thumbs-down emoji. She doesn't understand why we aren't moving forward until after we find the treasure, thinks it's all an excuse so he doesn't hurt my feelings. If I hadn't talked to Hanako yesterday and found out Quentin's interest in me dates back much farther than the last few weeks, I might agree. But, especially after last night when he held me and told me I was enough . . . I just don't see how it couldn't be real.

Then again, I couldn't see that what Cole and I had wasn't real either.

Dammit, Mom. Why did she have to choose this particular moment to be reticent for the first time in her life?

I try to think back to previous advice she's given me but can't seem to find anything relevant beyond how to tell if a watermelon is ripe. I don't think I can knock on Quentin's side to determine if he's a good pick. Even less so when it comes to taking Mrs. MacDonald's job.

Because maybe Quentin is right that I should be considering that more seriously than I have been. My mom might not have given me any words of wisdom that apply here, but Mrs. MacDonald did: *Figure out what it is you want in life before the real "can'ts" come to get you.*

It just so happens that the things I want in life are also the ones that might break me if I lose them.

FORM C–7

VII

Fear? Oh, I don't believe in that. I used to, of
course. Before I visited Edlo and saw how the
Edlosians live. I would say they are fearless, but
how do you live without a thing that doesn't exist
in the first place? It implies a defiance. Like
godlessness. What's the point of being godless if
there's no god to defy? That's how they are with
fear there, Mr. Aaron.

I see that you're skeptical. You're wondering:
How can fear not exist when I felt it only a few
moments ago? And, oh, you did jump quite high when
you entered this room and saw me here in my chair.
Hahaha. One of the best reactions I've had thus
far. Your face! You should have seen it. How I will
treasure the memory until the day I die.

What was I saying? Oh, yes. Fear does not exist
in Edlo, and I believe that is true here as well.
Fear is just love, Mr. Aaron, wrapped up in a bow
that isn't particularly pretty. Kind of like that
tie of yours.

30

SPEND THE NEXT Thursday with my mother, who finally convinces me to go to lunch with her and her friends. "They haven't seen you since you were small," she says.

"And they need proof that I'm bigger now?"

"Don't be churlish, Nina."

After an hour and a half of getting questioned by five retired women about my life choices and when I expect I'll be able to make better ones while a server comes by periodically to refill my Diet Coke and give me a sympathetic look, I'm dragged to the craft store beside the restaurant, where Mom loads up my arms with soft, beautiful skeins of yarn. She's perusing a wall of buttons when I get a text from Quentin.

Have any plans tomorrow night, cookiepuss?

I roll my eyes at the absurd term of endearment but can't help but smile anyway, remembering the affection that flashes over his face whenever he says it.

Tomorrow is July Fourth, and we've stocked up on various things to barbecue, but my parents aren't big on celebrations. My mom is suddenly really invested in grilling corn, I respond. But otherwise no. Why?

He quickly sends: It's a surprise. And I respond: A good one?

It takes much longer for him to reply this time, but eventually I get: Maybe.

He's going to tell me he's found a new job, that he's leaving. That's where my mind immediately jumps, and it sticks the landing so skillfully that my entire self holds up a card pronouncing it a ten out of ten mental maneuver. And that is *not* good news. No maybe about it.

I can't quite figure out why it hits me so hard. It isn't like I expected anything different. I knew Quentin would be leaving at some point. Hell, I probably will be too. I'm still mulling over the idea of taking the special collections job (if the library would even hire me; I definitely would need something more formal than Mrs. MacDonald pronouncing me heir to her archival throne to consider this seriously), but for some reason all of my thoughts about it have centered on the presupposition of Quentin still being around. Of him and me and more mornings like yesterday, with coffee in bed and attempting to pet Faustine without getting weirded out and him making fun of my snoring. Why I assumed that was something we could do, that he would be up for . . .

I guess I got ahead of myself. Let the concept of decisions based on maximum immediate happiness sweep away the logical part of my brain that always knew this summer was a temporary stopover, not the final destination.

Now there's that intense nausea again, the creeping hint of dread that tells me not to get too comfortable because something bad is coming.

Maybe it's because my only experience with Quentin is here. Historically, him leaving has not been conducive to our continued friendship. And this isn't just friendship anymore. It's . . . it's . . . I don't really know what to call it, how to label it, but it's something I'm not quite ready to give up exploring.

Best-case scenario: His surprise is that he did get a job offer, but it also happens to be in Boston, where he's happy to share his new apartment with me so I can work on reestablishing my career there, where I have the most connections. Worst-case: He's moving somewhere very far away, somewhere that would be difficult to visit even if we wanted to see if there was something more between us. Somewhere back in Europe, probably. There's pretty much no job for which I'm qualified that will pay enough for me to afford frequent transatlantic flights. Most likely: He got a job in, like, New York City, and we can try to figure it out. They do have those train ticket packages for frequent travelers and—

"Nina?"

"Hm?"

My mom stares at me, then down at my arms where I am holding several skeins of yarn like they are my babies, then at the checkout counter where a woman is waiting patiently for me to complete this transaction by providing the goods we would like to purchase.

"Oh. Sorry," I say. "Deep in thought about . . . crafts."

Quentin texts me around eight the next night, asking if I'm ready to go. I almost chicken out and tell him I'm not feeling well. Which, between the ever-present nausea of my current anxiety spike and all of the berry icebox cake I ate, isn't a complete lie, but is most likely to result in him coming over here to try to take care of me. And the last thing I need is him breaking the news of his imminent departure while rubbing my back and handing me some ginger ale to wash down my Pepto-Bismol. That would be so much worse, to have him actively caring for me while telling me he doesn't care *enough*. So I tell him I'll meet him out front and head down to the porch.

He's already standing on the sidewalk beside the Audi. "Hop in," he says.

"Where are we going?"

"You'll see."

I figure it out as soon as he turns right onto Carmichael Chapel Road. We're going to Sprangbur. Which closes, officially, at sundown.

"Ugh," I whine. "If I wind up spending the night in a jail cell, my parents are going to—"

"I promise that will not happen."

"You can't promise that. You can't even defend me if we get caught."

"Why not?"

"First of all, you don't even do that kind of law," I point out as we park in the lot at the edge of the property. "So you would probably not be very effective counsel."

He unbuckles his seat belt. "Wow, glad to know you have such faith in me."

"Second, would they even allow you to represent a co-conspirator in a crime?"

He shrugs. "Don't actually know. Like you said, I don't do that kind of law." Quentin flashes me an impish, if hesitant, smile.

Then it suddenly hits me, as I'm opening my car door carefully so as not to ding the truck beside us, that the parking lot is actually pretty full.

"What are we doing?" I ask in a sharp whisper as Quentin emerges from the driver's side. "Do you even know what kind of event we're crashing?" I look down at my navy sundress and sandals. I'm not sure if it's fancy enough to blend in at a wedding, but definitely better than the threadbare Old Navy flag shirt from 2003 I wore for most of the day after finding it buried deep, deep in my closet. I try to listen for any indication of what's taking place up ahead, but it's all crickets. Literal crickets. And maybe some cicadas. "Are we joining the local nocturnal wildlife for a game night?"

"Man, I hope not," he says. "You are the absolute worst charades partner."

"Just because I thought a chinchilla was a type of Mexican dish when we were ten . . ."

Quentin laughs as he takes my hand, leading me over a small rise beside the estate's pond. It's very dark, but he seems to know where we're going. As the ground evens out again, the crickets and cicadas are gradually drowned out by conversation and the occasional peal of a child's laugh. Ahead is a cluster of shadows, which, as we approach, turn out to be people—some sitting on blankets, some in chairs, and others (mostly kids) running around with sparklers.

"It's a good fireworks spot," he explains. Which makes sense, because they usually launch them east of downtown, right across the river. "Supposedly gets less crowded than Riverside Park or the Food Lion lot."

Except instead of staking out a spot of our own as I expect, Quentin leads me past the people and along the walkway that winds around the Castle.

"That isn't the surprise?" I ask.

"Nope."

"Oh. Where are you taking me?" But I don't need him to answer, because I can see exactly where we're headed—into the gardens.

31

QUENTIN USHERS ME inside the mushroom folly. The darkness and the massive rhododendron bushes surrounding the phallic stone structure make it feel like we've entered another world, thousands of miles away from another living soul. *I wonder if this is Edlo?* I think for a moment, and it sends a pleasant shiver down my spine. "What's this all about?" I ask, rotating in place before I turn back to where Quentin still stands at the entrance.

"Trying to fix some of my mistakes," he says cryptically. The word "mistakes" makes me swallow hard. He steps toward me, his gaze intent, and gently places his hands on my hips, before he walks me back against one of the pillars, the smooth concrete pleasantly cold against the exposed top of my back, my neck, my shoulders. "This is what I was going to do—what I'd planned to do—if you'd shown up that night." One of his hands drifts up, and his thumb softly lifts my chin, angling our mouths toward each other. My eyes close as our lips meet, and somehow, even though this isn't the first time we've kissed, this one feels like something new. Something different. More vulnerable.

"Nina." His smile is small, uncertain. No facade to be found here. This is pure Quentin, the boy, the man. The person some secret part of me has always and probably will always adore. "When you told me the other night that I made you feel like you weren't enough for me to want to stay in touch . . . God, that broke me. It shattered me, completely. Because it was so far from the truth, and I just didn't know how to tell you then. I barely know how to tell you now, but I'm trying. I'm trying to do better this time. Even though I know it's not enough to make up for everything we missed out on because I was too afraid, too stupid, to be honest about how I felt."

I reach out and run my fingers over his jaw, needing to lend my support in some way. (Also to feel the progress he's making on that beard. It's coming in quite nicely.) He closes his eyes against the touch, leaning into it, before taking my hand away and holding it.

"From the very first day we met," he continues, "I knew you were amazing. Like no other person I'd ever known. And, yeah, we were only five years old at the time, so that's probably not saying much, but you were so pretty and smart and we laughed at all the same things. I decided then and there I would do anything it took to make you want to be my friend." He stares down at where our fingers are intertwined. "But you didn't seem as interested in knowing me as I was in knowing you. Not until I started competing with you. Telling you I could do something better or faster or whatever lit this spark in your eyes, and it was so much easier to get your attention. By the time we were fifteen, I was absolutely head over heels in love with you."

Even though Hanako already revealed Quentin's crush, this confession makes my breath catch. He was *in love* with me?

"I wanted to tell you how I felt, but I was so scared you didn't feel the same way." He glances back up, into my eyes. "That's why I was so adamant we team up and look for the treasure that summer. Because I thought it would show you how good we could be together. So that once I left, you might not forget about me."

Forget about *him*? It makes no sense. "But you . . . You're the one who . . ." I start. "You never responded any of the times I tried to contact you."

"I know. I can never apologize enough, or express how much I regret that. First I was ignoring you because, yeah, I was a little mad. But mostly I was hurt. Heartbroken. Then embarrassed. You were the first girl I ever loved, Nina. You not showing up that night felt like a confirmation that all of my fears were completely founded. That you didn't feel the same way. That you were only looking for the treasure for the thrill of the competition, not because you cared about me."

"No, I—Quentin. I cared so much. I felt the exact same way. I just . . . I thought that I needed to impress you in order for *you* to like *me*. That if I found the treasure on my own, you would be so proud that you wouldn't forget *me*. And then it felt like that's exactly what you did." I shake my head, and my voice goes quieter. "I loved you too. That night we spent stargazing in your backyard, I wanted you to kiss me so badly."

"And I wanted to kiss you," he says.

"I know," I whisper. I respond to the question on his face. "Hanako might've let it slip."

"Ah." He rolls his eyes and quirks the corner of his mouth.

"So why didn't you?" I ask. "Why didn't you kiss me then?"

"I almost did. Really. But I kept chickening out. Why do

you think I wouldn't shut up about constellations? I was so freaking nervous. But the next night, when we were supposed to meet, I promised myself I was going to do it. That it was my last chance, and I was going to take it. To put it all out there, finally. Then you didn't show, and I felt like an absolute idiot." He releases my hand, and I reach for him, reluctant to lose his touch. "Kind of like I feel now, to be honest."

"Then we're both idiots," I say. "It's a perfect match, really."

We sigh deeply in unison, and silence stretches as we stare into each other's eyes, really seeing each other fully for the first time.

"So. Is the surprise that you're gonna fuck me here in the mushroom folly?" I joke.

This startles a laugh out of him that I've only heard once before—when we were fourteen and I wore a new bathing suit to a friend's birthday party at a water park. I thought he was laughing at the fact that I was a chubby girl in a two-piece. But I'm pretty sure now that it was actually the nervous laugh of someone confronted with something that's completely overwhelmed their system. "That is not the surprise," he says. I reach up and place my hand on the side of his neck so I can feel his flush even if I can't see it in the dark.

"Was it that you used to have a crush on me? Because it's flattering and I definitely had one on you too, but like, as far as *surprises* go . . ." I teeter my hand. "Meh."

"Maybe I will fuck you in the mushroom folly," he says, a glint in his eye that tells me he's joking but also definitely imagining it. His hands return to my hips, and he presses me slightly harder against the pillar. My heart flutters. At first I think it's a response to his touch and that look he's giving me, until I remember the worry that's been plaguing me since he texted yesterday.

"You got a job offer?" I blurt out.

His eyebrows dive, and that wolfish grin fades. "Did Patti tell you?"

"Wait. You told my mom before telling me?"

"I didn't exactly tell her so much as she overheard it. I was on the porch when the call came, and she was heading out. I asked her not to say anything to you."

"She didn't," I say. "I just guessed. Anyway, congratulations. So you're leaving, then? That's the surprise?"

"No," he says, lips curving again, less certain this time. "The job would be here, actually."

"What?"

"In Catoctin. It's a small, local firm that specializes in civil cases. They want someone to focus on landlord and tenant stuff, which I did way back in a law school clinic and really enjoyed. It's an opportunity to help people, and my dad is fine with me staying in the house, if I want, instead of selling it. Or I might still sell and find something else. I don't know yet."

He's staying here. Quentin is staying. A spark ignites in my heart, and I feel illuminated from the inside out. Because what is stopping me from staying too? From taking a chance on this, on us? I'm still terrified and overwhelmed by the concept of getting everything I want. What if I get it only to lose it like I did my old life? But this could also be a sign that my luck is turning around. That the losing streak is over. It feels like I've been lost in the woods for a month and have finally stumbled across a path; I would be a fool not to follow it. Besides, no matter where it spits me out, I'll at least know where I am, which is more than I had before.

His face goes very serious, his wide mouth a straight line as he readies himself to say more. "But if . . . or when . . . you leave, to go back to Boston or move somewhere else entirely, I still need you in my life, Neen. Whatever that looks like to you, and whether it be friendship or something more, I will do anything. Anything it takes to bridge the distance. I meant it when I said I don't want to lose you again."

His tone is firm, but there's tension in his jaw, around his eyes, that speaks of uncertainty. As if he thinks I might deny him, even now, after all we've shared.

"Quentin," I whisper as I place my hands on his shoulders. "If you were going to give me seventy percent of the reward money if we found the treasure within eight weeks, what would I get if I keep looking with you beyond that?"

"What?"

"What if I stick around? To keep looking for it."

"For how long?"

"Well, as long as it takes. Months. Years. Decades, if necessary. Do I get more then?"

It takes him a moment to process what I mean. Finally he says, "I'll go up to eighty-five percent, but no higher."

"God, you suck so much," I say, my smile giving away how little I mean that.

He grins back at me, then presses his forehead to mine. It feels like a secret world inside of a secret world inside of a magic one.

"I meant it too, when I said I don't want to lose you again either," I whisper, then press my mouth to his, cupping his face to keep it close to mine. I give and give and take and take until it's all inseparable, one and the same. Quentin is right that we're good together. In all sorts of ways, but especially this one. His fingers dig into my hips, stronger, deeper as my tongue strokes his. A loud *boom!* sounds in the distance, and for a moment I think we've somehow generated it until I remember: fireworks.

"Should we . . . Do you want to go watch?" I pant out.

"Not really. Do you?" he asks, his hand moving to rest on my upper thigh, skimming the hem of my dress.

"Nope."

He kisses me again as his fingers travel upward a few inches, finding the lace trim of my underwear and humming in approval. I hadn't realized how much he must've been holding back when he kissed me on the porch that night. Because now it feels like he's unleashing everything he has, and the passion, the intensity, crossed with what is almost desperation, stokes that flame that's been burning low inside of me for weeks. This is no longer a romantic kiss, or even a passionate make-out session. This is a precursor to more. And Quentin is showing no sign of stopping the natural progression this time around.

I have exactly one brain cell currently functioning enough to manage a "What are we . . . ?" as his lips leave mine and start exploring my neck.

"I know we were joking before. About the fucking in the mushroom folly. But I'm starting to feel sort of serious about it," he says, and the words vibrating against my skin make me feel molten from the stomach down.

"But . . . the treasure. You wanted to wait until—"

"Changed my mind," he says.

"Oh. Okay." My legs threaten to give out as his teeth lightly skim over my shoulder. I'm in no condition to question it beyond saying, "If you're sure."

"I am. Very sure. But you? You want to?"

I breathe in his enticing clean scent as I move my mouth to

the hollow of his throat. "Yes. More than anything." *Boom!* goes another firework, then a sizzling sound that feels like it's mimicking the sensations in my body.

"Then I think we're doing this." He hooks a finger into the band of my underwear as if he's about to tug them down, but stops himself as another firework bursts somewhere far beyond our sight. "Can I—?"

"Yeah. Yes. Please. Touch me. I need it. Need you."

He pulls the band down on just the one side, enough to bury his hand between my legs. I shift forward, trying to chase the pressure of his palm against me, and find that we're both moving our hips against it, grinding against his hand between us as our lips cling together, unmoving except for the exchange of gasps.

Then he backs off and runs a finger through my folds, collecting the moisture gathered there before slipping inside me. I arch into his touch, gasping at the sensation. He thrusts slowly, so slowly, that I find myself whimpering against his shoulder, begging for more. Instead of picking up speed or adding another finger like I'm hoping for, though, he takes his hand away altogether.

Before I can protest, Quentin sinks to his knees on the flagstone. "Been dreaming of this," he mutters. He reaches back under my dress and pulls the underwear down my legs now, helping me balance as I step out of them.

"What—" I start, but as he shoves the lace-trimmed satin into his pocket as if he plans on keeping them, my mind goes blank.

"Put your foot up on the bench," he orders.

I do, and even though I'm still covered completely by the skirt of my dress, I feel a bit of that warm, humid night air that tickled my skin the night in front of the window, and it brings back the memory of being someone brave and bold and sexy. Of feeling. Wanting. The way I'm feeling and wanting now.

I place a hand against the pillar for support, because I do not trust my legs to be the only things keeping me upright. Especially not when Quentin ducks beneath my dress, his head disappearing under the fabric, and I feel his fingers again, sliding over me in sensual observation, studying the terrain before his tongue sweeps over my center. As he continues, I feel a deep kinship with the fireworks I can hear bursting and then cascading down in bright fizzing streaks off in the distance.

"Please," I beg. "Quentin. Please."

"Please what?" he asks, reappearing with a wicked grin on his face. "Please stop?"

"No. I mean. Yes. I mean. Do you have a condom?"

The question seems to throw him. "Oh. Um. No. I, uh, I don't. Believe it or not, I really didn't *plan*—"

"That's okay. I have an IUD, and I haven't been with anyone since I was last tested. So if you also . . . we can keep going without."

"I got tested as soon as I got back to the States," he says. "On account of the, you know, being cheated on thing. Thought it was prudent."

"Oh. Right. Yeah." I cringe, lowering my foot back to the ground. Nothing hotter than the conversation turning toward perfidious exes mid–sexual activity.

I search for a joke to lighten the mood, but before I can find one, Quentin stands, then wraps his arms around my waist. "You know, it's funny," he says. "So many things that happened to me, things that I thought were awful at the time . . . Feel like silver linings when I'm with you. If everything hadn't gone to shit, I wouldn't be here right now, about to fuck the most amazing person I know in a penis-shaped gazebo."

"Am I not also the most amazing person you know *outside* of a penis-shaped gazebo?" I quip in time with another firework boom.

Quentin chuckles, his eyes crinkling as he does, and lightly taps my butt before taking a seat on the bench where my foot was before. "Get your pretty ass over here, Groucho Marx."

It's hard to mind the very unsexy nickname when he lounges back, arms spread on the railing behind the bench that's built into the structure's curve, looking at me like he isn't sure whether he wants to devour me or be devoured. It's so tempting to kneel in front of him, to use my mouth on him in return, but the fireworks seem to be increasing in frequency, shooting off not just in pairs but in threes and fours. This magical, private world will only exist a little while longer.

So I place my knee on the bench beside his thigh and swing my other leg over him. "It's . . . it's been a while for me," I confess, still keeping my distance from the bulge in his jeans. "Like, half a year or so." Until the night we broke up, I hadn't seen Cole for four months, and we didn't actually sleep together during that visit. Which isn't surprising looking back; sex was pretty far down on our hierarchy of relationship needs, and even the most pressing ones weren't exactly being met. "So, um, I might be . . ." I trail off as Quentin nods in understanding. I'm glad, because "rusty" was on the tip of my tongue and that is not at all a sexy description.

He strokes my sides as I reach between us to unzip his fly. He lifts his hips and tugs his pants and boxers down just enough to free his erection. The way his head falls back as I wrap my hand around his length is the most satisfying thing I've ever seen. He lets out an incredibly hot moan as I stroke him. "Take me however you need me, Nina. Please, I just need to be inside you."

"Maybe I'm trying to make you lose our competition," I say. "Remember. Whoever comes last this time." I position myself over him, lining us up, and carefully, gradually sink down onto his cock.

"Holy—" Quentin says as I let out a sound that I'm pretty sure rivals the one I made when he drove us really fast down Carmichael Chapel Road. Fully seated, I experiment with a few different movements, up and down, back and forth, circling my hips until I find the right pattern that has us both breathing heavier and unable to hold back the sounds of pleasure that are thankfully drowned out by the continued thundering of the fireworks display.

His hand slips between us, his thumb working in time with my movements, not giving me a chance to think about anything else, to get lost in thoughts of anything other than him and the pleasure steadily building low in my core. He moves so deliciously, so precisely. As if he wants nothing more than to find the exact frequencies I operate at and tune himself to where I am.

"Darling Nina," he says. "Smart Nina. Wet, tight, incredible Nina." I whimper as he whispers the words into my ear. "Funny Nina. Competitive Nina." He kisses me much more softly than I'm expecting. "Delicious Nina. Did you know that every single version of you . . ." His free hand reaches into my hair and directs my attention to his face. "Is the perfect one? Because they're all just *you*. My Nina."

His Nina.

Maybe that's who I've been all along.

I kiss him again, deeper this time, and find that there are still traces of me on his tongue.

"I'm . . . I'm so close," I sob into his shoulder.

"Me too."

"You first."

He shakes his head. "No."

I let out a moan that's equal parts frustration and pleasure. "Quentin, I swear to god. You better—"

His lips capture the rest of my protest. "Together," he says then. "I want . . . us together."

That could have many meanings, but regardless of which one or ones he intends, it contains something potent enough to send me over the edge at that exact instant. I'm unaware of what I'm saying, what sounds I'm making. The only thing I can latch onto is the pulsing, rippling heat as he stills deep inside me. The trembling of his body and the slow loosening of mine. The sweetest, softest kiss at the corner of my mouth and the nonstop explosions have reached a crescendo, leaving behind the faintest smell of smoke drifting over from the river and a satisfied, quiet peace that mirrors itself in my heart.

TEXT OF INTERVIEW (UNEDITED)

VIII

I feel you might need more convincing on the topic
of fear. [AA: Interviewer attempted to redirect
subject of the interview here, but informant put
fingers in his ears and sang until interviewer
stopped speaking.]

Are you quite done fussing at me now? Good. You
are worse than my instructors at the École des
Beaux-Arts--"Monsieur Fontaine, the assignment is
a theater, not a factory!" But what is a factory if
not a theater for industry?

As I was saying, fear is simply love wrapped up
in an ugly bow. Think about the times you have
thought you felt afraid. I would bet everything I
own that, if you are honest with yourself, every
moment of supposed fear is, beneath it, simply an
instinct to retain what you love and value in this
world--your wife, your son, your home, your
intellect, your very ability to draw breath.
These are the things I presume you value, Mr.
Aaron.

Yes, fear is simply a shorthand representation of all the things you love and want to keep. Which is why you can tell a lot about a man by what he believes he fears.

32

THE SILENCE LASTS only a moment before we hear distant clapping now that the fireworks show is over. Quentin and I stare at each other, eyes wide, me still straddling him.

"We should . . ." he starts.

"Yes. Before anyone . . ." I add.

My dismount isn't exactly graceful, and there's a bit of awkward laughter as we try to figure out how to handle cleanup. I wind up getting my underwear back and slip them on again.

"Ready to go," I say.

"Hold on." Quentin looks at me for a long time, lips parting as if he wants to say something. But instead he kisses me again, long and slow. "Neen . . ." he mutters against my lips. "I need—" His words cut out and his eyes squint against a sudden beam of light directed at his face.

"Hey," an unfamiliar voice says from a few yards outside the folly's entrance. I turn and find a security guard shining his flashlight on us. "Break it up, you two. This ain't no hanky-panky spot."

"Sorry. We just got engaged," Quentin lies smoothly. "We were just celebrating."

"Congratulations. But you're gonna have to celebrate elsewhere. Fireworks are over, and normal park rules and hours apply. Time to head home, folks."

"Of course," Quentin says. He and I share a smile as he takes my hand. "We'll follow you out."

Much later that night, as we lie with the covers thrown off of us in Quentin's bed, our bare skin sticking wherever we touch, I try to imagine the life I thought I wanted even a month ago. But it's fuzzy. Abstract. The same way it is if I try to imagine myself living in a lighthouse in Nova Scotia or becoming a chef. It's like a mental exercise I can perform but feel no real attachment to. No desire to find my way back to it.

It's nothing like when I imagine the life Quentin and I might build here. One that's comfortable. Soft and sweet and *easy*. Sunday mornings spent exploiting the online ordering loophole at Best That You Can Brew so that Quentin and I (and Faustine, who I admit is growing on me) can linger in bed and still have apple fritters for breakfast. A big pot of soup simmering on the stove for when my parents stop by for dinner. Maybe a couple of children with freckles and strawberry-blonde curls shrieking with joy in the backyard as they catch fireflies in their palms. It's a life that looks like the best memories of our childhood blended with every beautiful moment we've spent together this summer. All the things I think I've probably always wanted but was too afraid to accept could come so easily. I fall asleep to the idea playing in my mind like a pretty music box melody.

And wake up the next morning to two emails that are like monster trucks crushing the little dancing ballerina: one in my

308 · Sarah Adler

inbox from the dean of the School of Arts and Humanities at Malbyrne and one in Quentin's from Emily Aaron.

"Oh, hey," Quentin says. "Albert Aaron's great-granddaughter responded."

"They want me . . . to come back to Malbyrne," I say, staring at my phone's screen like the words on it might change at any minute. "In a different department, but still."

"Oh. Wow. And are you . . . happy about that?"

"I don't know," I admit. I read over the message again.

Dear Dr. Hunnicutt,

I hope you are well and enjoying your summer.

One of our associate professors in American studies has accepted a political appointment and will no longer be able to teach full-time during the 25–26 AY. We are in need of a one-year term lecturer to cover their courses, which include two sections of Intro to American Culture and one senior-level research methods course.

We were so disappointed when we were unable to renew your contract in history, but I hope that this might be an exciting opportunity for you to continue working with us here at Malbyrne. While I recognize this is not exactly your area of specialty, the interdisciplinary nature of the department creates significant flexibility in the way these courses can be taught. I'm attaching sample syllabi for each, and you can contact the department chair, Destiny Jones, with any questions you might have.

We look forward to having you back on campus!

Sincerely,
Hiba Bradbury, PhD
Dean of the School of Arts and Humanities
Malbyrne College

"Sounds like they need you to save their butts," Quentin says, reading over my arm. His voice is a strange mixture of pride and annoyance—not dissimilar to what I'm feeling.

I put my phone down and shift so that I can read Quentin's. "I'll deal with it later. What does Emily Aaron have to say?"

He turns his screen toward me more.

Hi Nina and Quentin,
    I'm so sorry for the delayed response. Your
message got stuck in my spam folder and I only
just discovered it. My grandfather, Eugene, would
be happy to share what he knows about Albert's
work with the WPA and, more specifically, his
interview with Julius Fountain. In fact, he has
something he thinks might interest you. We live
in Richmond and would prefer to meet in person at
his home if possible. If not, let me know and I'll
try to teach him how to do a video call. :)
    Cheers,
    Emily

"So . . ." I say. "Guess we're taking a day trip to Richmond?"

"Unless you need to get back to Boston . . ."

The urge to reassure Quentin—and myself—that I'm not going anywhere leads me to take the phone from his hand and place it beside mine at the edge of the mattress. I climb atop him, straddling his hips. "If you think you can get rid of me when we're on the verge of cracking this mystery . . . you have another think coming, mister."

"Is that . . . is that the correct saying?" he asks. "'Think,' not 'thing'?"

"Yeah. You didn't know that?"

"Huh. I did not."

And then I lean down and kiss him until thinking becomes a foreign concept to us both.

33

W E LEAVE CATOCTIN at seven on Monday morning but don't arrive at the address Emily Aaron gave us—an American foursquare-style single-family home scrunched in with its neighbors in the Museum District of Richmond, Virginia—until a little after ten thanks to a major accident shutting down a lane on the DC Beltway. Things between Quentin and me are feeling slightly off since I got the email from Malbyrne inviting me back. Nothing I can put my finger on exactly, just a sense that he's retreating again, ever so subtly, as if he might think I'm not serious about still wanting to stay in Catoctin with him. The fact that he's trying so hard to pretend everything is fine and good only makes it more obvious. It's like we're driving with an elephant in the back seat, a jacket thrown over its head as if that's enough to convince me it disappeared. However, not being an infant, I have object permanence and can't quite forget about its presence.

A woman around our age with light brown skin, large brown eyes, and long, dark, curly hair answers the door, and I recognize her from the headshot on her website as Emily. She shows us to the living room and says, "My grandfather will be down in just a minute. Can I get you anything?"

"A glass of water would be great," I answer as I lower myself onto the leather sofa. "Quentin?"

"Nothing for me, thank you." He remains standing awkwardly, like he's forgotten how to exist in someone else's space.

Emily leaves to grab my drink, and I tug Quentin's hand until he sits beside me. Almost immediately, his knee starts bouncing with the frantic energy of a dog having a dream about chasing rabbits. I'd hoped the elephant would stay in the car, give me a temporary reprieve from trying to ignore it, but it seems to have followed us into the Aaron residence.

I sigh as I lay a hand on his thigh and put a stop to the jiggling.

"Calm down," I say. "You're going to make them think we're here to case their house or something."

Quentin turns to face me, his eyes wide. "Nina. What if this is it? What if the Aarons know something that leads us to the treasure?"

"Then we find it. Yay."

"But then what? Do you . . . Would you still stay?" he asks. "Because you said the other night that you'd stay until it was found, and—"

He stops talking as Emily returns. She sits the glass of water on a coaster in front of me, politely not acknowledging that her grandfather's visitors appear to be having a tense discussion in his living room.

"I'll go see what's taking him so long," she says with a smile and points in the direction of the staircase we passed when we came inside.

Instead of resuming our conversation, we both stare straight ahead, waiting for our first glimpse of Mr. Aaron. Even though he's the son of the man who interviewed Fountain, not the man himself, this feels like a significant moment. Eugene may have been a baby at the time his father visited Sprangbur and diligently recorded everything the old seltzer magnate wanted to share with him, but he's still the closest we've come to talking to someone with a direct connection to Julius Fountain. And, according to the email Emily sent, Mr. Aaron has something he thinks may interest us. Something *has* to come of this.

"Stop," I whisper, taking Quentin's hand and giving it a squeeze.

"Stop what?"

"Worrying so much. The treasure isn't what's most important to me and you know it."

"But it is important," he says. "The treasure is still important even if it isn't the most important."

I give him a look like, *What are you even talking about?*

The sound of stairs creaking alerts us that our hosts are on their way. Emily rounds the corner first, followed closely by an elderly white man that must be Eugene Aaron. He walks hunched over slightly, as if the modest wisp of light gray hair swooping over the top of his head is some sort of antennae he uses to feel his way. His granddaughter helps him into a wingback chair, and he lets out a heavy exhale as he lifts his legs so that she can shift the ottoman under his feet.

"Mr. Aaron," I say, and lean forward with my hand extended. He takes it and gives it a stronger-than-expected shake. "So nice to meet you. I'm Nina Hunnicutt."

"Quentin Bell," Quentin says, that charming mask of his sliding back into place easily now that he's speaking to someone else. "Thank you for inviting us."

"Of course. I couldn't help but be intrigued. It isn't every day young folks reach out to me about my father's work."

"We'd love to hear all about it. But we're primarily interested in anything you can tell us about his experience interviewing Julius James Fountain in 1937. Especially anything you know about a place called Edlo?" On the way here, Quentin and I briefly discussed how much detail we wanted to give about the motivations behind our research. Mentioning that it had to do with a treasure hunt, we thought (or I thought, and Quentin sort of half-heartedly nodded in concurrence) might needlessly complicate matters. So we decided to be as vague as possible while still being honest.

Mr. Aaron smiles. "Ah, Edlo. Yes. Figured it might have something to do with that."

"Is this for a book or a podcast or something?" Emily asks from where she stands with her arms folded atop the back of the chair where Eugene Aaron sits. Her voice is light and breezy, the same as her emails inviting us to Richmond and then confirming the date and time, but there's an unmistakable undercurrent of protectiveness there too.

"I'm not sure where our research will—" I start, but Quentin cuts me off.

"It's more of a personal quest," he says.

"Well, now," Mr. Aaron says, raising his bushy eyebrows. "That sounds like a story of its own." His expression makes it clear that he now expects to hear all about it.

Quentin looks at me for a few seconds, searching for something. Finally, he turns back to Mr. Aaron and Emily. "Nina and I go way back," he explains. "Her family and mine shared a duplex, so we were next-door neighbors growing up. I wound up moving away when we were fifteen, but that last summer we lived beside each other, we spent a bunch of time exploring Julius Fountain's estate together. Which made us also want to know more about the man who built it. That's how we learned about your father's oral history interviews."

"Ah," Mr. Aaron says. "I never did get to go there, you know. But my father spoke of it often." He glances up at Emily. "Maybe we'll visit when it isn't so hot out."

"I don't know if you've read the interviews," Quentin continues.

Mr. Aaron nods. "Some time ago."

"In them, Fountain talks about this whole other side to Sprangbur, the fantasy world where he claimed to spend so much of his time. He called it Edlo. Seemed like a place where you could lose yourself in pretending, which was something I understood the appeal of. My parents were going through a divorce, and it was decided I would live with my mom in Michigan, where she'd gotten a new job. I was going to have to join her there at the end of that summer. I dreaded leaving the only home I really remembered having. My school, my friends. The pressures on me back then were very different from those on Fountain, but I could definitely empathize with wanting to get lost in a fantasy for a while." He glances at me again, that serious look on his face instead of the smile I'm expecting. "That was also the summer I realized I was in love with Nina. And spending time with her was the closest thing I'd ever found to how Fountain described Edlo—magical, delightful, a respite from everything that weighs on me. It's still the closest thing."

"Oh my god, that's so romantic," Emily says, then covers her mouth with her hand sheepishly. "Sorry."

Quentin simply smiles at her before returning his attention to Mr. Aaron. "There's an intellectual curiosity as well, of course. But Edlo and love have this inseparable connection in my mind, and I can't help but think that understanding Fountain's world better will also help me love better." He glances at me before taking my hand and, lowering his voice so I'm the only one who can hear his next words, says, "Love *you* better."

I cannot conjure even a single thought except *Quentin loves me.* He said the other night that he love*d* me. Back then. Past tense. Present tense is not something that's entered the conversation yet. And here he is, professing his love for me to this elderly man and his granddaughter as if it's a basic fact about him. His middle name is Foster. He went to the University of Michigan for undergrad. He doesn't like olives. And he loves me.

He *loves* me.

"Ah! Nothing quite like young love!" Mr. Aaron exclaims with a chuckle. "Let's get you the book, then."

Book? What book? My eyes go wide as Quentin whispers, "'Stiff of spine, body pale . . .'" and it all suddenly makes sense. The riddle was about a book. Maybe *this* book.

Eugene looks up at Emily, still leaning on the chair's back. "Sheyfele, it's on my bed. Get it, would you?" His granddaughter dutifully heads back upstairs.

"Did your father ever talk about Julius Fountain?" Quentin asks. I don't know how he's managing to carry on normal conversation when my heart is thudding so hard in my chest I'm worried it's visible on the outside, like a cartoon character's.

"Oh, yes. Even though they only spent that one day together, for the interview, Papa spoke of Mr. Fountain often and with great respect and affection."

The Albert Aaron in the interviews did not seem particularly impressed with his informant's personality. Not that I blame him. Fountain didn't hold much back, nor did he pass up an opportunity to amuse himself by embarrassing someone else.

"You're shocked," Eugene remarks, humor dancing in his dark brown eyes as he takes in my face, which I'm sure shows all sorts of emotions right now. Shocked is one of them, though.

"It didn't seem like they got along all that well," I say. "At least based on the transcripts we read."

Emily returns, a thin, purple, clothbound book reverently cradled in her hands.

"It's true that Mr. Fountain did not make a good first impression on my father," Mr. Aaron says, taking possession of the volume. He thanks his granddaughter before continuing, "But beyond his peculiar behavior and the occasional cutting remark, Julius Fountain was a good man. A kind one. Papa used to say that he left Sprangbur Castle equal parts annoyed and charmed. Then 'charmed' won out once this arrived at our apartment a few months later."

He reaches forward and lays the beautifully bound manuscript on the coffee table in front of us. I move my glass of water to the floor out of an abundance of caution before leaning in, my shoulder and leg pressed tightly to Quentin's as we both take in the book. I'm the first to reach out to touch it, but I pause with my fingers on the edge of the cover.

There's a handwritten note tucked inside. I carefully slip it out and unfold the paper, immediately recognizing the penmanship from a few of the documents in the Fountain collection at the library.

"Oh, wow."

318 · Sarah Adler

Mr. Aaron smiles as I glance up at him.

"'Dear Mr. Aaron,'" Quentin reads aloud. "'I send you this as . . .' I can't make out that word."

My graduate work might not be particularly useful in day-to-day circumstances, but it did give me substantial experience deciphering old cursive handwriting. It's beyond absurd, yet I have the sense that this is what the past two decades of my life were leading up to, readying me for this moment. I take over, reading, "'I send you this as promised during our meeting last June, and hope it finds you and yours well. Your boy must be toddling around and being quite a darling terror by now. I gift him these stories of my beloved second home of Edlo, inviting him into this place I hold so dear, with the wish that it will inspire joy and freedom in the tender years of his life and beyond. I remain—J. J. Fountain.'"

Quentin's finger hovers over a postscript written along the edge of the page. "Can you see what this says?"

I take a moment to decipher the much smaller writing, tilting my head as far to the side as it will go to turn it upright, then realizing belatedly that I can simply rotate the paper. "I think . . . 'P.S. What you said before you left Sprangbur, about love . . . I have come to find you were correct. Thank you, Albert, from the depths of my desiccated old heart, for showing me what I could never see clearly on my own.'"

"Do you have any idea what that means, Mr. Aaron?" Quentin asks.

Eugene shrugs a shoulder. "All my father would say was that they quarreled at the end of the visit, and that he said some things he had no right saying."

"Fountain apparently didn't mind," I say.

"Even so, my father was quite embarrassed about the outburst. He wouldn't tell me more than that, and I certainly tried to get it out of him. The idea of my mild-mannered father shouting at a rich old businessman felt as fantastical as the stories in this book." Eugene smiles. "Papa ultimately came around on the fellow, but apparently Fountain pushed his buttons like no one else in the short time they were in conversation. I think he almost admired him for it."

I refold the letter along its time-worn crease and place it back inside the book. Quentin and I both emit gasps as we take in the illustration we uncover as I carefully turn to the next page. Not terrible by any means, but certainly not the work of a professional artist. Maybe not even of an adult, actually. It shows three people—a princess flanked on either side by a king and a queen—standing together inside of a large bubble soaring above a few cloudlike trees.

Next is the title page:

A New Account of an Incredible Land
By L. M. Worman
1918

Written helpfully beneath in large cursive, with the same heavy ink as the drawing on the previous page, it says:

Illustrations by Isolde Fountain, age 8

And suddenly everything makes so much more sense. Because Edlo was *Louisa's* creation, not Fountain's. She must have come up with it out of a need to connect with the child that inadvertently wound up in her partial care. Edlo was a kind of play therapy for Isolde, and maybe for Julius Fountain too. This book must be the product of years of storytelling—a recording of the world they created at Sprangbur.

The realization makes me surprisingly emotional, thinking about how this woman—someone paid to be responsible for Fountain's daily business needs—wound up taking on this job of caring for the man and his young niece. Because I would bet anything that the princess on the first page is Isolde Fountain, the king is Julius Fountain, and the queen is Louisa Worman. This is a portrait of their family. Circumstances necessitated that Louisa slip into the role of matriarch without ever officially being part of it, and instead of refusing or resenting that role, she created something so absolutely beautiful for them to share.

"Look," Quentin says, pulling me from my thoughts. I refocus on the page in front of me and take in an illustration of the king speaking to a whale—about how anytime he leaves the kingdom, he should leave something valuable behind to comfort and assure the queen and the princess, according to the bit of story that goes with it. *You shall find what you seek beneath the whale* . . . Immediately below the rather rectangular body, in Isolde's youthful writing again, is a piece of dialogue from the story: *"Leave your heart tucked safely away in a bubble!"* Sprangbur has so many details, bas-reliefs and wood carvings and painted ceilings. Surely there are bubbles represented somewhere, overlooked while we were hyper-focused on finding whales.

"In a bubble," I say. "It's in a bubble."

"Found something interesting, did you?" Mr. Aaron says from where I thought he'd actually dozed off in his chair.

"Oh, it's all interesting," I say, my voice shaking at this slight dishonesty. "Thank you so much for sharing it with us. Do you mind if I take a few pictures as we flip through?"

"Be my guest."

I aim my phone over the page with the king and the whale and snap a shot of it. We continue flipping through the manuscript then, my fingers increasingly unsteady as the reality of our discovery sinks deeper. I keep an eye out for anything else that may fit the riddle, but Isolde didn't draw any other whales. It seems clearer than ever: All we have to do is go back to Sprangbur and look for anything that could represent a bubble. Then it's over. The treasure, the thing we've searched for all summer, and all those years ago, will be in our hands. It's the piece we've been missing, finally clicking into place.

After we've closed the book and given it back to Emily, who dutifully returns it to its place in her grandfather's bedroom, we both stand in front of Eugene's chair.

"Thank you again, Mr. Aaron," I say. "That was . . . an extremely special experience for us. I don't think I can express how much we appreciate your help with this."

He reaches out to squeeze my hands. "Maybe you'll name your firstborn after me." He gives me a wink and I laugh, not really sure what else to do.

But it does make me remember that there's a whole life I've made up in my head that I still have to actually talk to Quentin about. We discussed the past the other night in the gardens at Sprangbur, throwing out the clean slate for good. But we still need to have a real conversation about our future. About the fact that he apparently *loves* me. And that I definitely love him. I want him to know that before we find the treasure, so there's no doubt in his mind about my motives or my intentions for our post-hunt relationship. So we can talk about what's ahead for us.

There's the whole car ride home for me to figure out the right way to bring that all up, though. Right now I want to take a minute to bask in what we've accomplished.

After attempting to say our farewells but getting roped into a surprisingly long story about when Albert Aaron met President Truman's cousin, and then managing to cut the anecdote off before it subtly transitioned into another, we finally say goodbye for real. A quarter of the way down the block, out of view of Mr. Aaron's house so he and his granddaughter won't spot us, I stop walking and start jumping up and down, squeezing my eyes shut and my fists closed. "Ahhhh!" I scream in excitement. "Quentin!!" I grab his hands and jump up and down more, but he stays firmly planted on the sidewalk. "We did it! This is it! We've almost found it!"

"Calm," he orders like I'm a small child or a dachshund. "You need to calm down, Nina."

"Why? This has to be the answer! All we have to do is search Sprangbur and find the bubbles. Now that we know what to look for, surely it won't take long to figure out—"

"Nina. Stop." This time his voice is louder and even firmer. He frees his hands from mine and instead holds me by the upper arms to keep me from hopping around. Quentin looks into my eyes until he has my full attention. "It isn't there."

"Since when did you get so pessimistic?" I ask. "Of course it's there. It has to be. I know you've been worried about us, about if I really meant it about staying, but—"

"Nina Hunnicutt, would you *please* just fucking *listen* to me for once?!"

I freeze, noticing now that his eyes are devoid of any hint of the excitement and joy I feel. Instead, he looks absolutely miserable.

"It's not there." He drops both his gaze and his hands then, freeing me. His voice is soft now, pained. "Or it isn't anymore. Because I already found it."

34

Yｏｕ ... ᴡʜᴀᴛ?"

Quentin tries to take my hand again, but I shake him off. "Can we please get in the car and talk there? Mr. Aaron's neighbors—"

"Are you serious? What do I care about Mr. Aaron's neighbors? *Fuck* Mr. Aaron's neighbors!" I shout. An older woman pruning a bush two houses down gives me a look of betrayal and shock. My cheeks go extremely hot. "Not you, sorry," I tell her. "You're lovely." Quentin opens the passenger-side door, and I sink into the seat as if my blush weighs fifty pounds.

An even heavier silence settles as soon as we're both inside the car. Quentin grabs the steering wheel and leans forward until his head is resting on it.

"Please start explaining yourself," I say. "Because my mind is jumping to conclusions here."

Quentin lets out a long sigh before looking back up and staring out the windshield. "I found it that summer. In 2008." When he finally turns to me, his eyelids are heavy, as if talking is beyond exhausting and all he wants to do is take a nice long nap. Except, no, it's not tiredness. It's . . . weariness. "And I have been keeping it from you ever since."

"Jesus Christ, Quentin."

"I know. Please . . . just let me finish explaining, okay? And then you can be as mad as you want."

I stare him down for a good five seconds before glancing away, which he accepts as my agreement.

"Early that summer, sometime in June, I went to Sprangbur without you."

"Why?"

I can see him deciding whether or not he has room to snap at me for interrupting already, before wisely letting it go. "I told you, I felt like I needed to do whatever it took to make you want to be my friend. And I had this ridiculous idea that if I could find the treasure, I could steer us away from it until the last second."

"But why would you want to do that?" I demand. Then I remember everything he confessed the other night at Sprangbur and answer the question myself. "Because you convinced me to treasure hunt with you so we could spend the summer together, and you were worried we'd find it too quickly and I wouldn't want to hang out anymore."

"Yes. I'm not going to lie to you, Nina." I flash him a look and he winces. "I'm not going to lie to you *anymore*," he amends. "I didn't actually expect to find it. I had no ideas of my own, nothing new to investigate. But you were so brilliant. You always have been. I figured it was only a matter of time until you cracked the riddle and we'd be done searching, and then I wouldn't have an excuse to spend time with you."

"That is so stupid, Quentin," I say, burying my fingers in my hair.

"I'm very aware, thank you," he says. "I spent a very hot, sweaty hour combing Sprangbur for anything we missed. I was just about to give up when I noticed a stone right at the top of the cenotaph, along the roof, that seemed oddly loose. There was a log at the edge of the woods, so I dragged it over and climbed up to get a better look. There was a circle engraved in the stone, which was weird because the rest of the design on that part of the wall was stars. I pulled on it and . . . There was a small compartment behind, lined with some sort of nonmagnetic metal. Inside was a canister, and inside that, wrapped up inside several pieces of waxed canvas, was a wooden puzzle box."

"And?" I ask. "What was in it?"

"I don't know. I never opened it."

"Why not?"

"Because I didn't want to do it without you," he says, sounding distressed. "I meant it when I said I wanted the treasure to be something we did as a team. Sure, I was excited when I found it, because it meant I could keep us hunting all summer. But I was also so disappointed. Both in the fact that we hadn't gotten to experience the moment together, and in myself for taking that away from us."

He runs his fingers through his hair, making it stand on end. He looks absolutely as frazzled as I'm starting to feel. "I planned to re-hide it that last night, to try to re-create the moment with you. Then I would get to see your face light up . . . the way it started lighting up a minute ago before I made it go all . . . shuttered." He buries his head in his hands. "God, my plans really *have* always sucked. And I've gone and fucked this all up. Again."

There's simply nothing I can say. All this time. All this time he's been hiding the treasure. And the truth. All in some totally unnecessary attempt to get and keep my attention.

"I can't believe you," I say. "You've known where it was all along, and yet you let me spend weeks in Catoctin—weeks that I could have spent focused on rebuilding my life instead of wasting it."

His head snaps back up now. "You have to be fucking kidding me," he says with much more bitterness than I'm expecting. "*This* is why, Nina. This is why I did it! Because even now, even after everything we've said and done, everything we've shared, you're so obsessed with this bizarre notion that you're falling behind every moment you haven't reached some nebulous ideal version of yourself, that the only way I get to spend time with *you*—the person you truly are—is to trick you into it. Which sucks, because I happen to really fucking love the person you are, Nina. I always have and I always will, even if you don't."

"Don't say that to me. Don't say that you love me right now."

"It's only the truth."

"All this time," I whisper. "All this time you made me feel so horrible for going behind your back, but what do you call what you did, Quentin? You actually *found* the treasure and kept it a secret from me. How is that not infinitely worse?"

"It *is* worse. And I never said I didn't forgive you. You just assumed. It's true what I said before, that the reason I went silent was that you broke my heart and I was embarrassed. But then it was because I was absolutely, completely consumed by guilt. When I—in the police cruiser, when I said it was all a mistake, I was talking about what *I* had done. But you took it as . . . as about you, and the way your eyes filled with tears. My god, Nina. I'd seen my parents hurt each other with words countless times in my life, but I'd never once seen them make amends for it. I had no idea what to do. I figured I'd blown my chance to even be your friend, much less anything more." His eyes close as if remembering the moment.

"The only thing I could think of to make it right was to double down. When I came back to my dad's house to visit for Christmas, I would get you to go to Sprangbur with me, and I could just . . . try the whole thing again. I had no clue what to say to you in the interim, and I figured I could apologize for the silence once I saw you. It was only supposed to be a few months. But then my dad wound up getting a new job and moving away really soon after, and I never did get to come back to Catoctin. The plan fell apart again. I thought I had no way to make things better without being able to give you the treasure as a consolation prize. And a large part of me still figured you didn't care that much about me anyway, so it probably wasn't even bothering you that I was gone."

"Of course I cared about you, you fucking dumbass."

He throws up his hands. "Well, fifteen-year-old Quentin wasn't particularly convinced of that, and honestly, thirty-two-year-old Quentin has some major fucking doubts too. I know you didn't turn down the job offer from Malbyrne yet, Nina."

"Only because I'm still waiting to hear back from the library! I'm not about to dismiss an opportunity that might be the only one I have if this Mrs. MacDonald thing falls through."

"Sure. Tell yourself that," he says.

I scrub my hands over my face. I need to focus on the treasure instead of my emotions before I implode. "What did you do with the treasure after you found it?"

"Well, I wasn't able to go back for it the night we got caught since I was in a whole lot of trouble with my dad, so I left it at Sprangbur and figured either it would still be there when I returned or it wouldn't be. When I came back to town at the end of May and found out from your mom you were coming home, I immediately went to check. And it was right where I left it. So I grabbed it, figuring I'd tell you everything as soon as possible and give it to you to do with as you saw fit. To try to make amends for what happened between us. But then . . . the moment I saw you again, Nina, it was just like before. I was overcome by this absolute, all-encompassing desire to be near you, whatever it took. I was an awkward, gangly little boy again, wanting your attention and not knowing any other way to get it." He pauses. "The money . . ."

"You can't think that's my primary concern right now."

"It's just that . . . I lied about that too. Charlie's Law isn't real. I made it up when it seemed like you weren't going to agree to start looking again."

Of course. I knew it sounded too absurd. I should have followed my instincts. But I think part of me didn't want to examine it too closely. I wanted the excuse to say yes. "That explains why you had no problem going up to seventy percent, I guess. Because I was never meant to get anything at all, so it didn't really matter."

"I was going to give you the money when I sold Charlene's ring."

My head falls back against the seat. "God, Quentin. This is all kinds of fucked-up." My fingers curl, as if they wish they were claws.

"I know," he says.

There's a long silence as we both stew in various intense, uncomfortable emotions. And then something suddenly makes sense. "July Fourth," I say. "When you took me to Sprangbur and said you had a surprise . . ."

"Yes. I was going to tell you then. That was my intention at least, to take you there and tell you everything I felt so you would understand why I did it, and then, if that went well, I would show you the stone in the cenotaph. Beg for your forgiveness. But I hadn't expected you to return my feelings, then or now, and it was so overwhelming. To feel like you wanted to *choose* me, Nina, when that's all I'd ever wanted. And we . . . we got sidetracked."

"So you just decided to keep lying to me?" I ask.

"It wasn't a conscious decision. I really was trying to do better by you. I *want* to do better, to be better. But when I'm with you, sometimes 'better' gets fuzzy. Sometimes the stupid little boy part of my brain takes control instead of the man trying to be worthy of you and—"

"What you mean is that you thought you could get away with it." He opens his mouth to counter the accusation, but I cut in. "Stop. Just, stop." My fingernails dig into my palms as I squeeze my fists in my lap, the barrage of feelings overwhelming. "Where's the box now?" I ask. "You said it isn't at Sprangbur now. You moved it again?"

"It's at my house, in the kitchen. I went back for it while you were with your parents yesterday. Because I was going to tell you this morning."

"What's your excuse for not doing it that time?" I ask.

Quentin sighs heavily. "You seemed so excited about meeting Emily and Eugene. I didn't want to ruin it for you."

"Right, because this isn't ruining anything at all."

"I know that I messed this up," he says. "That I've been selfish, that I've hurt you. You have every right in the world to hate me."

I'm furious, hurt, confused, but no part of me *hates* Quentin Bell. Admitting that aloud feels a lot like forgiving him, though, which I am in no way willing to do yet. So instead of telling him that, despite everything, I can't help but *not* hate him, I say, "You are going to drive us back to Catoctin, and we are going to open that damn box. I want to be done with this, Quentin."

35

OUR JOURNEY FROM Richmond to Catoctin immediately
takes the prize for Most Uncomfortable Time I've Spent in
a Car. Which is impressive considering that, freshman year
of college, I carpooled with a girl from my dorm and her girl-
friend to get back to Maryland for winter break and they had a
massive blowout fight and broke up about twenty minutes into
the trip.

Quentin doesn't even try to talk to me. Which is good, because I am not at all in the mood for more conversation. He
stares out the windshield with the intensity of someone trying
to drive in whiteout conditions and grips the steering wheel so
tightly that his fingers become colorless from the knuckle down.
They don't regain blood flow until he parks in front of our duplex two hours later.

Wordlessly, I follow him into his house, where Faustine
greets us with a haunting and distressingly deep *meeeeewow*.
Quentin marches past her, through the dining room, and into
the kitchen. I follow him, somehow managing to avoid tripping

on the cat weaving through my legs as I walk. He slides open the drawer next to the sink, reaches into the very back, and pulls out what appears to be a wad of grocery bags. Those are peeled away to reveal a wooden box, approximately five inches by four inches, and another four inches high. It has stars carved into the top, reminiscent of Sprangbur's front door.

He hands it over to me. "Here," he says, not meeting my eyes. "It's all yours."

I examine it, looking for some clue as to how it opens. "Do you know how it might—"

"No."

"Okay. Well. Thanks."

He finally looks at me. "I'm sorry, Nina. I really am." His voice is full of pain, and regret, and shame.

"I know," I say softly, because I can tell how much he means it. There's something to be said for this genuine apology. It's much more than I got the last time things fell apart (and infinitely more than what I got from Cole when he lied to me). It doesn't mean it will be enough to repair what's broken, though. In this particular moment, my anger is outweighed by sorrow. That this is the conclusion of our treasure hunt, and probably of us—here, in Quentin's mostly empty kitchen with his naked cat noisily cleaning herself atop one of my feet.

The absurdity hurts so much that tears well in my eyes. Quentin takes a hesitant step forward, then a more determined and certain one. His hand comes to my face, gently cupping my cheek and swiping away the moisture with his thumb. He leans forward and kisses me, so gently that his lips are only a whisper against mine. Not the beginning of something, but an ending. And not the happily-ever-after kind in the romances my mom reads with her book club. Once again, I managed to convince myself this was a different kind of story than it actually was. To see things one way when the entire time they were really another.

Lesson finally learned.

Saying goodbye seems redundant since that's clearly what that kiss was meant to be, so I turn around, clutching the box to my chest, take a deep breath, and leave.

FOR A LONG time, I sit on the steps of my parents' porch, staring at the damn box as the Orioles game drifts across the street from Mr. Farina's radio. I can't muster up the curiosity to open it yet, although I am extremely close at one point to throwing it down on the walkway to crack it the hell open, just because I bet it would be cathartic. The only thing that stops me is that I've heard stories of tamper-proof puzzle boxes. Also the box is so beautiful that it really would be a shame to break it.

Quentin and I have already left enough broken things in our wake.

Man, how embarrassingly emo.

Eventually I take the box inside, barely acknowledge my mother when she calls a greeting from the kitchen, and go up to my room.

I consider calling Sabrina to tell her what happened, but I'm not ready to rehash it all yet. The pain after I broke up with Cole was delayed, and then when it hit it wasn't nearly as bad as I'd feared. This, on the other hand . . . This is a profound wound, a reopening of an old one that's even deeper and wider, new damage and old damage mixed together in a way that's turned a fading scar into a fresh one that I'm not sure will ever heal correctly. Even a best friend can't do much for that, and I don't want her digging around in there, thinking she's helping but only making it worse.

Instead, I sit with my orange-and-pink comforter wrapped around me like it's my own soft little cave and simply stare at the box where I've placed it on my nightstand.

With the drama of how I came to possess it, it still hasn't really hit me that this is Fountain's treasure. That it wasn't a practical joke after all. (Or, at least, not completely; the contents could still prove to be ridiculous, I suppose.) I can't believe it actually exists.

Right now, I kind of wish it didn't.

Time doesn't feel real, so I'm not sure how long it is before my mom calls up the stairs, telling me that dinner is ready. My stomach grumbles; Quentin and I didn't eat lunch. I trudge down to the dining room to find my mother placing bowls of macaroni and cheese on the table. "A recipe Aunt Joan sent me," she says, not yet looking up. "I haven't tried it before, so I hope it's good. More mustard powder than I—" The moment she sees me she stops talking and moves forward to wrap me in a hug. "Oh, sweet baby."

I thought I was going to be okay, but my mother's embrace is like the gentle version of a battering ram, slamming into the place storing all the hurt I've accumulated and stashed away. My sobs against her shoulder are ugly and violent. Nothing like the quiet, woe-is-me tears I shed after getting fired and break-ing up with Cole and leaving Boston. Jon Bon Jovi himself could show up at our front door right now to call me delusional in person, and I wouldn't even be able to manage a raised mid-dle finger. The anger just isn't there.

It turns out I was delusional after all, to think Quentin and

I could be together. That I could find happiness in this place where I'd only ever felt disappointment. Disappointment that's now crashing to the floor, taking me with it. Heavy, heavy, heavy. Duffle bags full of bowling balls and suitcases stuffed with bricks. A security envelope with its seams straining under the burden of twenty-six dollars in pennies and nickels, its single stamp guaranteeing it would never arrive at its destination, just thud and clang when it's slipped back through the mail slot.

My tears do eventually dry up, and my stomach's demands recapture my attention. Mom guides me to my dining chair as if I might not be able to find it on my own and whisks away the bowl of dried-out macaroni. She reappears a short time later with a fresh, steaming bowl in one hand and a bottle of wine and two glasses in the other.

I love this woman so much. I hate that it looks like I'm going to have to leave her and Dad again now that the life I wanted to build here has failed its permit inspection.

Turns out you can't build on quicksand. And quicksand is pretty good at pretending to be regular sand. And also that it loves you.

Okay, I am in absolutely no emotional condition for good metaphors right now.

As we eat, I gradually fill Mom in on what happened in Richmond. First, I tell her about meeting the son and great-granddaughter of the man who interviewed Julius Fountain in the thirties, which she pretends she finds interesting even though I know it's not the part of the story she cares about. Then I get to Quentin's confession.

"So he *did* goblin you!" she declares. "I must've known all along somehow."

"What does that even mean?" I ask, attempting to rub away my exasperation and sinus pressure with little circles of my fingertips on my forehead.

"He played a nasty trick. That's what goblins do, right?"

"I honestly could not tell you," I say.

"It's what they do," she says, bringing a self-satisfied forkful of noodles to her mouth. "I'm so sorry, though, Ninabean. I really thought he was better than that."

"Me too."

"Did he tell you why he did it?"

"Oh. Um." I can already tell what my mother's response is going to be if I tell her he did it because he wanted to spend time with me. She's going to switch sides so fast, and I want her on *my* side, dammit. "It's . . . complicated."

She gives me a look like she knows I'm not telling her everything, but all she says is, "Do you want me to make those brownies you like, with the salted caramel swirled on top?"

"Yes, please." My voice is small and childlike, but this time I'm fully embracing it. I'm going to let my mom take care of me, the way she wasn't able to the first time Quentin broke my heart—mostly because I wouldn't tell her what was wrong, but then also because she was so preoccupied dealing with the aftermath of Dad's accident. I was afraid to use up Mom's limited supply of love and care. But as she places a gentle kiss on my temple before making her way to the kitchen, I understand now it's the most limitless thing on the planet. That reverberations of it will remain even after she's gone, inside me where my own limitless supply has been growing, waiting for the moment it will be activated. First I need to find someone worthy of it.

Or maybe I should direct some of it toward myself. I'm going to need it back in Boston, when I'm alone again.

Mom's voice drifts into the dining room, interrupting my thoughts. "On the upside, at least you didn't get picked up by the police this time around."

Hold up, what!?

"Um, I don't know what you mean. I never . . ." I turn and meet her gaze through the open doorway. I'm not fooling her even a bit. "How long have you known?"

"Mr. Bell called us that night to tell us everything. Did you really think he wouldn't?"

"I mean, sort of. Yeah." I can't believe I've carried that secret for so many years and my parents knew all along. More to the point, I can't believe they didn't punish me. "Why weren't you mad?"

"Because you were a good kid, Nina. We knew your heart. We didn't think you'd be making a habit of it. Besides, you were always your own harshest critic. If you made a mistake, we knew you didn't need us to tell you."

She's right. I did make a mistake, and I did know it.

I just wish I had a better sense of if I'm making one now.

FOR THE NEXT five days, I cry and mope around the house like a woeful ghost. Mom must fill Dad in on the most basic details, because he tells me he's "sorry about what happened" when we pass in the hallway the first morning, then otherwise gives me an extra-wide berth. It isn't long before even hearing evidence of Quentin's existence next door starts making me too sad, and I haul my comforter down to the couch, where at least we aren't sharing a bedroom wall and my window can't taunt me with memories. I consider leaving and going back north, crashing on a friend's couch for a week or two until I have the offer letter from Malbyrne and can use it to get a new apartment. But this isn't over yet.

There's still the unopened puzzle box, up in my room. I occasionally sit on my bed, staring at it, considering how it might open and what it might contain. Then I inevitably get too annoyed and angry that I'm doing this alone and shove it back into the top drawer of my nightstand. I spend most of my time consoling myself with my favorite comfort foods (thanks to my mother), making a bunch of macramé plant hangers (also thanks to my mother), and getting way too into *Formula 1: Drive to Survive* (that one's actually thanks to Hanako; we've been texting).

But inevitably I hit the limit of how many baked goods I can possibly consume, and soon thereafter I run out of both string and episodes featuring horrific crashes and Guenther Steiner being eminently quotable. I take it as a sign that it's time to get myself together again. This was the type of all-encompassing sulking I came here hoping to partake of back in June, which Quentin ruined with his presence and talent for getting me to laugh and smile and agree to his stupid challenges. I finally got to do it, just not over the things I thought had made me sad. Now, though, I'm finished. Like Forrest Gump deciding he's run far enough. Time to do something else.

Like figure out how to open that damn box.

36

H ELLO!" I SHOUT down the basement stairs as I descend. "It's Nina Hunnicutt! Your daughter! I'm coming down!" My father is sometimes so focused on his work that he isn't aware of much else and will startle if you simply appear in his periphery. Considering he often works with things that are sharp or tiny, he's reasonably asked that we announce our presence loudly before visiting his workshop. I wait on the landing for him to respond before going any farther.

"Roger that," he calls back.

When I reach him, he's already turned around on his stool, wiping his hands on a cloth and waiting for me to tell him what I need.

"Hi, Dad," I say, dropping a small kiss on his temple where his hair has turned salt-and-pepper. "Know anything about puzzle boxes? I've got one here, and I'm worried about breaking it if I try to open it myself. It's an antique."

"Let's see." He holds out his large palm—stained slightly green from who knows what—and I sit the wooden box atop it.

My father studies it for a few minutes, turning it this way and that, tapping here and there, giving it a light shake beside his ear. It looks a little like a doctor giving a patient an examination; I'm half expecting him to ask the box if it hurts at all when he presses here. What about . . . here? "Hmm." He shakes it once more. "Ah. Okay."

"Do you know how to do it?" I ask.

"I have a guess. No clue if it's right, though. Shouldn't hurt to try it." He hands it back over to me. "Put it down over there," he says, flicking a finger in the direction of a large wooden table pressed up against the wall perpendicular to his workbench. "More space."

"And then . . . ?"

"Spin it," he says.

"Spin it?"

"Yep. Clockwise. Like a top. The lid should lift right off."

"Seriously? That's it?" I stare at the box, my hand hovering over it like a claw machine waiting for someone to put in a quarter. Could it really be that easy? I thought I was ready to find out, but maybe I'm not.

"Think so. Clever, huh?" Dad says. "Sometimes things aren't as complicated as we try to make them."

Something in me unlocks as simply as the puzzle box might as he says the words. This doesn't have to be complicated. Quentin and me—*we* don't have to be complicated. His stupid behavior and my stupid behavior came from the same stupid source: our teenage brains unable to navigate having feelings for each other. Admittedly, his continued into adulthood, but I can't completely blame him. Looking back, I see all of the times he tried to lead me to the answer, or tell me the truth, only for me to change the subject, or for him to chicken out the same way he did when he didn't kiss me that night on the blanket in his backyard. I can understand making a bad decision because you aren't sure you can catch and hold someone's attention otherwise. Because isn't that exactly the same reason I went behind his back that night at Sprangbur? Some foolish attempt to be remembered after it was all over?

I groan. I was fully planning on stretching out my anger, but it seems silly to fake it when every part of me wants to see Quentin and tell him how I feel about him. How I've felt that way about him for so long that it's become an inherent part of who I am, even when I tried to suppress it or become someone else. That I understand exactly what it's like to feel like you aren't enough as you are, and the ridiculous hoops a person might jump through in order to convince themselves and the world they're worthy.

"You, uh, gonna try it?" my father asks after a full thirty seconds of me standing there in silence.

"Not quite yet." I snatch up the puzzle box, careful *not* to let it spin. "Thanks, Dad," I yell as I scramble back up the stairs. His response comes in the form of a mumble that sounds like "Happy to help."

In my room, I place the box atop the nightstand and make my way to the window. It's about two in the afternoon, and the sun is beating down on the backyard. I haven't been outside today— or, um, for several days now—but my mother was fretting this morning about needing to water her tomato plants while it was still early enough to try to save them from getting too burned, so I presume it's toasty out there.

When I lift the sash, it doesn't let out its distinctive scream. Oh, right. I forgot that Dad came in and silently fixed it sometime early in the week, when I was still hiding under my comforter and crying between bites of chocolate cake.

Meeewow.

Faustine's distinctive greeting drifts over from next door, telling me that Quentin's window must already be open, which means he's probably in there with her. Maybe I should have just gone over and knocked on his front door like a normal person. This seemed more fitting, in a way, when I thought of it downstairs, but perhaps this conversation actually deserves direct sincerity.

But I also know that what Quentin told Eugene Aaron about his desire to get lost in the fantasy was true. He's a person who has always felt most comfortable when he can shield himself behind something—a joke, a competition, a too-charming smile, a window. And I can't blame him. This shit is scary. *Love* is scary, a risk, something that I suppose is slightly easier to stare down when you take some of the heaviness out of it and instead insert a horrible accent.

So I take a breath and quickly call out, "G'day, mate!" then squeeze my eyes closed.

". . . Nina?" Quentin sounds somehow equal parts confused and desperate as he says my name.

"Nah, no Nina here, mate. Just the Sun. Ya know, big round fella up there in da sky? Center of da solar system?"

"I'm familiar," he says slowly. "I just didn't realize the Sun was from . . . Chicago?"

"Chicago?" I protest in my regular voice. "I'm obviously going for Australia."

"I have literally never heard an Australian person sound like that."

"Come on. I sound *just* like Daniel Ricciardo!"

"Who?"

"Bloody 'ell, mate," I say, trying again.

"Are you going for Cockney now?"

"Quentin! I'm trying to grand gesture you. Shut up."

"Grand gesture me?"

"Yes! I am trying to tell you that I forgive you for hiding the treasure from me and that I understand why you did it. It's the same reason I tried to find it on my own that summer too—I was trying to get your attention, to prove myself worthy of it. And I want to learn from our past so we can maybe, just maybe, figure out how to have a future together."

"Oh."

"But I hoped to say all of that in a fun accent. To make it, like, I don't know, sweet? And you've screwed it all up."

"Sorry. But I'm actually glad you didn't do the accent," he says. "It was already pretty damned sweet as it was."

"Quentin." I sigh. "I know you. Which is how I know that you meant it when you said you were sorry. I hope you know that I'm genuinely sorry too."

"I do know that."

"Okay. Good. I'm tired of being mad at you now, and I'm about ninety-five percent sure I know how to open the puzzle box. Will you please open it with me?"

"I would be absolutely honored. Just give me one . . . second . . ."

There's a quiet grunt right before a metallic pop, then a scraping sound before one of Quentin's bare feet suddenly appears in my peripheral vision. "What the fuck!" I shout, leaning out to see one of his legs hanging against the brick and his head emerging. "Are you trying to *climb* over here?"

"Yeah," he says, like it's not a big deal that he's currently dangling half his body out of a second-story window. He did attempt this once before, actually—which is how he wound up with a broken arm that had him unable to go swimming for most of the summer of 2005. I bet him he couldn't do it, so I guess it was technically my fault it happened.

"Quentin Foster Bell, use the front door, you absolute clown!"

"Now who's screwing up whose grand gesture, hm?" he mumbles as he disappears back inside.

I'm only halfway down the stairs when the doorbell rings.

37

MY HEART SKIPS a beat, then feels like it might implode as I take in the full force of Quentin standing there in front of me. I flung the door open so quickly he didn't even have time to do anything with his hands, one still extended toward the doorbell.

I suddenly can't seem to form words. I am empty of thoughts, which are crowded out by the intense emotion taking up every available inch. I don't quite know how to describe it, except . . . well, I guess I do, actually.

My arms go around his neck and I bury my face in his shoulder.

He freezes at first, likely caught unawares by the intensity of the greeting. But he softens into my embrace and wraps me in his arms, holding me tightly and murmuring my name over and over into my hair as if it's an incantation that might keep me from ever disappearing from his life again.

"Quentin," I whisper. "I love you. I love you so much."

After a moment, he slides his hands to my shoulders and holds me just far enough away to look into my eyes. "I thought

I loved you before. When we were kids. But I understand now that I was wrong."

"Oh." The world comes crashing down, one of those controlled demolition videos taking place in my chest. Maybe that incantation was actually one of future banishment. Surely I haven't . . . There is absolutely no way I could have misread this. I glance away, quickly, in an attempt to hide how startled I am by his words, but he gently cradles my cheek and directs my face back toward his.

"It was only a pale imitation," he whispers, a slight smile forming at the corner of his mouth. "Because as gigantic of a feeling as it was, as all-encompassing and demanding . . . it's nothing compared to what I feel for you now. This thing that makes me simultaneously make the stupidest decisions and want to be the best version of myself. That makes me ache with need and hope. I am so, so gone for you, Neen, and I don't know what to do about it. I've never quite known what to do. But, if you'll let me, I promise I'll keep trying to get it right, with everything I've got, for my whole life."

The sweet, soft words reverberate inside me, an echoing ring that feels like it could continue for as long as I'll let it. "If it makes you feel better, I'm not sure I know what to do with any of this either," I confess. "But I think that the first step is probably . . . kissing me."

"That, I can do."

Quentin's lips brush against mine tentatively before settling into something deeper, something that feels certain and steady and like it could last a lifetime.

A throat clears somewhere in the room behind me. We turn our heads as one, our lips separating as we find my mother sitting on the couch. In my hurry to get to Quentin, her presence in the living room completely evaded my notice. "Oh, would you look at the time!" she says, not looking at anything that actually indicates it. She puts down her e-reader, stands, grabs her purse from its hook by the front door, and scoots around us, talking all the while. "I need to go to . . . the store! For . . . onions. Hope you'll join us for dinner tonight, Quentin. We're having . . . uh . . . something with onions, I guess! Six o'clock? Great! See you later."

Quentin and I exchange smiles, too amused to be annoyed by the interruption.

"Where's the box?" he asks.

"Upstairs, in my room."

He leans down and whispers into my ear, his words hot against my already flushed skin. "Funny, that's where I was going to suggest we go anyway."

Quentin stops on the threshold of my bedroom, his hands grabbing the doorframe as he peeks inside without entering. "I haven't been in here in a very long time."

"I guess you haven't." I didn't even realize that, of all the times he came over to my parents' house this summer, he never did have reason to venture upstairs. And when we were teenagers, there was a strict "No Quentin in Nina's Room" policy instituted when we turned ten. At the time I thought it was absolutely absurd. What did they even think we were going to get up to in there? But I understand the concern now. Because it turns out we were pretty much the last ones on earth to notice that we were into each other. My parents can be forgiven for assuming we were smarter than we apparently were. "Hasn't changed too much, to be honest."

"That comforter," he says.

"It's horrible, isn't it?"

"I kind of like it. I remember you being all excited when you told me you finally got your parents to buy it for you. Or, you told the Moon, rather."

"What? Why do you remember that?"

"Because you were happy, and it made me happy. And we were like, fourteen then, I guess, and I was just starting to understand that my feelings toward you were changing into something very different from the friendship I was familiar with, and I was *so* annoyed that I found you cute." He leans against the doorframe and flexes his hand in front of him. "I tried to punch a hole in my wall because I saw someone do it on TV and it seemed like what a tough guy would do. But these walls are lath and plaster and I wasn't even particularly strong, so all I did was make my knuckles bleed and probably get a hairline fracture in one of my thumb bones. Still doesn't always bend right." He grins at me. "I was not kidding when I said I've never known what to do with the way I feel about you."

"Wow. You really weren't." I press up against him in the doorway and take his hand. I place a gentle kiss on his knuckles. "I know I'm a bit late, but I hope that still helps make it better."

"Let me see." He cups one of my breasts and gently squeezes as his thumb swipes over where my nipple is beneath the fabric of my shirt and bra. "Hey. Look at that. It's a miracle."

I roll my eyes and reach for his face, kissing him until both of his hands find purchase on my body. "Do you want to open the puzzle box now?" I ask when his mouth drifts to my neck.

"No," he answers simply, walking us into my room and turning me toward the bed.

A short time later, stretched out atop my comforter on the floor—the bed wasn't anywhere near big enough—our clothes hanging in disarray from our bodies as if we tried to get dressed inside one of those hurricane-strength wind machines that used to be at the mall, Quentin traces the shell of my ear with his finger, then drifts down to my collarbone.

"Are you ready?" he asks.

"I'm . . . You . . . Too good. Can't again," I say, still too drunk on the aftermath of pleasure to express coherent thoughts. "Not yet."

He laughs. "That's very satisfying to hear. But I meant are you ready to open Fountain's box?"

"Oh." Best-case outcome: We open the box and there's something so incredibly wonderful and valuable inside that the Conservancy insists on giving us a reward even though they don't have to. Worst-case outcome: The treasure isn't a treasure at all, but a trap—something super toxic that causes a slow, painful death for everyone in the house. Most likely: It's . . . a coin? A tiny brass figurine of a whale? I don't know. I really never expected us to get this far, nor do I have any clue what someone as unpredictable as Fountain would find worth creating a whole posthumous treasure hunt around. But whatever is inside that box, once we see it . . . well, this is kind of all over, isn't it? Maybe not immediately, but soon.

Things will have to change, for better or worse.

Delaying opening the box isn't going to delay the inevitable, though. We've waited so long to know. "Okay," I say. "Let's do it."

Quentin reaches up to his right and grabs it from where I left it on my bookshelf. "I don't know if it'll work here . . ." I say, rising up on my knees. I clear the top of the nightstand to make space. "It may need a larger table."

Once there's nothing in the way, Quentin places the puzzle box in the center of the small surface. "Now what?" he asks.

"Now we . . . spin it," I say, gently pressing my fingertips to opposite sides of the box. I give it a good flick. It makes two rotations before stopping, right on the edge of the nightstand. Quentin nudges it back to its original starting point, and I try again. This time it flies off and lands on the floor, the comforter thankfully softening the blow.

"Maybe you should do it," I say. "This is apparently not an area in which I excel."

"Took a couple decades, but we finally found one," he teases, then leans over and kisses my shoulder. He keeps his head resting against mine and his other arm wrapped around my waist as he takes a deep breath and gives the puzzle box a proper spin. It comes to rest in approximately the same location it started.

"That was a good spin," I say quietly, as if my words might disturb it.

"Check it," he says, nudging me with his nose as he presses his mouth against my skin.

My hands shake as I reach for the box and find the top loose. I slowly, slowly raise it up, until the bottom sits there, open.

I look to Quentin to find him already looking back at me, his expression somewhere between victory and defeat. "There it is. That's the look I've always loved most," he whispers. "The one on your face right now. Like you've just conquered the world. Hard to mind you beating me at anything when it always put that look on your face."

It's hard to tear my eyes away from him, the deep longing and affection living in the space between us palpable enough that it feels like something I might be able to package up and carry with me. He smiles ruefully and says, "So what's inside, cookiepuss? Don't keep me waiting."

IX

Lou is leaving me at the end of this month.
Retiring. She's been in my employ for twenty-six
years--longer than anyone save Marshall, my butler,
whom you met when you arrived.

Have you ever had a secretary, Mr. Aaron? No,
no, indeed you haven't. Writers must be quite
successful before they can hire a person to do
their typing for them, I imagine. And if you were
so successful, you would not be doing this job. No
offense intended, of course!

Fordham was the one who hired Lou, but I
immediately knew we would suit. I'm a stubborn old
horse, Mr. Aaron--and this is hardly a new quality
of mine--but Lou is quite the formidable jockey.
She's one of only a few people I've ever met who
knows when to give me my head and when to rein me
in. And one of even fewer I will allow to do so!

It is hard to believe she will be off on her own
adventures soon. We've had so many of them
together, you see. The business. Raising Issy.
Ruling Edlo. In many ways, Lou has been my partner
in all of it. Perhaps a change in title and pay

would convince her to give it another year or two?
But no. No. She deserves her rest, and time to
enjoy the fruits of her labor instead of moldering
here with me.

It's only that . . . Well, Mr. Aaron, it is
strange to live so much of your life alongside
someone else, with them living theirs alongside
you, the two never quite coming to meet.

Lou and I were almost always in agreement about
Fountain Seltzer, and usually about Issy. We often
worked in such harmony that I sometimes did not
know where Lou ended and I began, and vice versa.
Yet there were also a handful of times that . . .
times I suppose when we did not see eye to eye on
things. And in those moments, ones when Lou and I
were not of one mind, it felt like being torn
asunder from myself.

I suppose that is often how I have felt lately.

Perhaps it's the change in the weather, or my new
chef's cooking. Entirely too many beans in the--

"Now, Mr. Aaron, why have you stopped typing?"

The young man looked up from his portable typewriter and
gave Julius Fountain a falsely pleasant smile. "Oh, I thought
perhaps you were finished deluding yourself. Were you not?"

To his credit, Fountain revealed no emotion in response to
this blatant disrespect. "Pardon?"

"Are you that deep in denial or simply the world's largest
fool? Which is it? No, no, I can answer that myself. It's both, sir.
Both." Albert jumped to his feet and hastily crossed the room,
only to turn on his heel and come straight back. Despite the

voice in his head that attempted to cool his frustration and warned that it was unforgivably impertinent for him to speak this way to an informant—and such a wealthy one at that—he found himself unable to stop. He extended an accusatory finger toward the absurd man sprawled across the garish armchair. "You go on and on about how you don't believe in fear, yet I've never met anyone more afraid of reality. You're so scared of it that you hide inside these ridiculous stories you tell yourself, so wrapped up in pretending that you've managed to miss what's real and right in front of you."

Fountain's words were quiet, but with an unmistakable edge. "And what, in your estimation, is that?"

"Love!" Albert shouted, throwing his arms into the air. "You're in love with your secretary, Mr. Fountain! You *love* Miss Worman. It is clear as anything, and yet you bury your head in the sand and speak of changes in weather and beans rather than acknowledge it. You needn't admit it to her, I suppose. But my god, man, at least admit it to yourself! Perhaps then you will be a modicum less insufferable."

"Is that all, Mr. Aaron?" Fountain asked, the edge to his voice even sharper now.

Surely he'd already said enough for Fountain to complain to his superiors, and then he would once again be unemployed. His wife would be so disappointed. Better make it worth it, then, he thought. "No. I have one more thing to say to you."

Fountain raised his eyebrows slightly in invitation.

"My tie might be ugly, but your pajamas are absolutely atrocious."

38

BRING THE BOX to my lap and stare down at its contents. "It's . . . it looks like it's just a piece of paper," I say.

"Maybe there's something beneath it?"

Gently, I tuck my fingertip into where the edge of the paper meets the box's edge and lift it out. "Nope," I say. "Just . . . this."

"Maybe it's a folded-up US bond worth like a million dollars?" Quentin says. "I might've been lying about Charlie's Law, but 'finders keepers' is actually sort of legit in certain circumstances . . ."

The fold is complicated—over this way, over that way—almost like an accordion. "It appears to be . . . a letter. At least this first page is. There are a couple sheets here."

He lets out a long sigh and rubs his hands through his hair. "If this is another riddle, I swear to god."

"No . . ." I say, my eyes dancing over it quickly, making out the words separately before putting them together.

My dearest Lou,

I'm certain you're the one who will find this first. Probably within the first week of searching. I tried to make it a challenge, something to keep you occupied for a while, but you're whip-smart and always did know me too well.

With that in mind, I'm aware I may be telling you things that are not news to you. Still, please humor an old dead man and continue reading this letter.

Lou. Louisa. I used to say that I couldn't do it without you. And I couldn't have. But it hit me much too late that what I meant by that shifted dramatically over time. It started as a way to acknowledge your invaluable help with the business. Then . . .

Then.

You remember those early days after Isolde arrived. How I walked around in a fog of grief without the first clue how to care for that sensitive, beautiful child.

And so you created the magical world of Edlo. A place for Isolde to grow up. A place for us to grow together.

Somewhere along the way you stopped being my secretary and became my partner. We built a family, ruled a great kingdom. We lived happily in the fantasy of it for a long time. But it wasn't enough to keep you content forever—nor should it have been! So you left the Castle, decided to exist on the periphery of the story you'd written for us instead of remaining at its center. It was a story that I'd grown too comfortable inside, forgetting it wasn't reality. That it wasn't something I could keep.

I learned much too late that the problem with living inside the stories we tell ourselves is that sometimes it obscures what's real and in front of us all along.

I'm both sorry and not, Lou, that I never told you how much I loved you when I was alive. It will come as no surprise, I'm sure, that I did not recognize the emotion in myself until it was too late to confess it. I loved my parents and my brother and Isolde, of course, but this particular variety was foreign to me. Something I didn't understand, thought was beyond my capacity. Yet it snuck up on me over time, soft and purring like a kitten, disguising itself as gratitude and friendly affection until one day a stranger came by and tore the cover off it. Made me see exactly what it was. By that time, you were preparing to leave, though. To have adventures in service of yourself instead of us. You were on your way to real happiness, and I knew I couldn't offer you anything more than a continuous game of pretend.

The King of Edlo could not leave his heart here, as he will not be returning this time. The truth is that the Queen and the Princess made up the entirety of it anyway.

I lived a life that was more wonderful than I ever could have dreamed. Some of it was luck, yes. Some of it was intelligence and business savvy.

But most of it, Louisa, was you.

I remain yours, in death as I was in life,

J. J.

Quentin and I sit there, contemplating the letter for a solid minute.

"So, Fountain's treasure is the love he found along the way?" he asks, breaking the silence.

"That certainly does seem to be the implication, yes."

"That's . . . beautiful," Quentin says. Then snorts—a laugh

filed under *When he inadvertently skipped Question 4 on a standardized test and saw that his grade was a 33 percent because all of his answers were one place off.* "And worth less than nothing on the free market."

"Probably." I can't quite tell how I feel. There's the pride of accomplishing what we set out to do, the disappointment that it was relatively anticlimactic, the finality of it all. And there's also the joy that Fountain, Louisa Worman, and Isolde had each other, even if Fountain only truly appreciated the role Louisa played in his life toward the end of it. Followed by intense sadness that it seems like Louisa never found this. Maybe never even looked for it, considering how dismissive she was in the newspaper article about the treasure.

"Do you think she knew that he loved her?" Quentin asks, as if reading my mind. He holds out his hand, wordlessly requesting a look at the letter.

"I don't know," I say, handing him the two pieces of paper. I'm not sure how she would have felt about it anyway. Her long-term employer declaring his love for her? At least he did it after his death, so she wouldn't have needed to respond if she didn't return the sentiment. Then again, based on everything I know about Fountain and Louisa Worman, they were very close. They practically raised a child together. There had to be *some* warm feeling there, even if it was only the kind born of shared experience.

"Nina," Quentin says. "Look. There's more on the back of the second page." He's turned it over, and there's more handwriting there that I missed, thinking the shadows of the words were simply the first page beneath it showing through. I reach for it, since I'm still the better cursive-reader between us.

J. J.,

    This is ludicrous, writing to you now, when you live well beyond the delivery capabilities of the US Mail. Yet I do it, for the same reason I have done every ludicrous thing in my adult life: because of my deep and abiding respect and affection for you.

    I knew we weren't meant to be together in the traditional way. I never had any illusions that we might become husband and wife, so you need not feel as if you disappointed me. You see, we were something that brought me even more joy: Isolde's safe harbor and the very closest of friends.

    Believe it or not, before I was in your employ, I did not take notes sitting atop tables, or conclude my days tangoing about the library, or write stories about kings and queens and princesses in magical lands. My time with you made me someone else entirely, someone my younger self would barely recognize. It made me a dreamer, a believer. A mother. A partner. You made me those things, J. J. Through you, I became much more than what I'd imagined for myself. And I am forever grateful.

    We had our differences, especially at the end. It wasn't always easy. But much of the time, it was perfect.

    I have decided to leave this here, not out of any belief that you might come back for your heart someday (for I know where that will be, as I carry it with me, always, in my own, and know Issy does as well), but that someone else might find this and know love for the invaluable treasure that it is.

    With all of mine,
    Lou

39

QUENTIN AND I lay on the comforter-covered floor of my bedroom for a long time, mostly silent, staring up at the ceiling.

"What should we do with it?" he asks finally. "Put it back?"

I tuck away the part of me that feels slightly bruised by our find—both the one-two punch of Fountain's and Louisa's letters, and the end of our adventure—and put on my more objective historian hat. "I think we should contact Sharon at the Sprangbur Conservancy and see if they want the letters and box for their collections. The way they talked about Louisa during the tour, as if she were just Fountain's secretary . . . I think this might help them reinterpret the relationship and make it known how important she was to both his business and his life. That would make me feel moderately better, to get her some acknowledgment. Maybe we can even ask Eugene and Emily if they would mind someone making a copy of the Edlo manuscript. That could be nice for the Conservancy to have too. After all, Louisa was the author, and for all intents and purposes, she was the lady of the house."

"If they ask how we found it . . . ?"

"Maybe we give them a truncated version of the truth," I say. "We were interested in the legend of Fountain's treasure, we did some research, and we found it in a compartment hidden in the outer wall of the cenotaph. We don't need to mention that you were sitting on the information for almost two decades."

Quentin pillows his hands beneath his head and stares up at the ceiling again, contemplating. Is he thinking about Fountain and Louisa, about us, or about something else altogether?

He starts talking slowly, as if still putting together his thoughts. "What Fountain said . . . about missing what's real and in front of us because we're busy living inside the stories we tell ourselves."

"Yeah?"

"I think that's what happened to us. We got too wrapped up in the stories we were telling ourselves about . . . well, ourselves. And each other." He turns toward me now and rests a hand on my hip. "My biggest regret in life is that I missed what was real and right in front of me back then. That I didn't see you trying to prove yourself to me the same way I was trying to prove myself to you. That I ghosted you instead of facing what I'd done. That I wasn't around when you needed me, when your dad got hurt. I will never forgive myself for that."

"Quentin . . ."

"I told myself you couldn't possibly want me unless I hoodwinked you into it. Part of me still thinks that, if I'm being honest. But I'm going to try so hard, Nina, to stop telling myself that story now. I'm hoping we might start a new one together. I know you might have changed your mind about staying—"

"I haven't," I say. "I haven't changed my mind at all. In fact, the library formally offered me Mrs. MacDonald's position yesterday morning. I've already accepted."

It's true that I considered taking the job at Malbyrne and going back to Boston in the immediate aftermath of our fight. But then the other day, staring at that puzzle box on my nightstand, I found myself thinking about Julius James Fountain, wearing pink paisley pajamas that matched his chair. He believed that fear was just a shorthand way to discover everything you loved and would do anything to keep. And that made me realize that, even without Quentin in the picture, what I was most afraid of losing were my parents and apple fritters and Hanako's bar. The special collections room and Mr. Farina's booty shorts and the scent of honeysuckle. I think my heart is here now, whether it's broken or whole.

Obviously I prefer whole. But as much as I want to be Quentin's Nina, I know I don't *have* to be in order to find happiness. I understand now that love, when it's real, doesn't require you to be someone different. It just makes you even more solidly yourself.

And the fear of getting it all wrong, getting hurt . . . Maybe it's just a sign that you're doing it right.

"You . . . you did?" There's so much hope in his expression that it's a physical pain inside my breastbone.

I nod. "It's what I want. I want to be here. And I prefer it to be with you. Because I love you, Quentin. And I'm sorry that the treasure wasn't worth more, but—"

I'm kissed silent, the rest of my words swallowed up before

they make it past my lips. "The treasure is worth everything," he says. "Because for me the treasure is you, Nina. And it always has been." Quentin punctuates the sweetest thing anyone has ever said to me with a small laugh that rises to the very top of my mental catalog's *Favorites* list, filed under *The moment I knew, deep in my soul, that there would never be anyone else for me.*

EPILOGUE

—

Two months later . . .

OH MY GOD, Quentin, you didn't," I groan, slapping a hand over my eyes as if I haven't seen my boyfriend's naked body a million times. Though, to be fair, I have not seen it sketched out in pencil by my *mother* and hanging in a gallery. Except . . . wait . . . I peek through my fingers. "Oh. You . . . actually didn't?" Because that is definitely Quentin Bell's face, including the scatter of faded freckles beneath his eyes, and that rarely seen serious, almost warrior-like expression. But that is *not* Quentin's chest, or his stomach, or his penis. And I should know.

He takes a sip of his champagne. "Patti ran out of time in class and was left with a headless man. So I agreed to be the head."

"You seem very nonchalant about this."

Quentin shrugs. "I'm comfortable in my own skin," he says.

"Except that isn't even your skin," I point out.

"Guess I'm comfortable in other people's too." There's a wink and a grin before he wraps his arms around me and pulls me back against his chest. "Does that sound like a sexy thing or a murder-y thing?" he asks, lips brushing my ear.

"Kind of both?"

"Neat."

"When did you even pose for her without me noticing?"

"While you were in Belfast."

Sabrina and Malcolm eloped last month, and I was extremely honored when they asked me if I could hop on a plane to be one of their witnesses. I was worried that things with Sabrina would change when I decided to turn down the new term position at Malbyrne, officially closing the door on my career in academia. That we wouldn't be friends in the same way now that we weren't on the exact same trajectory. But, of course, the only difference is that the small sting of envy I sometimes had to hide from her has dissipated. Now we're closer than ever.

I sigh. "I really should know by now not to leave you alone with my parents."

"There you are, Ninabean!" Quentin releases me and my mom wraps me in a big hug, greeting me as if I didn't see her two hours ago when she left the house to get drinks with her classmates before the community center's end-of-summer art show. "What do you think?"

"I think you drew my boyfriend's head on someone else's nude body."

"I did!" she confirms, filled with glee.

My father has fully turned away, pretending to look at a painting of a dog.

"Isn't that a little . . . Dr. Frankenstein of you?" I ask.

She pauses, considering, as if she's an art critic and not the artist herself. "I think it makes it more interesting. And Quentin is so handsome." Her fingers dart out and he allows her to pinch his cheek. "Much handsomer than the model was, no offense to him."

"Well, my extreme discomfort aside, it's well done, Mom. Good job."

She beams. "Thank you, baby."

"We're going to have to head out, though," I say. "We're supposed to meet our realtor to check out another house." Quentin and I are in the early stages of looking for a place of our own. At first we considered staying at 304 West Dill, and maybe eventually buying it from his dad. Wouldn't that be fun, we thought, to turn the place into ours, to continue filling it with happier memories than the ones that lingered there from Quentin's childhood? But after we moved the bed into the master bedroom at the front of the house and realized that our headboard would be sharing a wall with my parents' headboard—meaning the possibility of them hearing us, or maybe worse, us hearing *them*—we decided to see what else we could find in the area. Still close to my family, just not literally next door. In the meantime, we've still been living in our respective sides of the duplex. At least officially. In practice, he's at my parents' whenever he's not at C. A. Howe, the local boutique law firm where he's already making a name for himself in the field of tenants' rights, and I'm over at his house pretty much every night. I have to admit, I've grown quite attached to sleeping with a curled-up Faustine snoring loudly beside my head.

"How exciting! Well, thanks for coming." Mom stretches out her arms to encompass us both in her farewell embrace. Quentin lets out something almost like a quack as the air is squeezed out of him, but when we're released he has a massive grin on his face. It is weird how much he and my mom adore each other, but also undeniably nice.

"Bye, Dad," I say as Quentin says, "See ya, Dave." My father's hug is much looser, and he gives Quentin a firm handshake. But with the goodbyes out of the way, we're free to leave.

I breathe in the late September air, enjoying the crispness of it. The community center is on a farm about fifteen miles south of Catoctin, and it's beautiful out here. There's a bonfire going somewhere nearby, and the warm, smoky scent feels like it heralds the arrival of fall. I forgot how much I love Maryland when it isn't humid and sweltering. The last hot day, in fact, was the one when we met with Sharon, whose maiden name we were surprised to learn is Worman. Apparently, Louisa was her great-aunt. Considering the personal connection, she was particularly thrilled by the letters we found. Then she actually cried when we told her about the Edlo manuscript and gave her Eugene and Emily Aaron's contact information. The puzzle box turned out to be nothing particularly noteworthy in her opinion, as it was a duplicate of another they already had in their collection; Fountain apparently had several made and often gave them as presents to friends and loved ones. So once we told her our abridged version of how we came to be in possession of Fountain's treasure (omitting, of course, the trespassing and lying portions of the story), she suggested we keep the box as a memento. Mostly I think she was trying to get rid of us at that point, because she was eager to reread the letters and get in touch with the Aarons. Very understandable.

And we did get to do an interview with a local news outlet about our find, so that was cool.

"You know my mom is going to try to gift us that picture," I say.

"Oh, I was hoping so," Quentin says. "This house we're going to check out has a fireplace, and it would be perfect over the mantel." I nudge him in the ribs with my elbow and he laughs. I've stopped cataloging his laughter over the last few weeks, because it's no longer something that feels like it might one day be in short supply. There's an abundance of it in my life, and I don't count on that changing as long as we're both around. Besides, now I spend my days reorganizing actual collections, and I don't feel a particular need to take my work home with me.

The same cannot be said for Quentin, I guess, because as soon as we're in the car, the light around us taking on a pinkish tinge as the sun begins to set, he's checking his email on his phone. It's true that, occasionally, his new job does have time-sensitive issues, but his paralegal is supposed to text him about those.

"Hey, what's so important that—"

"Shh."

". . . I'm sorry, did you just shush me?"

Quentin flaps his hand, adding a dismissive gesture to the dismissive noise.

I narrow my eyes, a little offended.

But then I notice that his are growing wider by the millisecond. "Neen. Read this." He passes the phone to me.

Dear Mr. Bell,

    My name is Birch Norwood, Esquire—

"Birch Norwood. Ha. That's a fun name," I say.

"Keep reading," Quentin urges, impatient.

    I represent Mr. John Francis Bongiovi—

Isn't that . . . ?

It cannot be.

Shit.

"Is being mean to Jon Bon Jovi a crime in New Jersey?" I ask Quentin, the words coming out in a panicked hurry.

His eyebrows dive in confusion. "What?"

But I'm already back to reading.

. . . who recently came across a news feature online about your and Dr. Hunnicutt's discovery of a new document belonging to industrialist Julius James Fountain. Is it true you still have the puzzle box in which it was contained? Please let me know if this is accurate. Mr. Bongiovi would like to discuss purchasing it for his private collection.

My head jerks up as the words on the screen register. "Does this say . . . that Jon Bon Jovi wants to buy Fountain's puzzle box from us?"

"It . . . it seems so." Quentin's mouth quirks, bemusement and delight competing for dominance. "What do you think? Are you particularly attached to it?"

"Have to be honest," I say. "I'm finding I'm less attached to it than I was a minute ago." I'm also finding that my animosity toward Jon Bon Jovi has suddenly dissipated. Write it in pencil? Solid advice, actually! Sometimes plans change, and I've learned that it isn't always for the worst.

Quentin and I lean in closer, our grins mirroring each other.

"I didn't know Jon Bon Jovi was a puzzle box guy," he says.

"Maybe he isn't. Maybe he's a seltzer-industry-memorabilia guy."

"A things-that-contained-treasure guy? That would be a fun niche collection." Quentin plants a small kiss on the tip of my nose, then one at the corner of my eye. "How much do you think he'll offer?"

"Hopefully enough to add to the money from the ring and your portion of the proceeds from your dad's house so we have more available for our down payment."

"Oh," he says. "I was thinking we'd put it toward a wedding."

"A wedding?!" I ask, laughing. "Hold your horses, man, it's been like three seconds since we got together."

"I've loved you for a lot longer, though," he says, his lips now at my cheek.

"Yeah?"

"Yeah. Like a full minute. Maybe even two."

We share another long, silent smile, where we exist in our own fantastic world of magic and joy. Being with Quentin sometimes feels like I've stumbled into Edlo, except I know none of this is make-believe. It's real and enduring, made up of every moment we have ever loved each other, and all the moments we ever will. And I'll forever be glad we found it together.

ACKNOWLEDGMENTS

Working on this book was a bit like treasure hunting in that there was a good bit to keep track of and a lot of digging around, all fueled by the belief that we'd uncover something wonderful at the end. I like to think we got there eventually!

Thank you so much to Sareer Khader for her endless patience as each round of revisions somehow turned into me deciding to rewrite half the manuscript—you are worth a bajillion jewels and bars of gold. Also invaluable are Jessica Mangicaro, Kim-Salina I, Anna Venckus, Vikki Chu, Megha Jain, Christine Legon, Jeanne-Marie Hudson, Craig Burke, Claire Zion, Christine Ball, and all of the other excellent people at Berkley and Penguin Random House who helped make *Finders Keepers* and get it into readers' hands.

Massive thanks to my agent, Taylor Haggerty, for getting me through selling on proposal for the first time, and to Jasmine Brown, Alice Lawson, and Heather Baror-Shapiro.

It has been so exciting seeing my work reach readers all around the globe. Thank you to Kat Burdon at Quercus and to my other international editors and translators for believing in my stories.

I am forever grateful to have so many incredible friends, old and new. I must explicitly shout out Amber Roberts and Regine Darius for being my Bad Cats for the past five years, Jamie Harrow and Claire Griggs for talking to me about treasure trove law and the rule of perpetuities, Alexandra Kiley and Jenny Lane for helping me fix up my first draft, Esther Reid for helping me fix up my third, and Amy Langford, PhD, for her helpful notes on my behind-the-book essay. And to all of my fellow authors who don't seem to mind when I'm being goofy in their DMs: I love you.

To Houston and Hazel—my love for you both is endless and absolutely the treasure I found along the way. Also, I want to thank my parents for their love and continued support of me and this strange career of mine. I would be remiss not to mention that I appreciate Noodle and her frequent willingness to keep me company while I work, though she is a cat and will probably not read this.

Booksellers, librarians, and bookish influencers—I am always so touched and grateful when you recommend my books, and it has been a real joy to get to know so many of you during the past few years.

And, as always, thank *you* for picking up this book. Readers are the best part of this whole business, and it is an absolute pleasure and privilege to get to share my words with you all.

FINDERS KEEPERS

SARAH ADLER

BEHIND THE BOOK

—

A RANDOM WOMAN ON the internet once inexplicably chided me under the guise of providing feedback: "You're a storyteller. Your job is to tell a story." So, here's one, and it's actually true:

In 1935, the federal government under President Franklin D. Roosevelt created the Works Progress Administration—a program under the New Deal that aimed to provide employment to millions of Americans during the Great Depression. The WPA's projects were more of a mixed bag than we generally acknowledge, in that they included good and useful things like building bridges but also horrible and racist ones like managing Japanese American internment camps. Pretty on-brand for the United States!

Anyway, one of the (somewhat less problematic) aspects of the WPA that has long fascinated me is the Federal Writers' Project. Nested under what they called Federal Project Number One, which was the umbrella for arts initiatives, the Federal Writers' Project gave out-of-work authors, journalists, lawyers, teachers, librarians, and others who could capably put pen to paper an opportunity to support their families.

Some of these writers worked on guidebooks, which provided tourists with both practical and cultural information on various states, cities, and regions, while other writers—including well-known names such as Ralph Ellison, Saul Bellow, and May Swenson—were assigned to interview individuals around the country and collect their responses for posterity with the goal of ultimately having a number of accounts to draw upon to describe the unique experiences of various groups of Americans.

Maybe you've heard about this before, as over two thousand of these interviews were conducted with formerly enslaved people and are now frequently used in high school and college history classes as primary sources. It's quite likely that if you've studied slavery in the United States, you've encountered or at least heard of these interviews. The slave narratives were only one aspect of the important oral history work done by those in the Federal Writers' Project's employ. Another three thousand more of these documents are at the Library of Congress under a collection titled "American Life Histories." And it was in browsing through these interviews with shrimpers and clock-makers and sign painters, these accounts of the day-to-day experiences and the extraordinary moments that make a life, that made me think about how I might one day use the transcript format as a framing device in a book. Then I came up with the premise for *Finders Keepers*, and the idea I'd been carrying around to include an oral history component in my writing suddenly seemed like the perfect addition to the plot.

Fiction, though, is much more malleable than reality, easily reshaped to serve the author's purposes. And so, for mine, I took some liberties when creating my WPA-inspired interviews. Most significantly, were Julius James Fountain a real person, he would not have been a likely interview candidate under the American Life Histories project, as the genuine oral histories mostly focused on working-class people, not wealthy business owners. In fact, the power imbalance between Fountain and Albert Aaron in this book is the inverse of how it often was in reality, as interviewers were mostly educated white people recording the experiences of marginalized and/or financially precarious informants. This would have influenced what questions were asked and how they were answered in a way that does not apply to these fictional interviews. Another difference is that Albert Aaron tends to be more detail-oriented and verbose than his real-life counterparts; while some of the transcripts in the Library of Congress collection are on the longer side, most are only a few pages, and in many, Forms A and B—"Circumstances of Interview" and "Personal History of Informant," respectively—are either not included or are not filled out in much detail. But I tried to, in general, remain faithful to the formatting and spirit of the documents where it made sense to do so.

It's true that I'm a storyteller. My job *is* to tell stories. (Random Internet Woman definitely got me there!) But I also have this instinct that I'm pretty sure stems from my training as a historian, and it's to ensure that whenever I create, I also remember. So, yes, this book is primarily a romantic comedy about made-up people. But it's also an homage to thousands of other stories—ones about real individuals who worked and struggled and laughed and loved, dictated in their own words and by the historical moment, recorded on portable typewriters and now digitized for easy access.

Because every person has a story to tell; it just comes down

to whose we deem worth remembering, and whose we let ourselves forget.

You can learn more about and view the primary source
documents that inspired the oral history sections of this
book by visiting loc.gov/collections/federal-writers-project
/about-this-collection/.
This and other resources are also linked in the FAQ sec-
tion of my website at sarahadlerwrites.com/faq.

DISCUSSION QUESTIONS

---

1. Have you ever hunted for treasure? What were the circumstances, and did you find it?
2. Nina returns to Catoctin and finds it much different from what she remembers. Has your hometown changed much since you were growing up there? Is it a place you like or would like to live now?
3. Do you believe it's possible to meaningfully reconnect with someone who ghosted you?
4. If you were to create a treasure hunt of your own hoping someone specific found it, what clue(s) would you give them?
5. Nina and Hanako become friends as adults, though they were only acquaintances when they were in school together. Are you close with anyone from your childhood that you weren't really friends with back then?
6. Would you go to a nude drawing class with your mother, or would you just happen to be busy that night?

7. If you were an eccentric millionaire at the turn of the century, what odd or extravagant feature(s) would you want to include on your estate?

8. If Edlo were a real place, do you think you'd enjoy traveling by bubble?

9. Which character do you relate to most and why?

10. Quentin learns about a life hack to procure apple fritters without waking up early. Are there any similar tricks only locals know about where you live?

USA Today bestselling author **Sarah Adler** writes romantic comedies about lovable weirdos finding their happily ever afters. She lives in Maryland with her husband, daughter, and very mischievous cat. When not working, you can find her attempting to course-correct an ill-advised late-afternoon nap with an equally ill-advised late-afternoon coffee, as she is incapable of ever learning a lesson.

Visit Sarah Adler Online

SarahAdlerWrites.com
SarahAdlerWrites

Ready to find
your next great read?

Let us help.

Visit prh.com/nextread

Penguin
Random
House